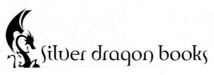

Silver dragon books

BUCKHAM MEMORIAL LIBRARY
FARIBAULT, MN 55021

Creators

Pat Shand

Sarah Dill

Writer

Pat Shand

Artwork

Sarah Dill

Letters

Jim Campbell

Editor

Ralph Tedesco

Trade Design

Christopher Cote

Silver dragon books

WWW.SILVERDRAGONBOOKS.COM
FACEBOOK.COM/SILVERDRAGONBOOKS

SILVER DRAGON BOOKS, INC.

Joe Brusha • President & Publisher
Ralph Tedesco • Editor-in-Chief
Jennifer Bermel • VP Business Affairs
Christopher Cote • Art Director & Graphic Designer

This volume contains the comic series Family Pets issues #1-6 published by Silver Dragon Books.
First Edition, June 2015 • ISBN 978-1-939683-64-9

FAMILY PETS

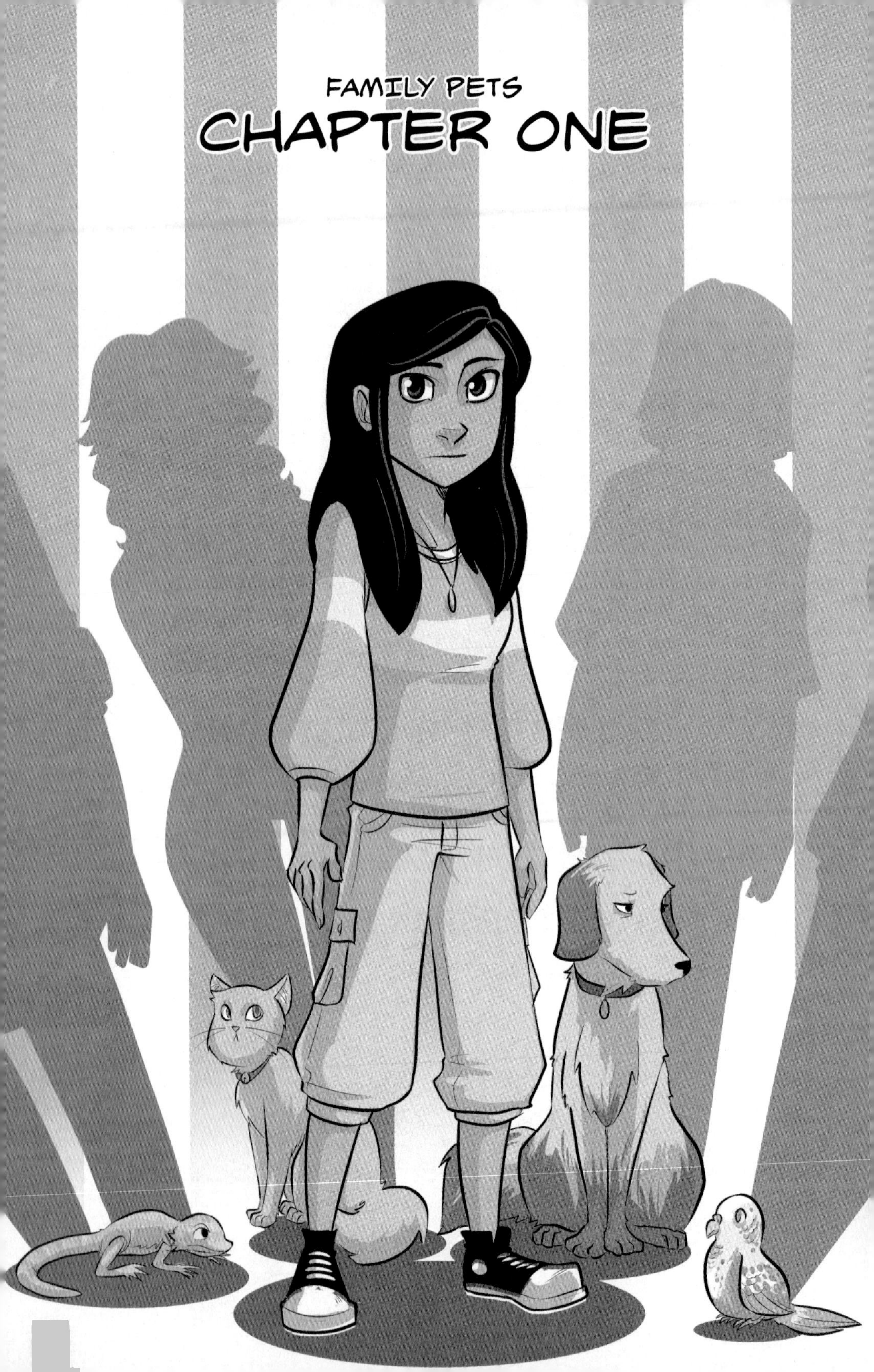
FAMILY PETS
CHAPTER ONE

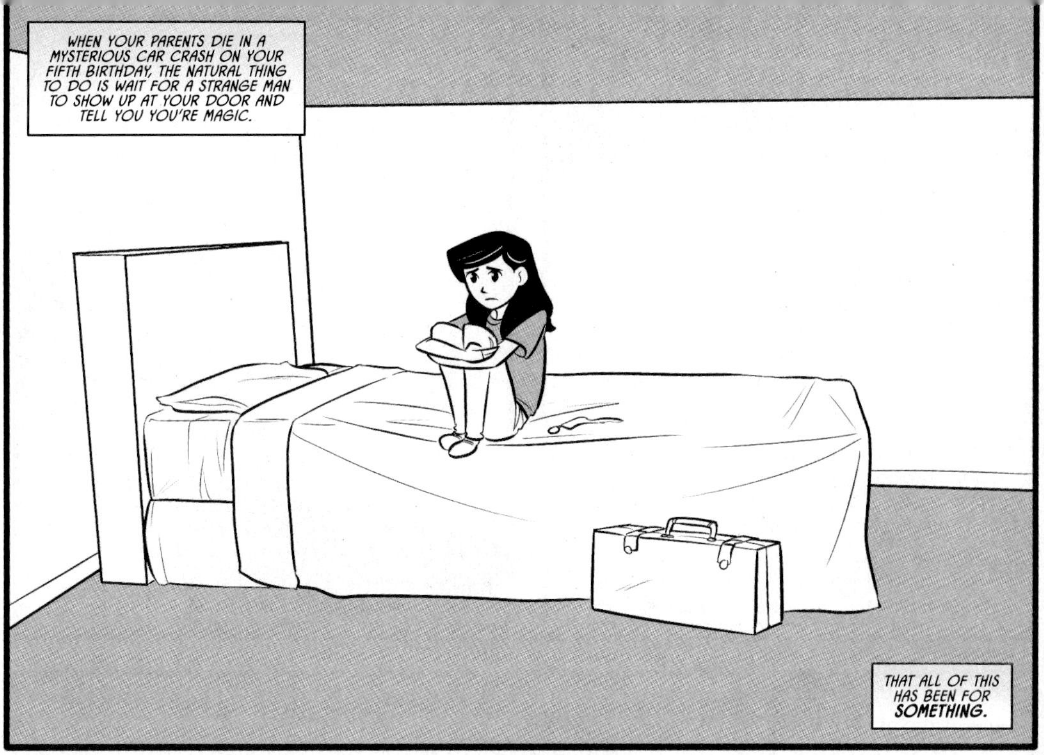
WHEN YOUR PARENTS DIE IN A MYSTERIOUS CAR CRASH ON YOUR FIFTH BIRTHDAY, THE NATURAL THING TO DO IS WAIT FOR A STRANGE MAN TO SHOW UP AT YOUR DOOR AND TELL YOU YOU'RE MAGIC.
THAT ALL OF THIS HAS BEEN FOR SOMETHING.

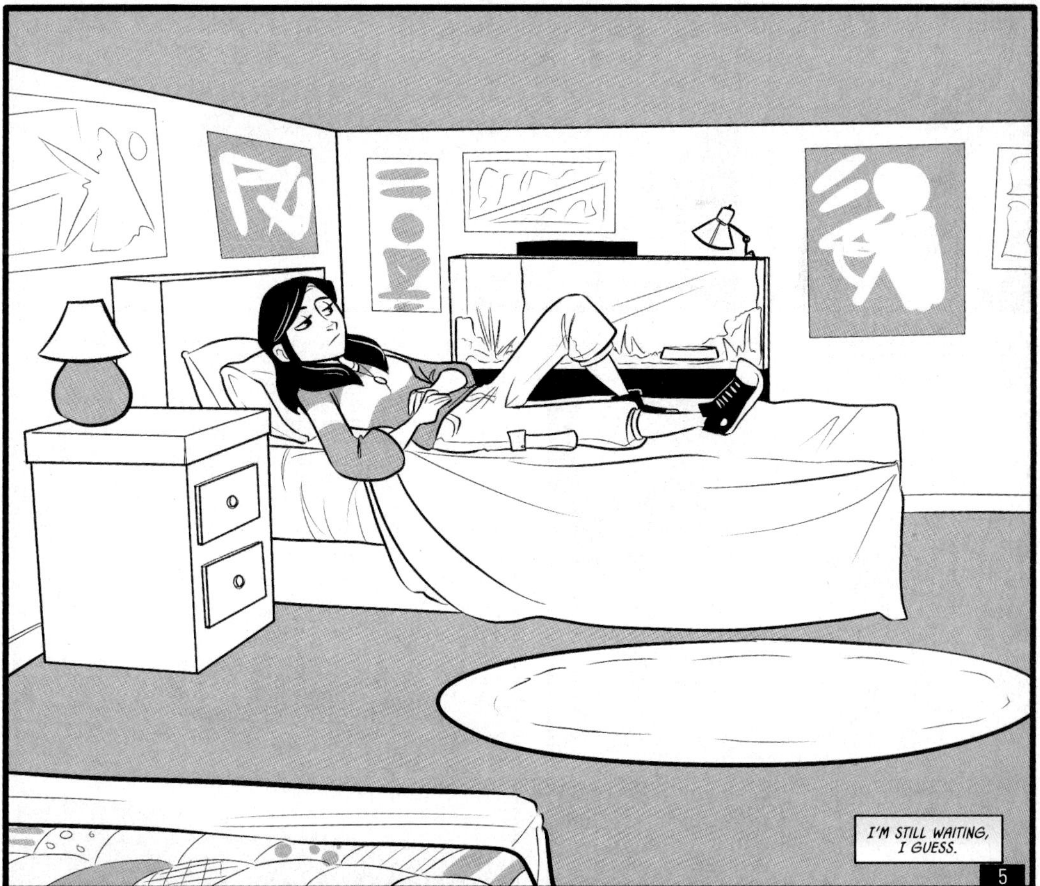
I'M STILL WAITING, I GUESS.

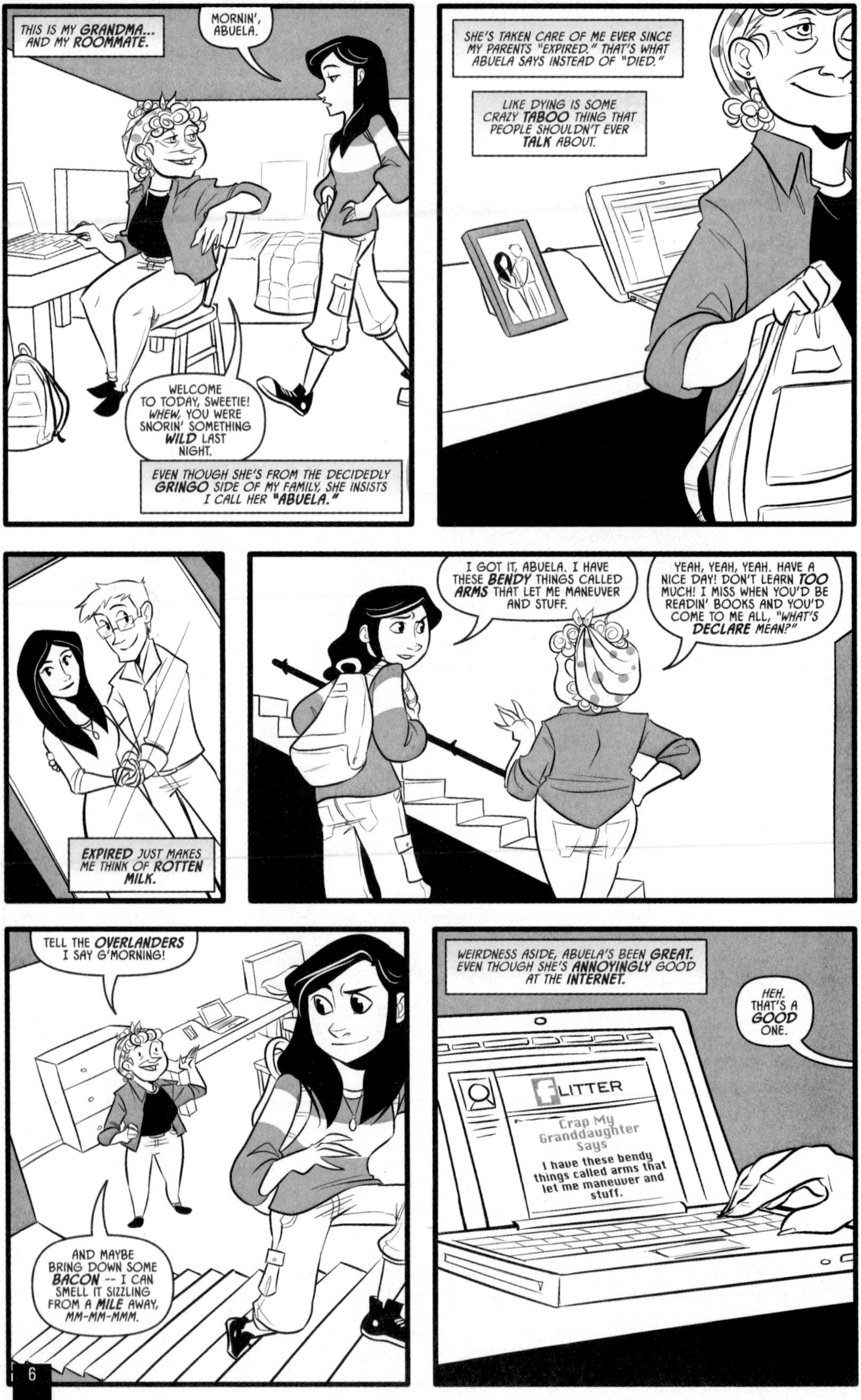

THIS IS MY GRANDMA... AND MY ROOMMATE.
MORNIN', ABUELA.
WELCOME TO TODAY, SWEETIE! WHEW, YOU WERE SNORIN' SOMETHING WILD LAST NIGHT.
EVEN THOUGH SHE'S FROM THE DECIDEDLY GRINGO SIDE OF MY FAMILY, SHE INSISTS I CALL HER "ABUELA."
SHE'S TAKEN CARE OF ME EVER SINCE MY PARENTS "EXPIRED." THAT'S WHAT ABUELA SAYS INSTEAD OF "DIED."
LIKE DYING IS SOME CRAZY TABOO THING THAT PEOPLE SHOULDN'T EVER TALK ABOUT.
EXPIRED JUST MAKES ME THINK OF ROTTEN MILK.
I GOT IT, ABUELA. I HAVE THESE BENDY THINGS CALLED ARMS THAT LET ME MANEUVER AND STUFF.
YEAH, YEAH, YEAH. HAVE A NICE DAY! DON'T LEARN TOO MUCH! I MISS WHEN YOU'D BE READIN' BOOKS AND YOU'D COME TO ME ALL, "WHAT'S DECLARE MEAN?"
TELL THE OVERLANDERS I SAY G'MORNING!
AND MAYBE BRING DOWN SOME BACON -- I CAN SMELL IT SIZZLING FROM A MILE AWAY, MM-MM-MMM.
WEIRDNESS ASIDE, ABUELA'S BEEN GREAT. EVEN THOUGH SHE'S ANNOYINGLY GOOD AT THE INTERNET.
HEH. THAT'S A GOOD ONE.
FLITTER
Crap My Granddaughter Says
I have these bendy things called arms that let me maneuver and stuff.

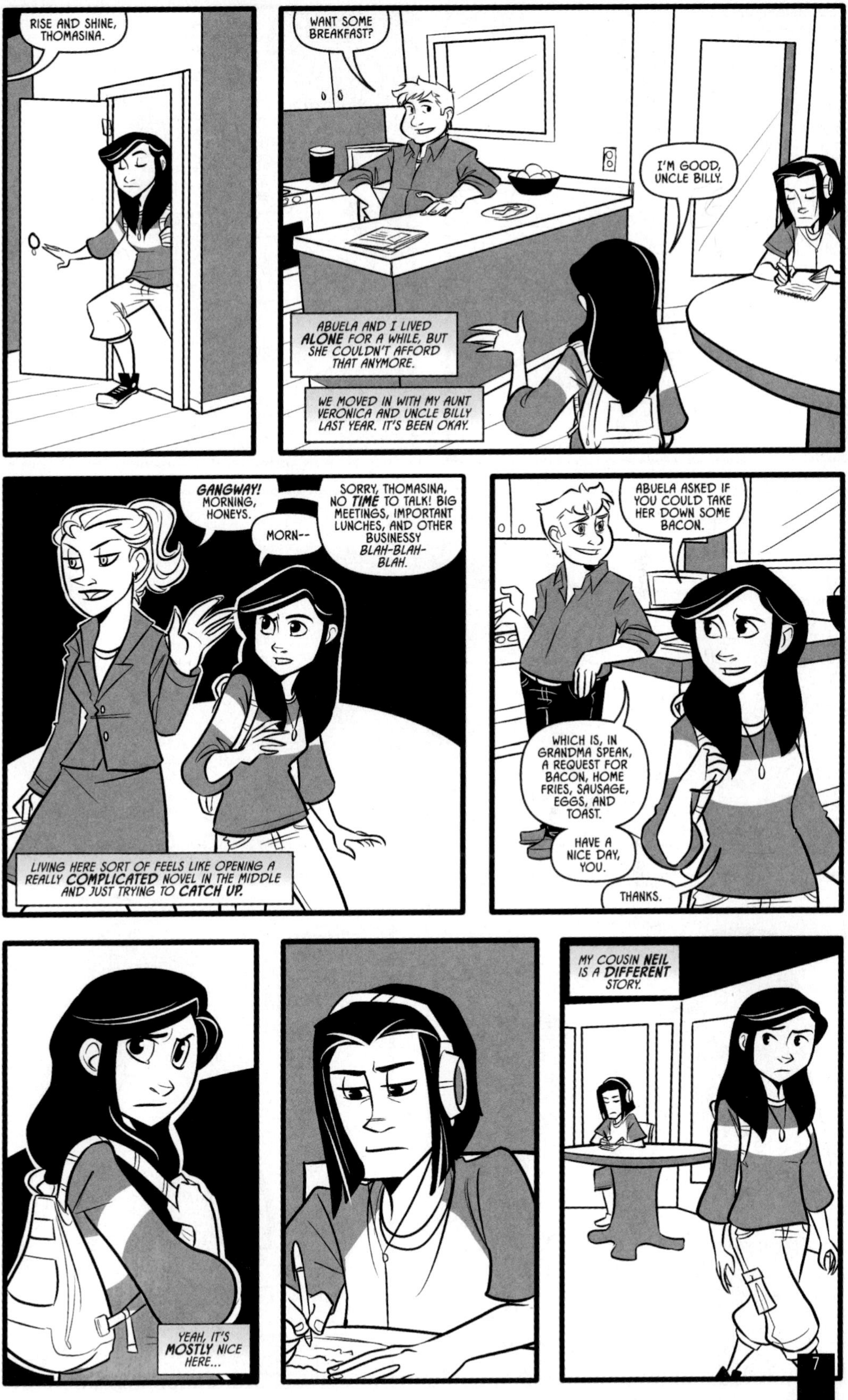
RISE AND SHINE, THOMASINA.
WANT SOME BREAKFAST?
I'M GOOD, UNCLE BILLY.
ABUELA AND I LIVED ALONE FOR A WHILE, BUT SHE COULDN'T AFFORD THAT ANYMORE.
WE MOVED IN WITH MY AUNT VERONICA AND UNCLE BILLY LAST YEAR. IT'S BEEN OKAY.
GANGWAY! MORNING, HONEYS.
MORN--
SORRY, THOMASINA, NO TIME TO TALK! BIG MEETINGS, IMPORTANT LUNCHES, AND OTHER BUSINESSY BLAH-BLAH-BLAH.
LIVING HERE SORT OF FEELS LIKE OPENING A REALLY COMPLICATED NOVEL IN THE MIDDLE AND JUST TRYING TO CATCH UP.
ABUELA ASKED IF YOU COULD TAKE HER DOWN SOME BACON.
WHICH IS, IN GRANDMA SPEAK, A REQUEST FOR BACON, HOME FRIES, SAUSAGE, EGGS, AND TOAST.
HAVE A NICE DAY, YOU.
THANKS.
YEAH, IT'S MOSTLY NICE HERE...
MY COUSIN NEIL IS A DIFFERENT STORY.

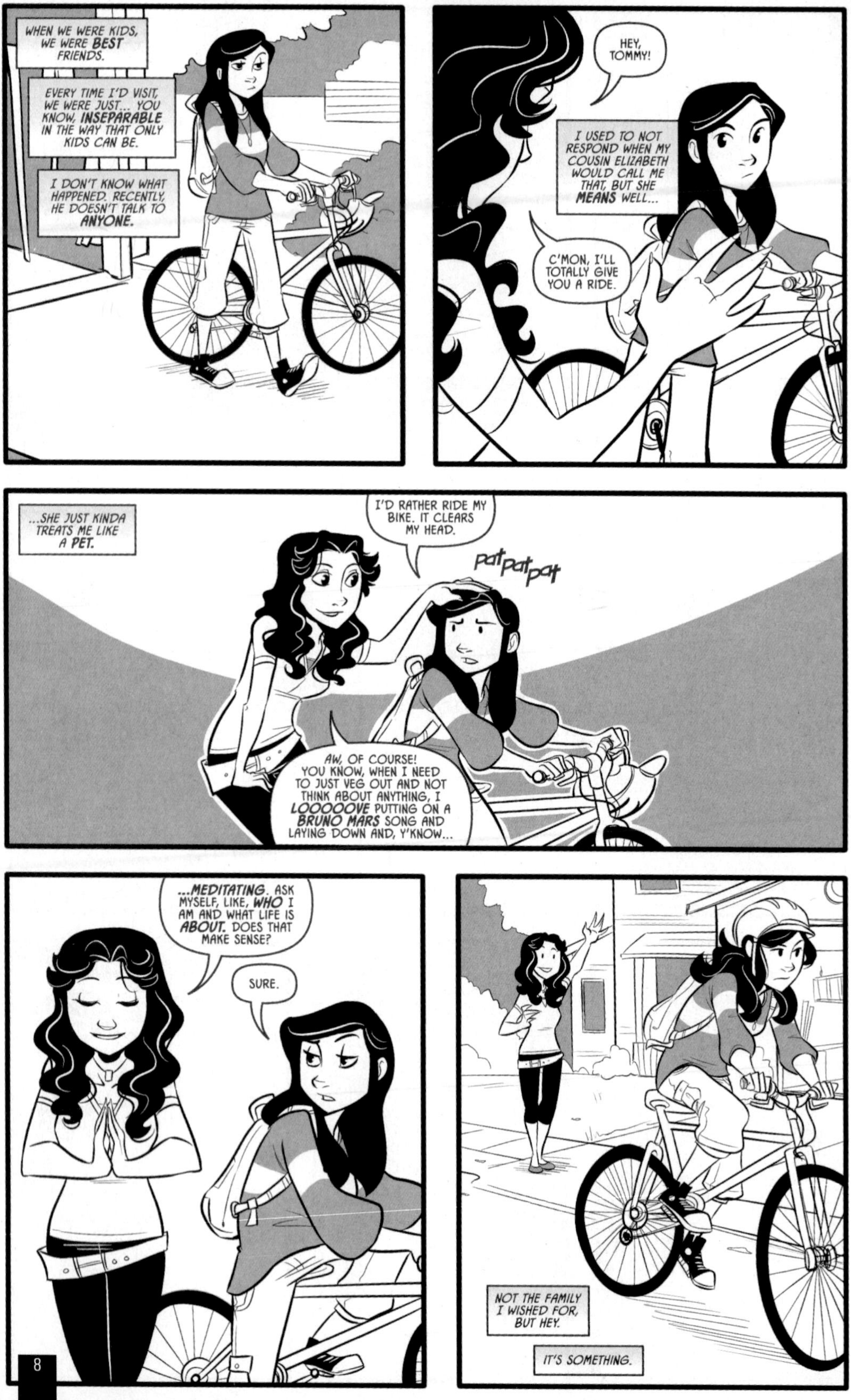
WHEN WE WERE KIDS, WE WERE BEST FRIENDS.
EVERY TIME I'D VISIT, WE WERE JUST... YOU KNOW, INSEPARABLE IN THE WAY THAT ONLY KIDS CAN BE.
I DON'T KNOW WHAT HAPPENED. RECENTLY, HE DOESN'T TALK TO ANYONE.
HEY, TOMMY!
I USED TO NOT RESPOND WHEN MY COUSIN ELIZABETH WOULD CALL ME THAT, BUT SHE MEANS WELL...
C'MON, I'LL TOTALLY GIVE YOU A RIDE.
...SHE JUST KINDA TREATS ME LIKE A PET.
I'D RATHER RIDE MY BIKE. IT CLEARS MY HEAD.
pat pat pat
AW, OF COURSE! YOU KNOW, WHEN I NEED TO JUST VEG OUT AND NOT THINK ABOUT ANYTHING, I LOOOOOVE PUTTING ON A BRUNO MARS SONG AND LAYING DOWN AND, Y'KNOW...
...MEDITATING. ASK MYSELF, LIKE, WHO I AM AND WHAT LIFE IS ABOUT. DOES THAT MAKE SENSE?
SURE.
NOT THE FAMILY I WISHED FOR, BUT HEY.
IT'S SOMETHING.

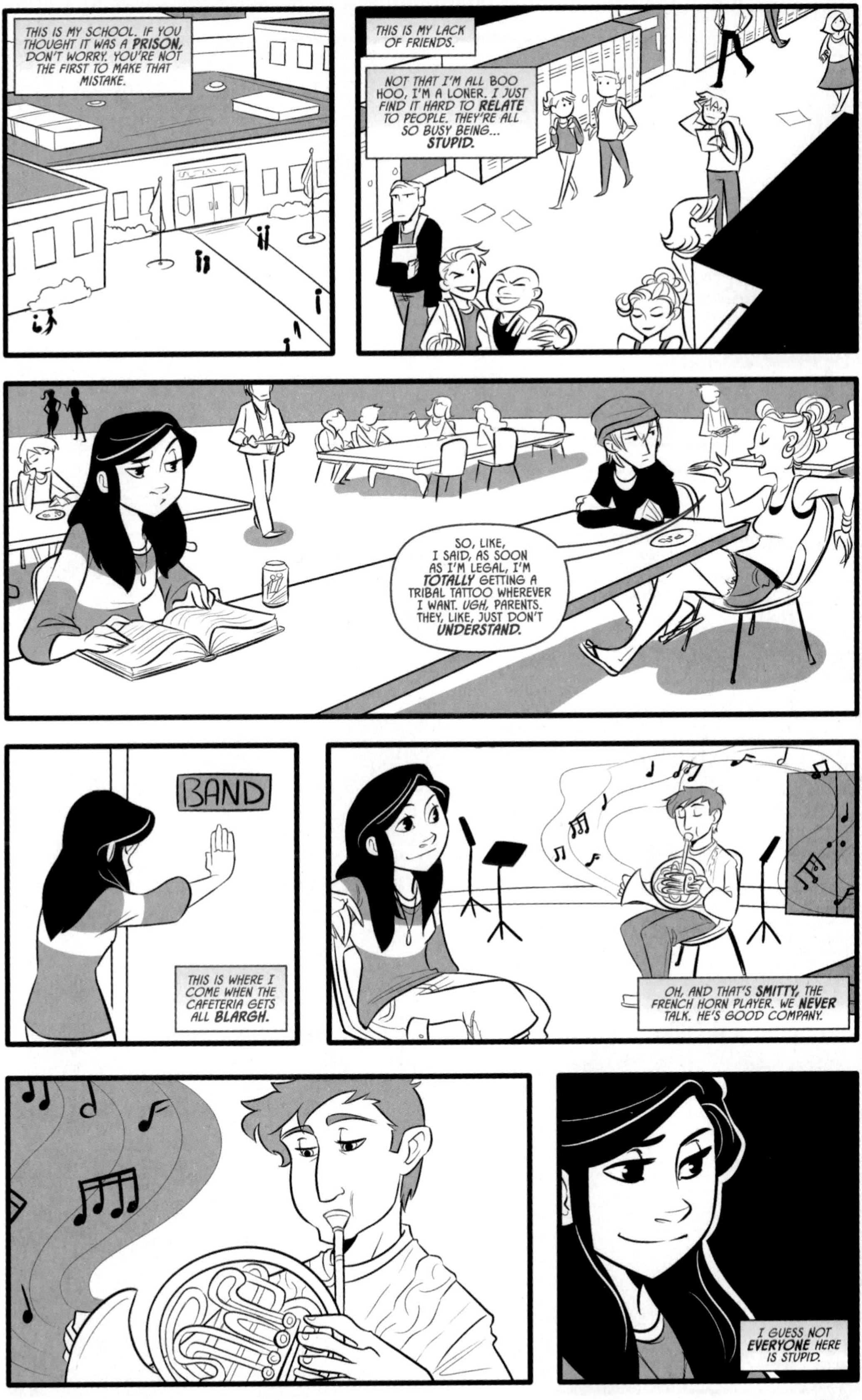
THIS IS MY SCHOOL. IF YOU THOUGHT IT WAS A **PRISON,** DON'T WORRY. YOU'RE NOT THE FIRST TO MAKE THAT MISTAKE.
THIS IS MY LACK OF FRIENDS.
NOT THAT I'M ALL BOO HOO, I'M A LONER. I JUST FIND IT HARD TO **RELATE** TO PEOPLE. THEY'RE ALL SO BUSY BEING... **STUPID.**
SO, LIKE, I SAID, AS SOON AS I'M LEGAL, I'M **TOTALLY** GETTING A TRIBAL TATTOO WHEREVER I WANT. *UGH,* PARENTS. THEY, LIKE, JUST DON'T **UNDERSTAND.**
BAND
THIS IS WHERE I COME WHEN THE CAFETERIA GETS ALL **BLARGH.**
OH, AND THAT'S **SMITTY,** THE FRENCH HORN PLAYER. WE **NEVER** TALK. HE'S GOOD COMPANY.
I GUESS NOT **EVERYONE** HERE IS STUPID.

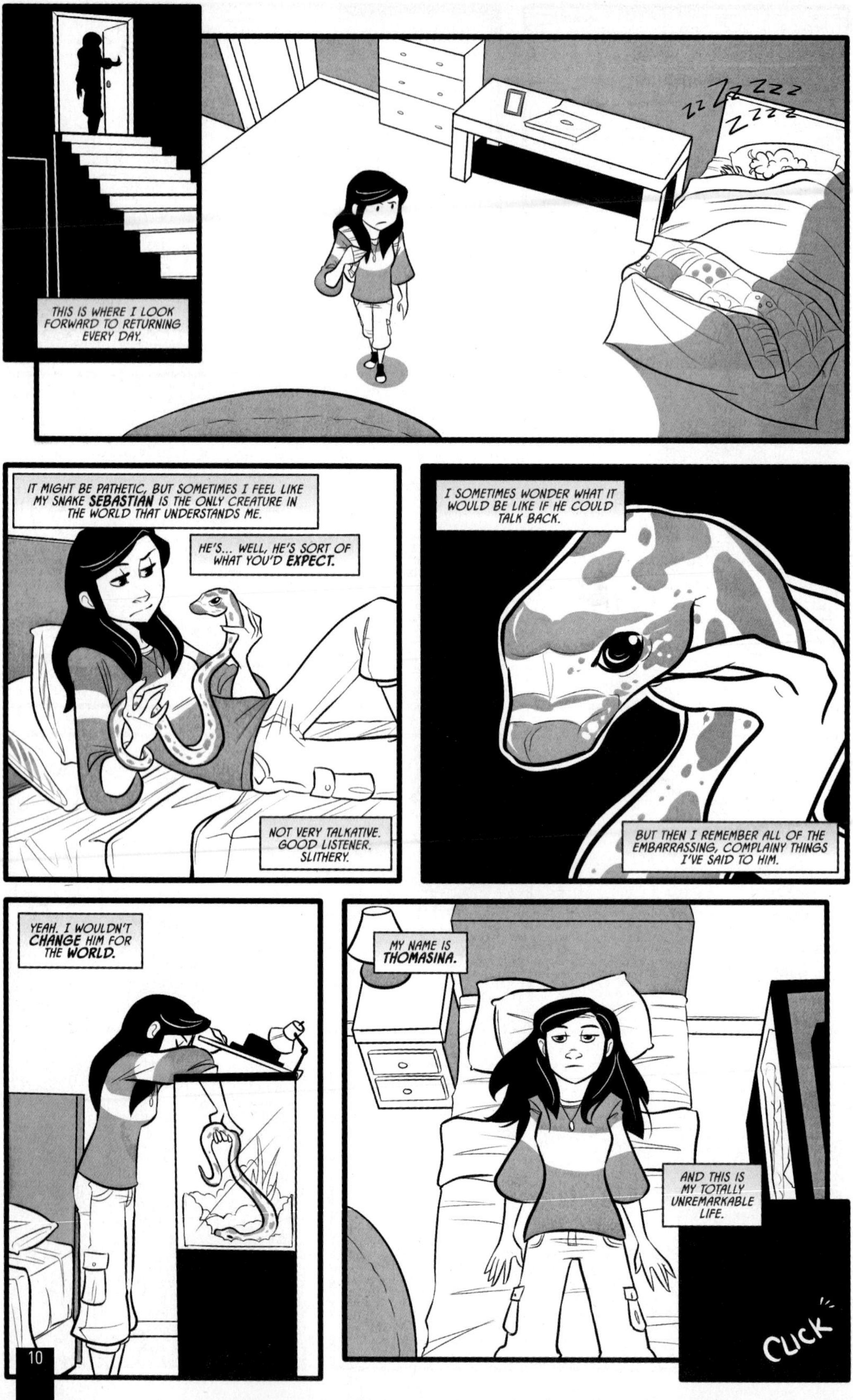
THIS IS WHERE I LOOK FORWARD TO RETURNING EVERY DAY.
ZZ ZZZZ ZZZZ
IT MIGHT BE PATHETIC, BUT SOMETIMES I FEEL LIKE MY SNAKE SEBASTIAN IS THE ONLY CREATURE IN THE WORLD THAT UNDERSTANDS ME.
HE'S... WELL, HE'S SORT OF WHAT YOU'D EXPECT.
NOT VERY TALKATIVE. GOOD LISTENER. SLITHERY.
I SOMETIMES WONDER WHAT IT WOULD BE LIKE IF HE COULD TALK BACK.
BUT THEN I REMEMBER ALL OF THE EMBARRASSING, COMPLAINY THINGS I'VE SAID TO HIM.
YEAH. I WOULDN'T CHANGE HIM FOR THE WORLD.
MY NAME IS THOMASINA.
AND THIS IS MY TOTALLY UNREMARKABLE LIFE.
CLICK

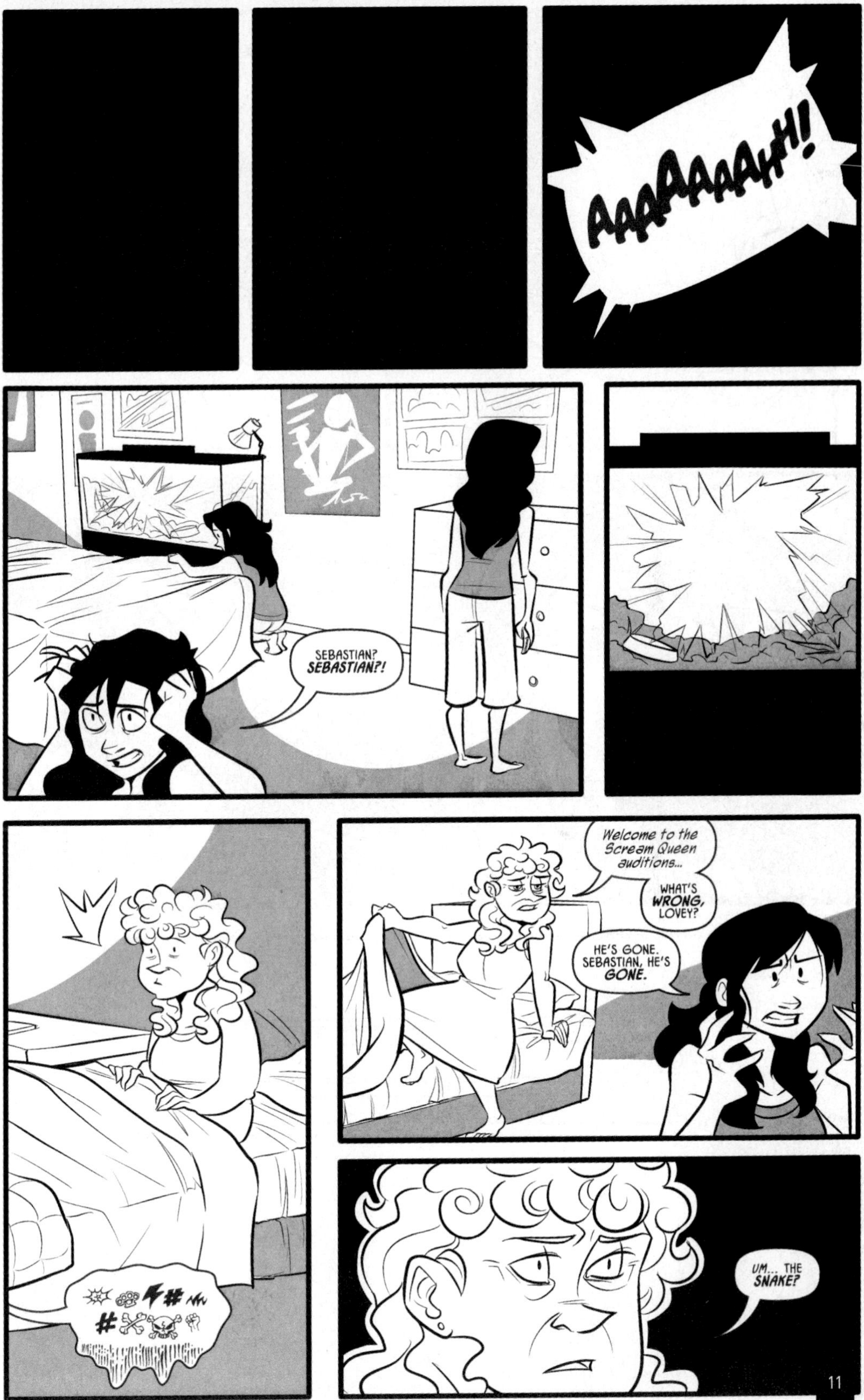
AAAAAAAAH!
SEBASTIAN? SEBASTIAN?!
Welcome to the Scream Queen auditions...
WHAT'S WRONG, LOVEY?
HE'S GONE. SEBASTIAN, HE'S GONE.
UM... THE SNAKE?

HE'S NOT GOING TO SIZE YOU UP OR *EAT* YOU OR, OR, OR... ANY OF THOSE DUMB MYTHS.

HE COULDN'T HURT A *FLY*. WELL, HE COULD, HE HURTS *MICE* KIND OF A LOT, BUT THAT'S NOT THE ISSUE.

I KNOW HOW MUCH HE MEANS TO YOU--

HOW COULD THIS HAVE HAPPENED?

HE CAN'T JUST SHATTER THE GLASS, HE...

WAIT, WHAT THE HECK!?

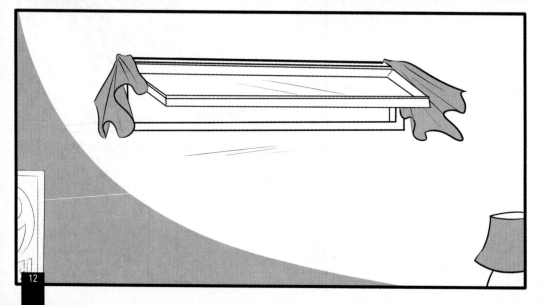

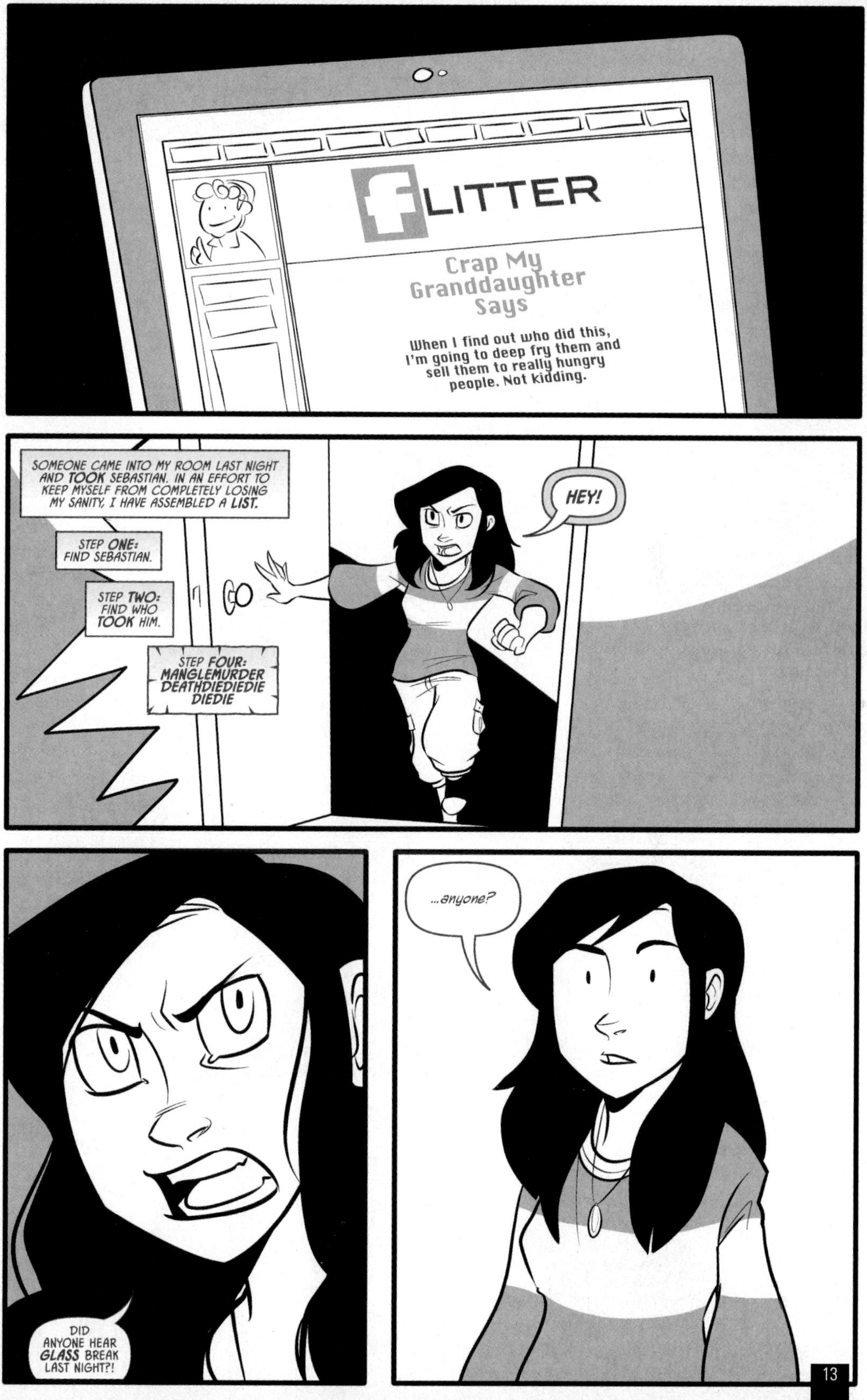
FLITTER
Crap My Granddaughter Says
When I find out who did this, I'm going to deep fry them and sell them to really hungry people. Not kidding.
SOMEONE CAME INTO MY ROOM LAST NIGHT AND TOOK SEBASTIAN. IN AN EFFORT TO KEEP MYSELF FROM COMPLETELY LOSING MY SANITY, I HAVE ASSEMBLED A LIST.
STEP ONE: FIND SEBASTIAN.
STEP TWO: FIND WHO TOOK HIM.
STEP FOUR: MANGLEMURDER DEATHDIEDIEDIE DIEDIE
HEY!
DID ANYONE HEAR GLASS BREAK LAST NIGHT?!
...anyone?

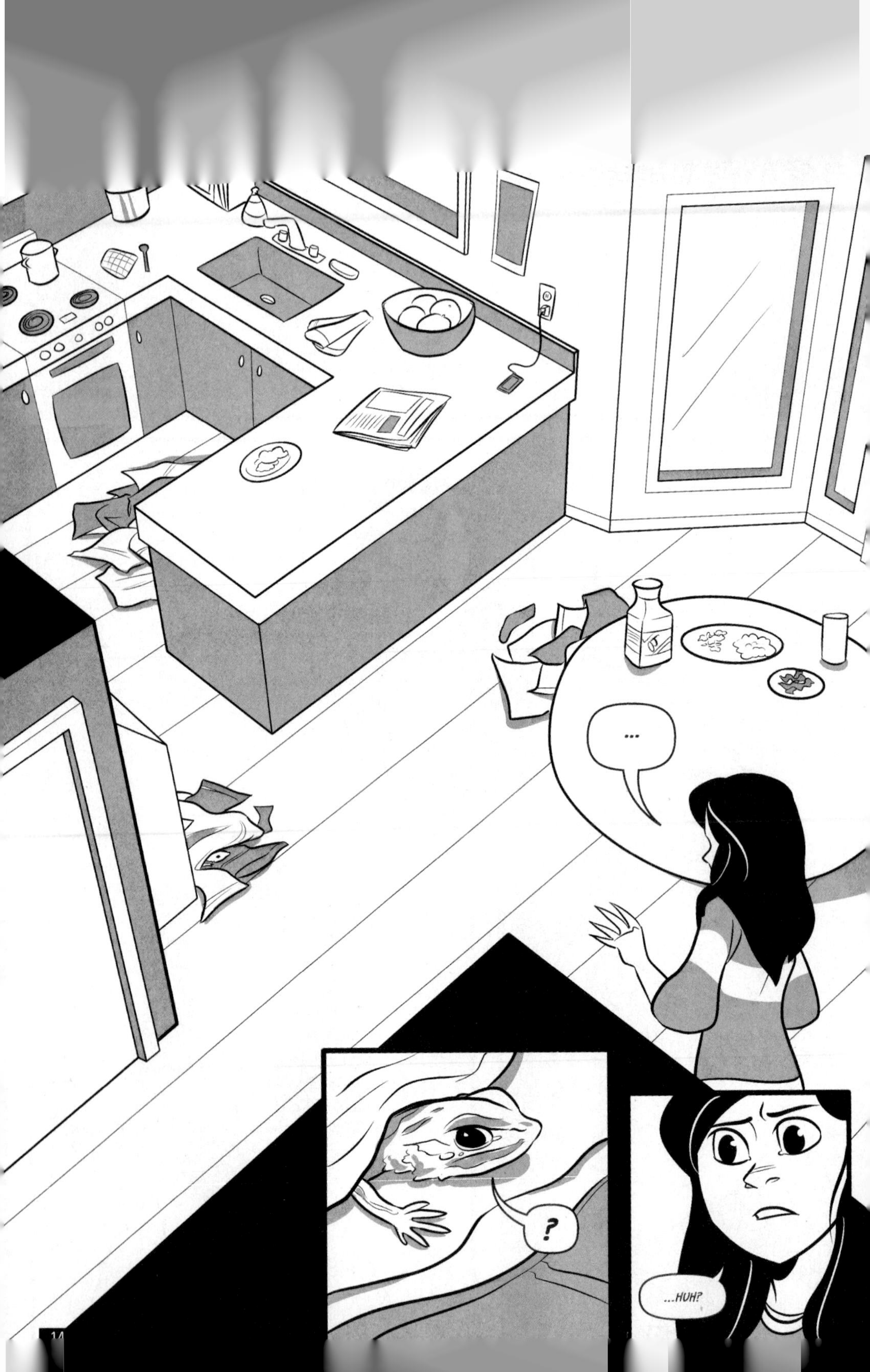
...
?
...HUH?

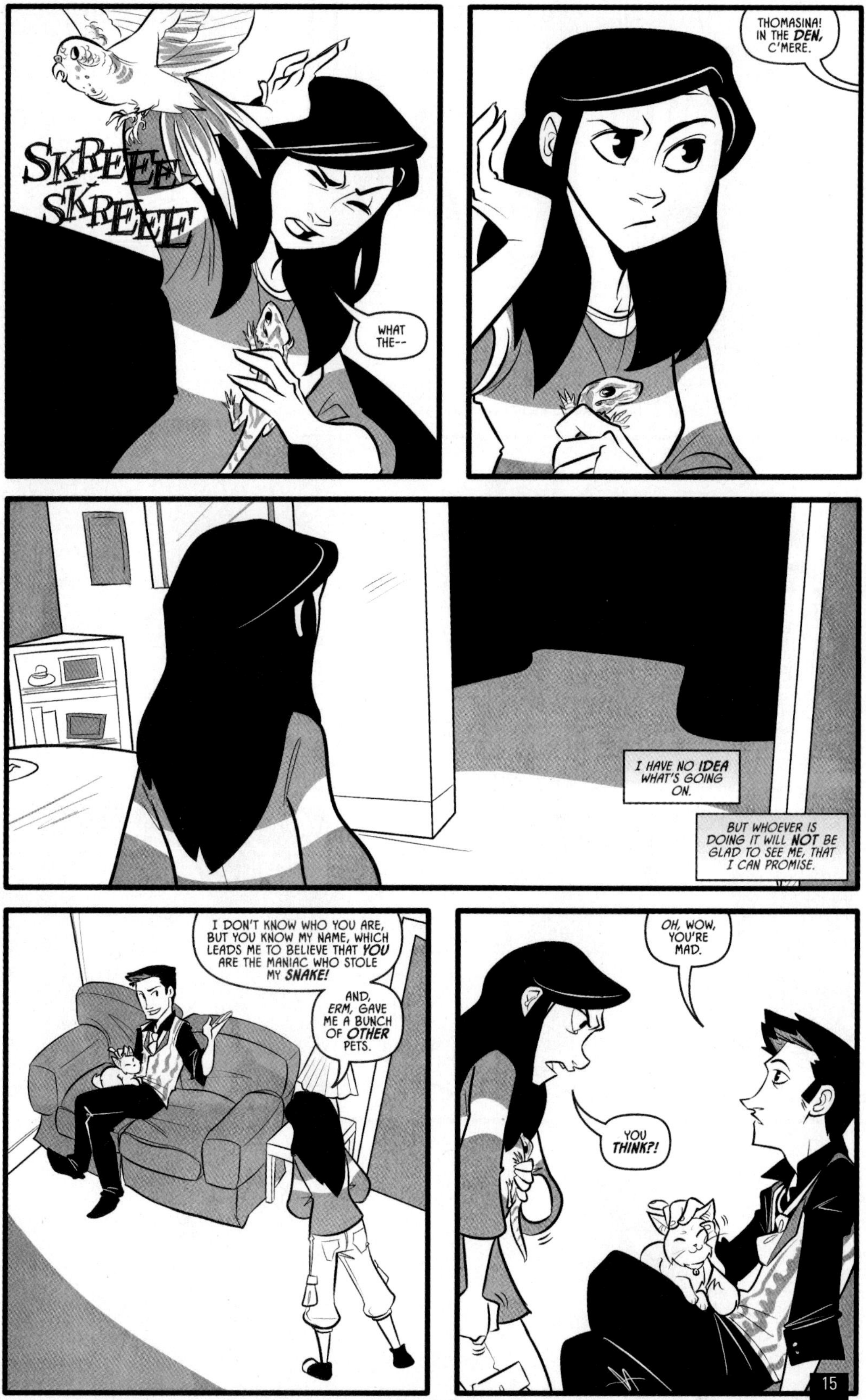
SKREEEE SKREEEE
WHAT THE--
THOMASINA! IN THE DEN, C'MERE.
I HAVE NO IDEA WHAT'S GOING ON.
BUT WHOEVER IS DOING IT WILL NOT BE GLAD TO SEE ME, THAT I CAN PROMISE.
I DON'T KNOW WHO YOU ARE, BUT YOU KNOW MY NAME, WHICH LEADS ME TO BELIEVE THAT YOU ARE THE MANIAC WHO STOLE MY SNAKE!
AND, ERM, GAVE ME A BUNCH OF OTHER PETS.
OH, WOW, YOU'RE MAD.
YOU THINK?!

I DIDN'T **STEAL** ANYTHING, THOMASINA...

AND **WHERE** IS THE **REST** OF MY FAMILY?

AND **WHY** ARE YOU IN MY **HOUSE?**

WHAT'S ALL THIS YELLIN' UP HERE?

OH, **BRILLIANT!** HI THERE, ABUELA!

HOW DO YOU KNOW WHO SHE IS?!

IT'LL ALL MAKE **SENSE** IN A MOMENT.

YOU SEE, LOVE, MY NAME IS **SEBASTIAN.**

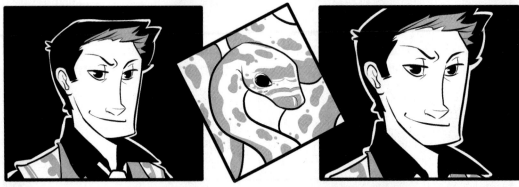

...wha?

o_0

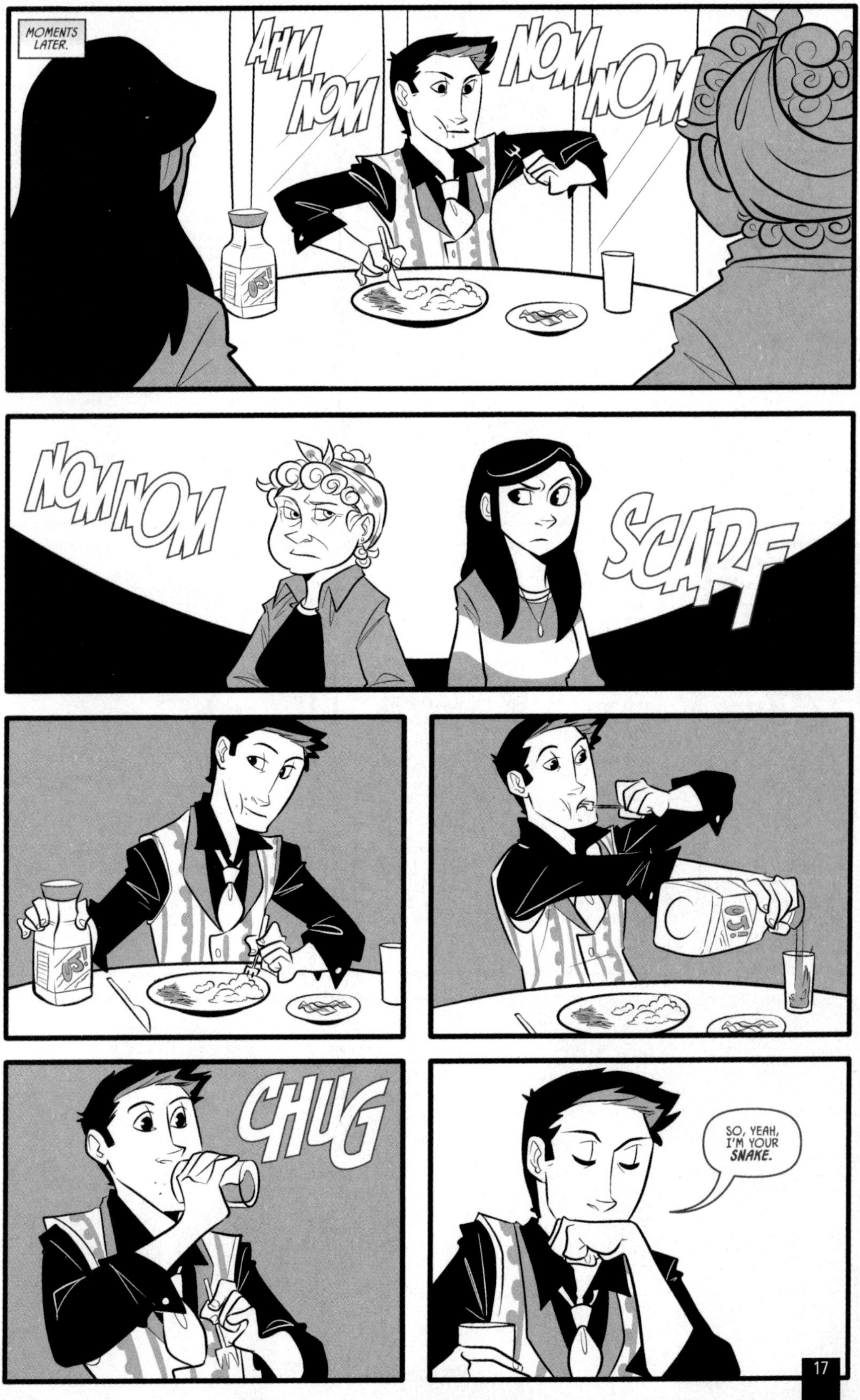
MOMENTS LATER.
AHM NOM
NOM NOM
NOM NOM
SCARF
OJ!
CHUG
SO, YEAH, I'M YOUR *SNAKE*.

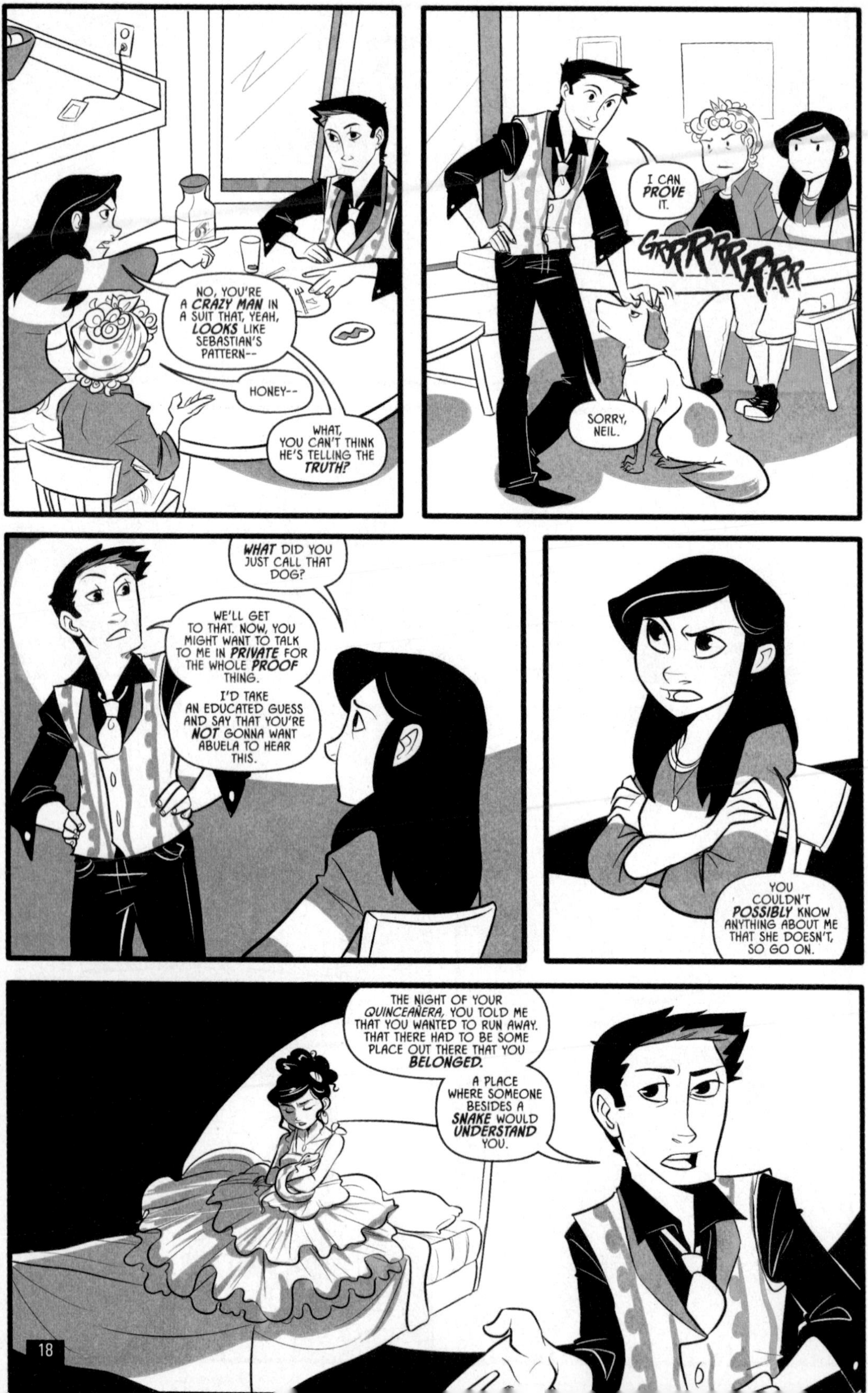
NO, YOU'RE A CRAZY MAN IN A SUIT THAT, YEAH, LOOKS LIKE SEBASTIAN'S PATTERN--
HONEY--
WHAT, YOU CAN'T THINK HE'S TELLING THE TRUTH?
I CAN PROVE IT.
GRRRRRRRRR
SORRY, NEIL.
WHAT DID YOU JUST CALL THAT DOG?
WE'LL GET TO THAT. NOW, YOU MIGHT WANT TO TALK TO ME IN PRIVATE FOR THE WHOLE PROOF THING.
I'D TAKE AN EDUCATED GUESS AND SAY THAT YOU'RE NOT GONNA WANT ABUELA TO HEAR THIS.
YOU COULDN'T POSSIBLY KNOW ANYTHING ABOUT ME THAT SHE DOESN'T, SO GO ON.
THE NIGHT OF YOUR QUINCEAÑERA, YOU TOLD ME THAT YOU WANTED TO RUN AWAY. THAT THERE HAD TO BE SOME PLACE OUT THERE THAT YOU BELONGED.
A PLACE WHERE SOMEONE BESIDES A SNAKE WOULD UNDERSTAND YOU.

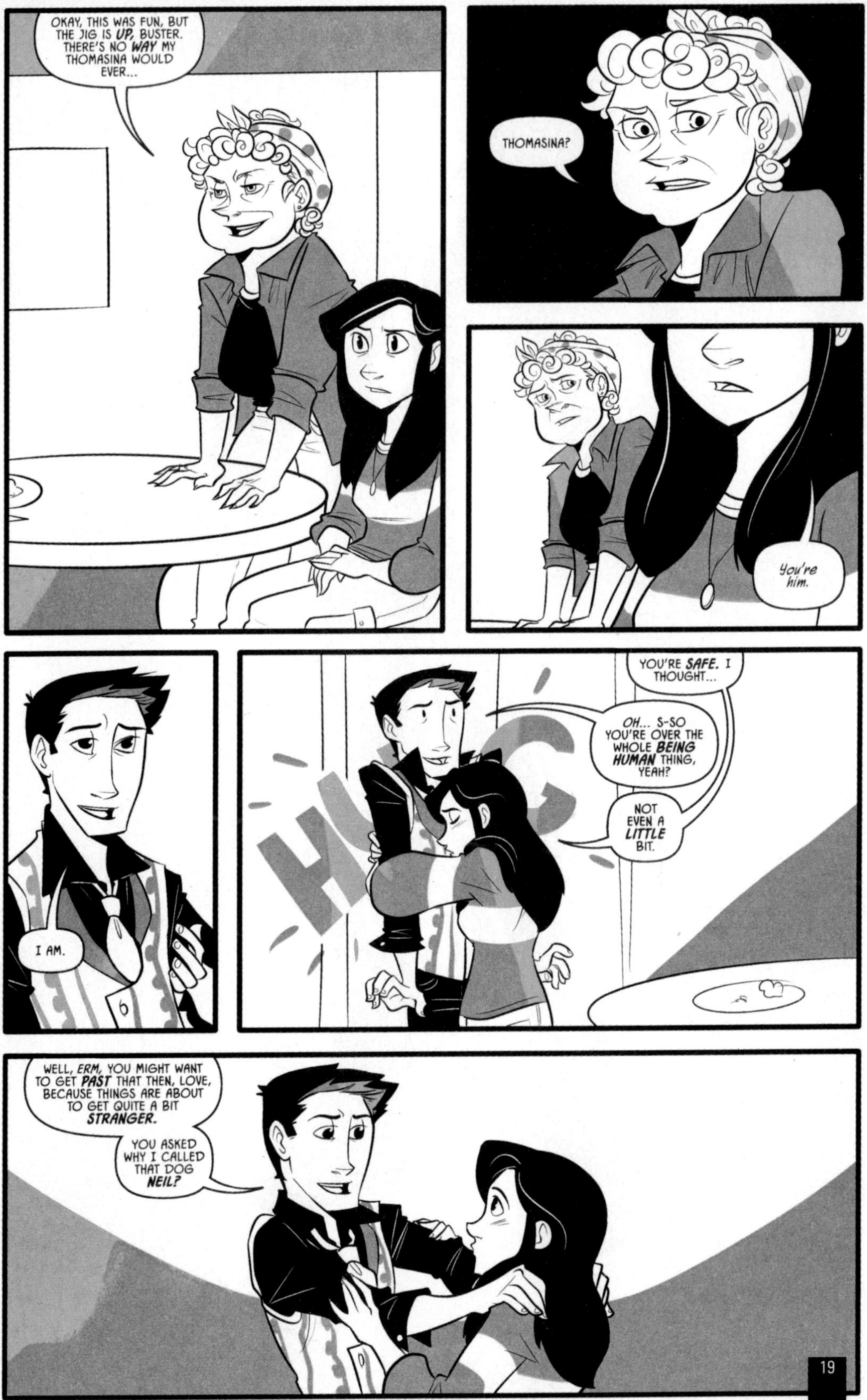

OKAY, THIS WAS FUN, BUT THE JIG IS UP, BUSTER. THERE'S NO WAY MY THOMASINA WOULD EVER...
THOMASINA?
You're him.
I AM.
YOU'RE SAFE. I THOUGHT...
OH... S-SO YOU'RE OVER THE WHOLE BEING HUMAN THING, YEAH?
NOT EVEN A LITTLE BIT.
HUG
WELL, ERM, YOU MIGHT WANT TO GET PAST THAT THEN, LOVE, BECAUSE THINGS ARE ABOUT TO GET QUITE A BIT STRANGER.
YOU ASKED WHY I CALLED THAT DOG NEIL?

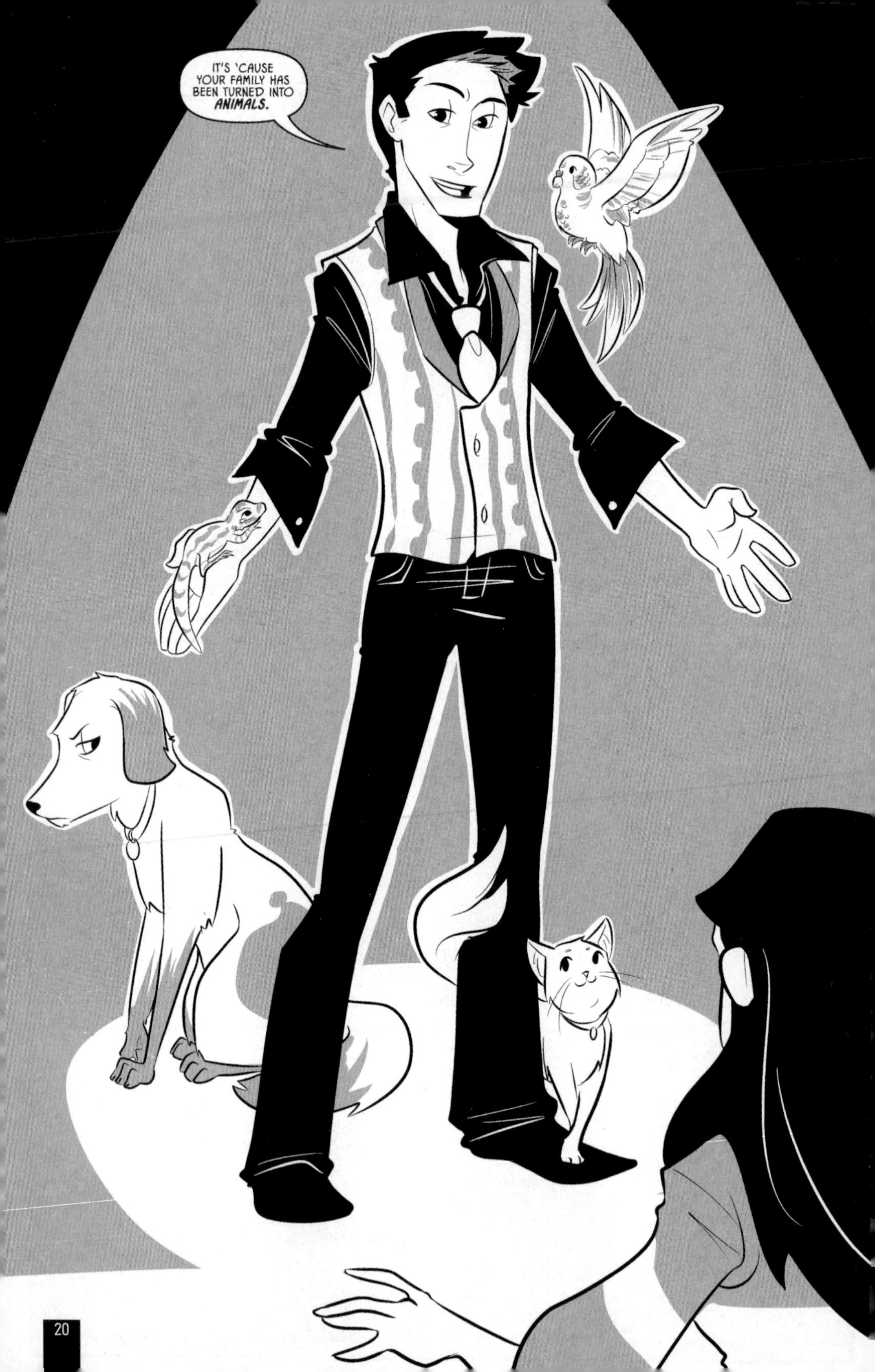
IT'S 'CAUSE YOUR FAMILY HAS BEEN TURNED INTO ANIMALS.

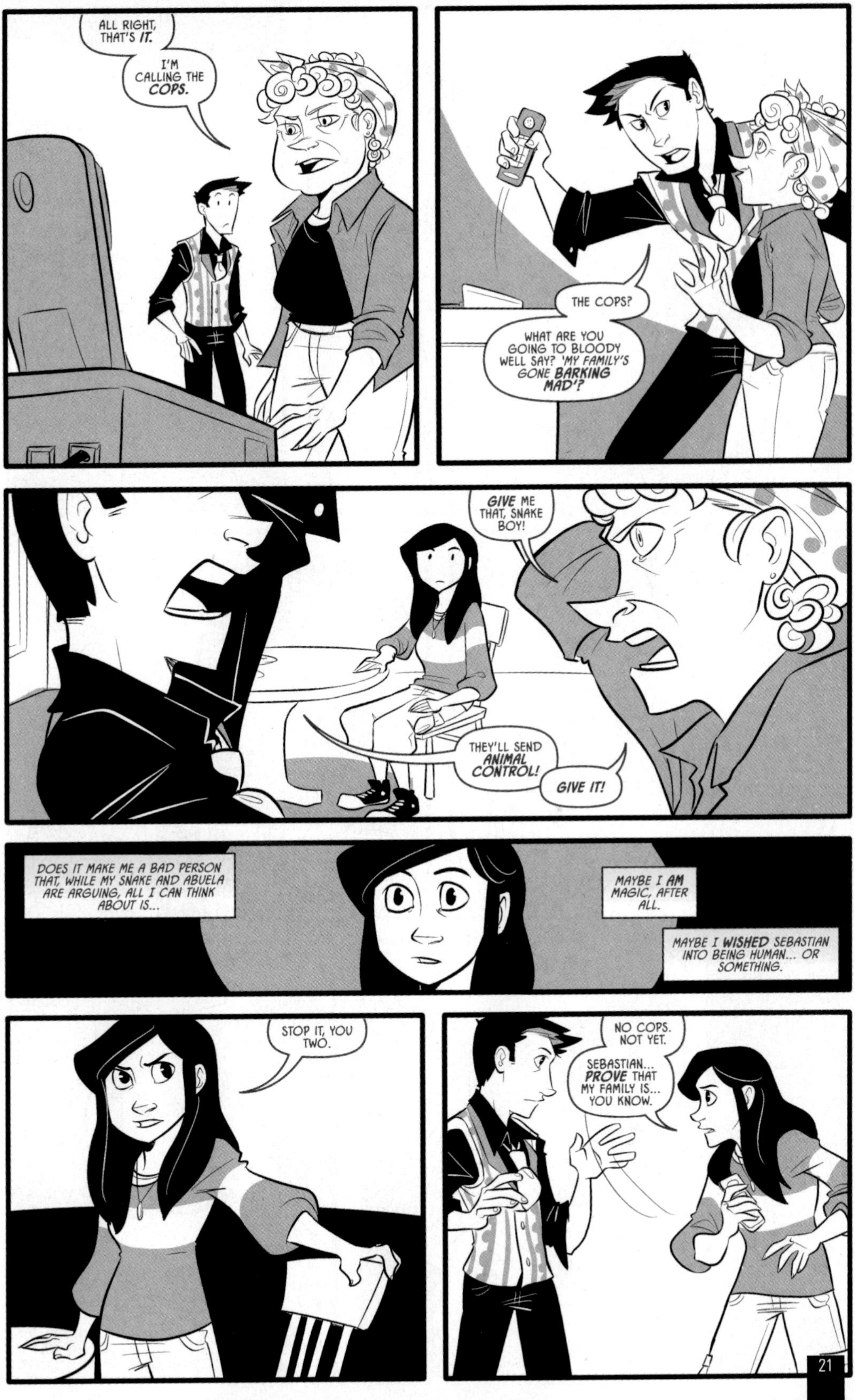
ALL RIGHT, THAT'S IT.
I'M CALLING THE COPS.
THE COPS?
WHAT ARE YOU GOING TO BLOODY WELL SAY? 'MY FAMILY'S GONE BARKING MAD'?
GIVE ME THAT, SNAKE BOY!
THEY'LL SEND ANIMAL CONTROL!
GIVE IT!
DOES IT MAKE ME A BAD PERSON THAT, WHILE MY SNAKE AND ABUELA ARE ARGUING, ALL I CAN THINK ABOUT IS...
MAYBE I AM MAGIC, AFTER ALL.
MAYBE I WISHED SEBASTIAN INTO BEING HUMAN... OR SOMETHING.
STOP IT, YOU TWO.
NO COPS. NOT YET.
SEBASTIAN... PROVE THAT MY FAMILY IS... YOU KNOW.

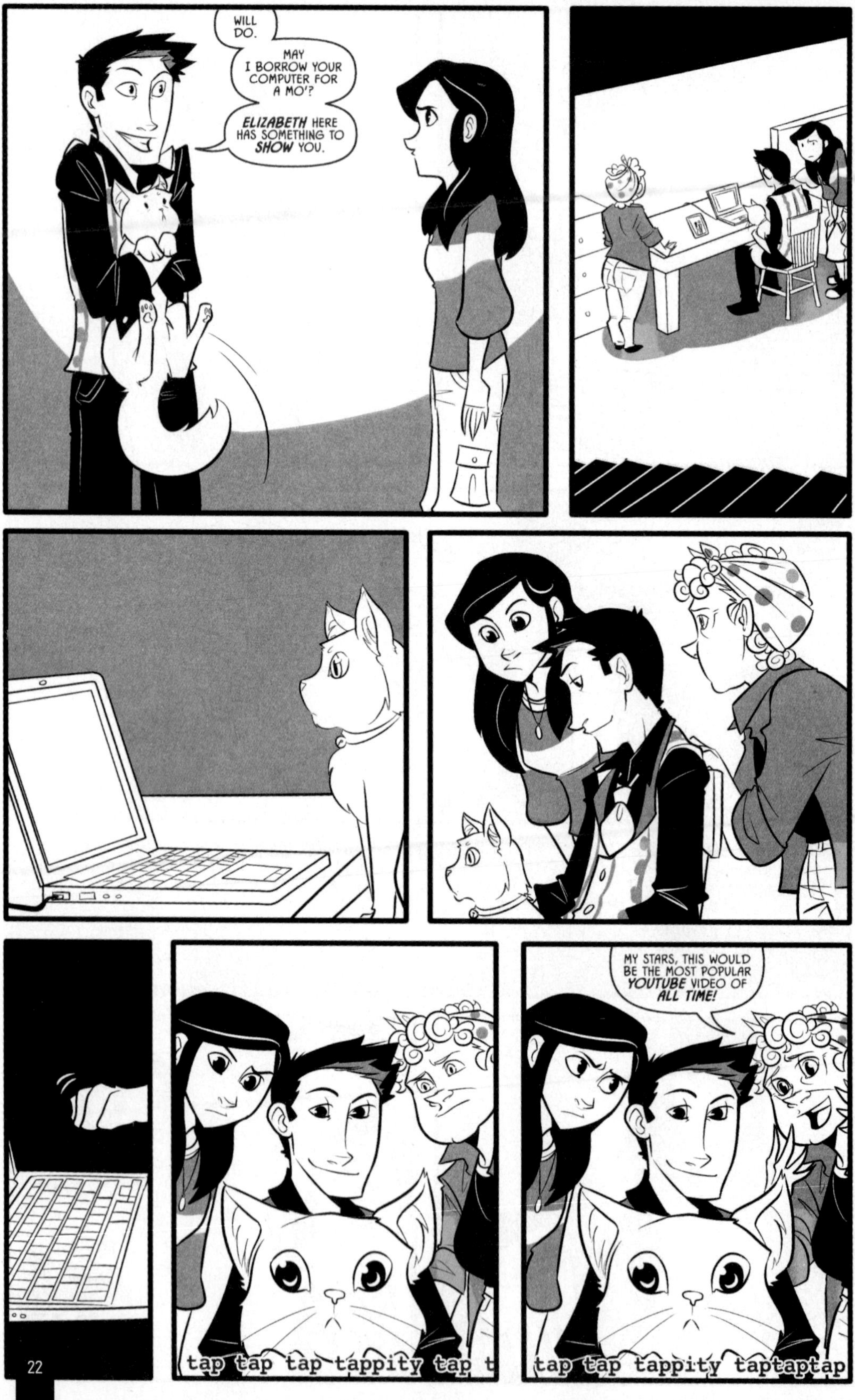
WILL DO.
MAY I BORROW YOUR COMPUTER FOR A MO'?
ELIZABETH HERE HAS SOMETHING TO SHOW YOU.
tap tap tap tappity tap t
MY STARS, THIS WOULD BE THE MOST POPULAR YOUTUBE VIDEO OF ALL TIME!
tap tap tappity taptaptap

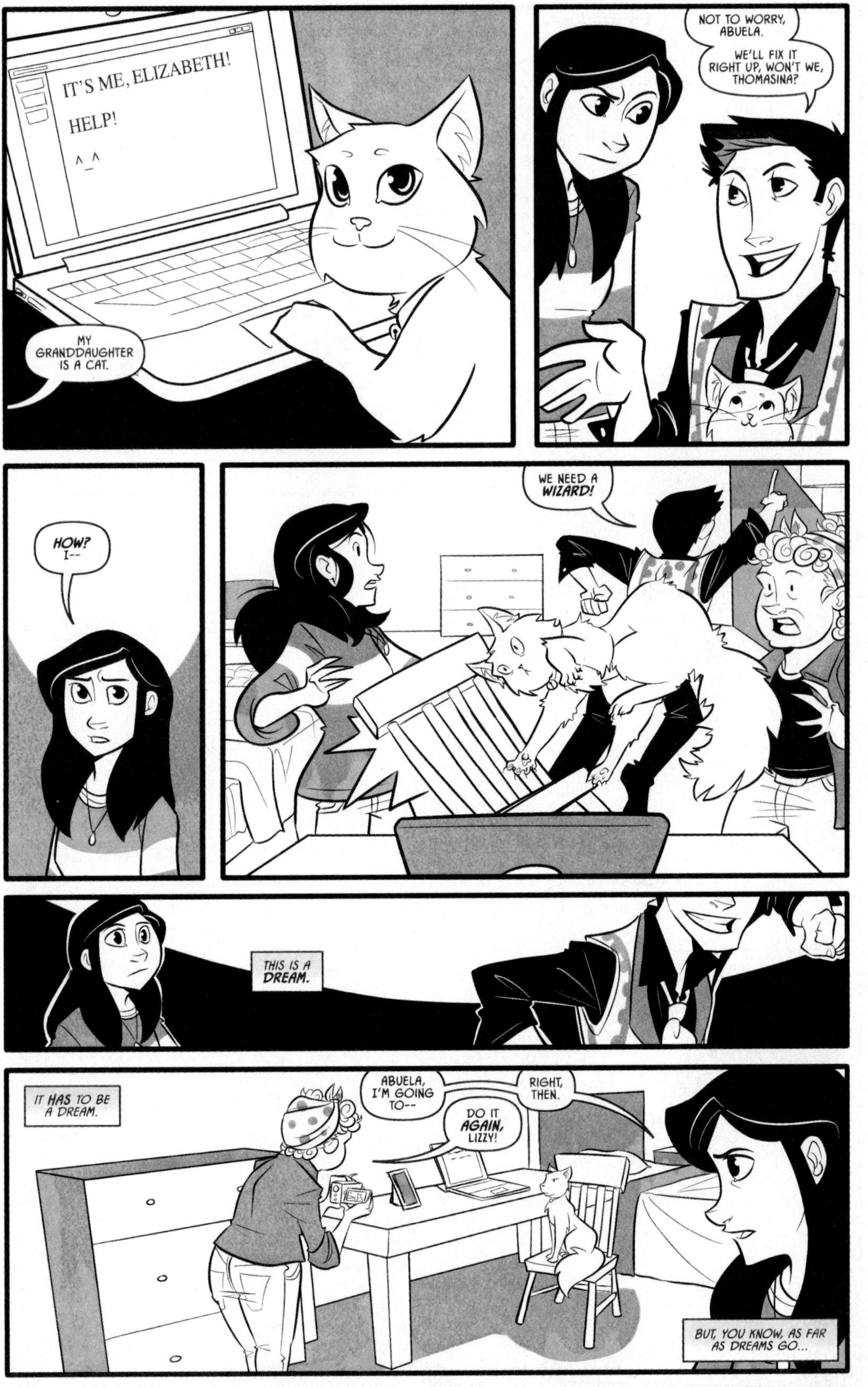
IT'S ME, ELIZABETH!
HELP!
^_^
MY GRANDDAUGHTER IS A CAT.
NOT TO WORRY, ABUELA.
WE'LL FIX IT RIGHT UP, WON'T WE, THOMASINA?
HOW? I--
WE NEED A WIZARD!
THIS IS A DREAM.
IT HAS TO BE A DREAM.
ABUELA, I'M GOING TO--
RIGHT, THEN.
DO IT AGAIN, LIZZY!
BUT, YOU KNOW, AS FAR AS DREAMS GO...

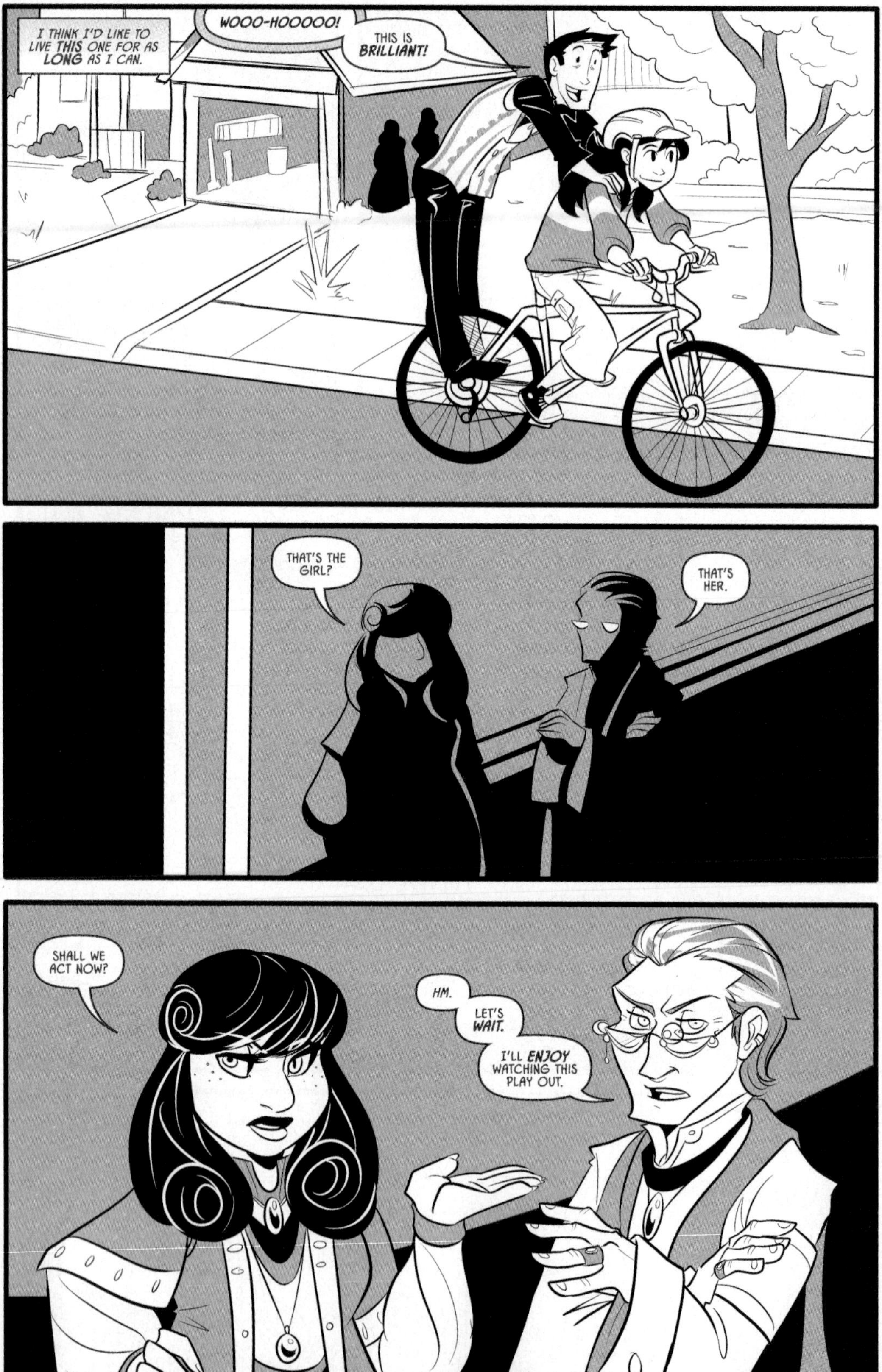

I THINK I'D LIKE TO LIVE **THIS** ONE FOR AS **LONG** AS I CAN.
WOOO-HOOOOO!
THIS IS **BRILLIANT!**
THAT'S THE GIRL?
THAT'S HER.
SHALL WE ACT NOW?
HM.
LET'S **WAIT.**
I'LL **ENJOY** WATCHING THIS PLAY OUT.

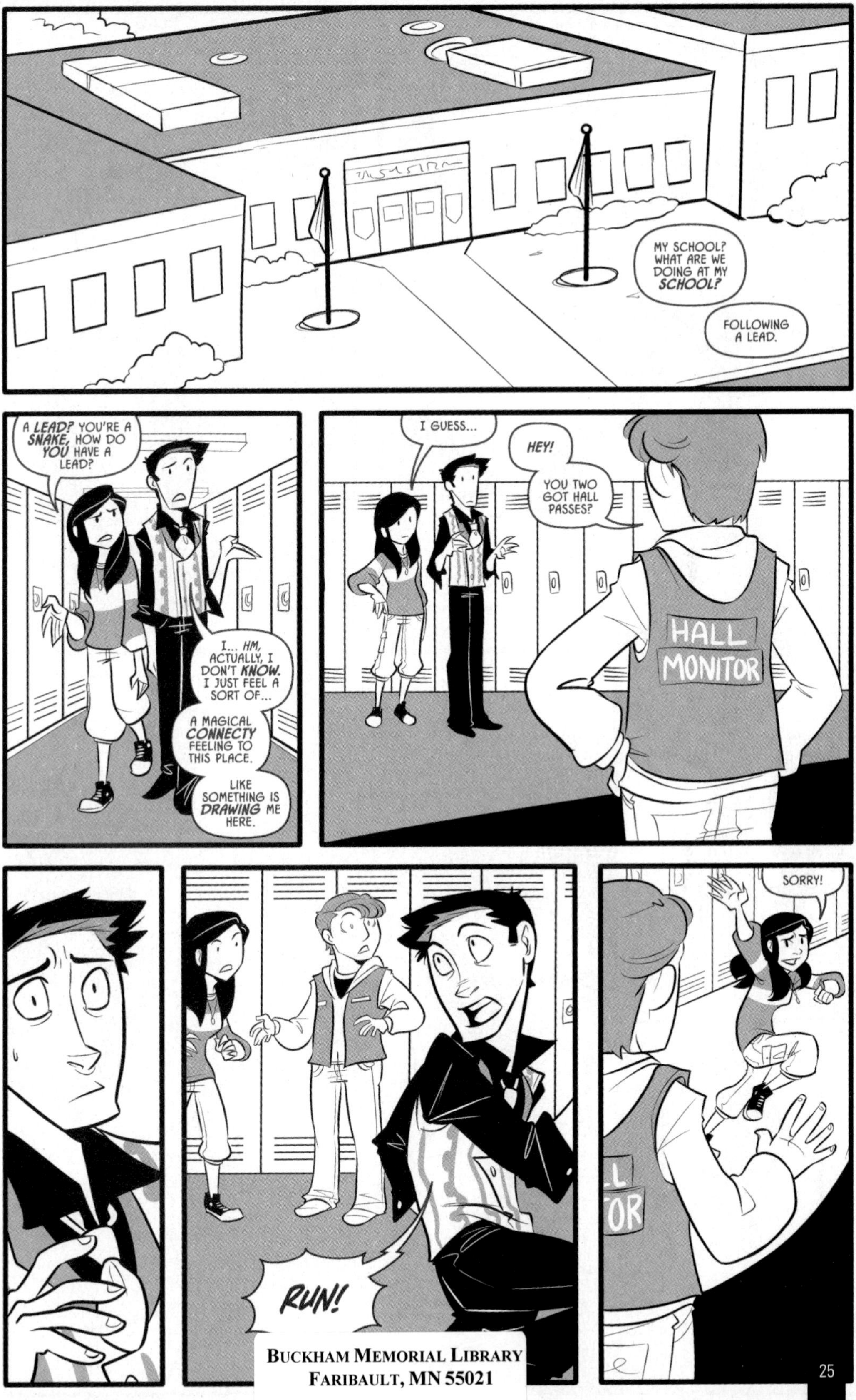
MY SCHOOL? WHAT ARE WE DOING AT MY SCHOOL?
FOLLOWING A LEAD.
A LEAD? YOU'RE A SNAKE, HOW DO YOU HAVE A LEAD?
I... HM, ACTUALLY, I DON'T KNOW. I JUST FEEL A SORT OF...
A MAGICAL CONNECTY FEELING TO THIS PLACE.
LIKE SOMETHING IS DRAWING ME HERE.
I GUESS...
HEY!
YOU TWO GOT HALL PASSES?
HALL MONITOR
RUN!
SORRY!

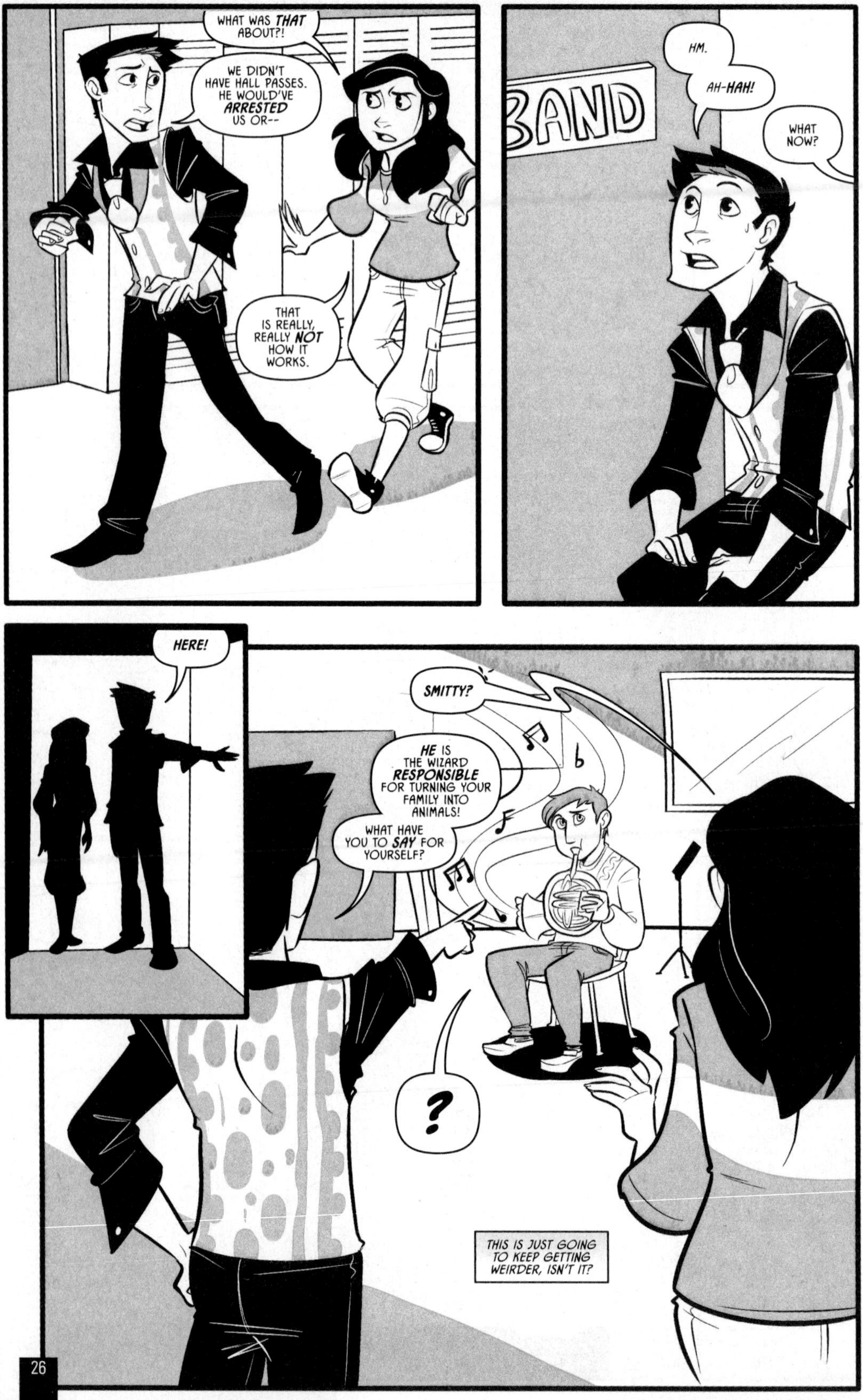
WHAT WAS THAT ABOUT?!
WE DIDN'T HAVE HALL PASSES. HE WOULD'VE ARRESTED US OR--
THAT IS REALLY, REALLY NOT HOW IT WORKS.
BAND
HM.
AH-HAH!
WHAT NOW?
HERE!
SMITTY?
HE IS THE WIZARD RESPONSIBLE FOR TURNING YOUR FAMILY INTO ANIMALS!
WHAT HAVE YOU TO SAY FOR YOURSELF?
?
THIS IS JUST GOING TO KEEP GETTING WEIRDER, ISN'T IT?

FAMILY PETS

FAMILY PETS
CHAPTER TWO

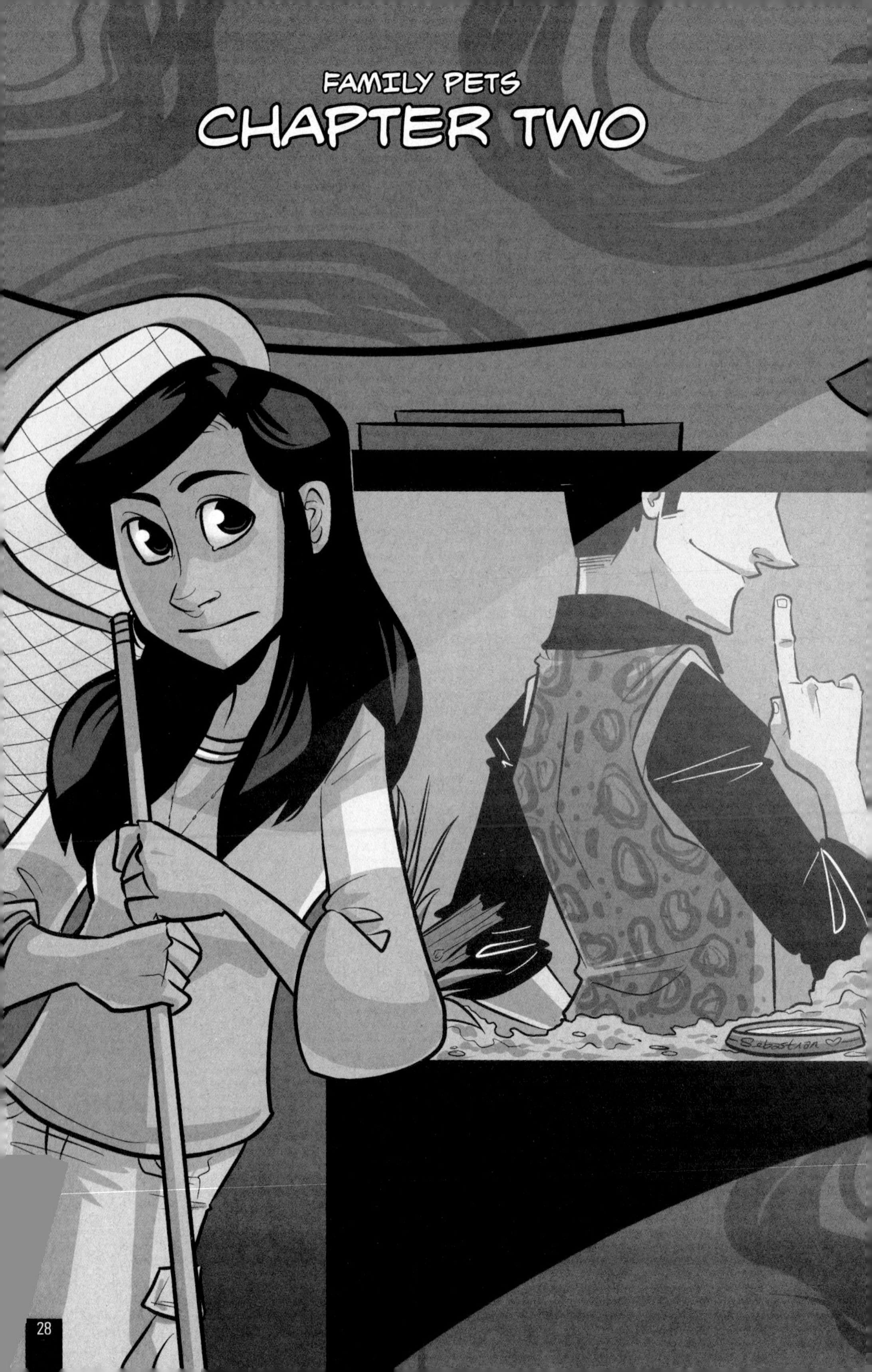

Sebastian

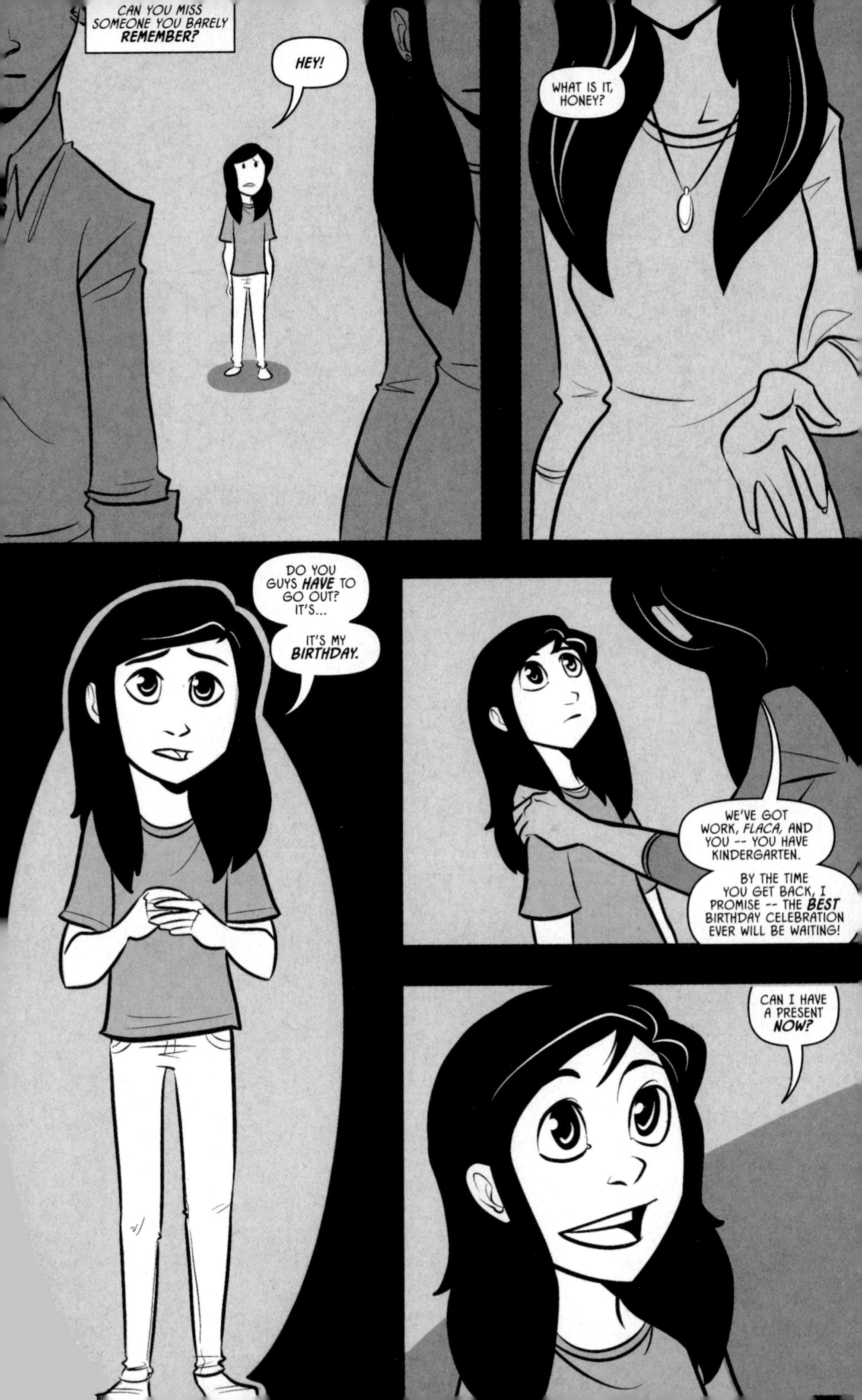
CAN YOU MISS SOMEONE YOU BARELY **REMEMBER?**
HEY!
WHAT IS IT, HONEY?
DO YOU GUYS **HAVE** TO GO OUT? IT'S...
IT'S MY **BIRTHDAY.**
WE'VE GOT WORK, *FLACA,* AND YOU -- YOU HAVE KINDERGARTEN.
BY THE TIME YOU GET BACK, I PROMISE -- THE **BEST** BIRTHDAY CELEBRATION EVER WILL BE WAITING!
CAN I HAVE A PRESENT **NOW?**

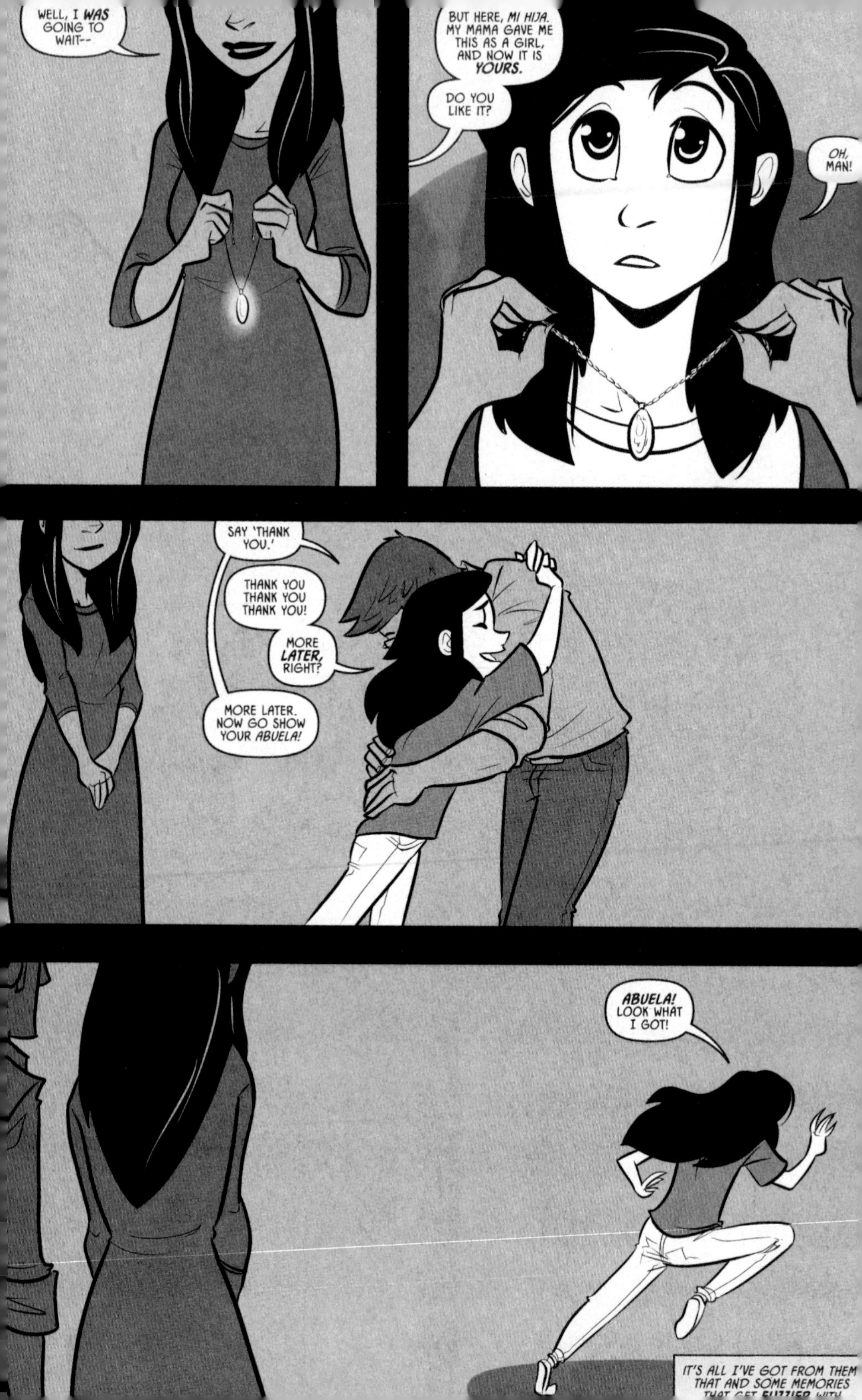
WELL, I **WAS** GOING TO WAIT--
BUT HERE, *MI HIJA.* MY MAMA GAVE ME THIS AS A GIRL, AND NOW IT IS ***YOURS.***
DO YOU LIKE IT?
OH, MAN!
SAY 'THANK YOU.'
THANK YOU THANK YOU THANK YOU!
MORE ***LATER,*** RIGHT?
MORE LATER. NOW GO SHOW YOUR *ABUELA!*
ABUELA! LOOK WHAT I GOT!
IT'S ALL I'VE GOT FROM THEM
THAT AND SOME MEMORIES

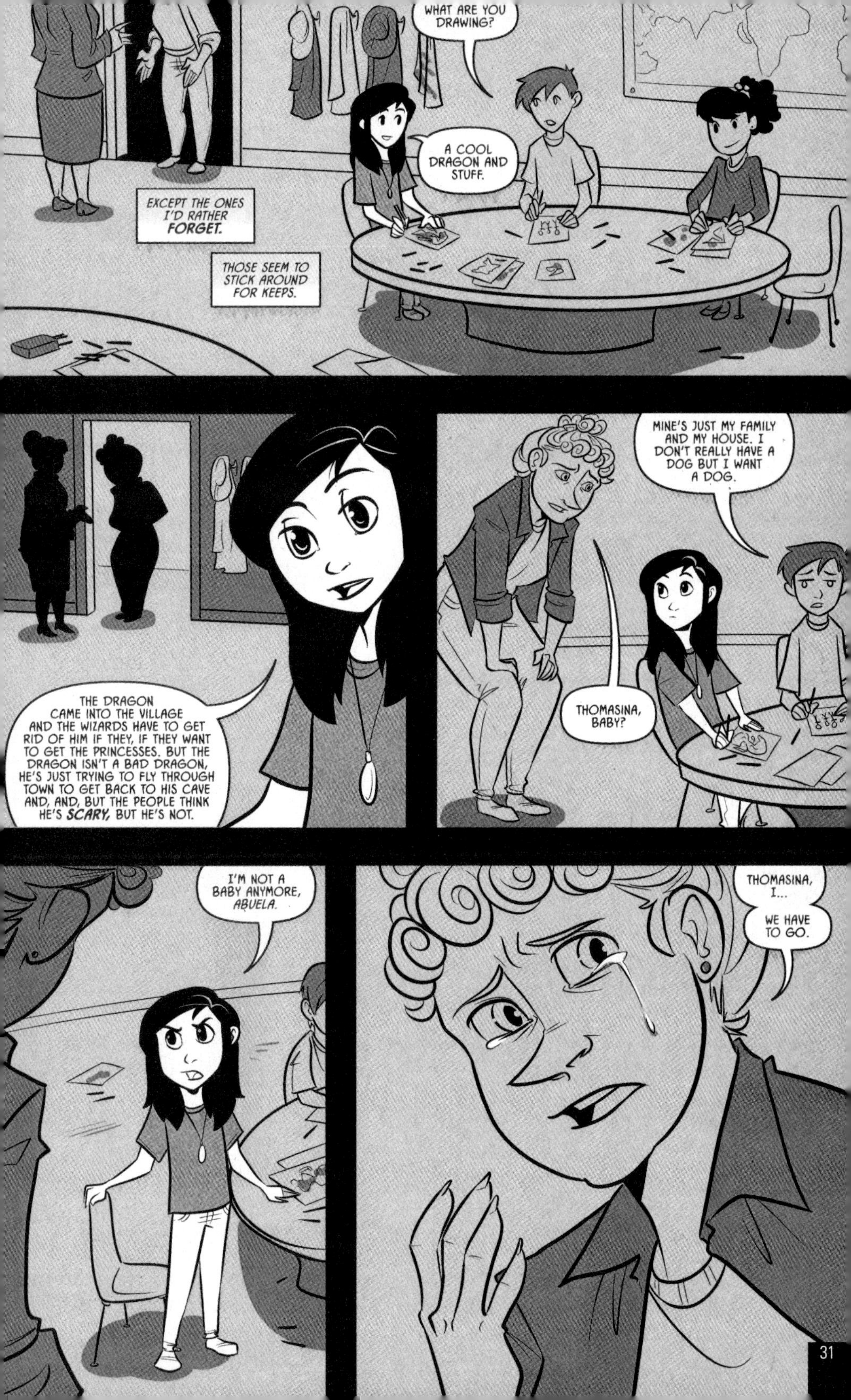
WHAT ARE YOU DRAWING?
A COOL DRAGON AND STUFF.
EXCEPT THE ONES I'D RATHER **FORGET.**
THOSE SEEM TO STICK AROUND FOR KEEPS.
THE DRAGON CAME INTO THE VILLAGE AND THE WIZARDS HAVE TO GET RID OF HIM IF THEY, IF THEY WANT TO GET THE PRINCESSES. BUT THE DRAGON ISN'T A BAD DRAGON, HE'S JUST TRYING TO FLY THROUGH TOWN TO GET BACK TO HIS CAVE AND, AND, BUT THE PEOPLE THINK HE'S *SCARY,* BUT HE'S NOT.
MINE'S JUST MY FAMILY AND MY HOUSE. I DON'T REALLY HAVE A DOG BUT I WANT A DOG.
THOMASINA, BABY?
I'M NOT A BABY ANYMORE, *ABUELA.*
THOMASINA, I...
WE HAVE TO GO.

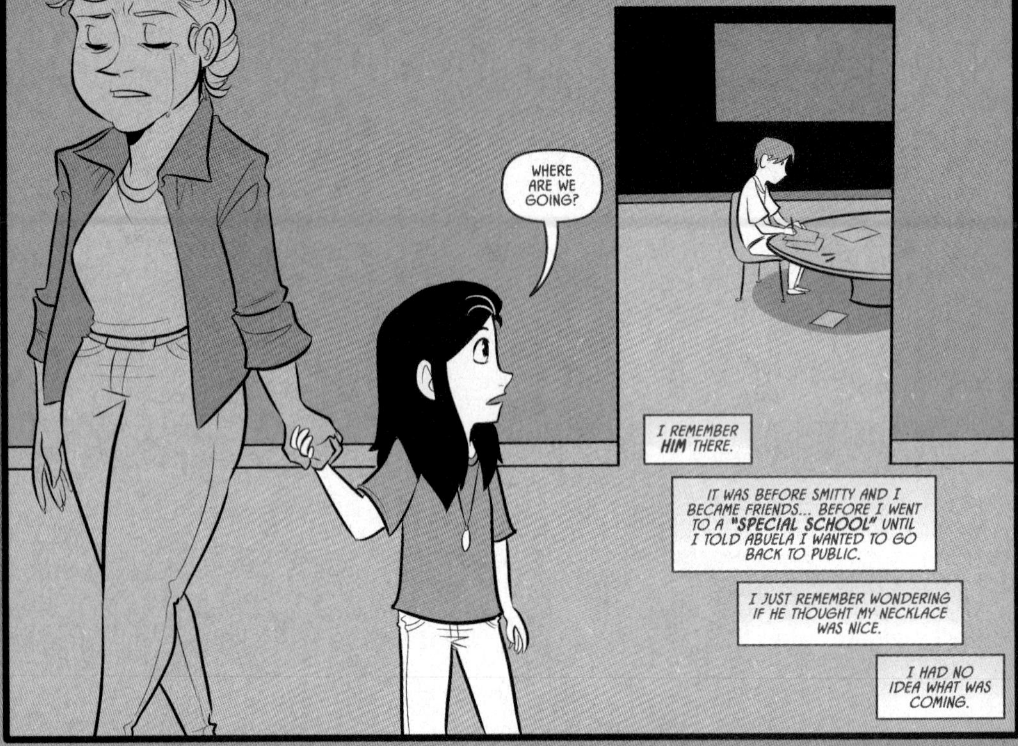
WHERE ARE WE GOING?
I REMEMBER HIM THERE.
IT WAS BEFORE SMITTY AND I BECAME FRIENDS... BEFORE I WENT TO A "SPECIAL SCHOOL" UNTIL I TOLD ABUELA I WANTED TO GO BACK TO PUBLIC.
I JUST REMEMBER WONDERING IF HE THOUGHT MY NECKLACE WAS NICE.
I HAD NO IDEA WHAT WAS COMING.

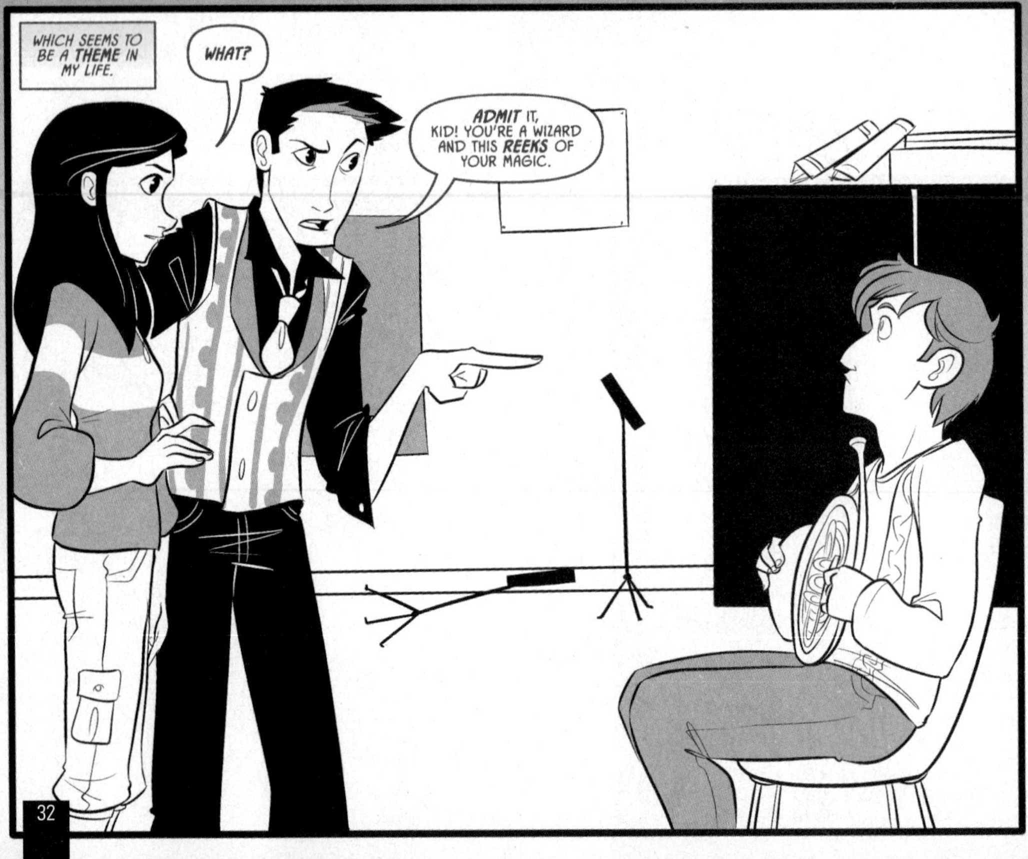
WHICH SEEMS TO BE A THEME IN MY LIFE.
WHAT?
ADMIT IT, KID! YOU'RE A WIZARD AND THIS REEKS OF YOUR MAGIC.

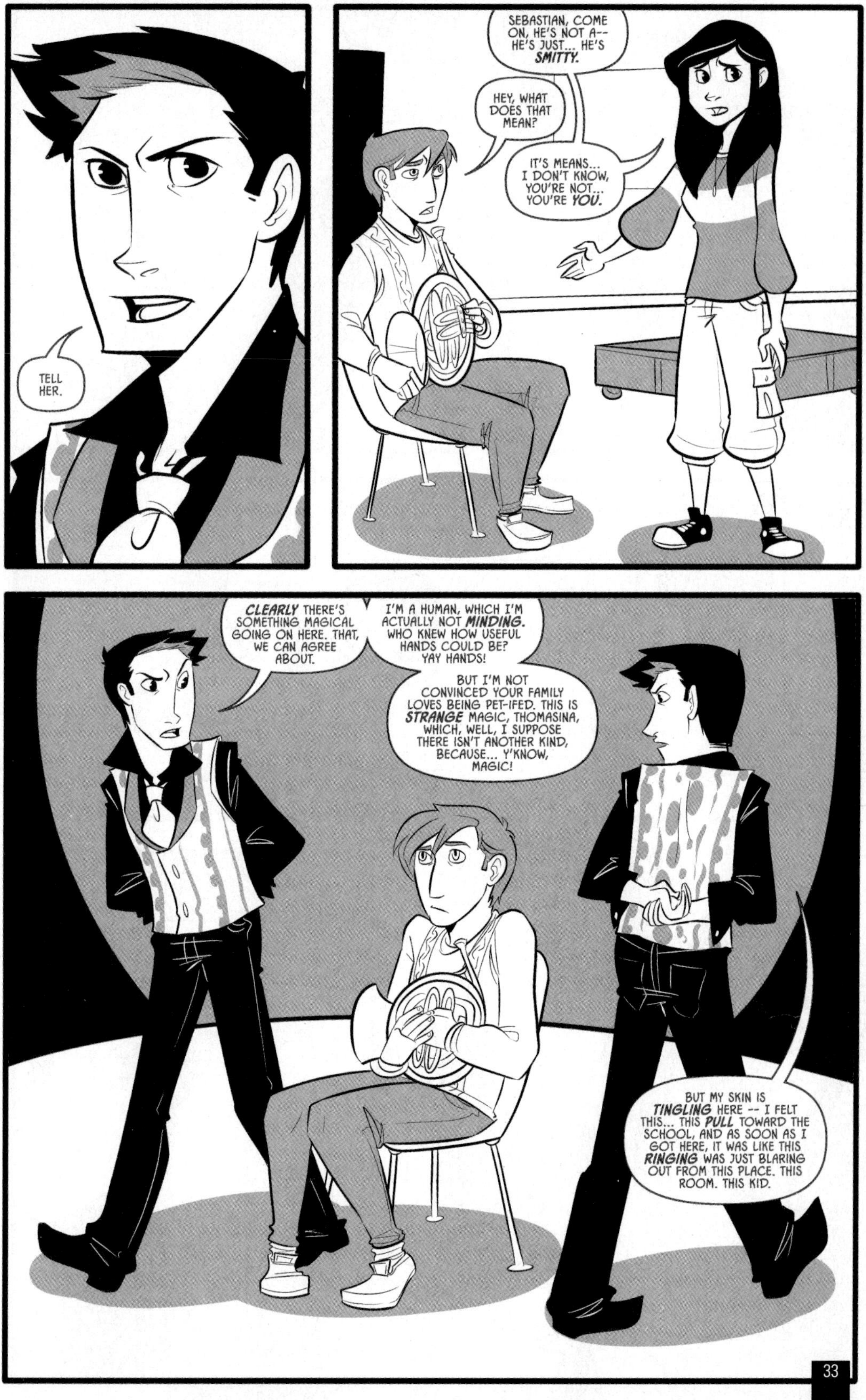
TELL HER.
SEBASTIAN, COME ON, HE'S NOT A-- HE'S JUST... HE'S SMITTY.
HEY, WHAT DOES THAT MEAN?
IT'S MEANS... I DON'T KNOW, YOU'RE NOT... YOU'RE YOU.
CLEARLY THERE'S SOMETHING MAGICAL GOING ON HERE. THAT, WE CAN AGREE ABOUT.
I'M A HUMAN, WHICH I'M ACTUALLY NOT MINDING. WHO KNEW HOW USEFUL HANDS COULD BE? YAY HANDS!
BUT I'M NOT CONVINCED YOUR FAMILY LOVES BEING PET-IFED. THIS IS STRANGE MAGIC, THOMASINA, WHICH, WELL, I SUPPOSE THERE ISN'T ANOTHER KIND, BECAUSE... Y'KNOW, MAGIC!
BUT MY SKIN IS TINGLING HERE -- I FELT THIS... THIS PULL TOWARD THE SCHOOL, AND AS SOON AS I GOT HERE, IT WAS LIKE THIS RINGING WAS JUST BLARING OUT FROM THIS PLACE. THIS ROOM. THIS KID.

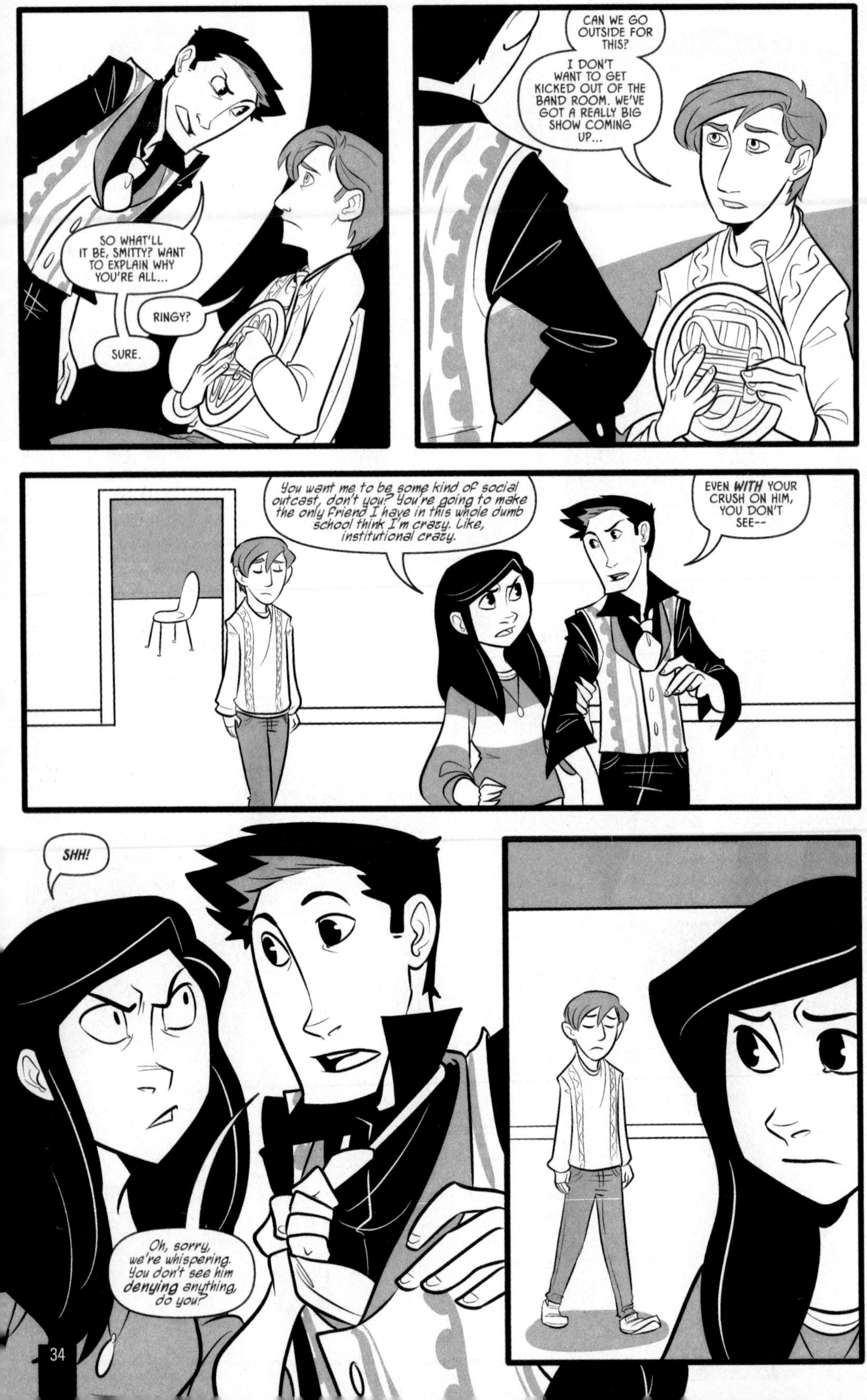
SO WHAT'LL IT BE, SMITTY? WANT TO EXPLAIN WHY YOU'RE ALL...
RINGY?
SURE.
CAN WE GO OUTSIDE FOR THIS?
I DON'T WANT TO GET KICKED OUT OF THE BAND ROOM. WE'VE GOT A REALLY BIG SHOW COMING UP...
You want me to be some kind of social outcast, don't you? You're going to make the only friend I have in this whole dumb school think I'm crazy. Like, institutional crazy.
EVEN WITH YOUR CRUSH ON HIM, YOU DON'T SEE--
SHH!
Oh, sorry, we're whispering. You don't see him denying anything, do you?

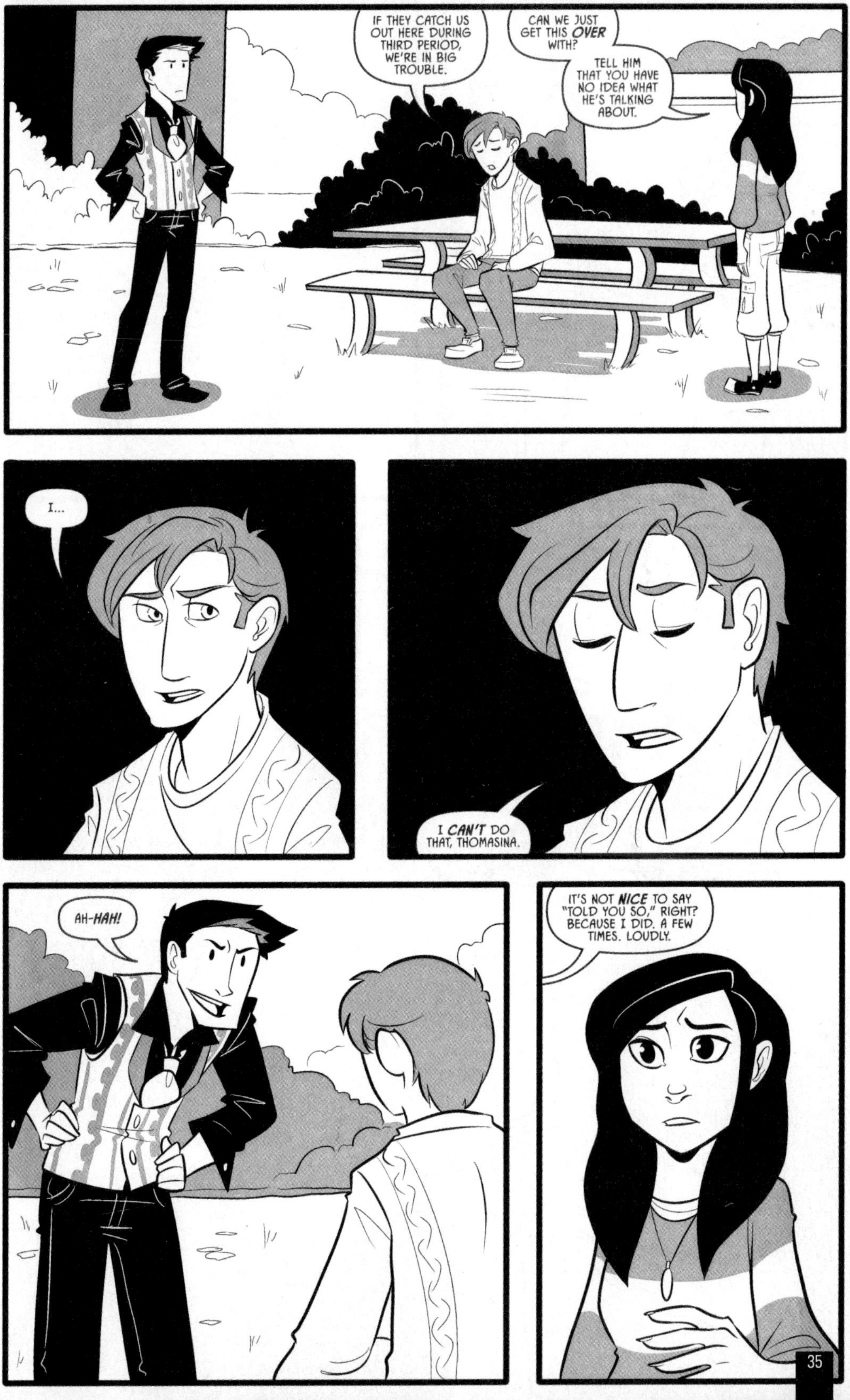
IF THEY CATCH US OUT HERE DURING THIRD PERIOD, WE'RE IN BIG TROUBLE.
CAN WE JUST GET THIS OVER WITH?
TELL HIM THAT YOU HAVE NO IDEA WHAT HE'S TALKING ABOUT.
I...
I CAN'T DO THAT, THOMASINA.
AH-HAH!
IT'S NOT NICE TO SAY "TOLD YOU SO," RIGHT? BECAUSE I DID. A FEW TIMES. LOUDLY.

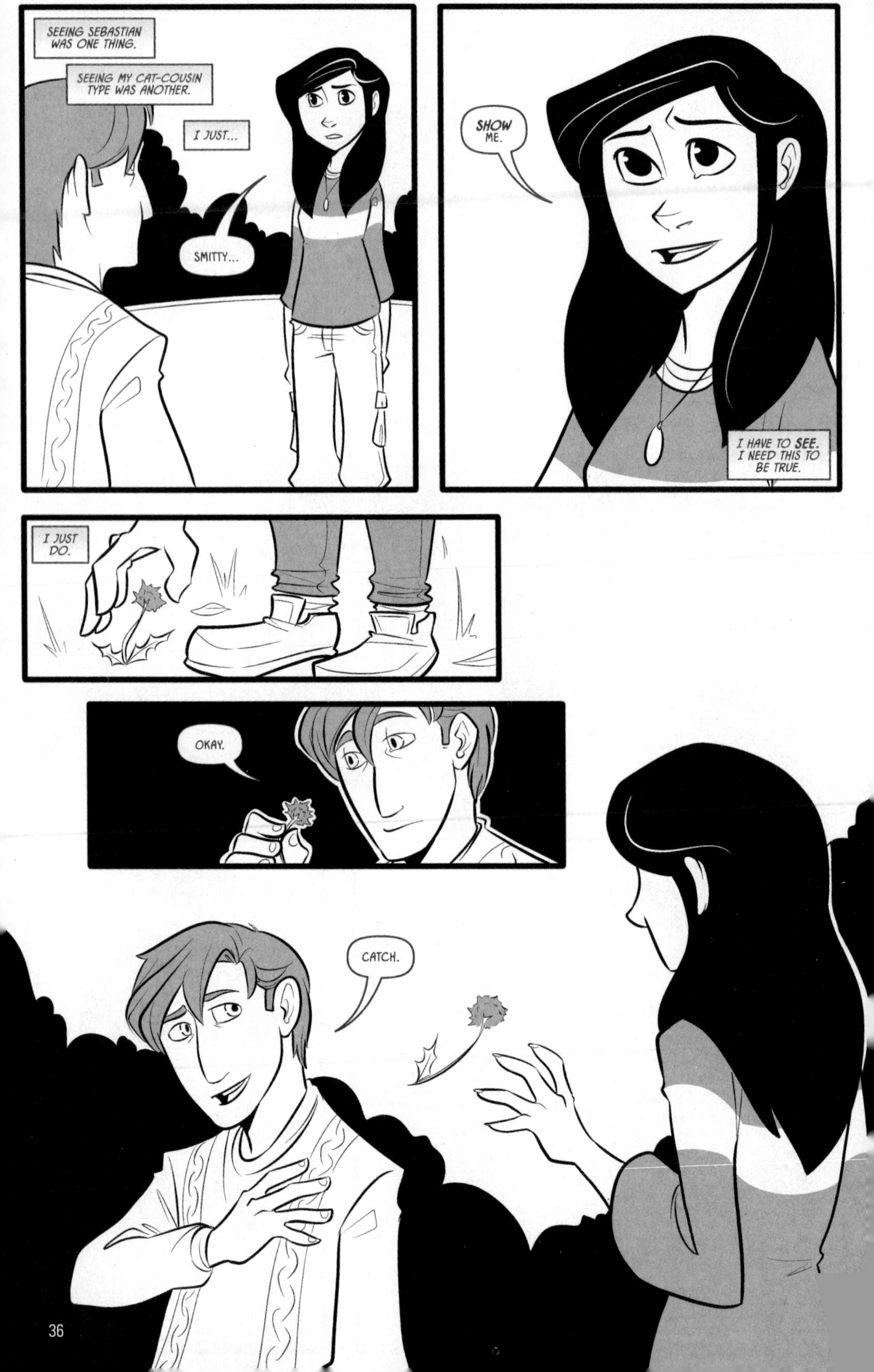
SEEING SEBASTIAN WAS ONE THING.
SEEING MY CAT-COUSIN TYPE WAS ANOTHER.
I JUST...
SMITTY...
SHOW ME.
I HAVE TO SEE. I NEED THIS TO BE TRUE.
I JUST DO.
OKAY.
CATCH.

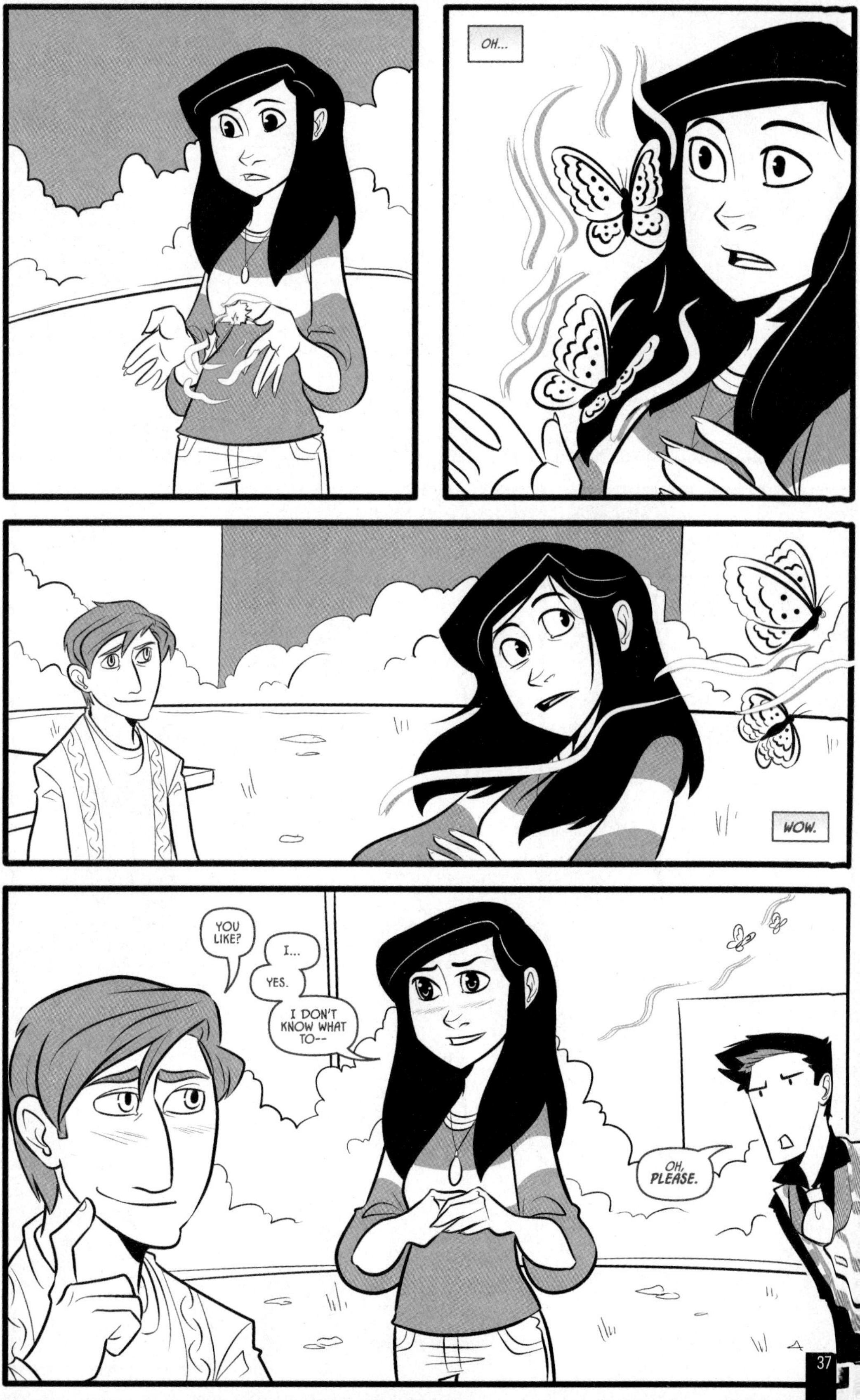
OH...
WOW.
YOU LIKE?
I...
YES.
I DON'T KNOW WHAT TO--
OH, PLEASE.

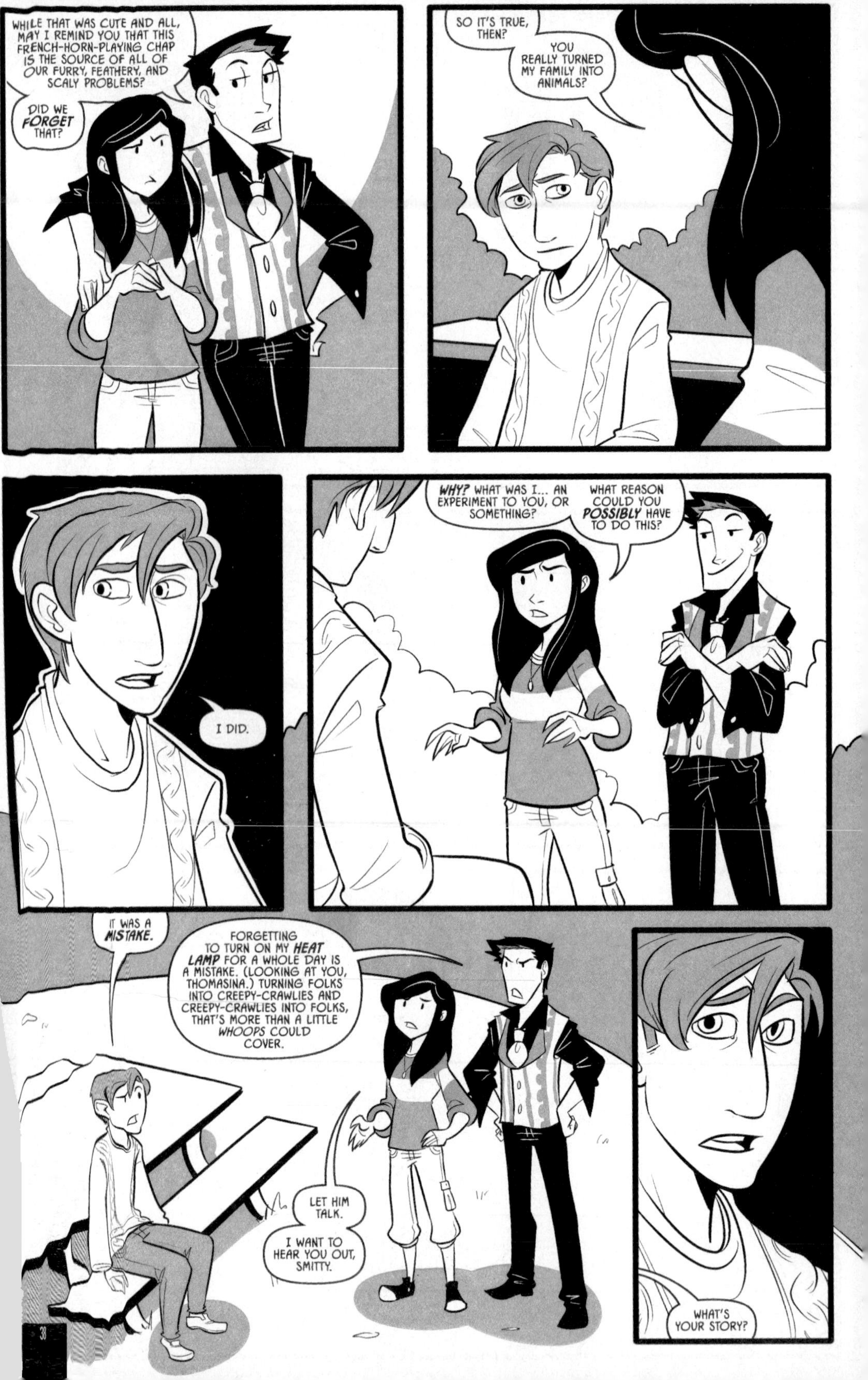
WHILE THAT WAS CUTE AND ALL, MAY I REMIND YOU THAT THIS FRENCH-HORN-PLAYING CHAP IS THE SOURCE OF ALL OF OUR FURRY, FEATHERY, AND SCALY PROBLEMS?
DID WE FORGET THAT?
SO IT'S TRUE, THEN?
YOU REALLY TURNED MY FAMILY INTO ANIMALS?
I DID.
WHY? WHAT WAS I... AN EXPERIMENT TO YOU, OR SOMETHING?
WHAT REASON COULD YOU POSSIBLY HAVE TO DO THIS?
IT WAS A MISTAKE.
FORGETTING TO TURN ON MY HEAT LAMP FOR A WHOLE DAY IS A MISTAKE. (LOOKING AT YOU, THOMASINA.) TURNING FOLKS INTO CREEPY-CRAWLIES AND CREEPY-CRAWLIES INTO FOLKS, THAT'S MORE THAN A LITTLE WHOOPS COULD COVER.
LET HIM TALK.
I WANT TO HEAR YOU OUT, SMITTY.
WHAT'S YOUR STORY?

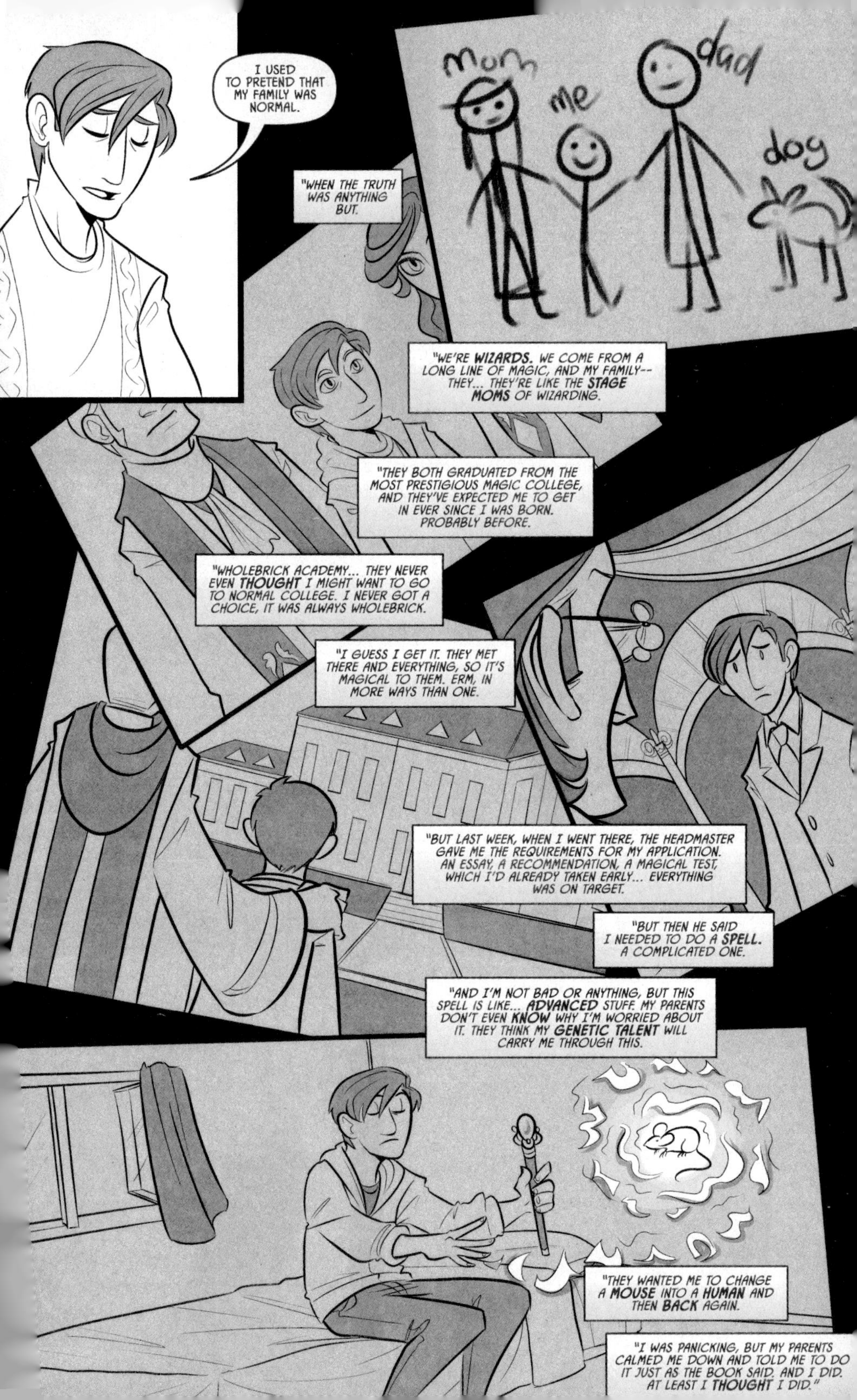
I USED TO PRETEND THAT MY FAMILY WAS NORMAL.
mom
me
dad
dog
"WHEN THE TRUTH WAS ANYTHING BUT.
"WE'RE WIZARDS. WE COME FROM A LONG LINE OF MAGIC, AND MY FAMILY-- THEY... THEY'RE LIKE THE STAGE MOMS OF WIZARDING.
"THEY BOTH GRADUATED FROM THE MOST PRESTIGIOUS MAGIC COLLEGE, AND THEY'VE EXPECTED ME TO GET IN EVER SINCE I WAS BORN. PROBABLY BEFORE.
"WHOLEBRICK ACADEMY... THEY NEVER EVEN THOUGHT I MIGHT WANT TO GO TO NORMAL COLLEGE. I NEVER GOT A CHOICE, IT WAS ALWAYS WHOLEBRICK.
"I GUESS I GET IT. THEY MET THERE AND EVERYTHING, SO IT'S MAGICAL TO THEM. ERM, IN MORE WAYS THAN ONE.
"BUT LAST WEEK, WHEN I WENT THERE, THE HEADMASTER GAVE ME THE REQUIREMENTS FOR MY APPLICATION. AN ESSAY, A RECOMMENDATION, A MAGICAL TEST, WHICH I'D ALREADY TAKEN EARLY... EVERYTHING WAS ON TARGET.
"BUT THEN HE SAID I NEEDED TO DO A SPELL. A COMPLICATED ONE.
"AND I'M NOT BAD OR ANYTHING, BUT THIS SPELL IS LIKE... ADVANCED STUFF. MY PARENTS DON'T EVEN KNOW WHY I'M WORRIED ABOUT IT. THEY THINK MY GENETIC TALENT WILL CARRY ME THROUGH THIS.
"THEY WANTED ME TO CHANGE A MOUSE INTO A HUMAN AND THEN BACK AGAIN.
"I WAS PANICKING, BUT MY PARENTS CALMED ME DOWN AND TOLD ME TO DO IT JUST AS THE BOOK SAID. AND I DID. AT LEAST I THOUGHT I DID."

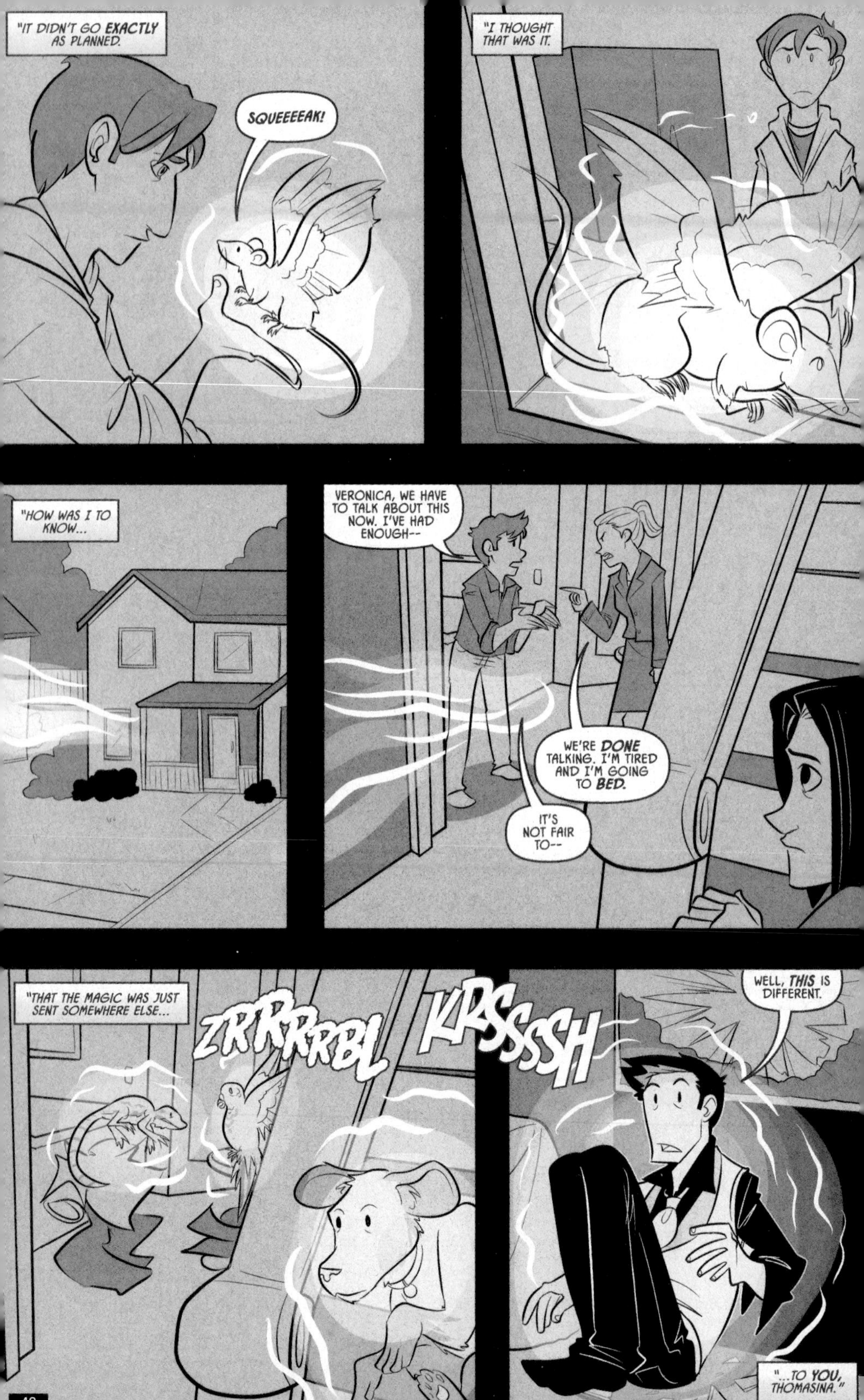
"IT DIDN'T GO EXACTLY AS PLANNED.
SQUEEEEAK!
"I THOUGHT THAT WAS IT.
"HOW WAS I TO KNOW...
VERONICA, WE HAVE TO TALK ABOUT THIS NOW. I'VE HAD ENOUGH--
WE'RE DONE TALKING. I'M TIRED AND I'M GOING TO BED.
IT'S NOT FAIR TO--
"THAT THE MAGIC WAS JUST SENT SOMEWHERE ELSE...
ZRRRRRBL
KRSSSSH
WELL, THIS IS DIFFERENT.
"...TO YOU, THOMASINA."

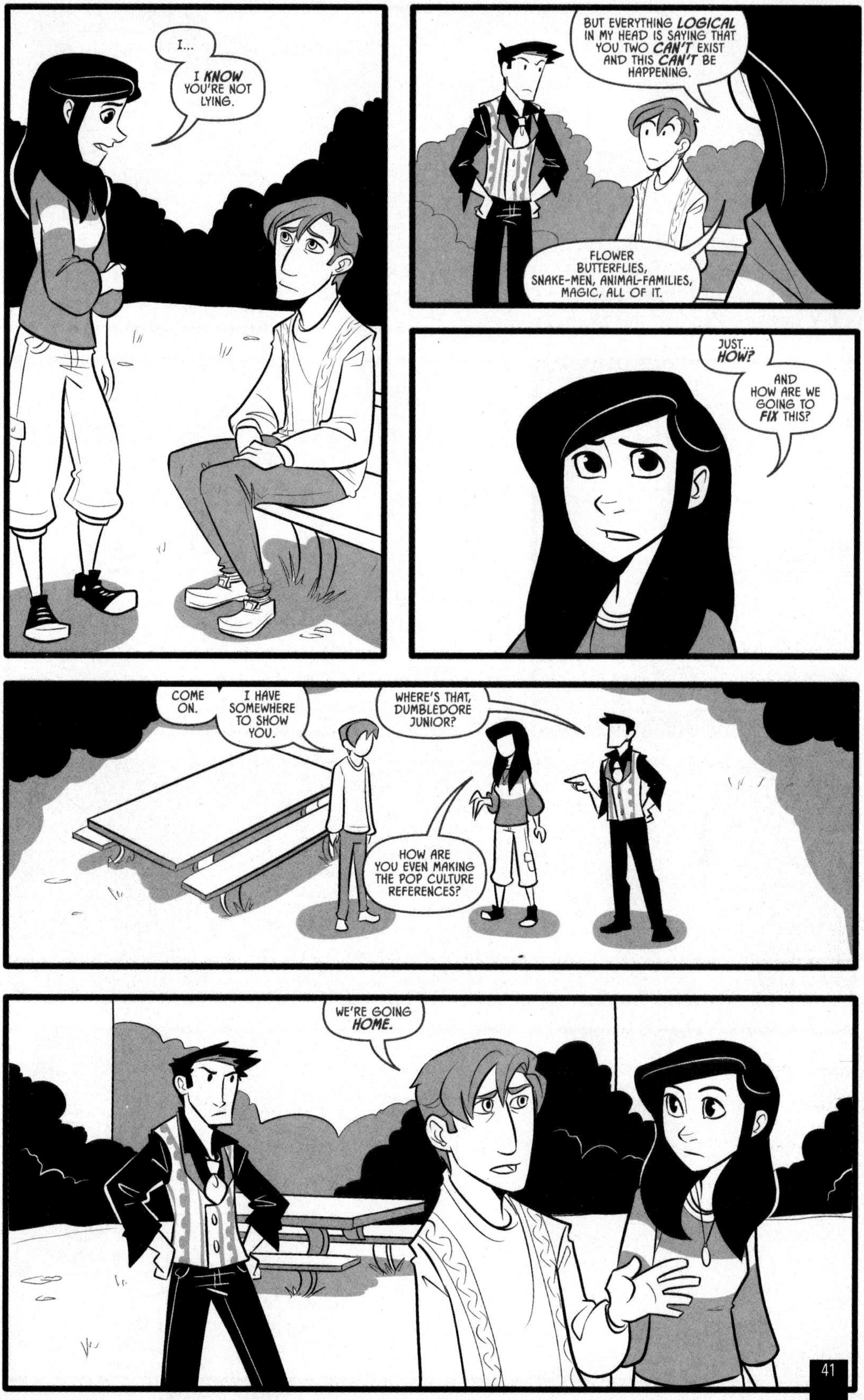
I...
I KNOW YOU'RE NOT LYING.
BUT EVERYTHING LOGICAL IN MY HEAD IS SAYING THAT YOU TWO CAN'T EXIST AND THIS CAN'T BE HAPPENING.
FLOWER BUTTERFLIES, SNAKE-MEN, ANIMAL-FAMILIES, MAGIC, ALL OF IT.
JUST... HOW?
AND HOW ARE WE GOING TO FIX THIS?
COME ON.
I HAVE SOMEWHERE TO SHOW YOU.
WHERE'S THAT, DUMBLEDORE JUNIOR?
HOW ARE YOU EVEN MAKING THE POP CULTURE REFERENCES?
WE'RE GOING HOME.

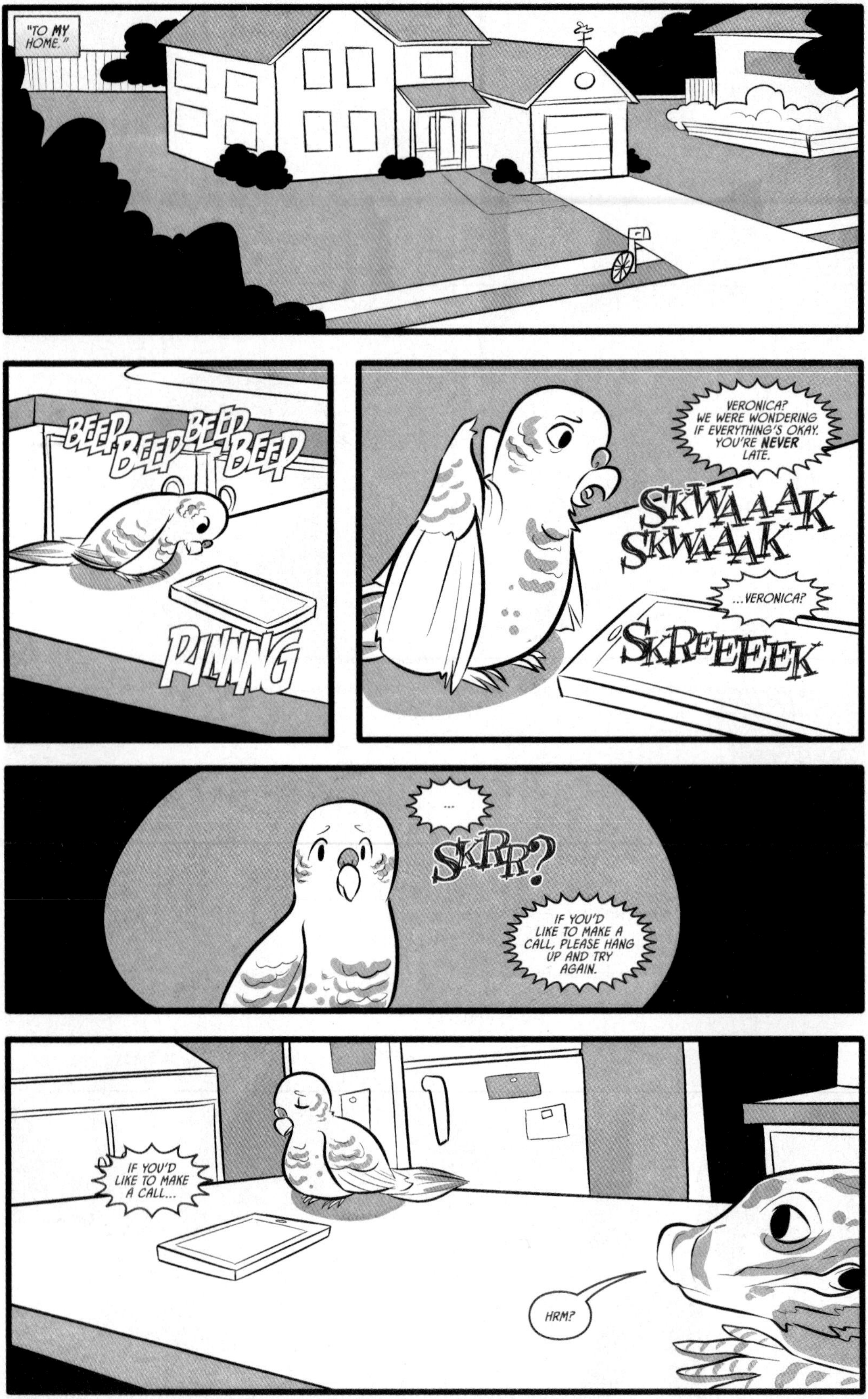
"TO MY HOME."
BEEP BEEP BEEP BEEP
RINNNG
VERONICA? WE WERE WONDERING IF EVERYTHING'S OKAY. YOU'RE NEVER LATE.
SKWAAAK SKWAAAK
...VERONICA?
SKREEEEK
...
SKRR?
IF YOU'D LIKE TO MAKE A CALL, PLEASE HANG UP AND TRY AGAIN.
IF YOU'D LIKE TO MAKE A CALL...
HRM?

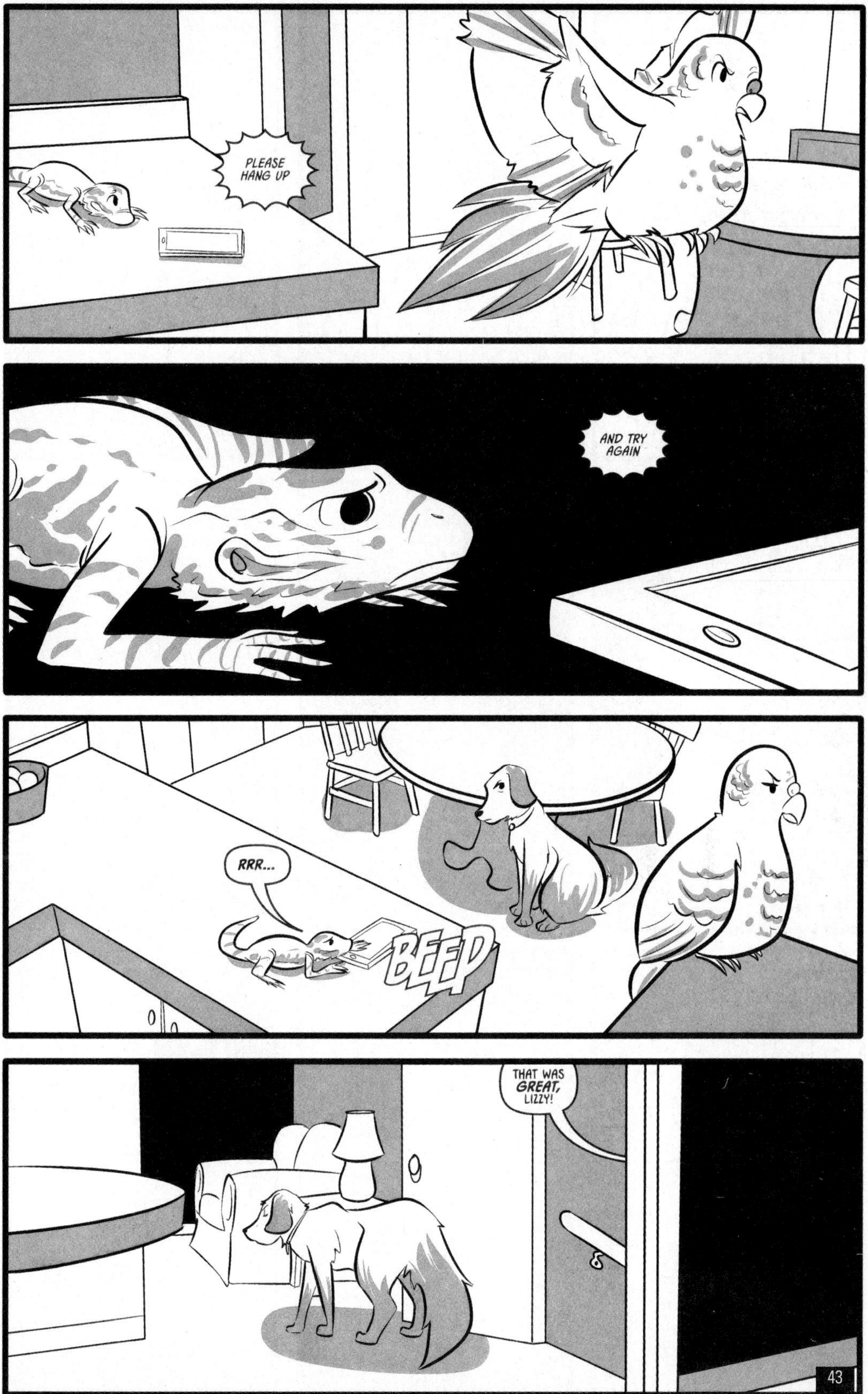
PLEASE HANG UP
AND TRY AGAIN
RRR...
BEEP
THAT WAS GREAT, LIZZY!

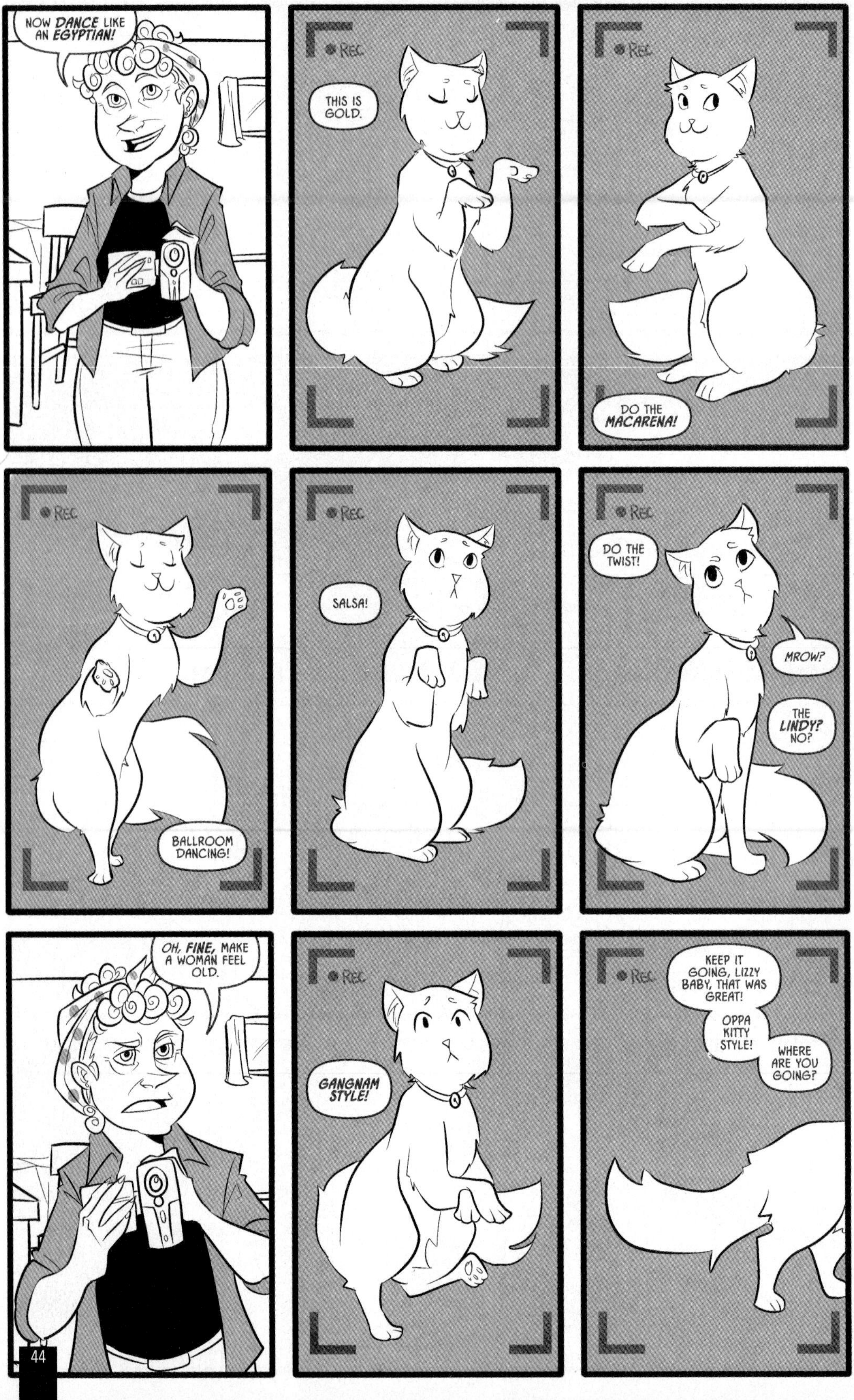
NOW DANCE LIKE AN EGYPTIAN!
REC
THIS IS GOLD.
REC
DO THE MACARENA!
REC
BALLROOM DANCING!
REC
SALSA!
REC
DO THE TWIST!
MROW?
THE LINDY? NO?
OH, FINE, MAKE A WOMAN FEEL OLD.
REC
GANGNAM STYLE!
REC
KEEP IT GOING, LIZZY BABY, THAT WAS GREAT!
OPPA KITTY STYLE!
WHERE ARE YOU GOING?

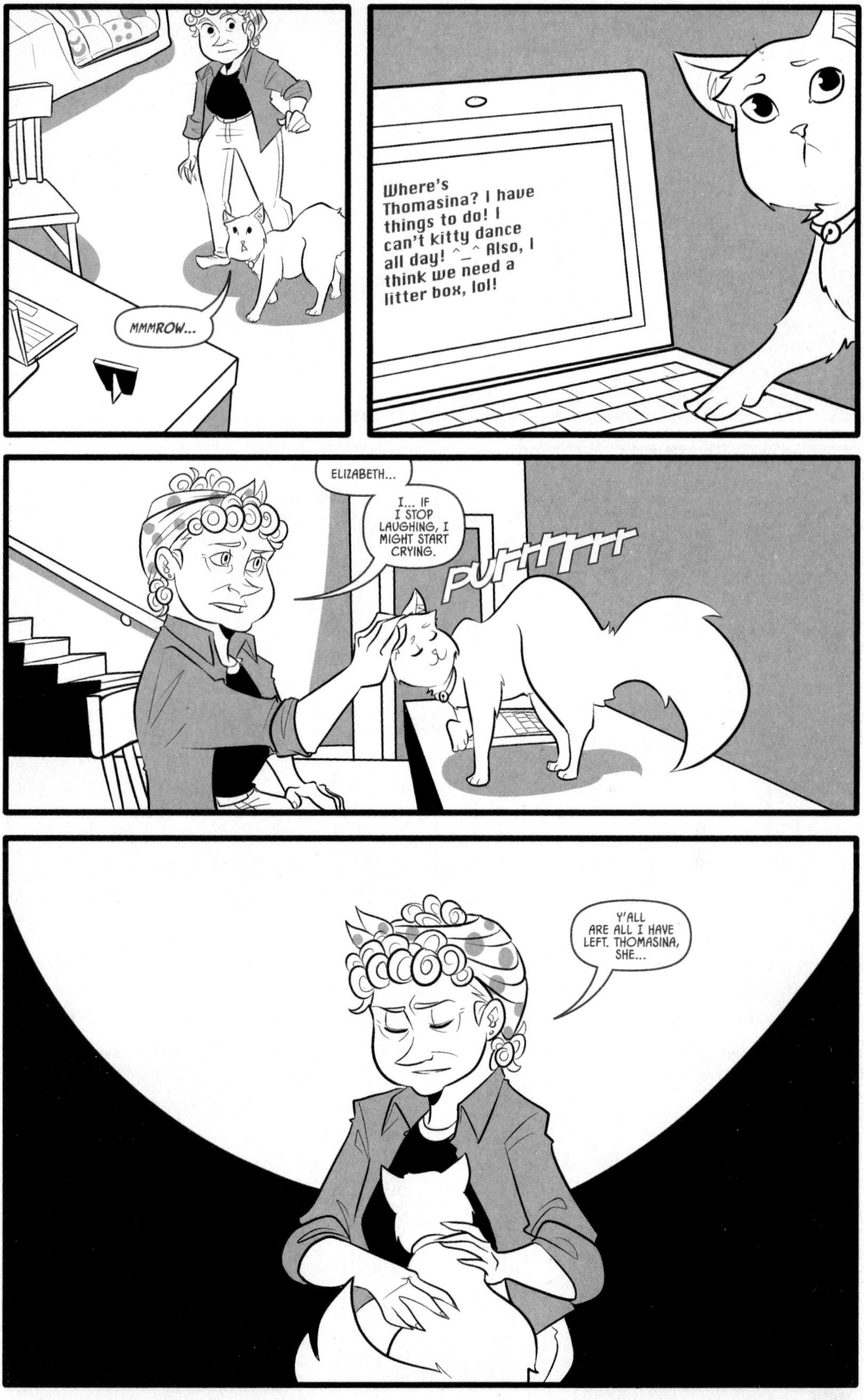

MMMROW...
Where's Thomasina? I have things to do! I can't kitty dance all day! ^_^ Also, I think we need a litter box, lol!
ELIZABETH...
I... IF I STOP LAUGHING, I MIGHT START CRYING.
PURRRRRRR
Y'ALL ARE ALL I HAVE LEFT. THOMASINA, SHE...

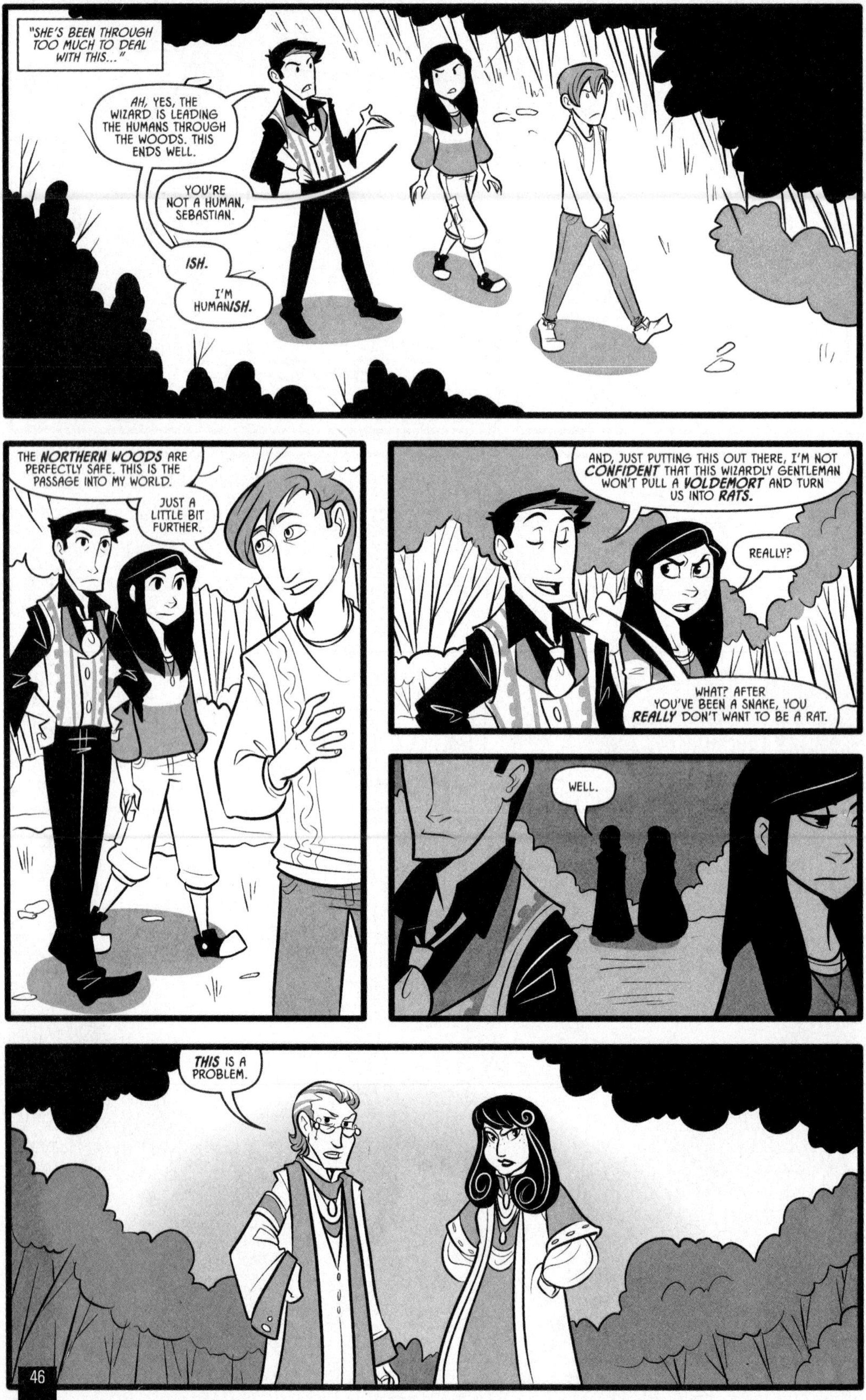
"SHE'S BEEN THROUGH TOO MUCH TO DEAL WITH THIS..."
AH, YES, THE WIZARD IS LEADING THE HUMANS THROUGH THE WOODS. THIS ENDS WELL.
YOU'RE NOT A HUMAN, SEBASTIAN.
ISH.
I'M HUMANISH.
THE NORTHERN WOODS ARE PERFECTLY SAFE. THIS IS THE PASSAGE INTO MY WORLD.
JUST A LITTLE BIT FURTHER.
AND, JUST PUTTING THIS OUT THERE, I'M NOT CONFIDENT THAT THIS WIZARDLY GENTLEMAN WON'T PULL A VOLDEMORT AND TURN US INTO RATS.
REALLY?
WHAT? AFTER YOU'VE BEEN A SNAKE, YOU REALLY DON'T WANT TO BE A RAT.
WELL.
THIS IS A PROBLEM.

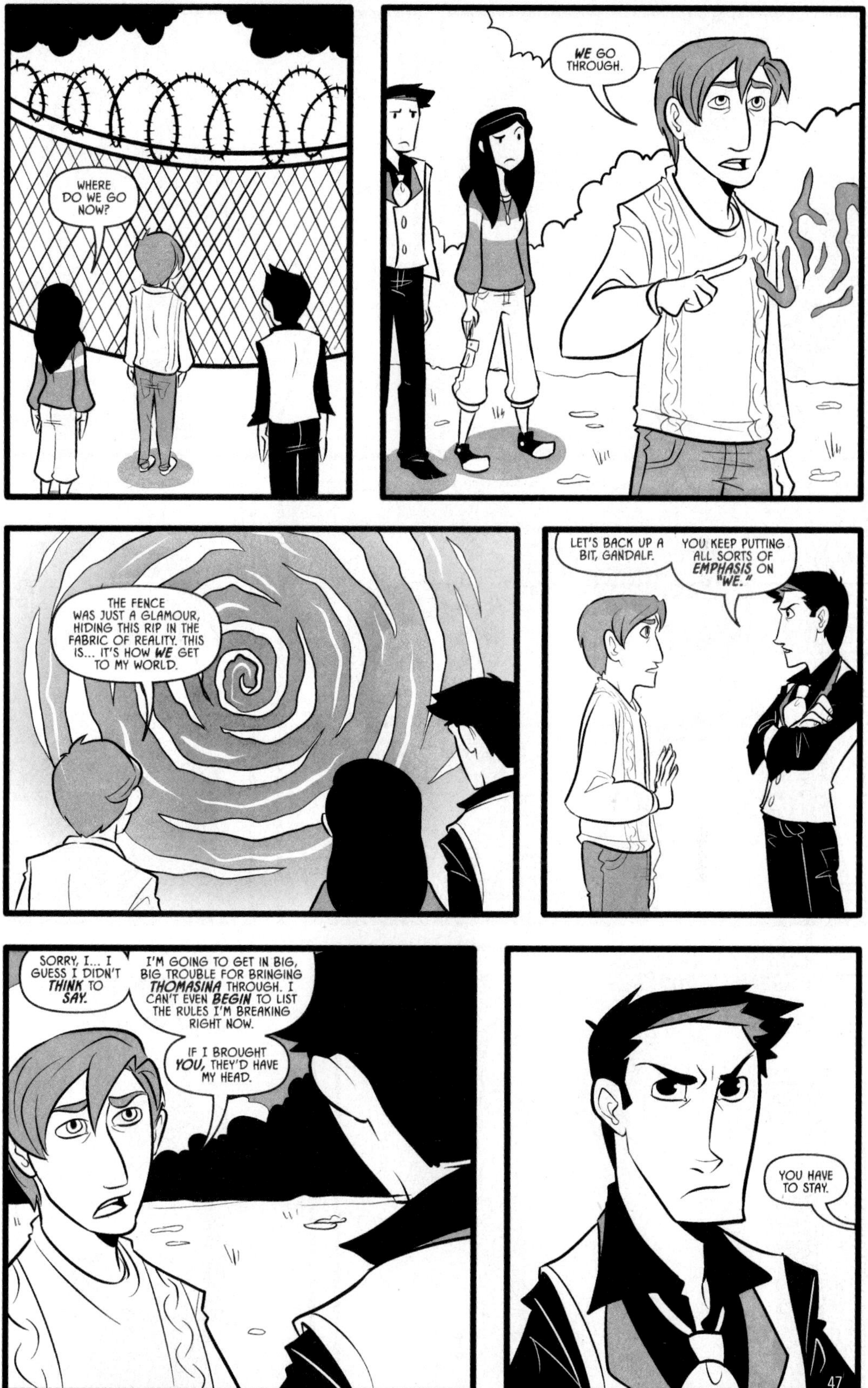

WHERE DO WE GO NOW?
WE GO THROUGH.
THE FENCE WAS JUST A GLAMOUR, HIDING THIS RIP IN THE FABRIC OF REALITY. THIS IS... IT'S HOW WE GET TO MY WORLD.
LET'S BACK UP A BIT, GANDALF.
YOU KEEP PUTTING ALL SORTS OF EMPHASIS ON "WE."
SORRY, I... I GUESS I DIDN'T THINK TO SAY.
I'M GOING TO GET IN BIG, BIG TROUBLE FOR BRINGING THOMASINA THROUGH. I CAN'T EVEN BEGIN TO LIST THE RULES I'M BREAKING RIGHT NOW.
IF I BROUGHT YOU, THEY'D HAVE MY HEAD.
YOU HAVE TO STAY.

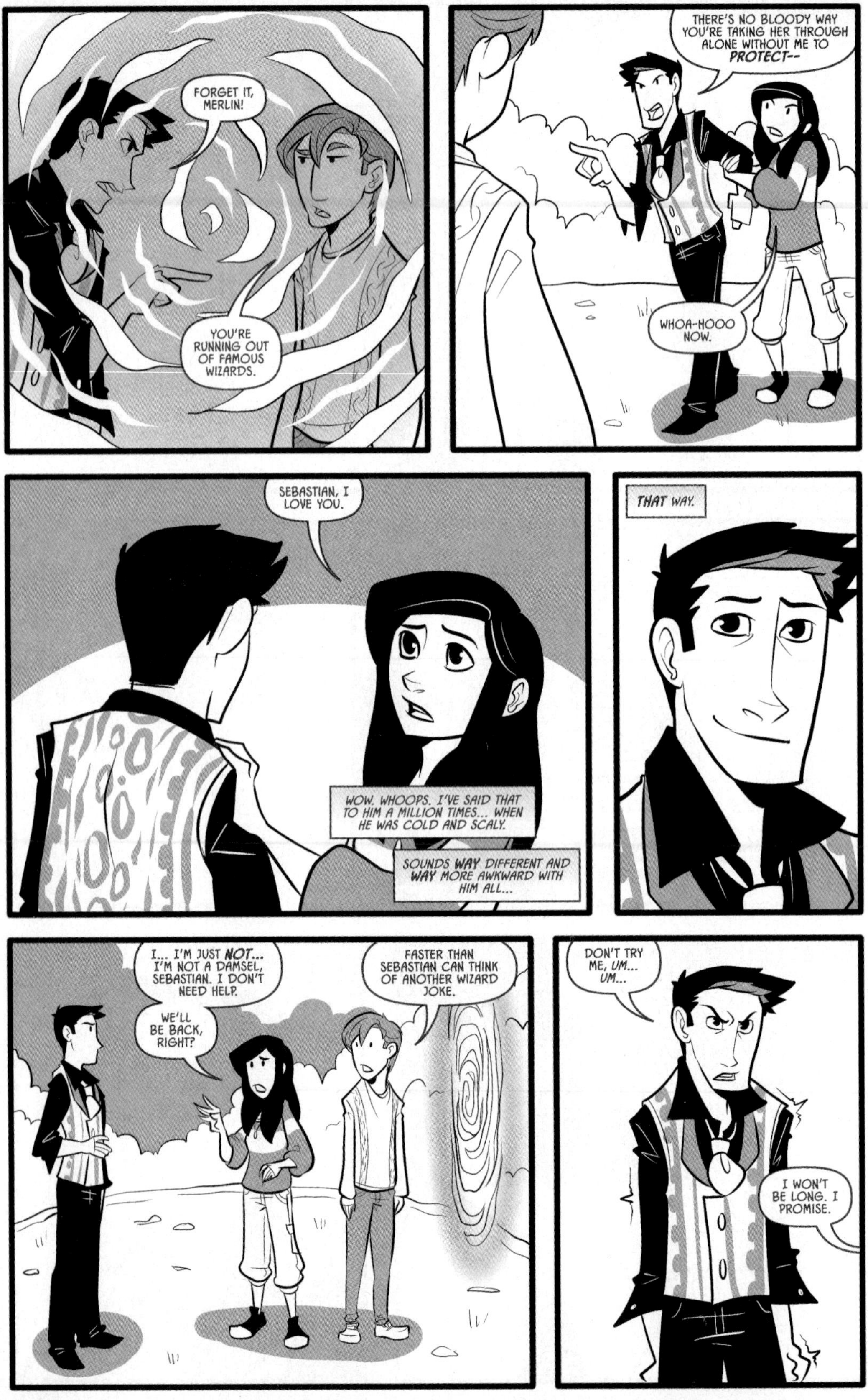
FORGET IT, MERLIN!
YOU'RE RUNNING OUT OF FAMOUS WIZARDS.
THERE'S NO BLOODY WAY YOU'RE TAKING HER THROUGH ALONE WITHOUT ME TO PROTECT--
WHOA-HOOO NOW.
SEBASTIAN, I LOVE YOU.
WOW. WHOOPS. I'VE SAID THAT TO HIM A MILLION TIMES... WHEN HE WAS COLD AND SCALY.
SOUNDS WAY DIFFERENT AND WAY MORE AWKWARD WITH HIM ALL...
THAT WAY.
I... I'M JUST NOT... I'M NOT A DAMSEL, SEBASTIAN. I DON'T NEED HELP.
WE'LL BE BACK, RIGHT?
FASTER THAN SEBASTIAN CAN THINK OF ANOTHER WIZARD JOKE.
DON'T TRY ME, UM... UM...
I WON'T BE LONG. I PROMISE.

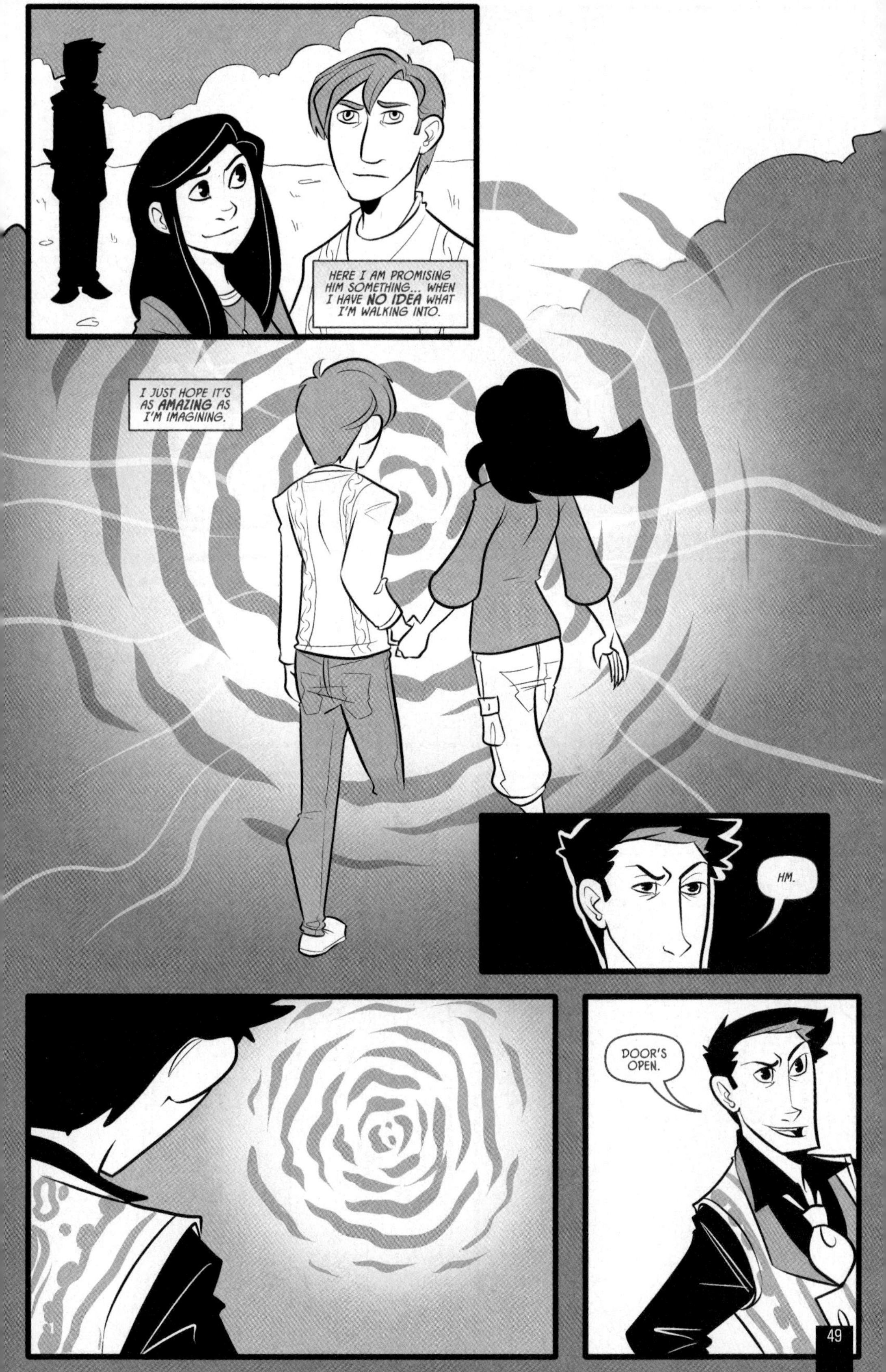

HERE I AM PROMISING HIM SOMETHING... WHEN I HAVE NO IDEA WHAT I'M WALKING INTO.
I JUST HOPE IT'S AS AMAZING AS I'M IMAGINING.
HM.
DOOR'S OPEN.

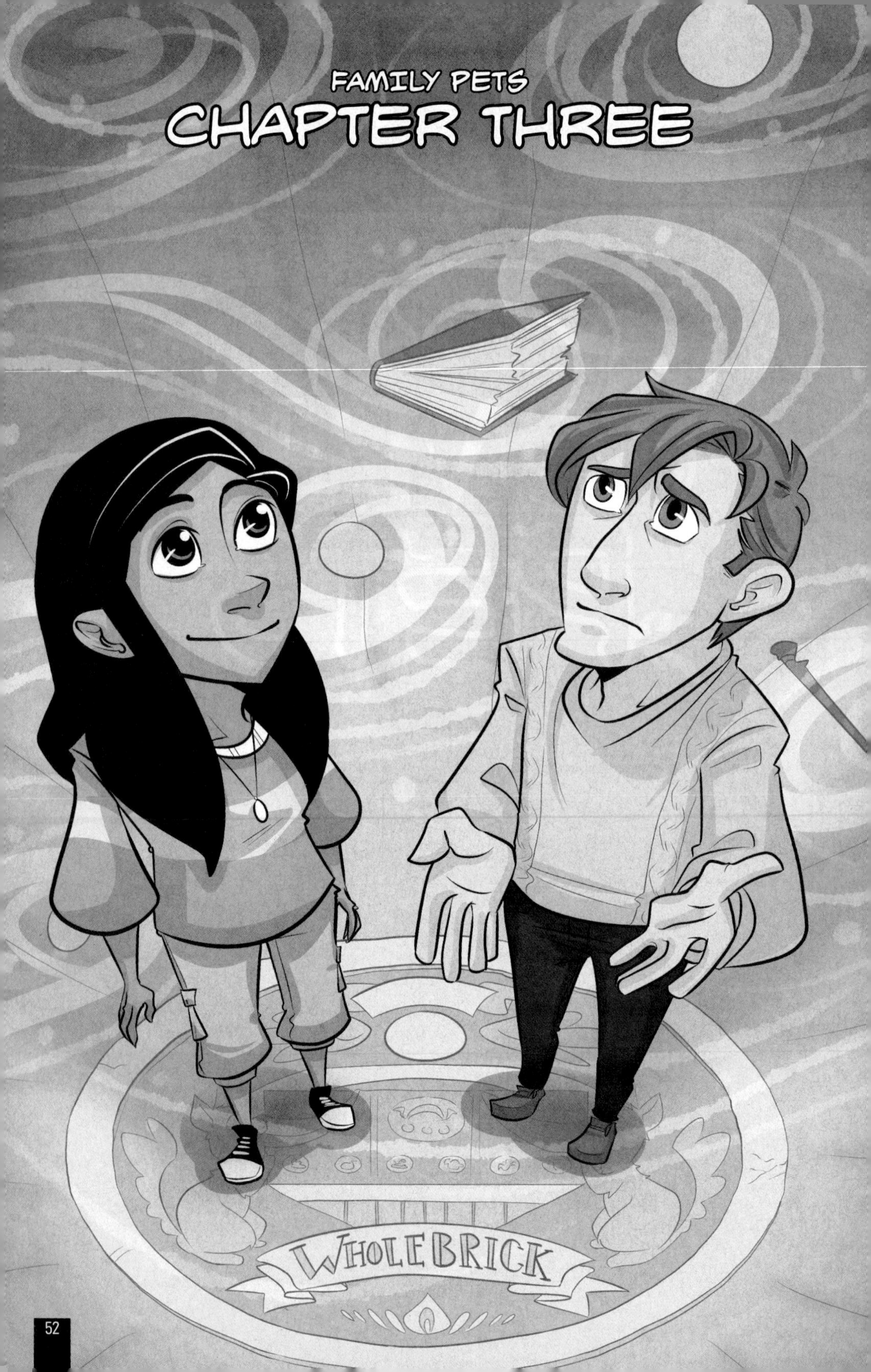
FAMILY PETS
CHAPTER THREE
WHOLEBRICK

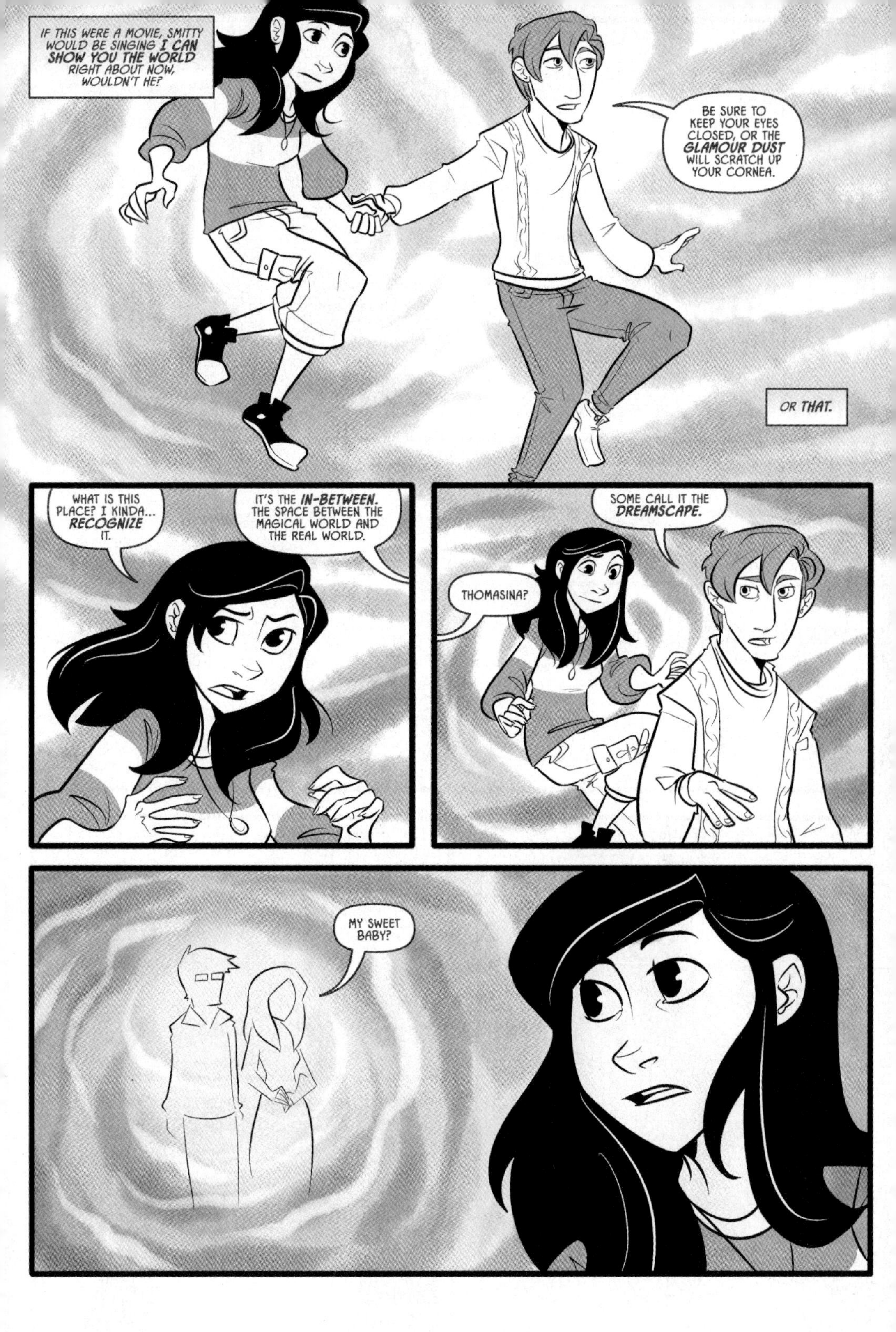
IF THIS WERE A MOVIE, SMITTY WOULD BE SINGING I CAN SHOW YOU THE WORLD RIGHT ABOUT NOW, WOULDN'T HE?
BE SURE TO KEEP YOUR EYES CLOSED, OR THE GLAMOUR DUST WILL SCRATCH UP YOUR CORNEA.
OR THAT.
WHAT IS THIS PLACE? I KINDA... RECOGNIZE IT.
IT'S THE IN-BETWEEN. THE SPACE BETWEEN THE MAGICAL WORLD AND THE REAL WORLD.
SOME CALL IT THE DREAMSCAPE.
THOMASINA?
MY SWEET BABY?

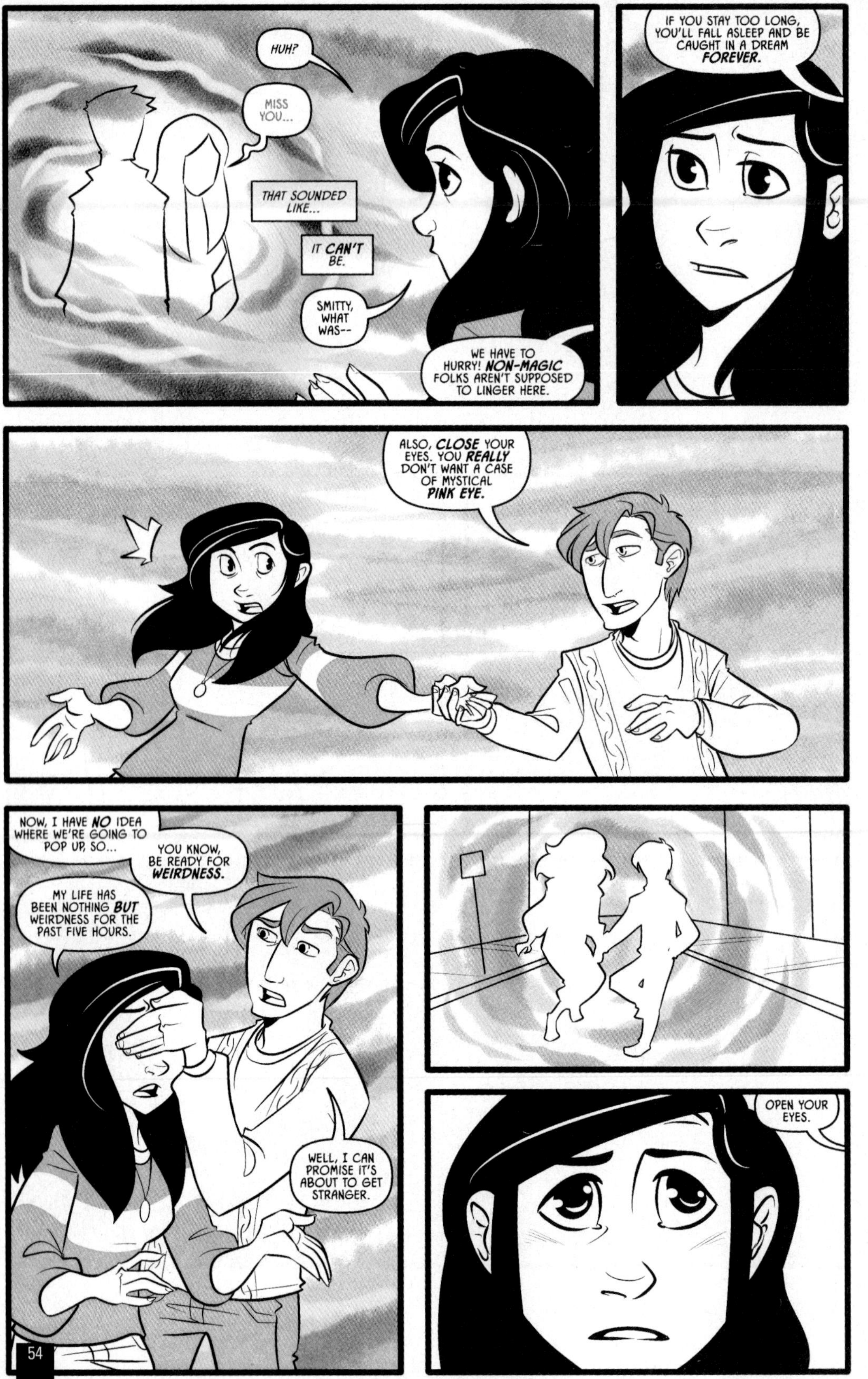
HUH?
MISS YOU...
THAT SOUNDED LIKE...
IT CAN'T BE.
SMITTY, WHAT WAS--
WE HAVE TO HURRY! NON-MAGIC FOLKS AREN'T SUPPOSED TO LINGER HERE.
IF YOU STAY TOO LONG, YOU'LL FALL ASLEEP AND BE CAUGHT IN A DREAM FOREVER.
ALSO, CLOSE YOUR EYES. YOU REALLY DON'T WANT A CASE OF MYSTICAL PINK EYE.
NOW, I HAVE NO IDEA WHERE WE'RE GOING TO POP UP, SO...
YOU KNOW, BE READY FOR WEIRDNESS.
MY LIFE HAS BEEN NOTHING BUT WEIRDNESS FOR THE PAST FIVE HOURS.
WELL, I CAN PROMISE IT'S ABOUT TO GET STRANGER.
OPEN YOUR EYES.

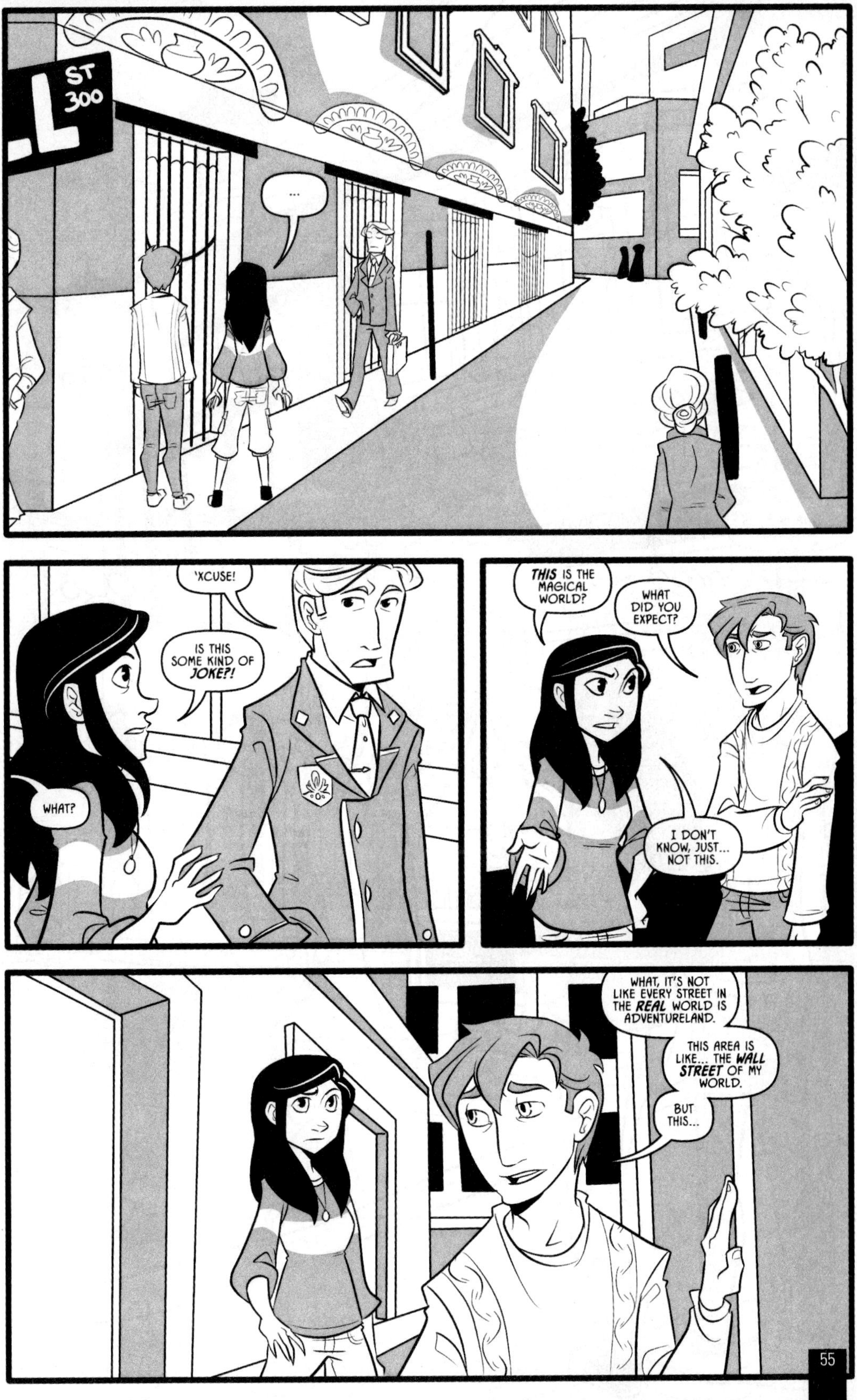
...
'XCUSE!
IS THIS SOME KIND OF JOKE?!
WHAT?
THIS IS THE MAGICAL WORLD?
WHAT DID YOU EXPECT?
I DON'T KNOW, JUST... NOT THIS.
WHAT, IT'S NOT LIKE EVERY STREET IN THE REAL WORLD IS ADVENTURELAND.
THIS AREA IS LIKE... THE WALL STREET OF MY WORLD.
BUT THIS...

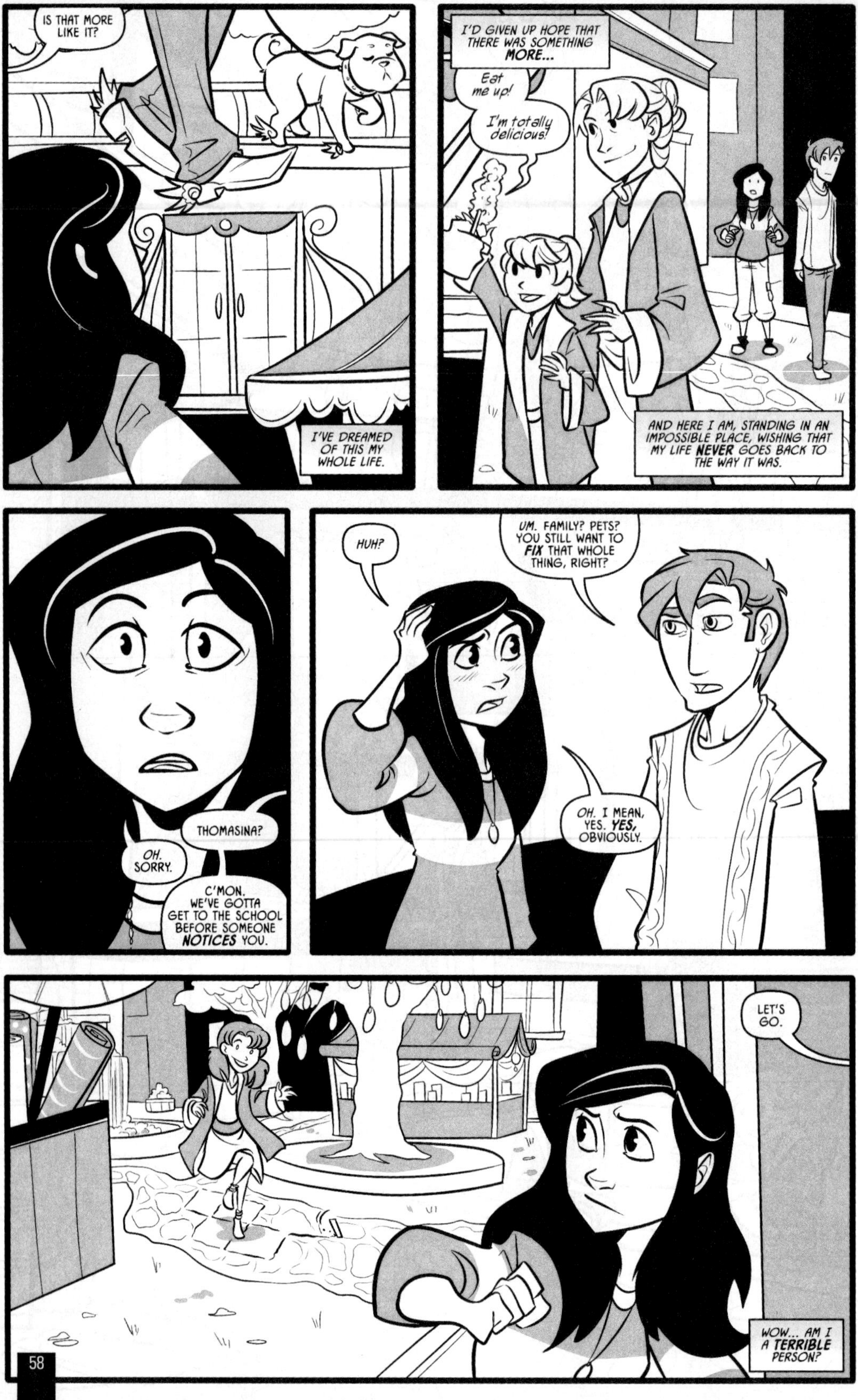
IS THAT MORE LIKE IT?
I'VE DREAMED OF THIS MY WHOLE LIFE.
I'D GIVEN UP HOPE THAT THERE WAS SOMETHING MORE...
Eat me up!
I'm totally delicious!
AND HERE I AM, STANDING IN AN IMPOSSIBLE PLACE, WISHING THAT MY LIFE NEVER GOES BACK TO THE WAY IT WAS.
THOMASINA?
OH. SORRY.
C'MON. WE'VE GOTTA GET TO THE SCHOOL BEFORE SOMEONE NOTICES YOU.
HUH?
UM. FAMILY? PETS? YOU STILL WANT TO FIX THAT WHOLE THING, RIGHT?
OH. I MEAN, YES. YES, OBVIOUSLY.
LET'S GO.
WOW... AM I A TERRIBLE PERSON?

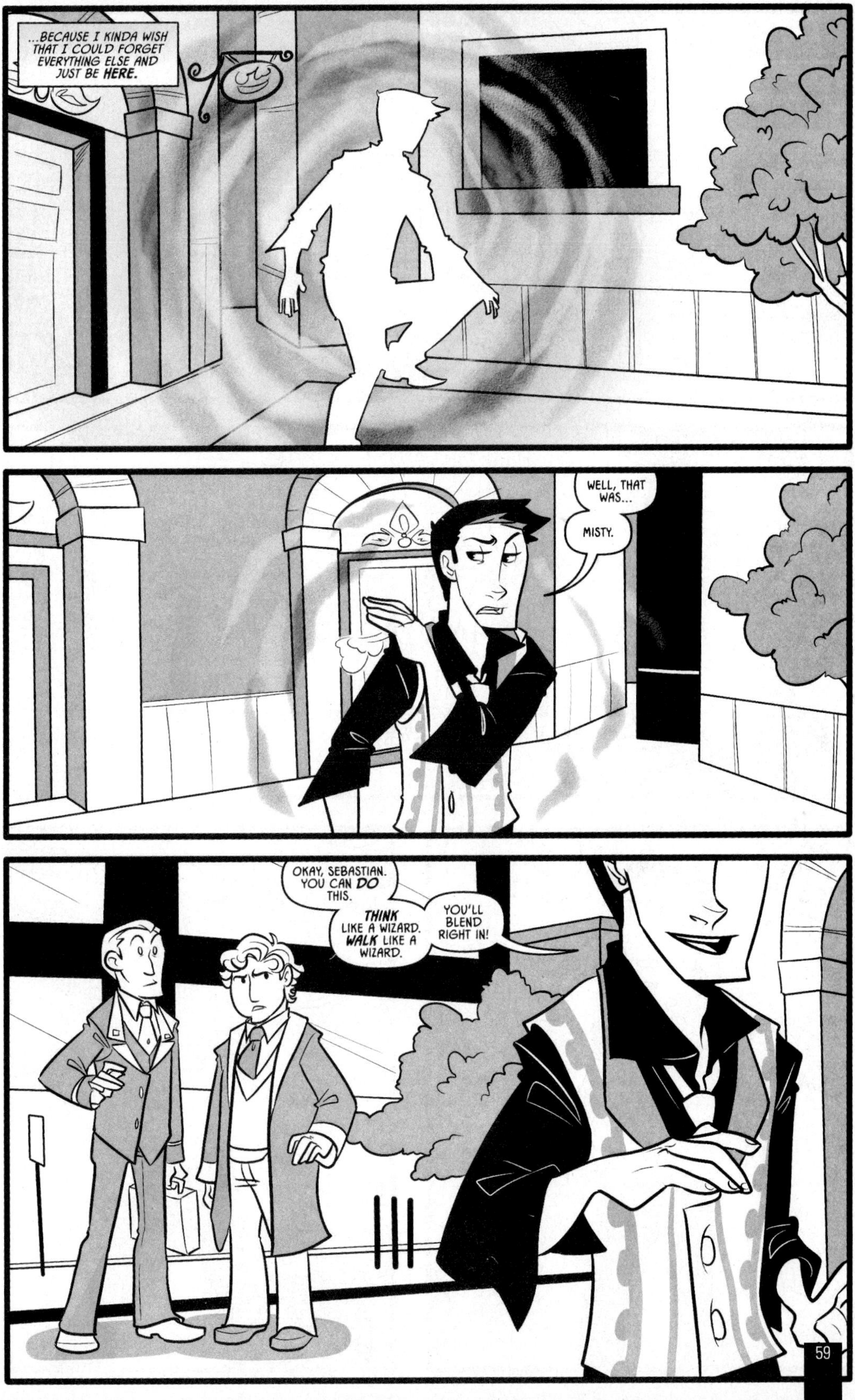
...BECAUSE I KINDA WISH THAT I COULD FORGET EVERYTHING ELSE AND JUST BE **HERE.**
WELL, THAT WAS...
MISTY.
OKAY, SEBASTIAN. YOU CAN **DO** THIS.
THINK LIKE A WIZARD. **WALK** LIKE A WIZARD.
YOU'LL BLEND RIGHT IN!

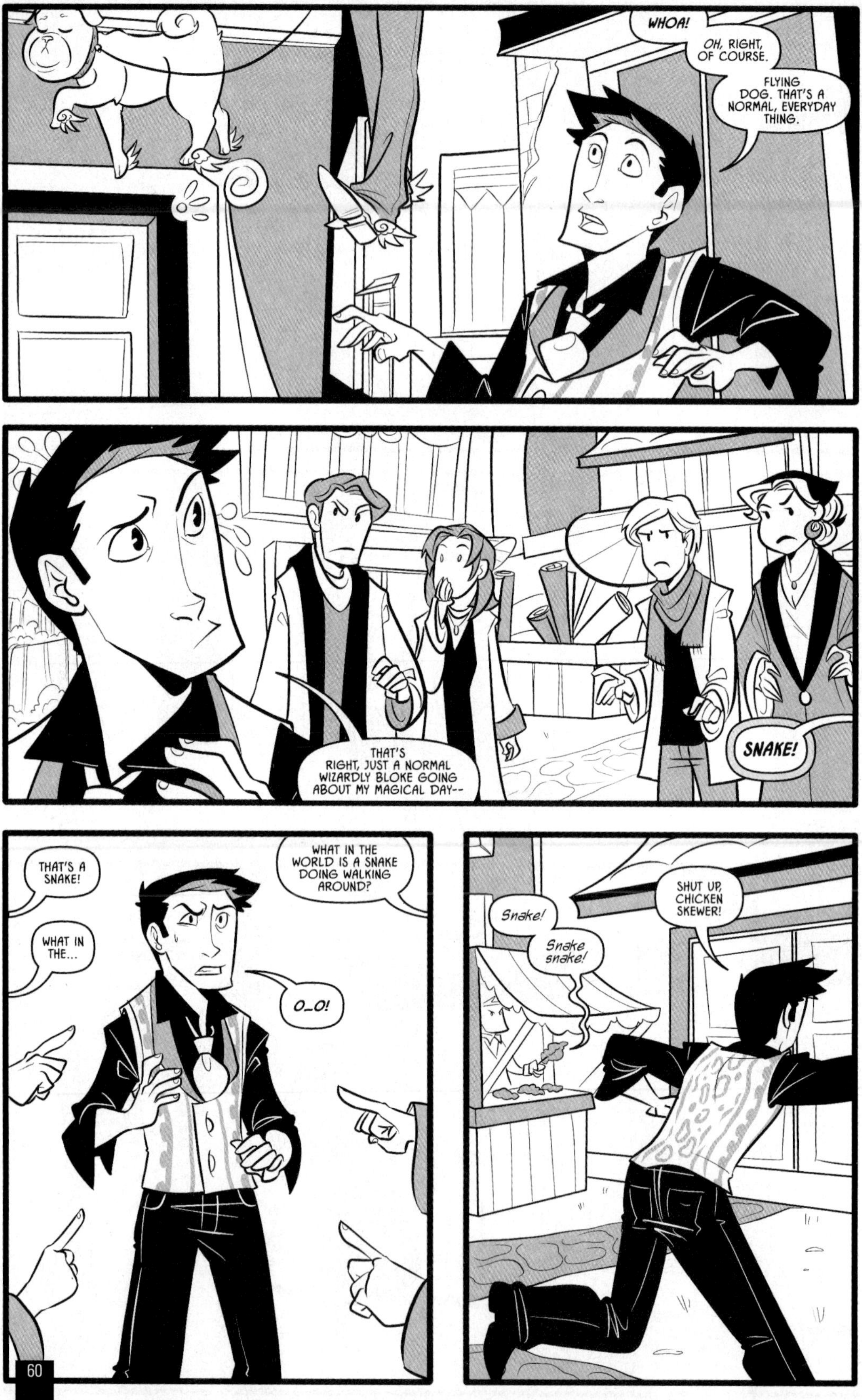
WHOA!
OH, RIGHT, OF COURSE.
FLYING DOG. THAT'S A NORMAL, EVERYDAY THING.
THAT'S RIGHT, JUST A NORMAL WIZARDLY BLOKE GOING ABOUT MY MAGICAL DAY--
SNAKE!
THAT'S A SNAKE!
WHAT IN THE...
WHAT IN THE WORLD IS A SNAKE DOING WALKING AROUND?
O_O!
Snake!
Snake snake!
SHUT UP, CHICKEN SKEWER!

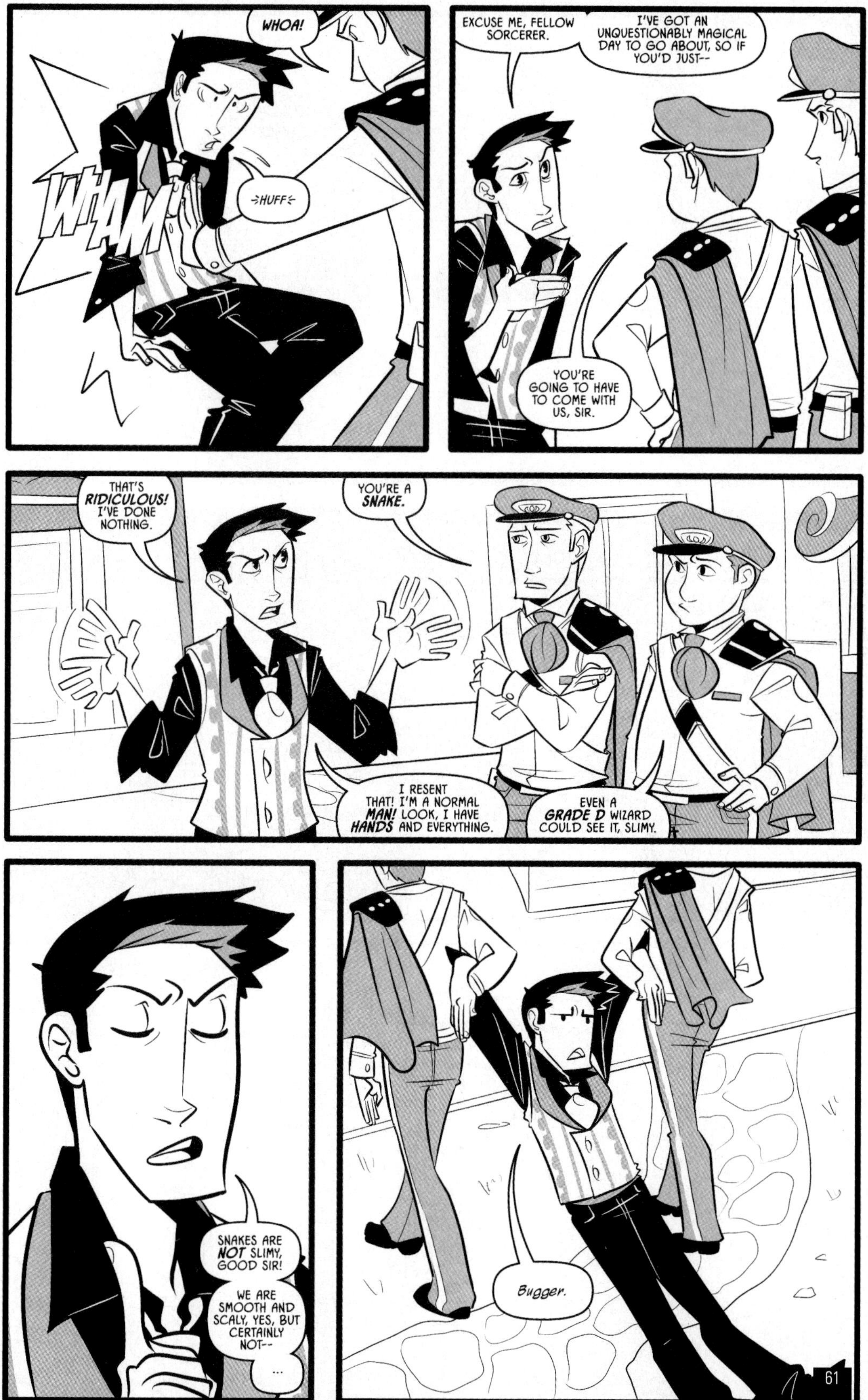
WHOA!
WHAM!
HUFF
EXCUSE ME, FELLOW SORCERER.
I'VE GOT AN UNQUESTIONABLY MAGICAL DAY TO GO ABOUT, SO IF YOU'D JUST--
YOU'RE GOING TO HAVE TO COME WITH US, SIR.
THAT'S RIDICULOUS! I'VE DONE NOTHING.
YOU'RE A SNAKE.
I RESENT THAT! I'M A NORMAL MAN! LOOK, I HAVE HANDS AND EVERYTHING.
EVEN A GRADE D WIZARD COULD SEE IT, SLIMY.
SNAKES ARE NOT SLIMY, GOOD SIR!
WE ARE SMOOTH AND SCALY, YES, BUT CERTAINLY NOT--
...
Bugger.

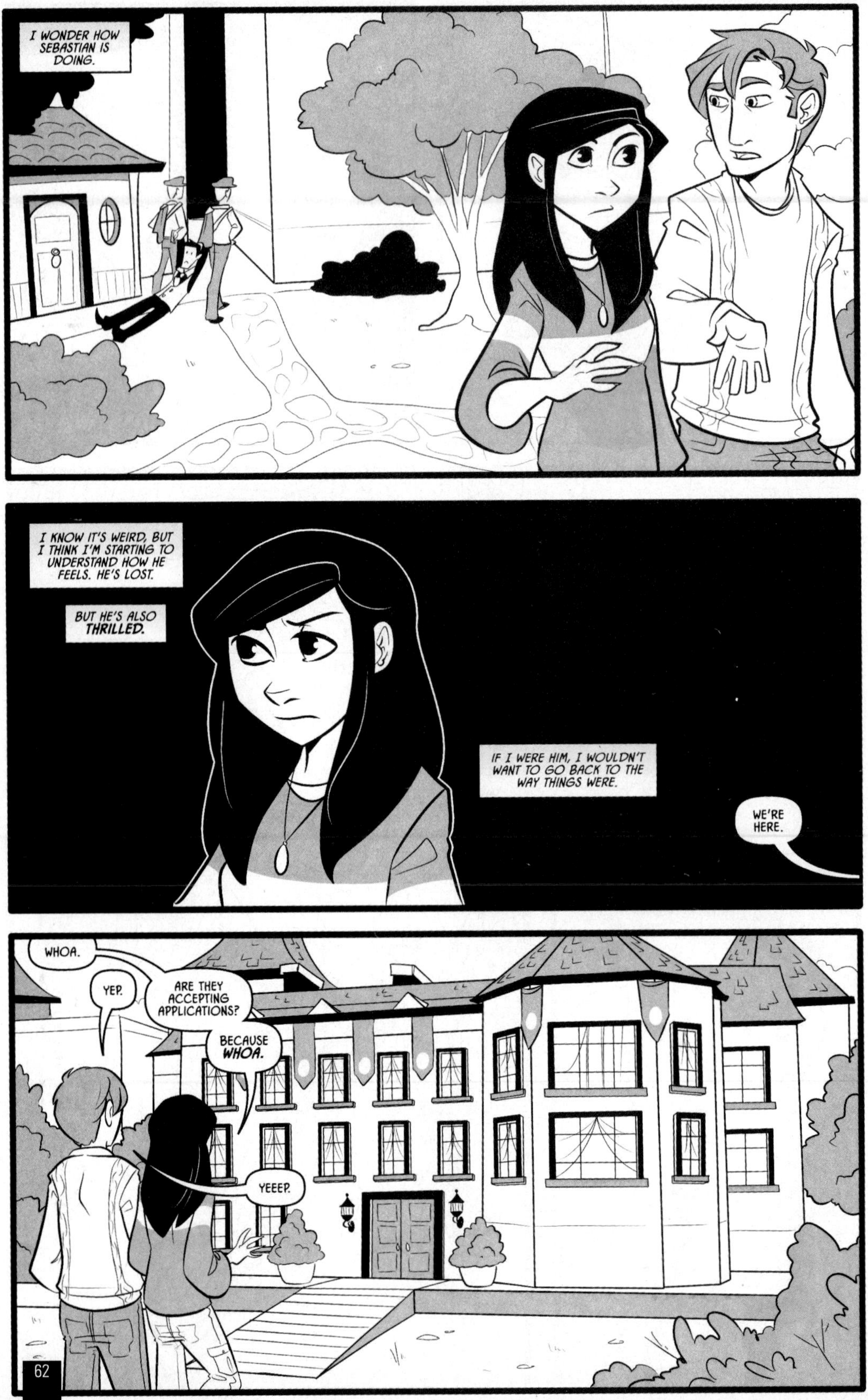
I WONDER HOW SEBASTIAN IS DOING.
I KNOW IT'S WEIRD, BUT I THINK I'M STARTING TO UNDERSTAND HOW HE FEELS. HE'S LOST.
BUT HE'S ALSO **THRILLED.**
IF I WERE HIM, I WOULDN'T WANT TO GO BACK TO THE WAY THINGS WERE.
WE'RE HERE.
WHOA.
YEP.
ARE THEY ACCEPTING APPLICATIONS?
BECAUSE **WHOA.**
YEEEP.

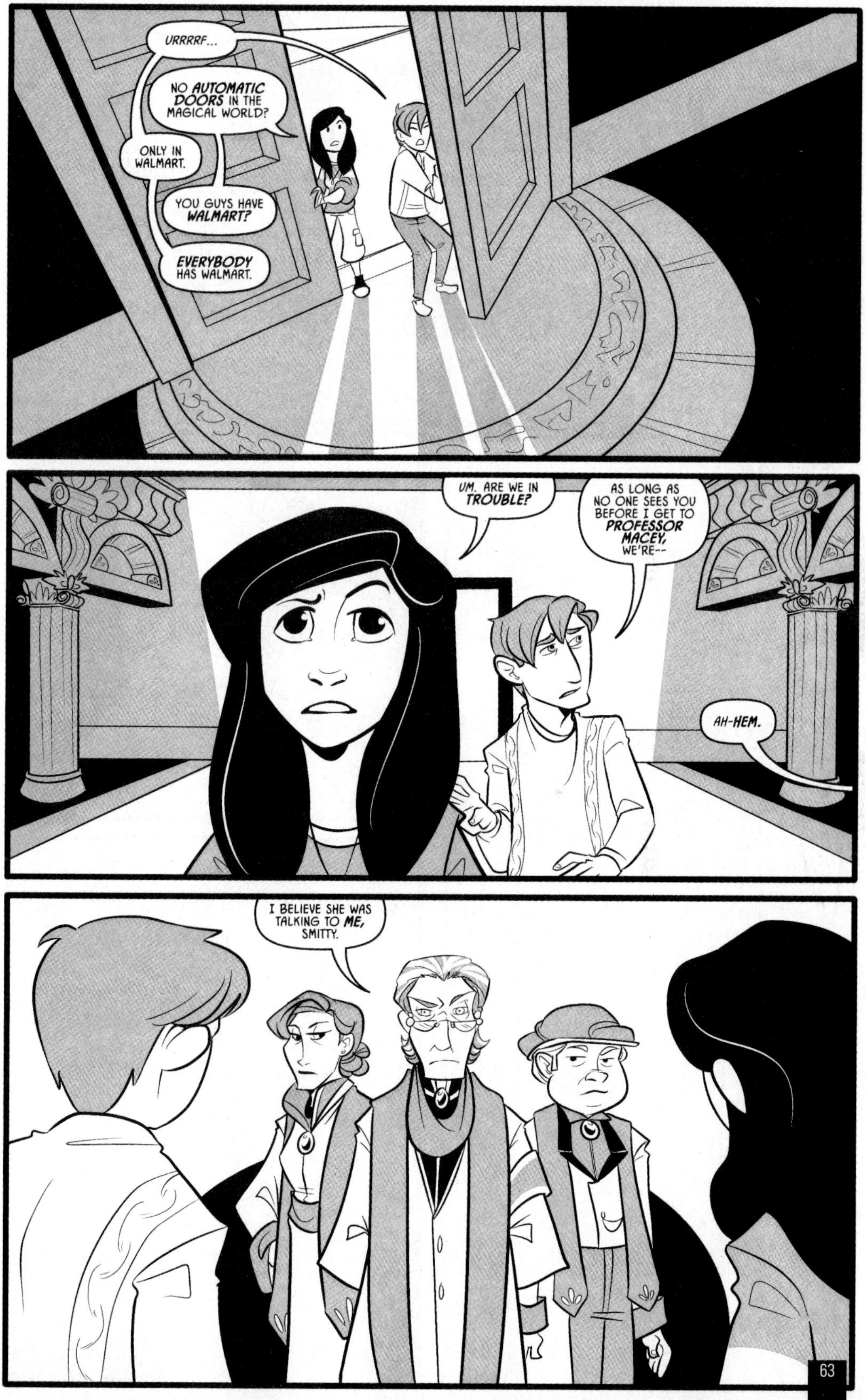
URRRRF...
NO AUTOMATIC DOORS IN THE MAGICAL WORLD?
ONLY IN WALMART.
YOU GUYS HAVE WALMART?
EVERYBODY HAS WALMART.
UM. ARE WE IN TROUBLE?
AS LONG AS NO ONE SEES YOU BEFORE I GET TO PROFESSOR MACEY, WE'RE--
AH-HEM.
I BELIEVE SHE WAS TALKING TO ME, SMITTY.

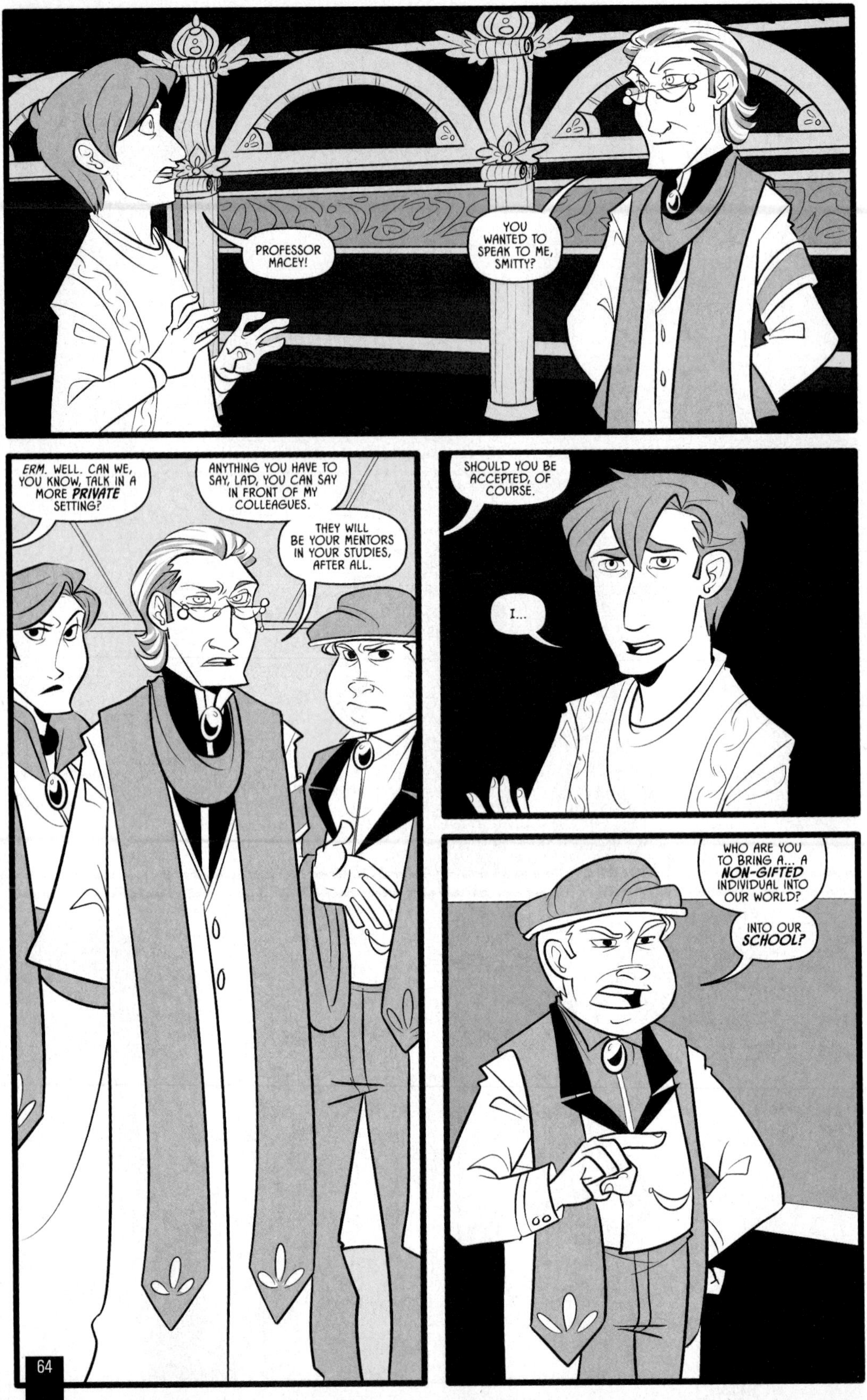
PROFESSOR MACEY!
YOU WANTED TO SPEAK TO ME, SMITTY?
ERM. WELL. CAN WE, YOU KNOW, TALK IN A MORE ***PRIVATE*** SETTING?
ANYTHING YOU HAVE TO SAY, LAD, YOU CAN SAY IN FRONT OF MY COLLEAGUES.
THEY WILL BE YOUR MENTORS IN YOUR STUDIES, AFTER ALL.
SHOULD YOU BE ACCEPTED, OF COURSE.
I...
WHO ARE YOU TO BRING A... A ***NON-GIFTED*** INDIVIDUAL INTO OUR WORLD?
INTO OUR ***SCHOOL?***

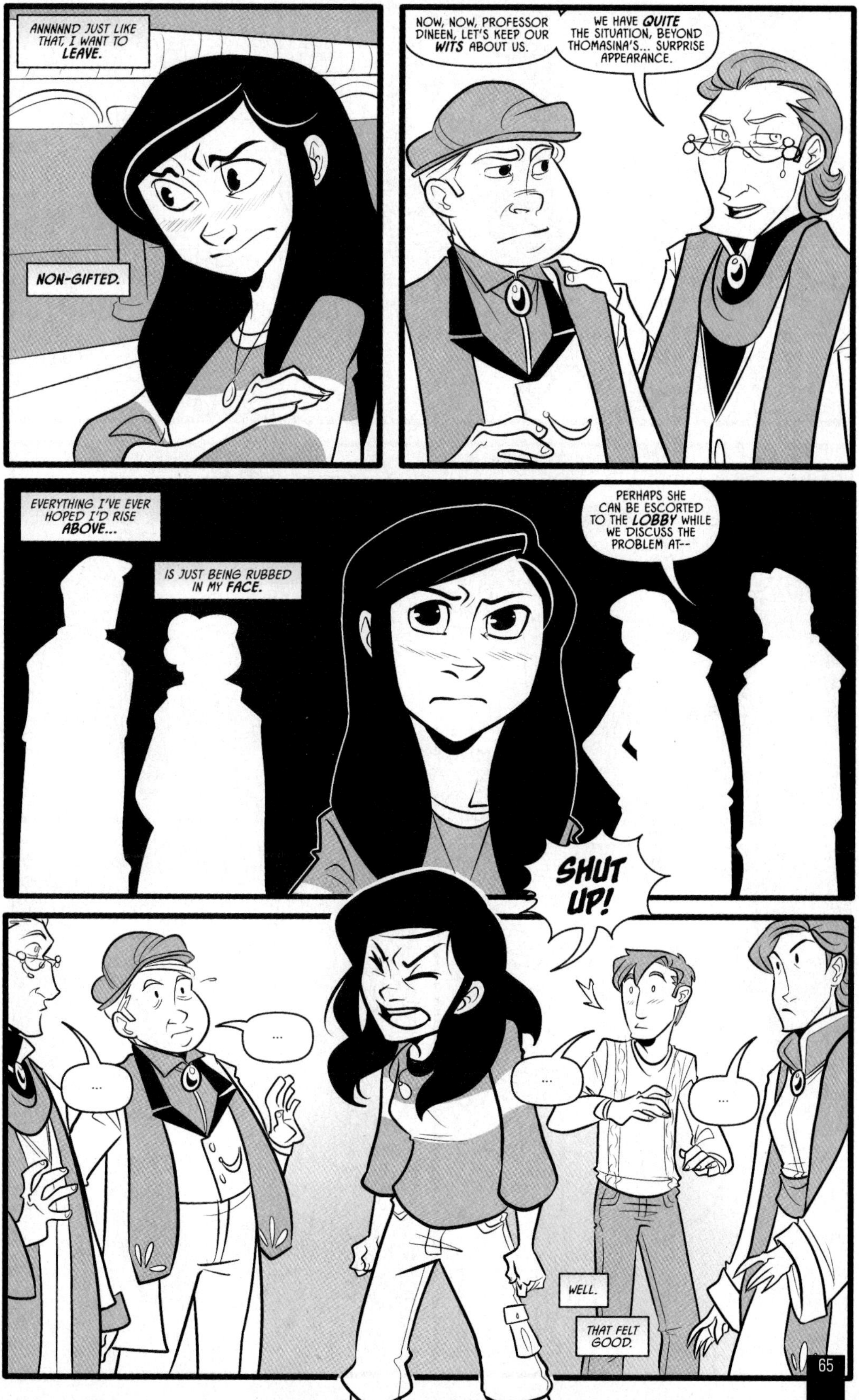
ANNNNND JUST LIKE THAT, I WANT TO LEAVE.
NON-GIFTED.
NOW, NOW, PROFESSOR DINEEN, LET'S KEEP OUR WITS ABOUT US.
WE HAVE QUITE THE SITUATION, BEYOND THOMASINA'S... SURPRISE APPEARANCE.
EVERYTHING I'VE EVER HOPED I'D RISE ABOVE...
IS JUST BEING RUBBED IN MY FACE.
PERHAPS SHE CAN BE ESCORTED TO THE LOBBY WHILE WE DISCUSS THE PROBLEM AT--
SHUT UP!
...
...
...
...
WELL.
THAT FELT GOOD.

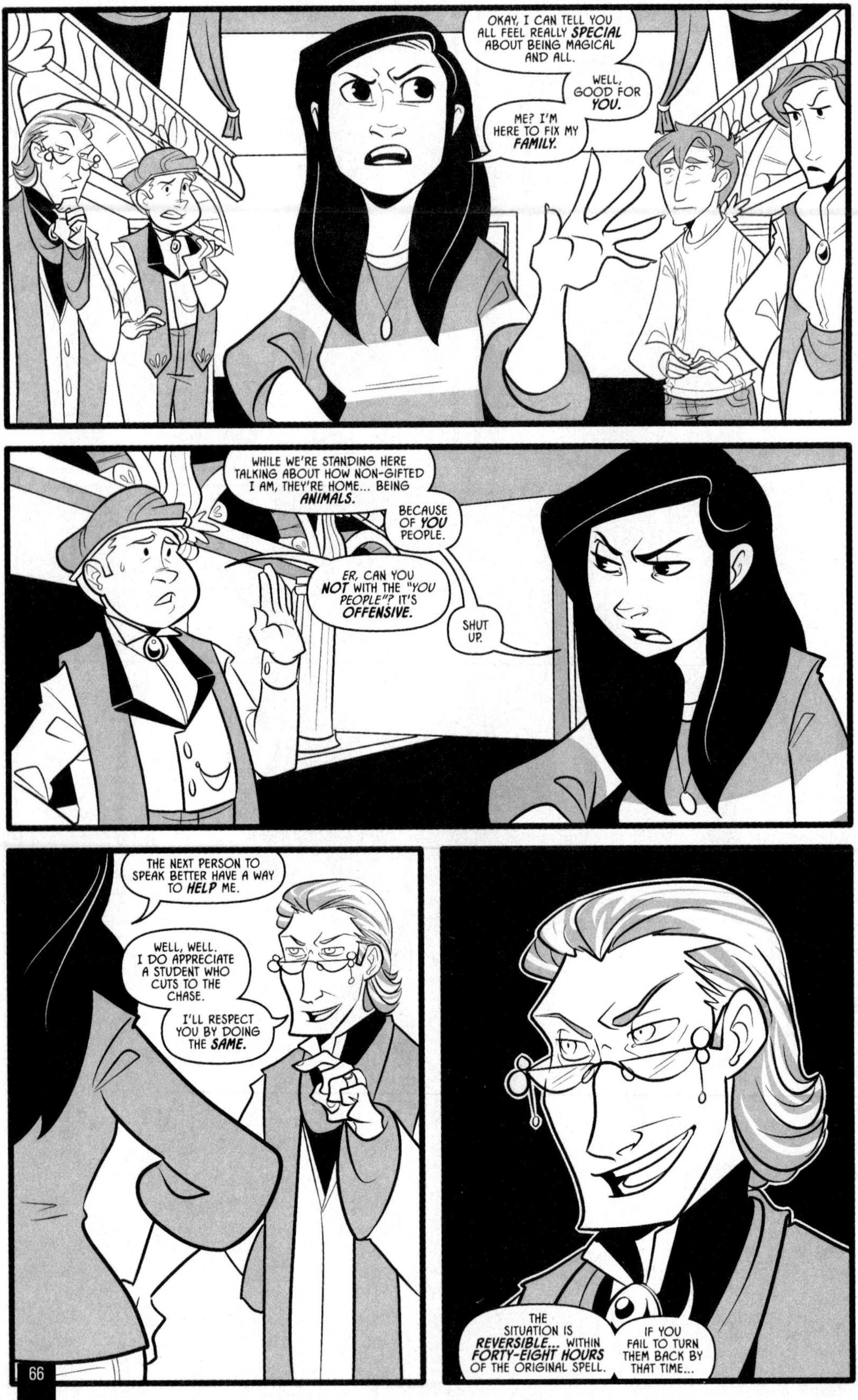
OKAY, I CAN TELL YOU ALL FEEL REALLY SPECIAL ABOUT BEING MAGICAL AND ALL.
WELL, GOOD FOR YOU.
ME? I'M HERE TO FIX MY FAMILY.
WHILE WE'RE STANDING HERE TALKING ABOUT HOW NON-GIFTED I AM, THEY'RE HOME... BEING ANIMALS.
BECAUSE OF YOU PEOPLE.
ER, CAN YOU NOT WITH THE "YOU PEOPLE"? IT'S OFFENSIVE.
SHUT UP.
THE NEXT PERSON TO SPEAK BETTER HAVE A WAY TO HELP ME.
WELL, WELL. I DO APPRECIATE A STUDENT WHO CUTS TO THE CHASE.
I'LL RESPECT YOU BY DOING THE SAME.
THE SITUATION IS REVERSIBLE... WITHIN FORTY-EIGHT HOURS OF THE ORIGINAL SPELL.
IF YOU FAIL TO TURN THEM BACK BY THAT TIME...

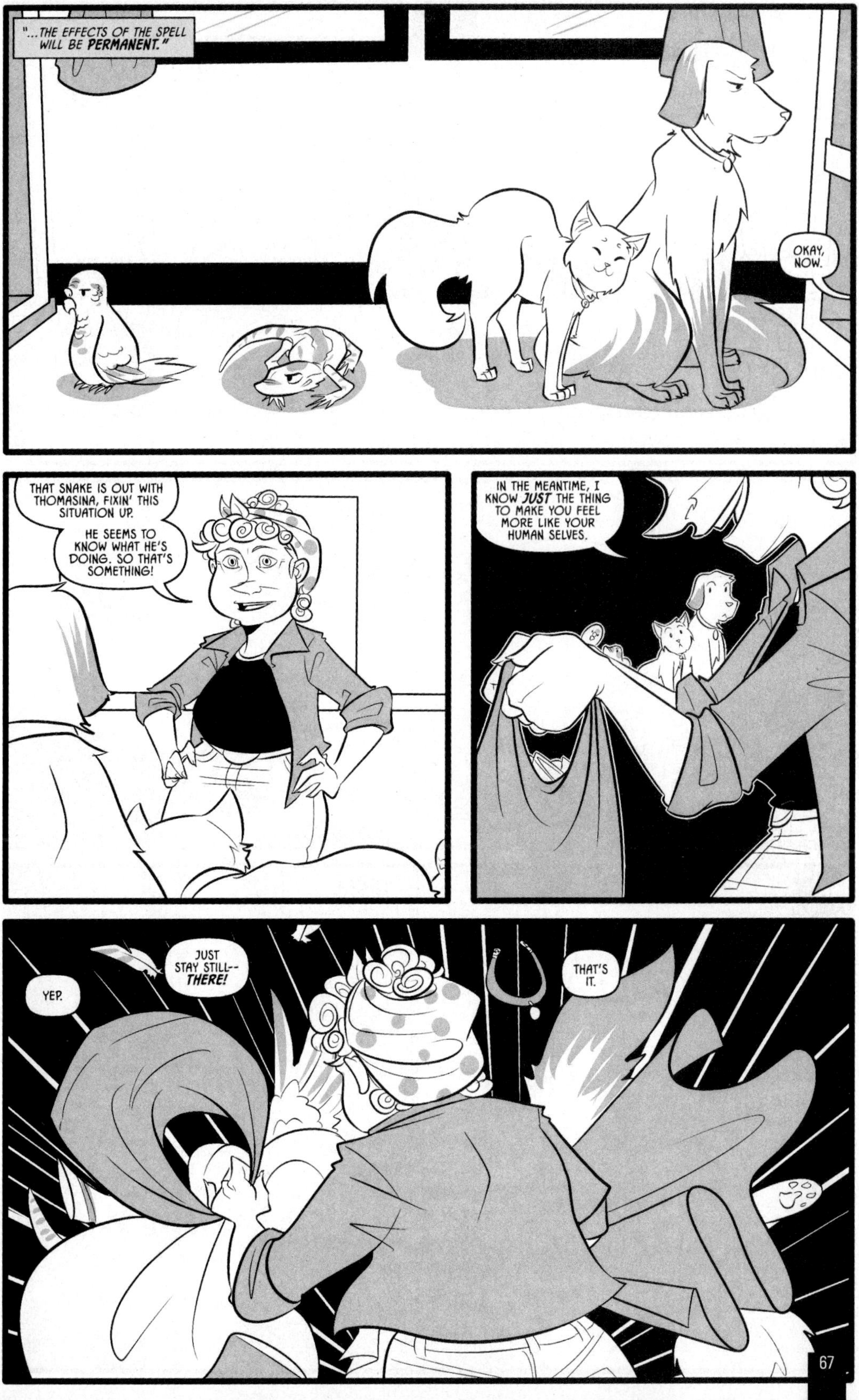
"...THE EFFECTS OF THE SPELL WILL BE PERMANENT."
OKAY, NOW.
THAT SNAKE IS OUT WITH THOMASINA, FIXIN' THIS SITUATION UP.
HE SEEMS TO KNOW WHAT HE'S DOING. SO THAT'S SOMETHING!
IN THE MEANTIME, I KNOW JUST THE THING TO MAKE YOU FEEL MORE LIKE YOUR HUMAN SELVES.
YEP.
JUST STAY STILL-- THERE!
THAT'S IT.

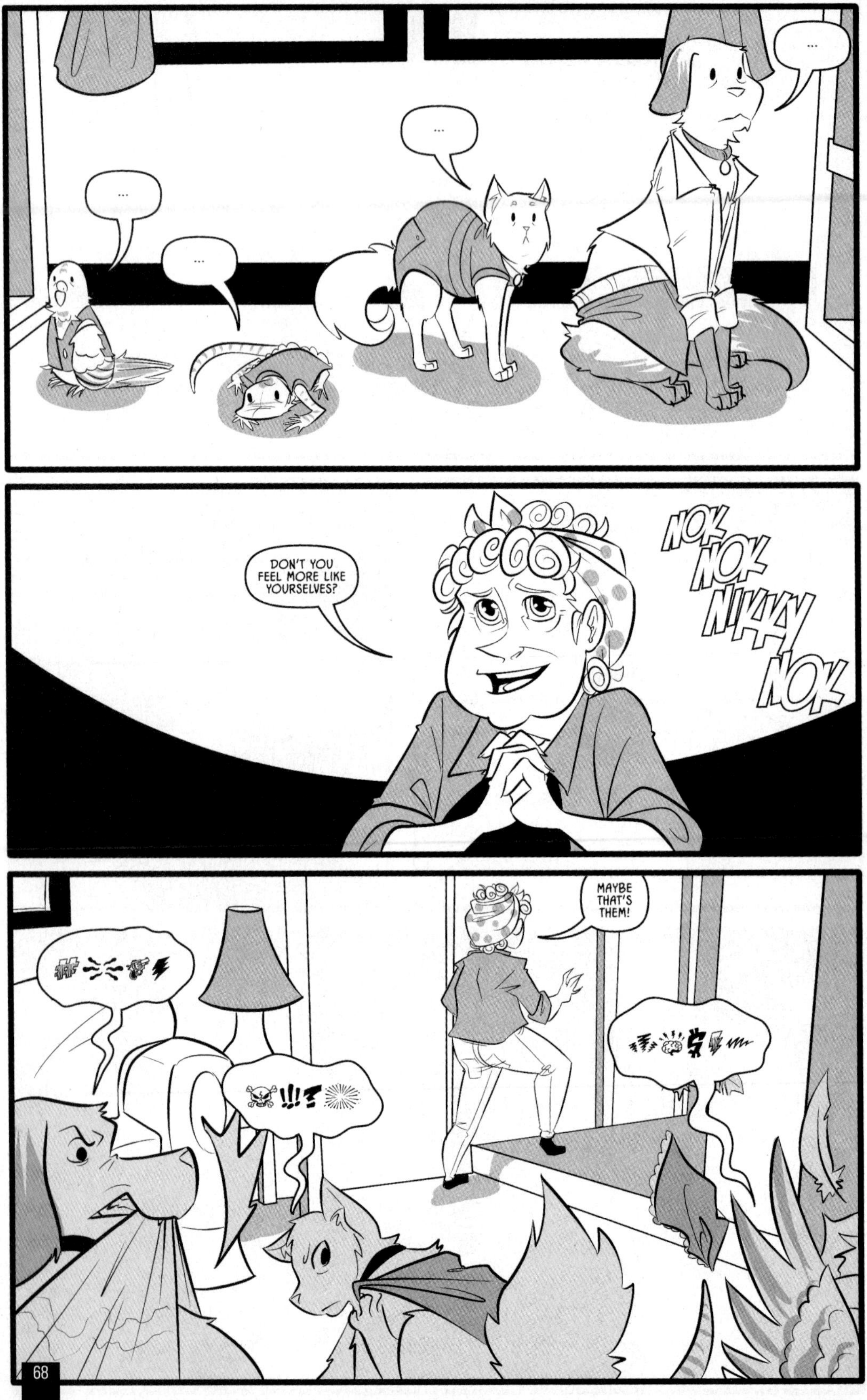
...
...
...
...
DON'T YOU FEEL MORE LIKE YOURSELVES?
NOK NOK NIKKY NOK
MAYBE THAT'S THEM!

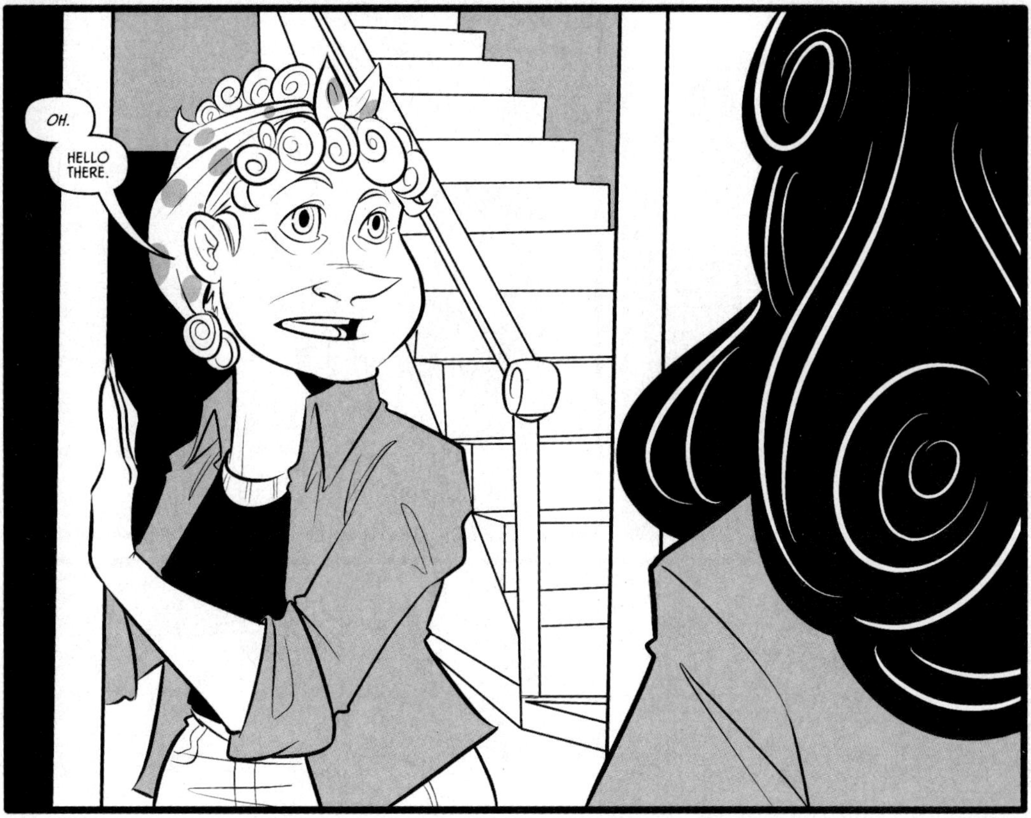
OH.
HELLO THERE.

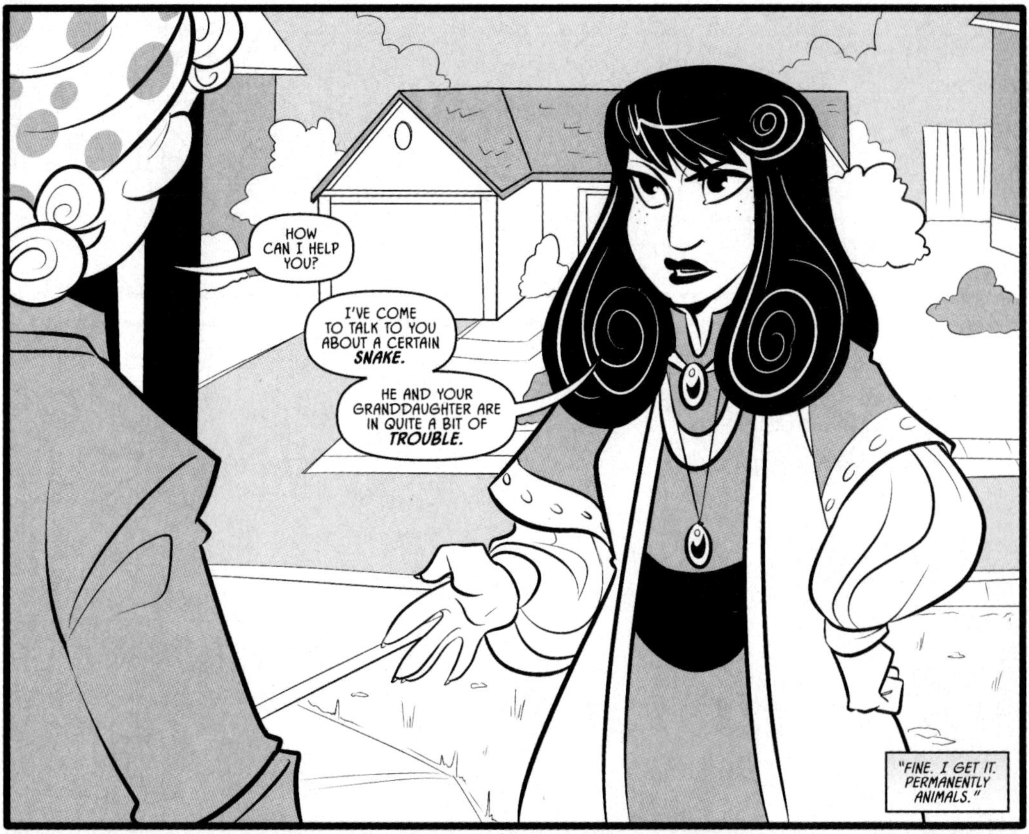
HOW CAN I HELP YOU?
I'VE COME TO TALK TO YOU ABOUT A CERTAIN SNAKE.
HE AND YOUR GRANDDAUGHTER ARE IN QUITE A BIT OF TROUBLE.
"FINE. I GET IT. PERMANENTLY ANIMALS."

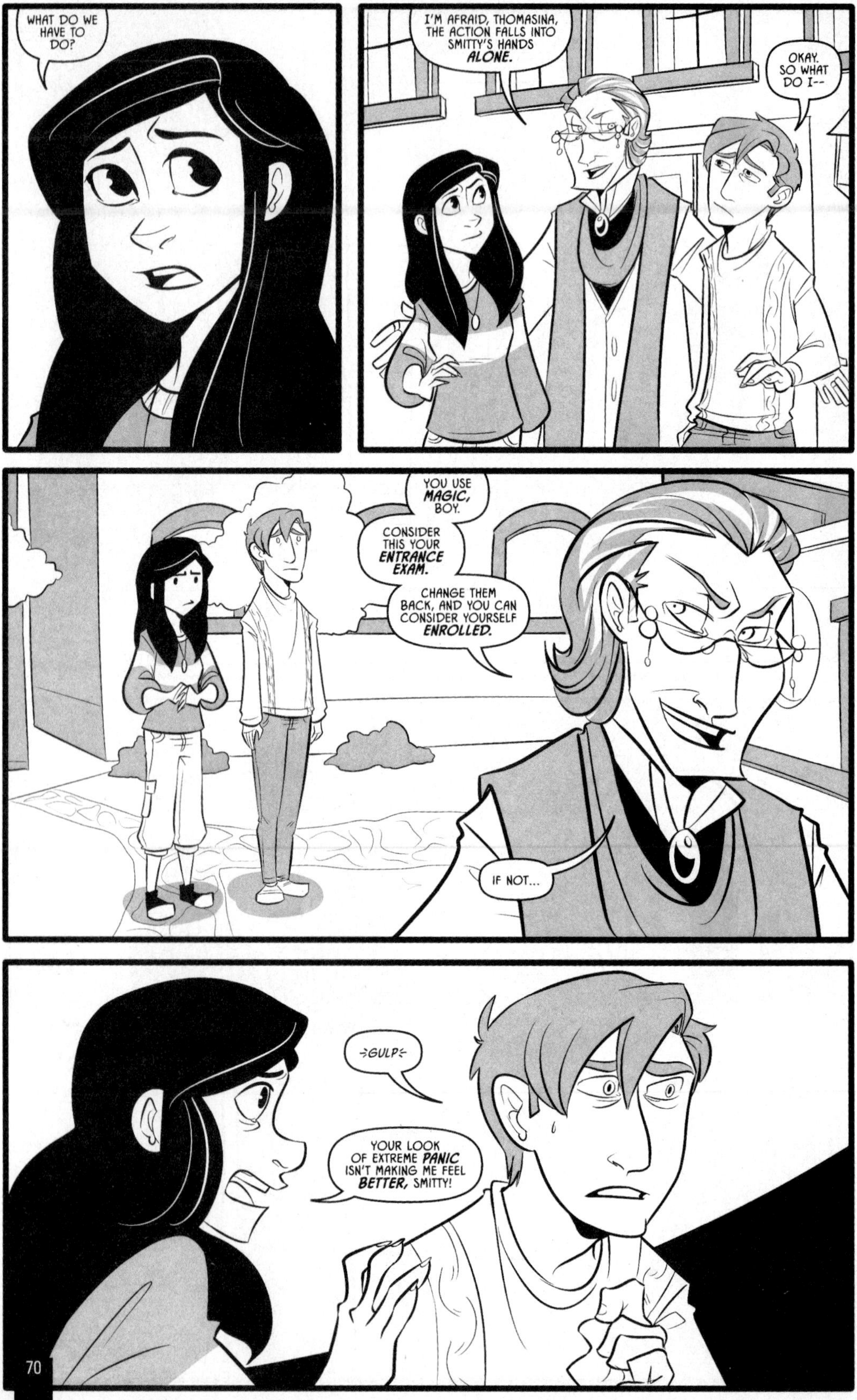
WHAT DO WE HAVE TO DO?
I'M AFRAID, THOMASINA, THE ACTION FALLS INTO SMITTY'S HANDS **ALONE.**
OKAY. SO WHAT DO I--
YOU USE **MAGIC,** BOY.
CONSIDER THIS YOUR **ENTRANCE EXAM.**
CHANGE THEM BACK, AND YOU CAN CONSIDER YOURSELF **ENROLLED.**
IF NOT...
GULP
YOUR LOOK OF EXTREME **PANIC** ISN'T MAKING ME FEEL **BETTER,** SMITTY!

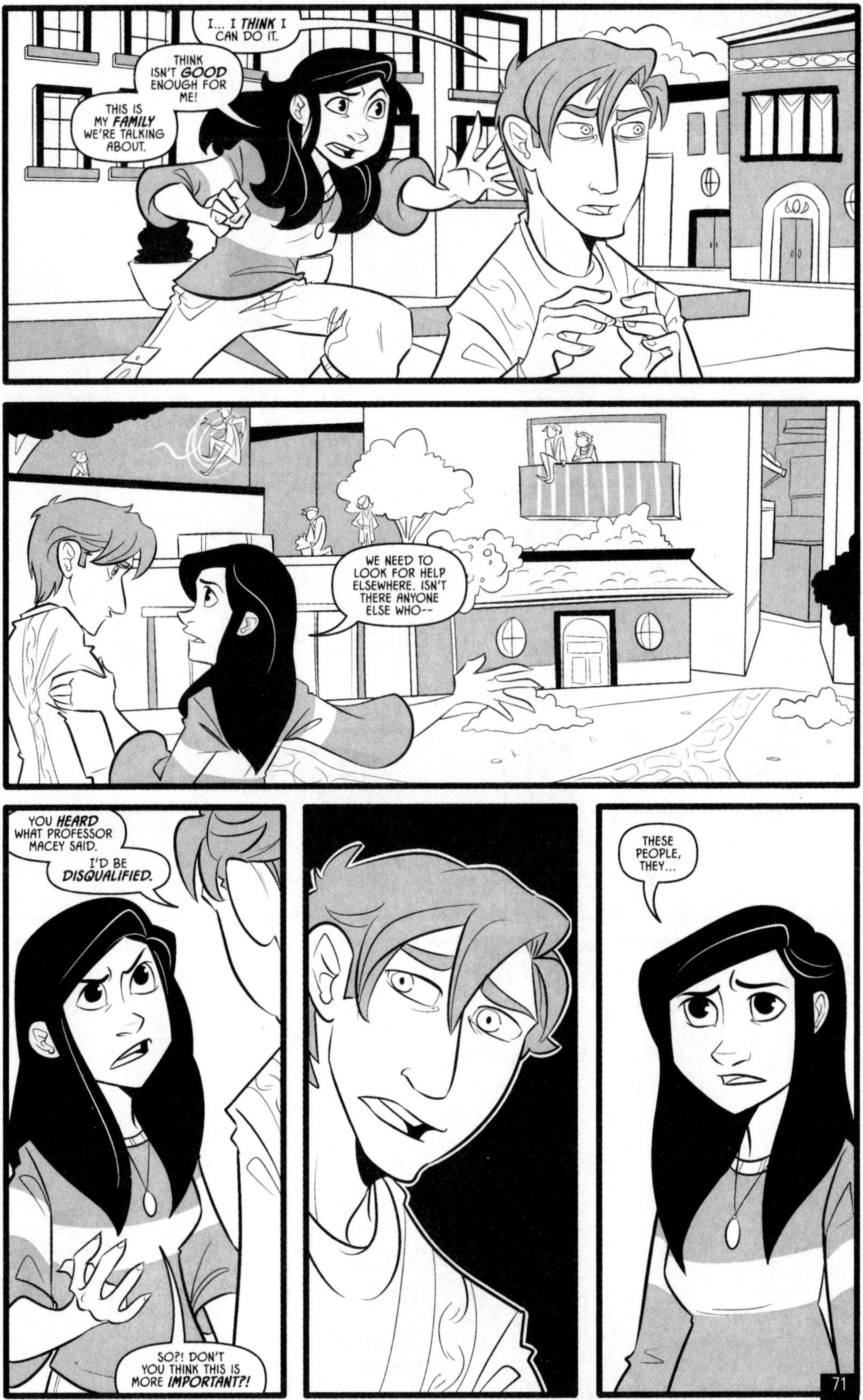

I... I *THINK* I CAN DO IT.
THINK ISN'T *GOOD* ENOUGH FOR ME!
THIS IS MY *FAMILY* WE'RE TALKING ABOUT.
WE NEED TO LOOK FOR HELP ELSEWHERE. ISN'T THERE ANYONE ELSE WHO--
YOU *HEARD* WHAT PROFESSOR MACEY SAID.
I'D BE *DISQUALIFIED.*
SO?! DON'T YOU THINK THIS IS MORE *IMPORTANT?!*
THESE PEOPLE, THEY...

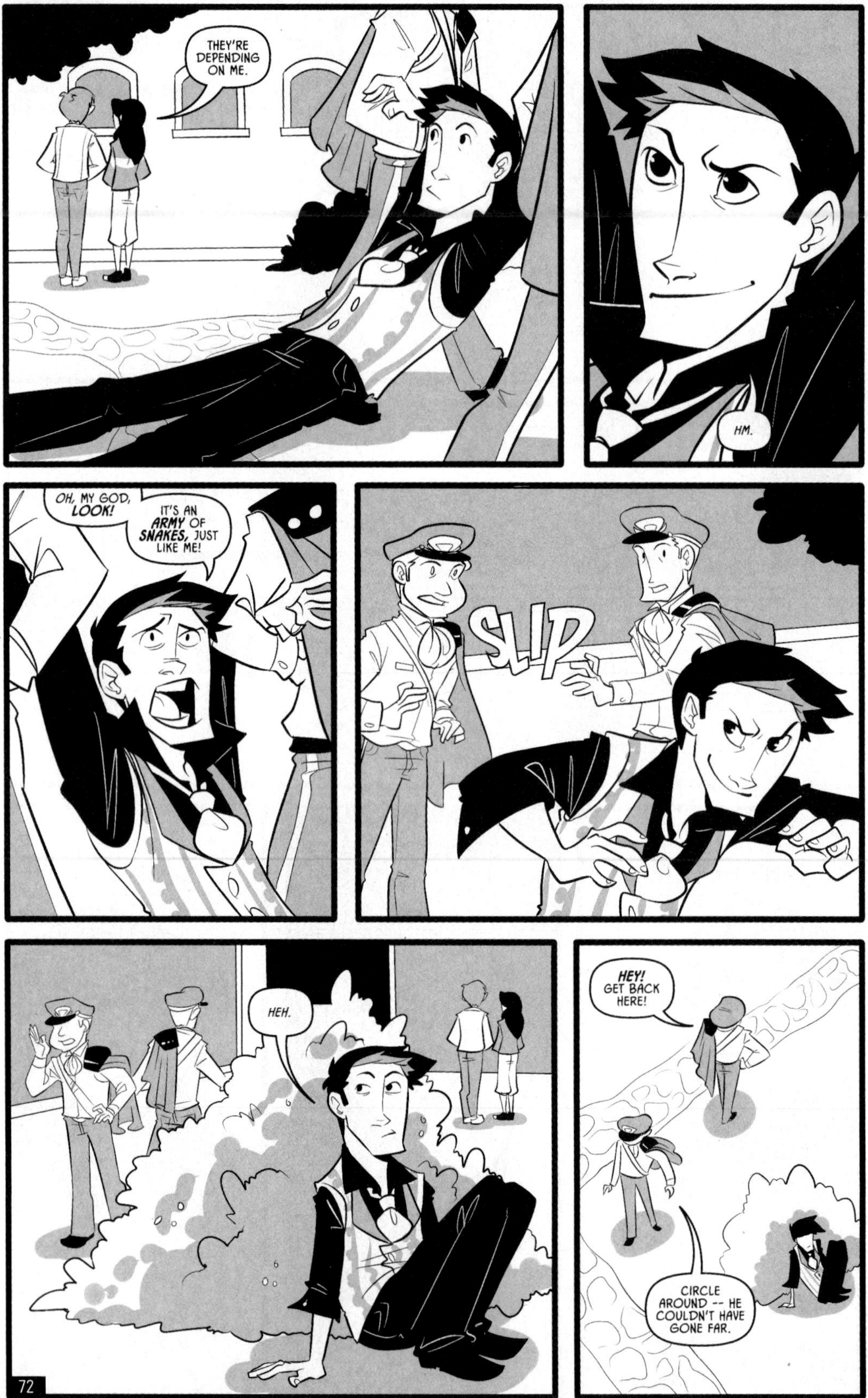
THEY'RE DEPENDING ON ME.
HM.
OH, MY GOD, LOOK!
IT'S AN ARMY OF SNAKES, JUST LIKE ME!
SLIP
HEH.
HEY! GET BACK HERE!
CIRCLE AROUND -- HE COULDN'T HAVE GONE FAR.

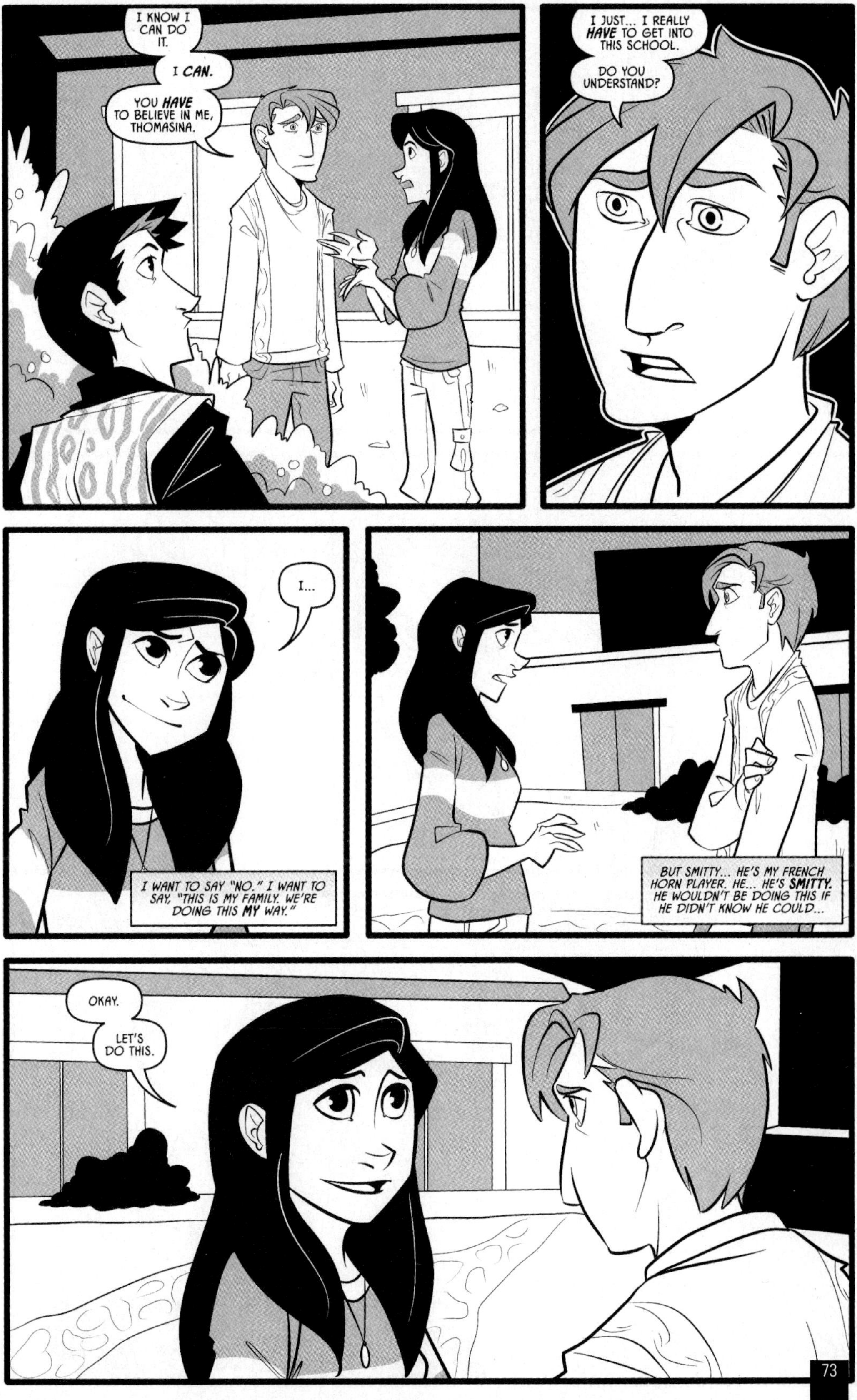
I KNOW I CAN DO IT.
I **CAN.**
YOU **HAVE** TO BELIEVE IN ME, THOMASINA.
I JUST... I REALLY **HAVE** TO GET INTO THIS SCHOOL.
DO YOU UNDERSTAND?
I...
I WANT TO SAY "NO." I WANT TO SAY, "THIS IS MY FAMILY. WE'RE DOING THIS **MY** WAY."
BUT SMITTY... HE'S MY FRENCH HORN PLAYER. HE... HE'S **SMITTY.** HE WOULDN'T BE DOING THIS IF HE DIDN'T KNOW HE COULD...
OKAY.
LET'S DO THIS.

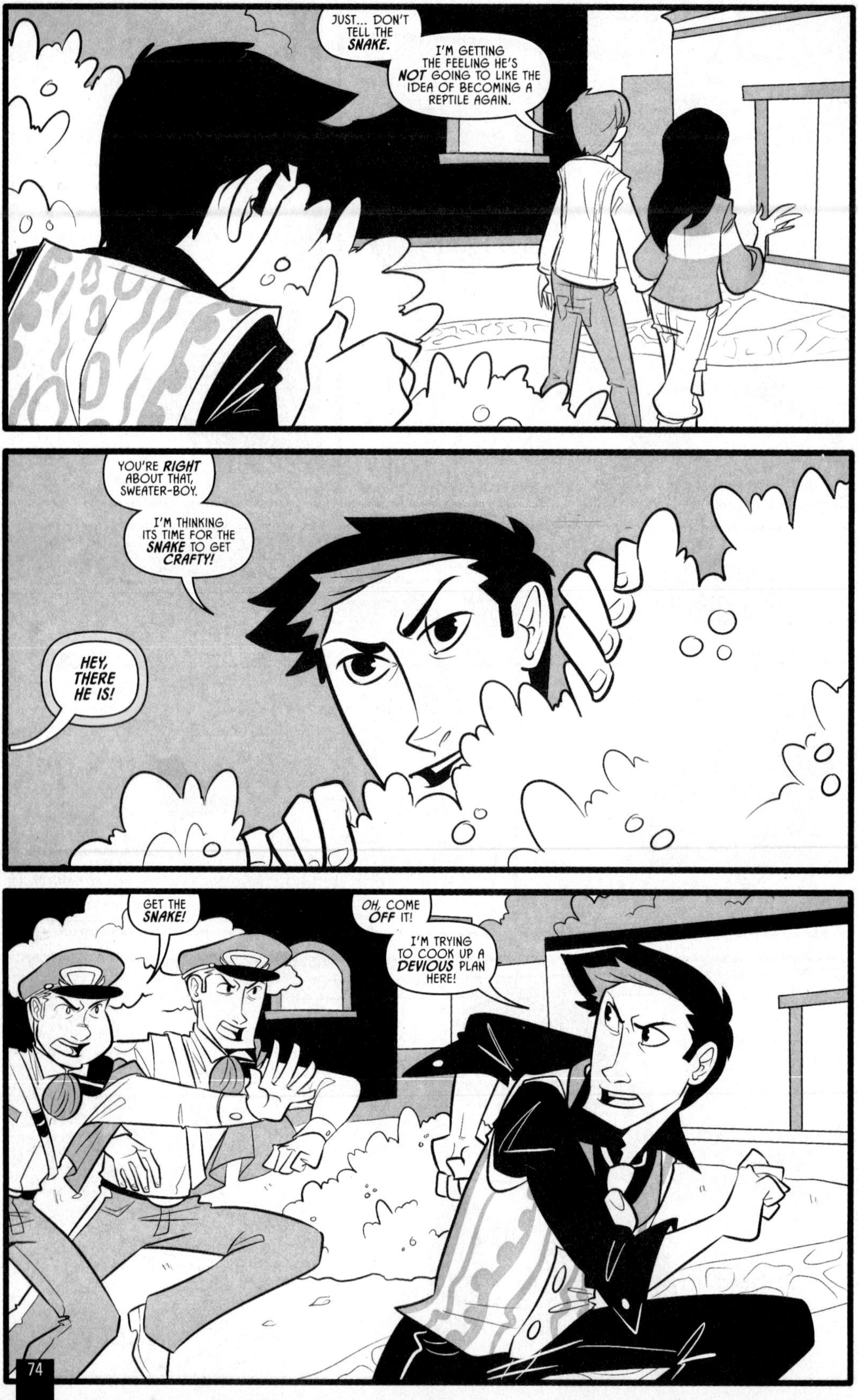
JUST... DON'T TELL THE SNAKE.
I'M GETTING THE FEELING HE'S NOT GOING TO LIKE THE IDEA OF BECOMING A REPTILE AGAIN.
YOU'RE RIGHT ABOUT THAT, SWEATER-BOY.
I'M THINKING ITS TIME FOR THE SNAKE TO GET CRAFTY!
HEY, THERE HE IS!
GET THE SNAKE!
OH, COME OFF IT!
I'M TRYING TO COOK UP A DEVIOUS PLAN HERE!

FAMILY PETS

FAMILY PETS
CHAPTER FOUR

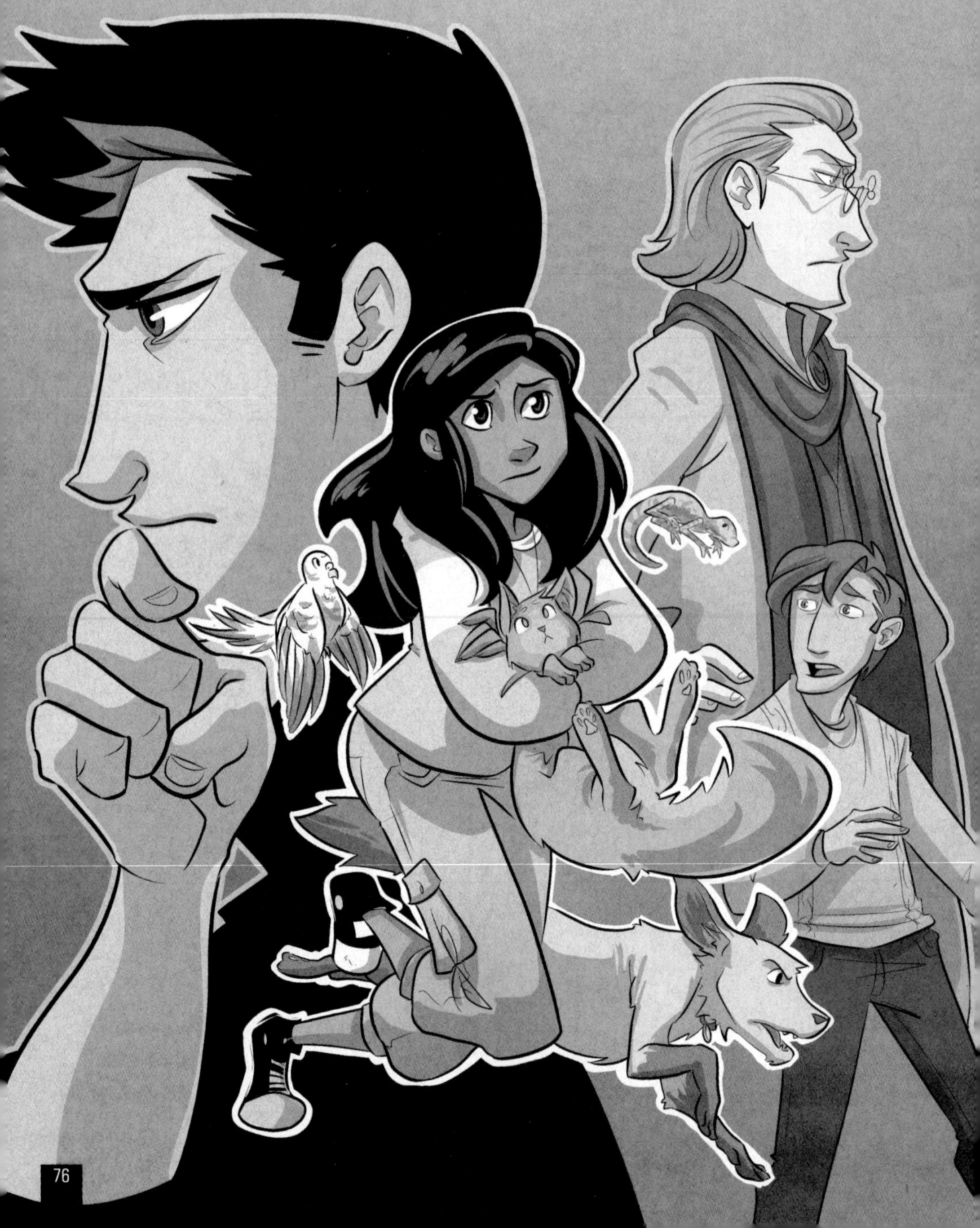

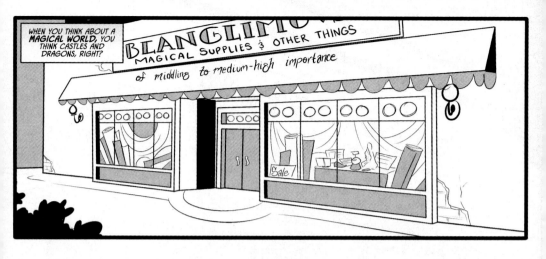

WHEN YOU THINK ABOUT A **MAGICAL WORLD**, YOU THINK CASTLES AND DRAGONS, RIGHT?

BLANGLIM
MAGICAL SUPPLIES & OTHER THINGS
of middling to medium-high importance

Sale

WIZARDS AND WITCHES, ROBES AND WANDS, WHIMSY AND ADVENTURE.

Sale

RUN!

I'M **RUNNING!** WE'RE RUNNING!

WHY ARE WE **RUNNING?!**

OH...

YOU NEVER REALLY WONDER...

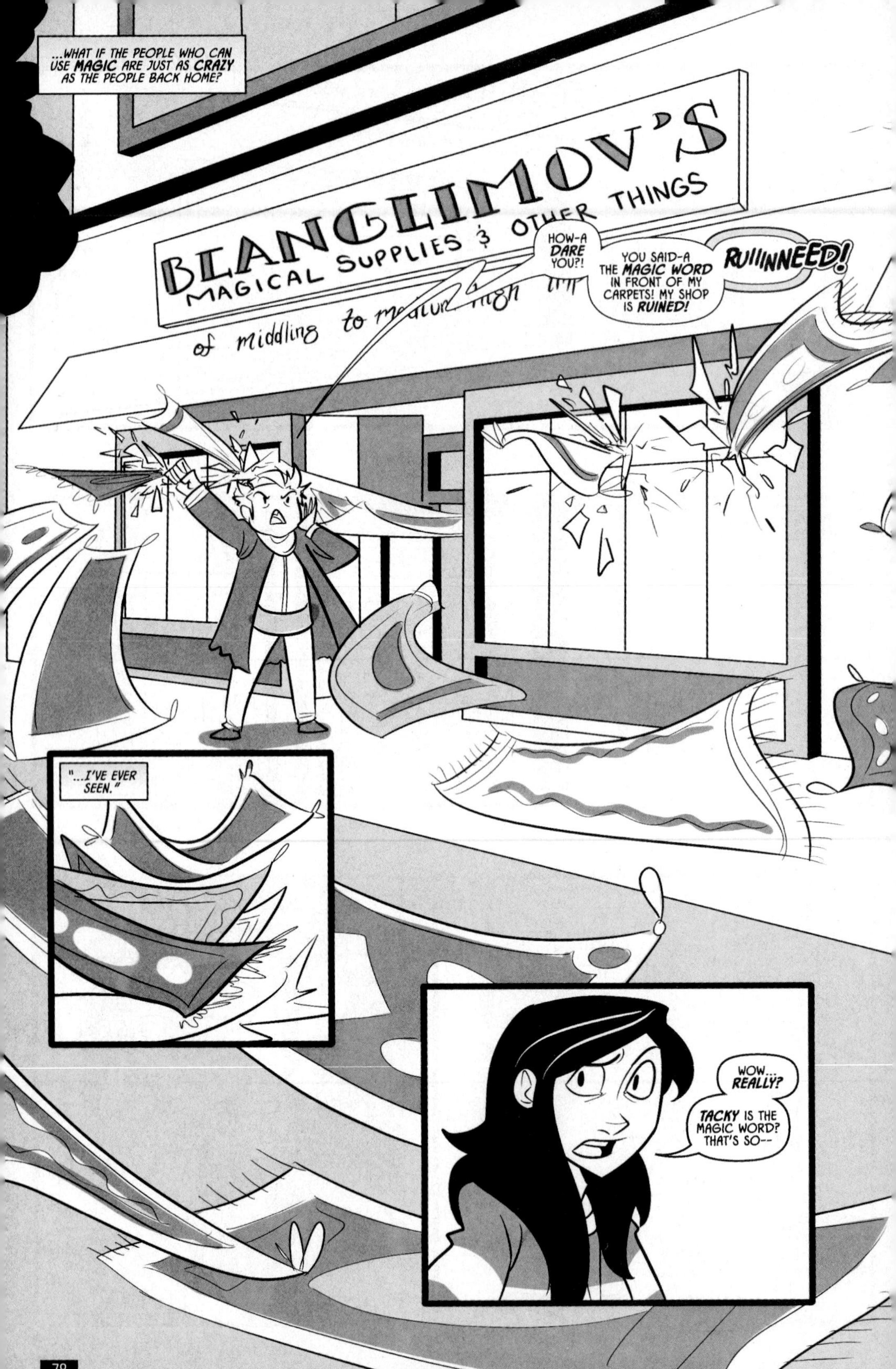
...WHAT IF THE PEOPLE WHO CAN USE MAGIC ARE JUST AS CRAZY AS THE PEOPLE BACK HOME?
BLANGLIMOV'S
MAGICAL SUPPLIES & OTHER THINGS
of middling to medium high
HOW-A DARE YOU?!
YOU SAID-A THE MAGIC WORD IN FRONT OF MY CARPETS! MY SHOP IS RUINED!
RUIIINNEED!
"...I'VE EVER SEEN."
WOW... REALLY?
TACKY IS THE MAGIC WORD? THAT'S SO--

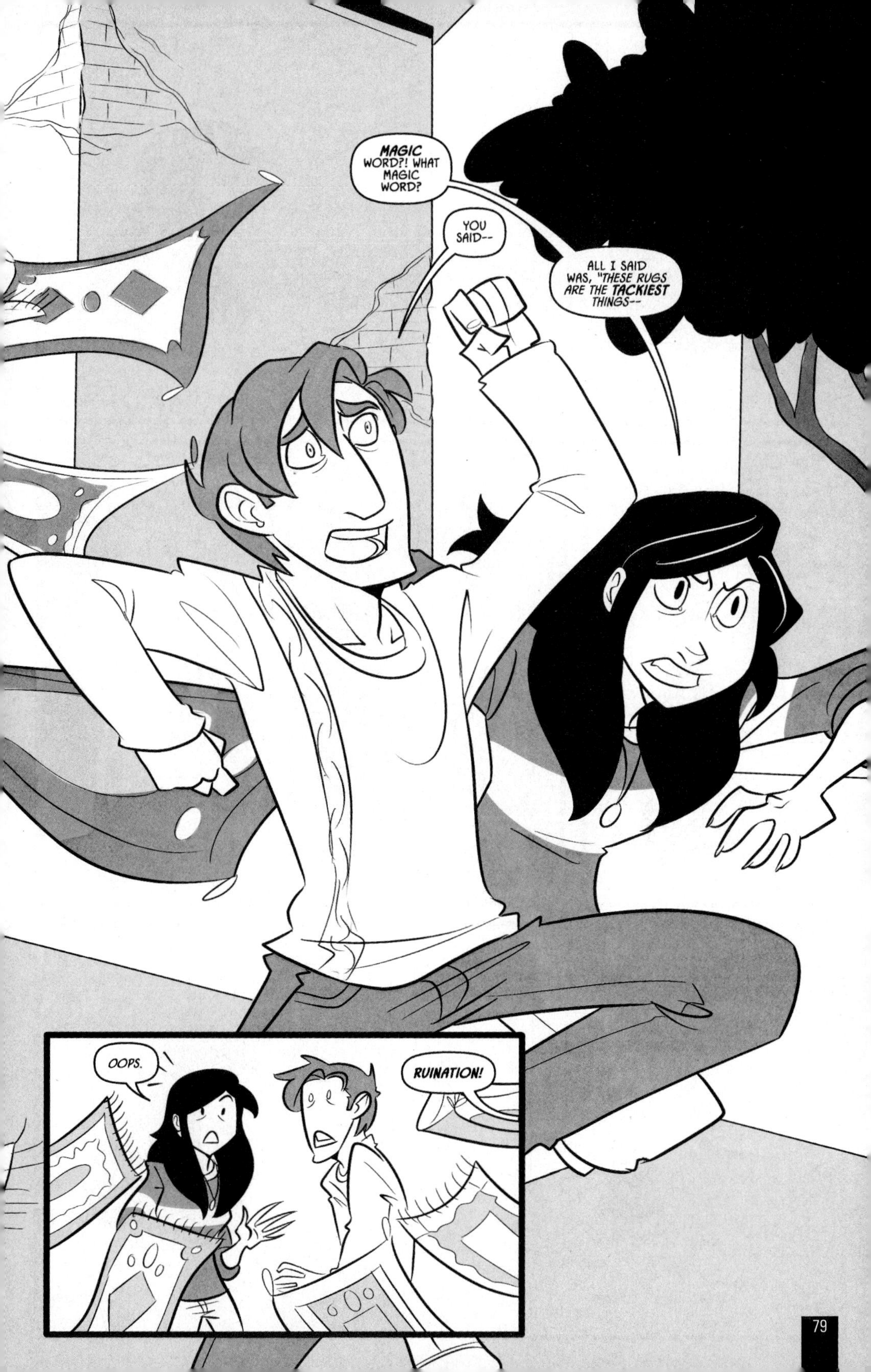
MAGIC WORD?! WHAT MAGIC WORD?
YOU SAID--
ALL I SAID WAS, "THESE RUGS ARE THE TACKIEST THINGS--
OOPS.
RUINATION!

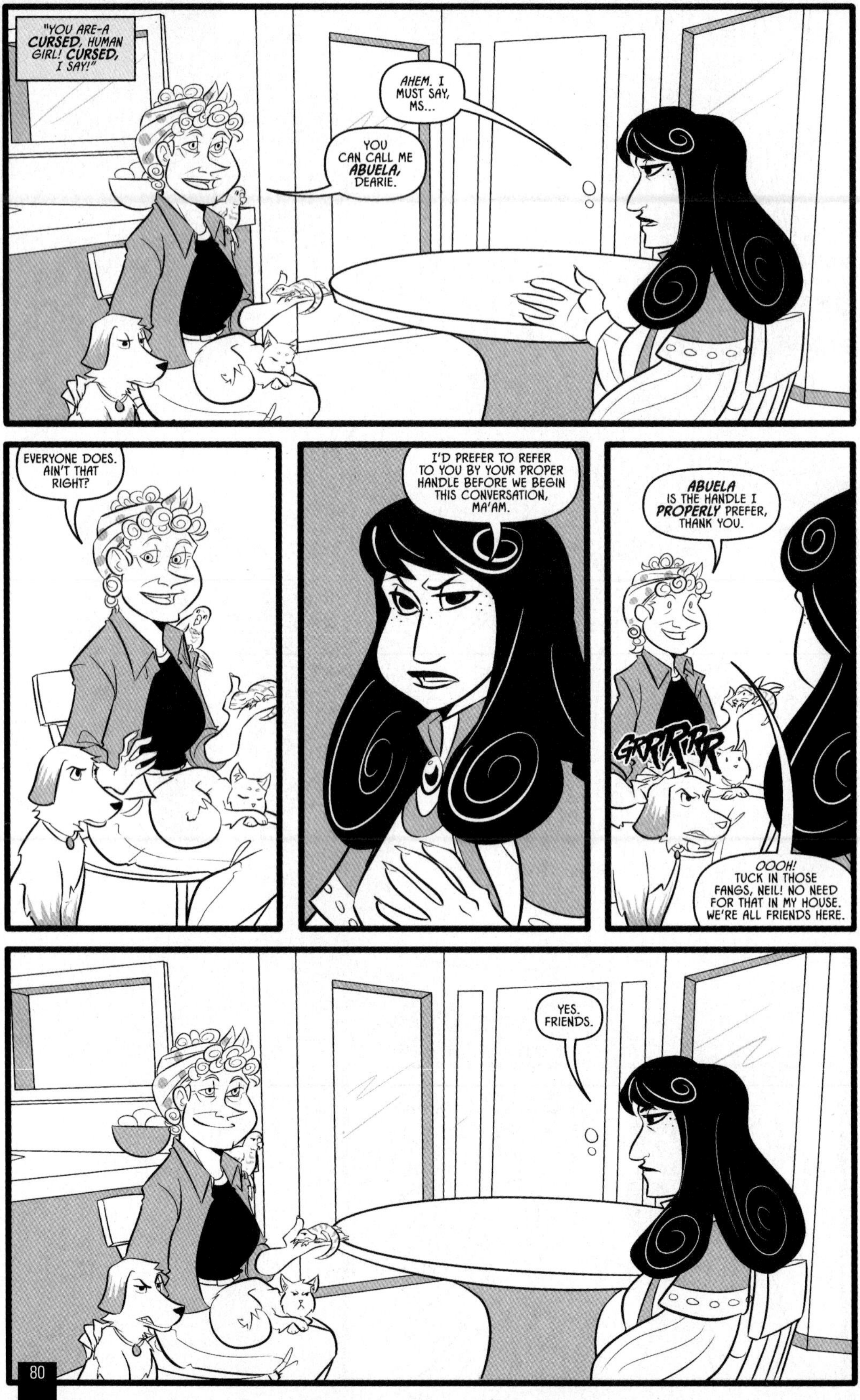
"YOU ARE-A CURSED, HUMAN GIRL! CURSED, I SAY!"
AHEM. I MUST SAY, MS...
YOU CAN CALL ME ABUELA, DEARIE.
EVERYONE DOES. AIN'T THAT RIGHT?
I'D PREFER TO REFER TO YOU BY YOUR PROPER HANDLE BEFORE WE BEGIN THIS CONVERSATION, MA'AM.
ABUELA IS THE HANDLE I PROPERLY PREFER, THANK YOU.
GRRRRRR
OOOH! TUCK IN THOSE FANGS, NEIL! NO NEED FOR THAT IN MY HOUSE. WE'RE ALL FRIENDS HERE.
YES. FRIENDS.

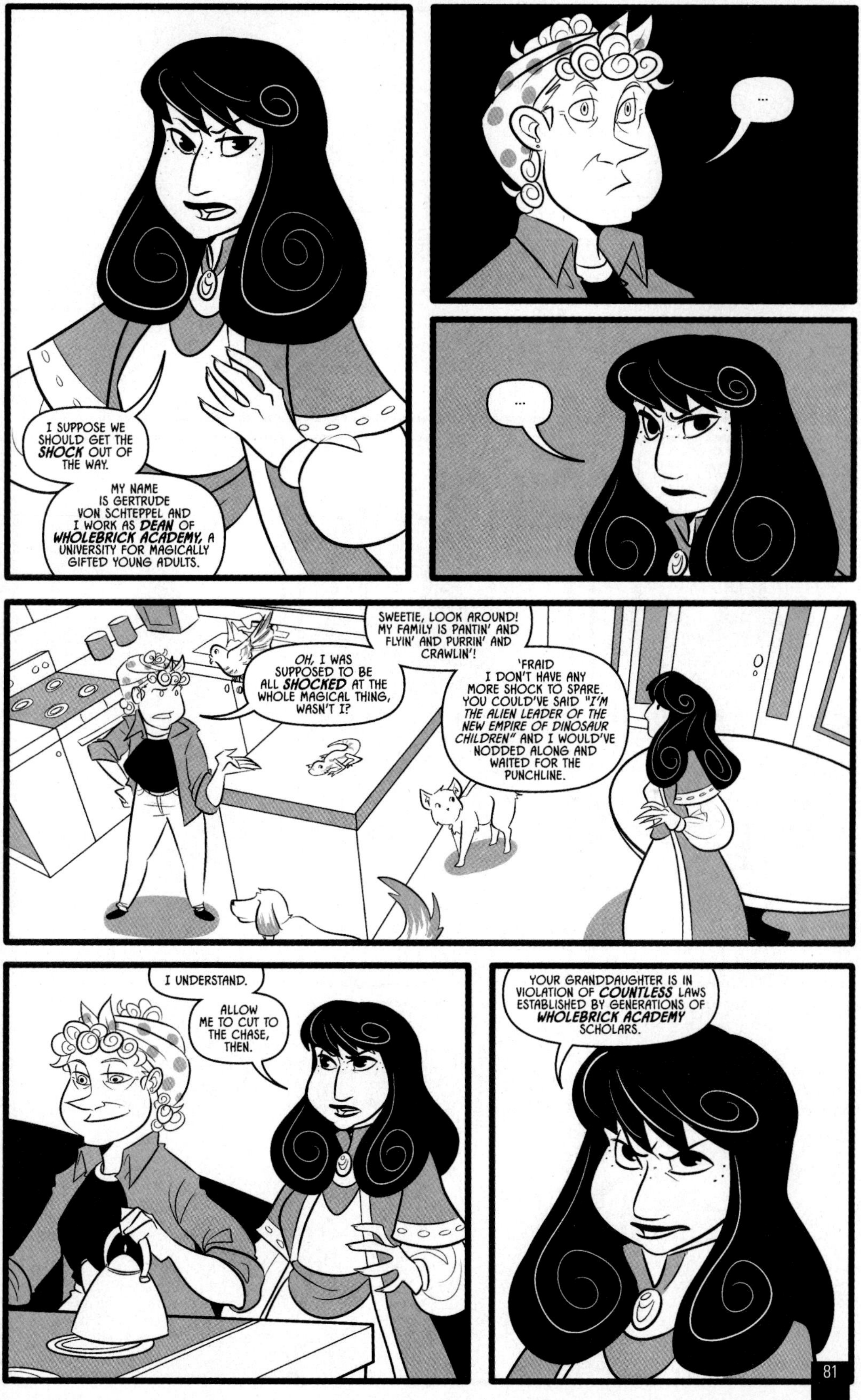
I SUPPOSE WE SHOULD GET THE SHOCK OUT OF THE WAY.
MY NAME IS GERTRUDE VON SCHTEPPEL AND I WORK AS DEAN OF WHOLEBRICK ACADEMY, A UNIVERSITY FOR MAGICALLY GIFTED YOUNG ADULTS.
...
...
OH, I WAS SUPPOSED TO BE ALL SHOCKED AT THE WHOLE MAGICAL THING, WASN'T I?
SWEETIE, LOOK AROUND! MY FAMILY IS PANTIN' AND FLYIN' AND PURRIN' AND CRAWLIN'!
'FRAID I DON'T HAVE ANY MORE SHOCK TO SPARE. YOU COULD'VE SAID "I'M THE ALIEN LEADER OF THE NEW EMPIRE OF DINOSAUR CHILDREN" AND I WOULD'VE NODDED ALONG AND WAITED FOR THE PUNCHLINE.
I UNDERSTAND.
ALLOW ME TO CUT TO THE CHASE, THEN.
YOUR GRANDDAUGHTER IS IN VIOLATION OF COUNTLESS LAWS ESTABLISHED BY GENERATIONS OF WHOLEBRICK ACADEMY SCHOLARS.

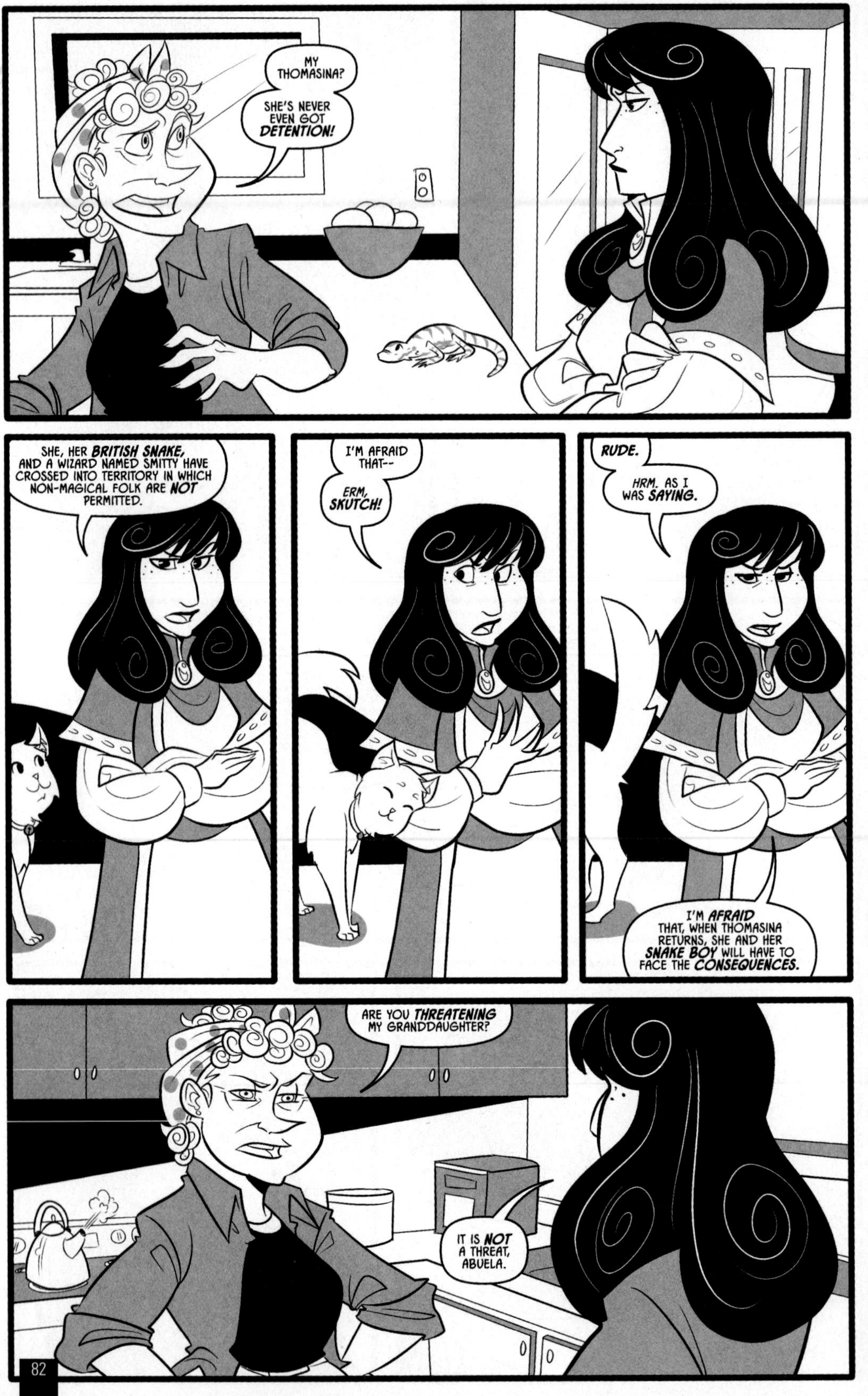

MY THOMASINA?
SHE'S NEVER EVEN GOT DETENTION!
SHE, HER BRITISH SNAKE, AND A WIZARD NAMED SMITTY HAVE CROSSED INTO TERRITORY IN WHICH NON-MAGICAL FOLK ARE NOT PERMITTED.
I'M AFRAID THAT--
ERM, SKUTCH!
RUDE.
HRM. AS I WAS SAYING.
I'M AFRAID THAT, WHEN THOMASINA RETURNS, SHE AND HER SNAKE BOY WILL HAVE TO FACE THE CONSEQUENCES.
ARE YOU THREATENING MY GRANDDAUGHTER?
IT IS NOT A THREAT, ABUELA.

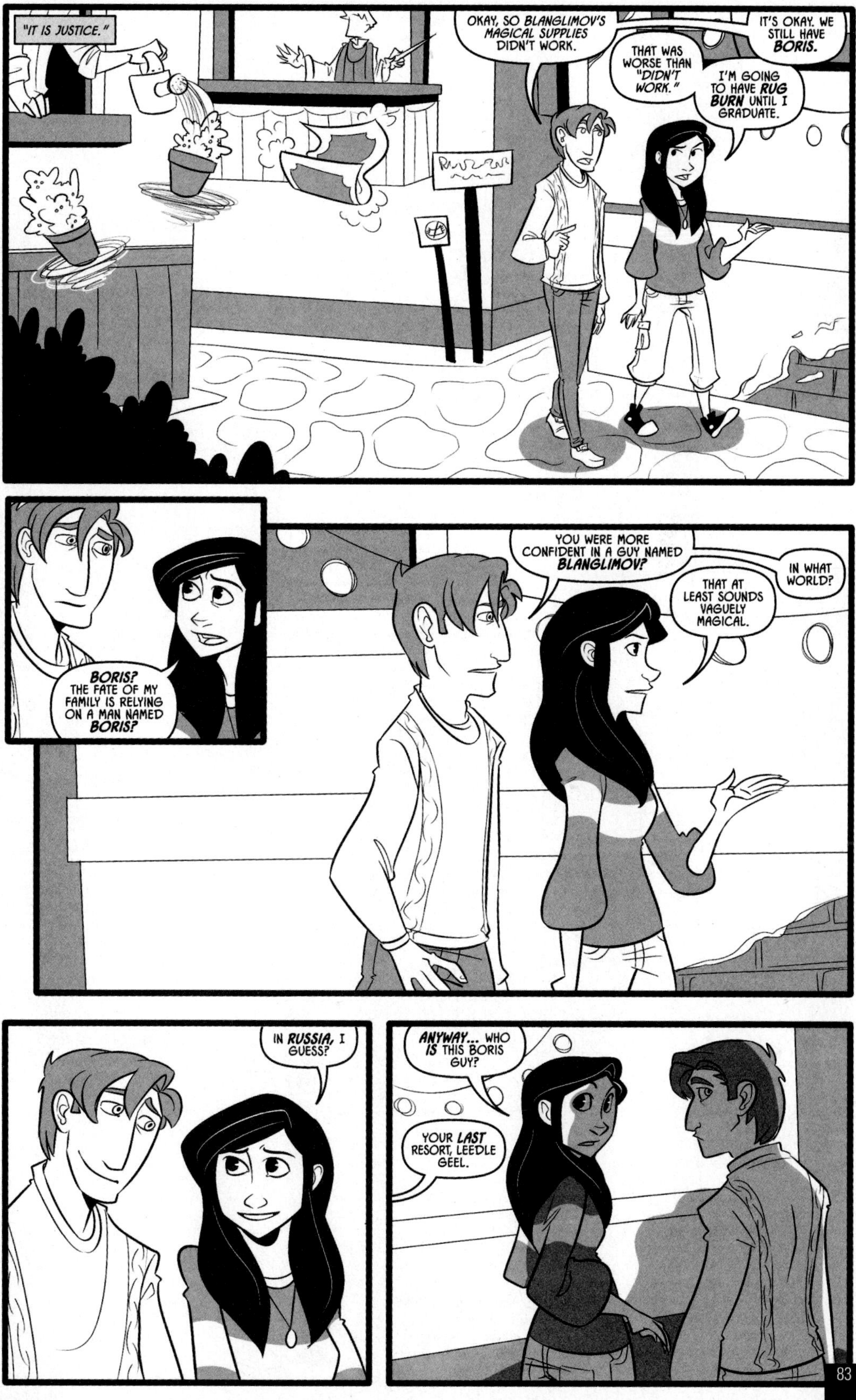
"IT IS JUSTICE."
OKAY, SO BLANGLIMOV'S MAGICAL SUPPLIES DIDN'T WORK.
IT'S OKAY. WE STILL HAVE BORIS.
THAT WAS WORSE THAN "DIDN'T WORK."
I'M GOING TO HAVE RUG BURN UNTIL I GRADUATE.
BORIS? THE FATE OF MY FAMILY IS RELYING ON A MAN NAMED BORIS?
YOU WERE MORE CONFIDENT IN A GUY NAMED BLANGLIMOV?
THAT AT LEAST SOUNDS VAGUELY MAGICAL.
IN WHAT WORLD?
IN RUSSIA, I GUESS?
ANYWAY... WHO IS THIS BORIS GUY?
YOUR LAST RESORT, LEEDLE GEEL.

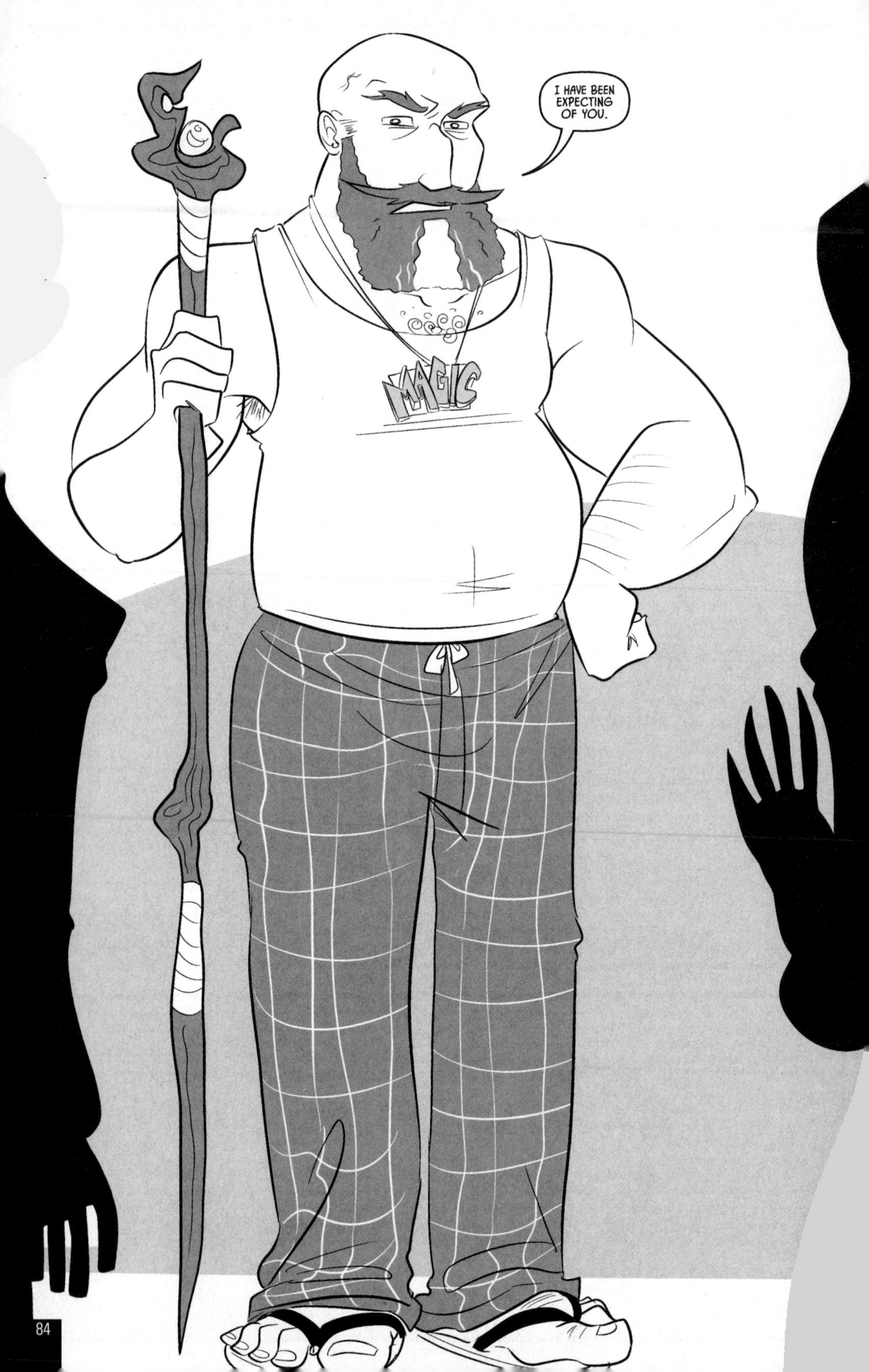
I HAVE BEEN EXPECTING OF YOU.
MAGIC

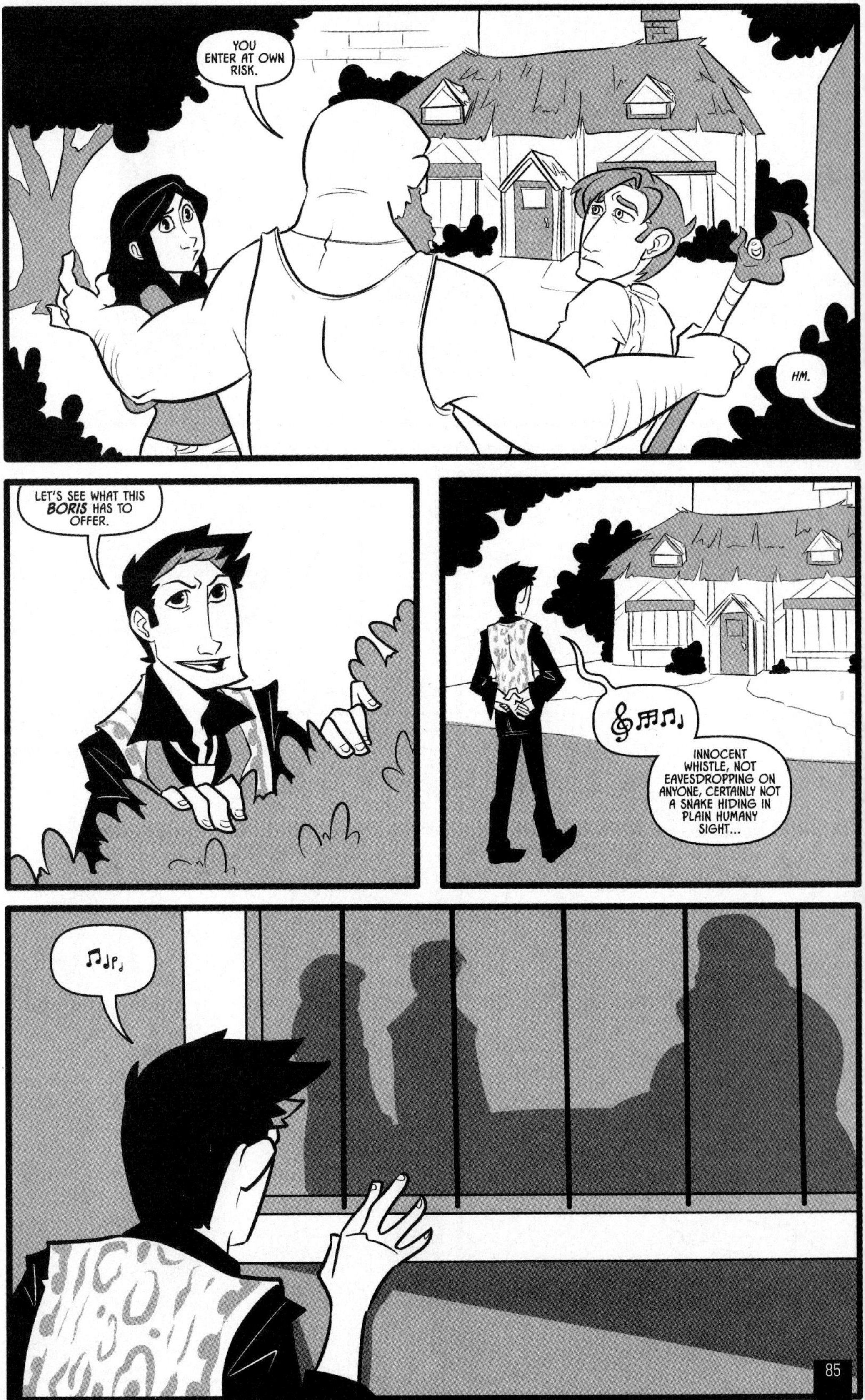
YOU ENTER AT OWN RISK.
HM.
LET'S SEE WHAT THIS BORIS HAS TO OFFER.
INNOCENT WHISTLE, NOT EAVESDROPPING ON ANYONE, CERTAINLY NOT A SNAKE HIDING IN PLAIN HUMANY SIGHT...

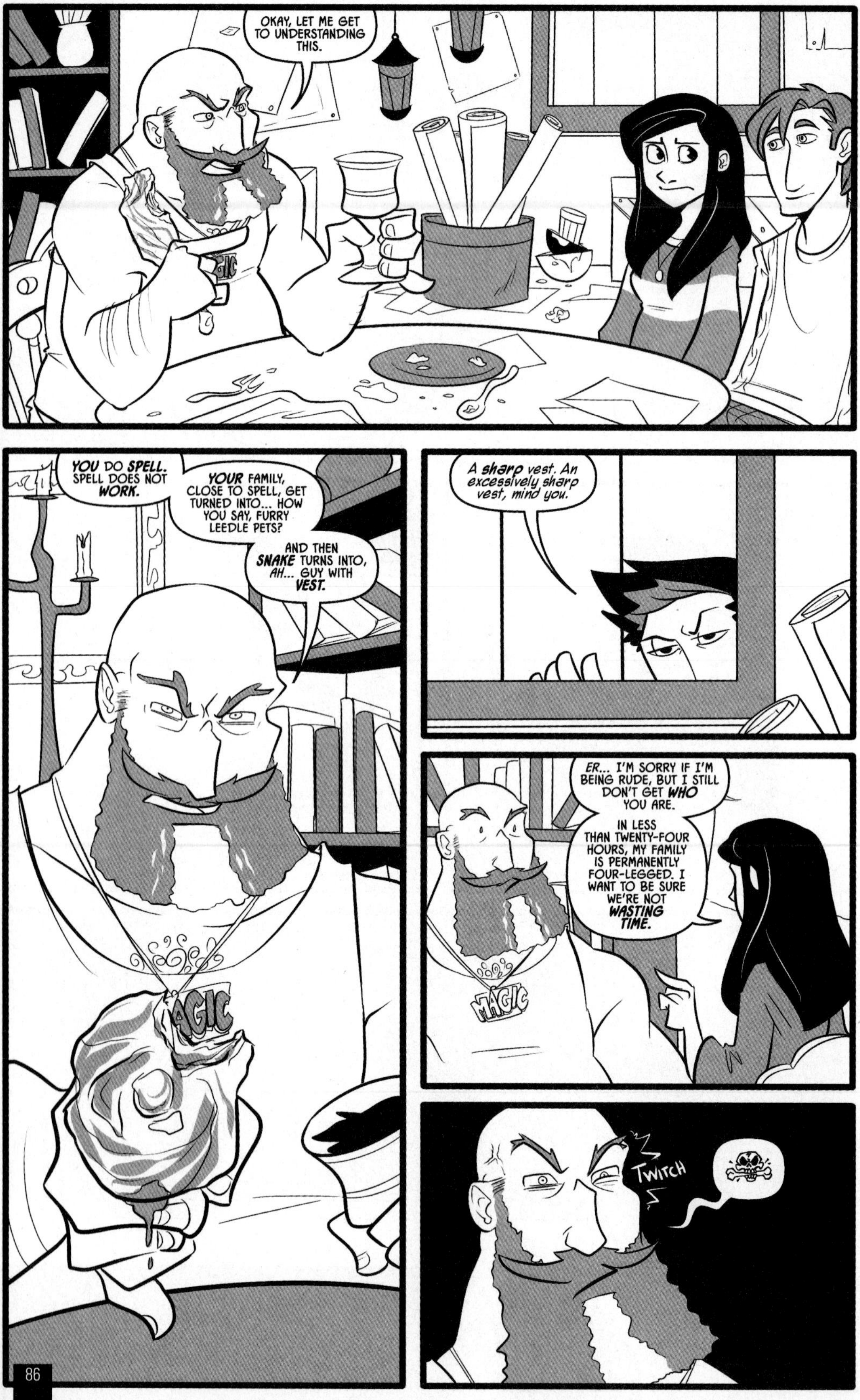

OKAY, LET ME GET TO UNDERSTANDING THIS.
YOU DO SPELL. SPELL DOES NOT WORK.
YOUR FAMILY, CLOSE TO SPELL, GET TURNED INTO... HOW YOU SAY, FURRY LEEDLE PETS?
AND THEN SNAKE TURNS INTO, AH... GUY WITH VEST.
A sharp vest. An excessively sharp vest, mind you.
ER... I'M SORRY IF I'M BEING RUDE, BUT I STILL DON'T GET WHO YOU ARE.
IN LESS THAN TWENTY-FOUR HOURS, MY FAMILY IS PERMANENTLY FOUR-LEGGED. I WANT TO BE SURE WE'RE NOT WASTING TIME.
TWITCH

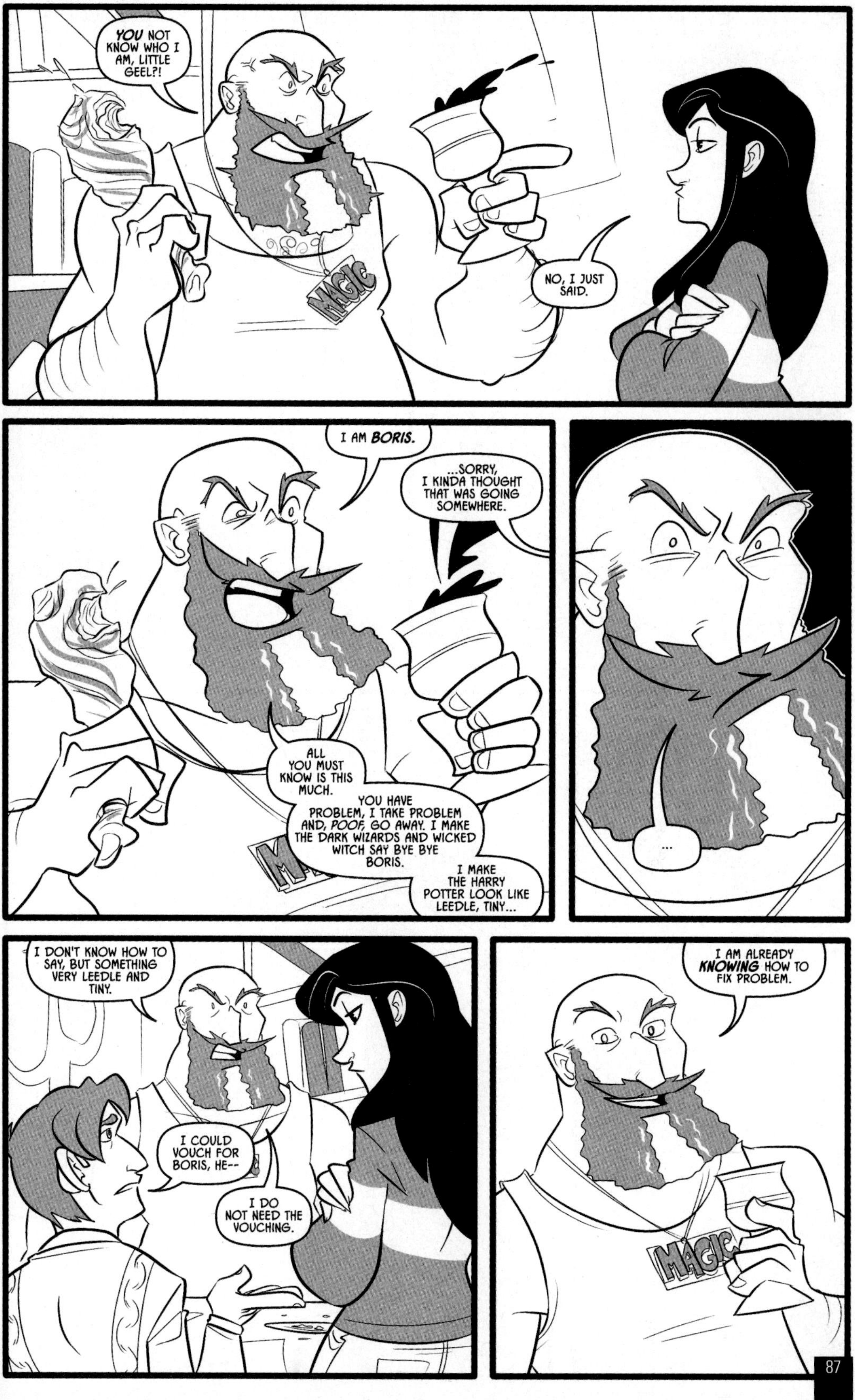
YOU NOT KNOW WHO I AM, LITTLE GEEL?!
NO, I JUST SAID.
I AM BORIS.
...SORRY, I KINDA THOUGHT THAT WAS GOING SOMEWHERE.
ALL YOU MUST KNOW IS THIS MUCH.
YOU HAVE PROBLEM, I TAKE PROBLEM AND, POOF, GO AWAY. I MAKE THE DARK WIZARDS AND WICKED WITCH SAY BYE BYE BORIS.
I MAKE THE HARRY POTTER LOOK LIKE LEEDLE, TINY...
...
I DON'T KNOW HOW TO SAY, BUT SOMETHING VERY LEEDLE AND TINY.
I COULD VOUCH FOR BORIS, HE--
I DO NOT NEED THE VOUCHING.
I AM ALREADY KNOWING HOW TO FIX PROBLEM.

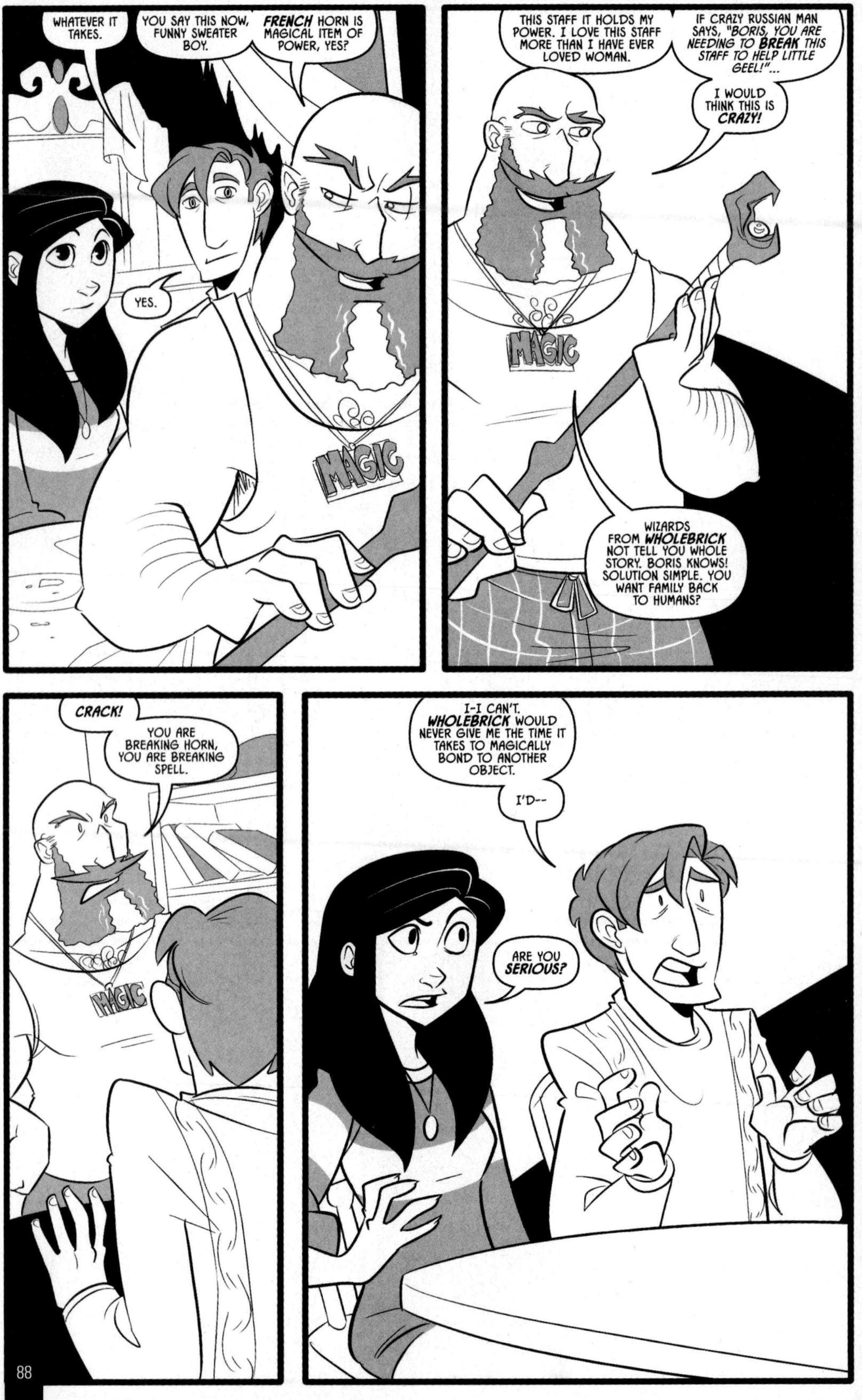
WHATEVER IT TAKES.
YOU SAY THIS NOW, FUNNY SWEATER BOY.
FRENCH HORN IS MAGICAL ITEM OF POWER, YES?
YES.
MAGIC
THIS STAFF IT HOLDS MY POWER. I LOVE THIS STAFF MORE THAN I HAVE EVER LOVED WOMAN.
IF CRAZY RUSSIAN MAN SAYS, "BORIS, YOU ARE NEEDING TO BREAK THIS STAFF TO HELP LITTLE GEEL!"...
I WOULD THINK THIS IS CRAZY!
MAGIC
WIZARDS FROM WHOLEBRICK NOT TELL YOU WHOLE STORY. BORIS KNOWS! SOLUTION SIMPLE. YOU WANT FAMILY BACK TO HUMANS?
CRACK!
YOU ARE BREAKING HORN, YOU ARE BREAKING SPELL.
MAGIC
I-I CAN'T. WHOLEBRICK WOULD NEVER GIVE ME THE TIME IT TAKES TO MAGICALLY BOND TO ANOTHER OBJECT.
I'D--
ARE YOU SERIOUS?

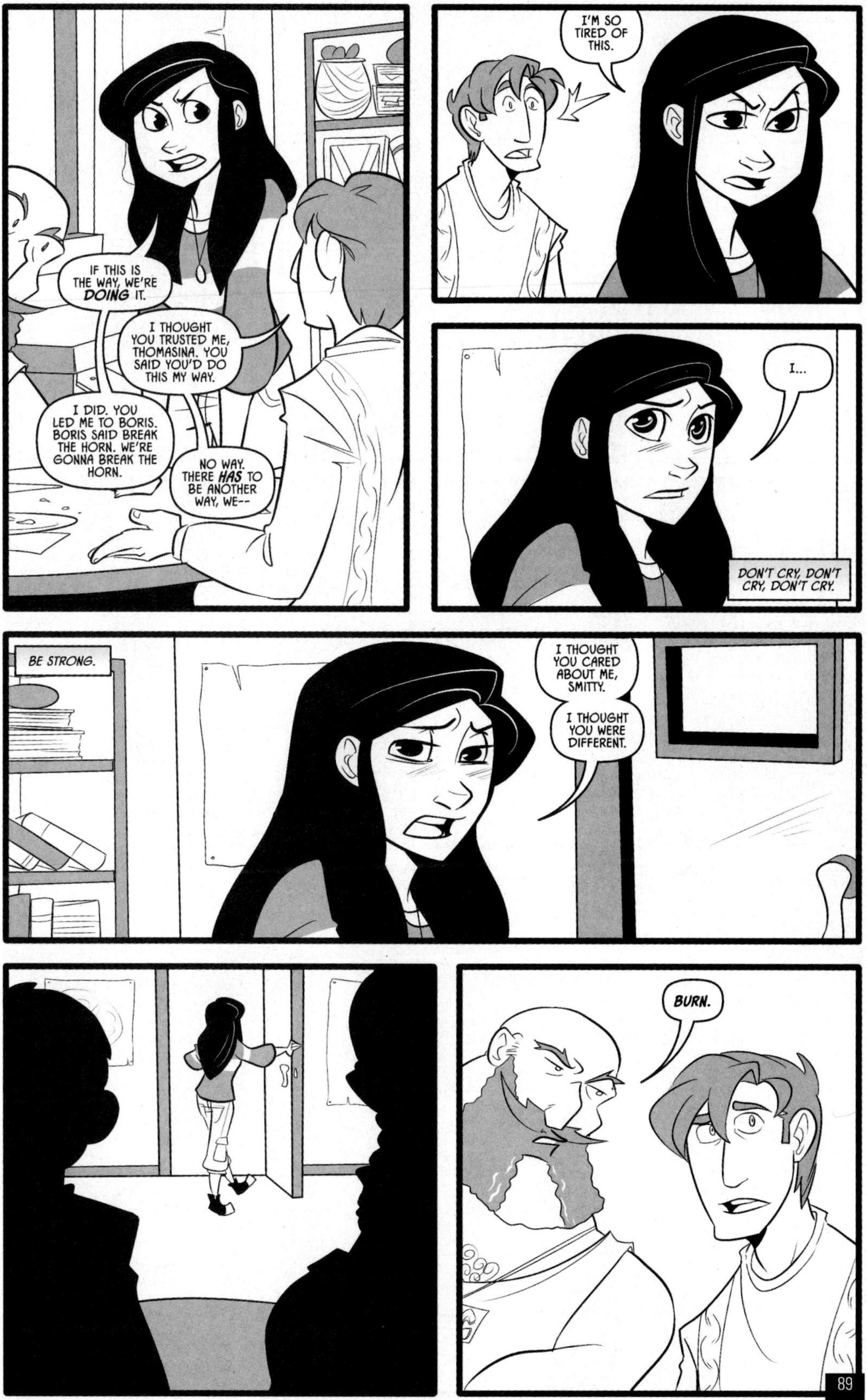
IF THIS IS THE WAY, WE'RE **DOING** IT.
I THOUGHT YOU TRUSTED ME, THOMASINA. YOU SAID YOU'D DO THIS MY WAY.
I DID. YOU LED ME TO BORIS. BORIS SAID BREAK THE HORN. WE'RE GONNA BREAK THE HORN.
NO WAY. THERE **HAS** TO BE ANOTHER WAY, WE--
I'M SO TIRED OF THIS.
I...
DON'T CRY, DON'T CRY, DON'T CRY.
BE STRONG.
I THOUGHT YOU CARED ABOUT ME, SMITTY.
I THOUGHT YOU WERE DIFFERENT.
BURN.

SMITTY.

MY **FRENCH HORN** PLAYER.

HE CARES MORE ABOUT GETTING INTO SOME **SCHOOL** THAN HE DOES ABOUT MY FAMILY.

ABOUT **ME**.

I SHOULD HAVE **STAYED** WITH SEBASTIAN. I SHOULD HAVE...

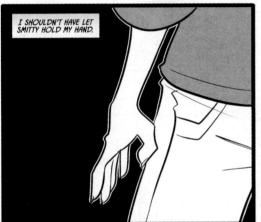

I SHOULDN'T HAVE LET SMITTY HOLD MY HAND.

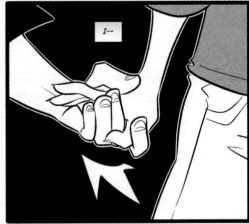

I--

FANCY MEETING YOU HERE.

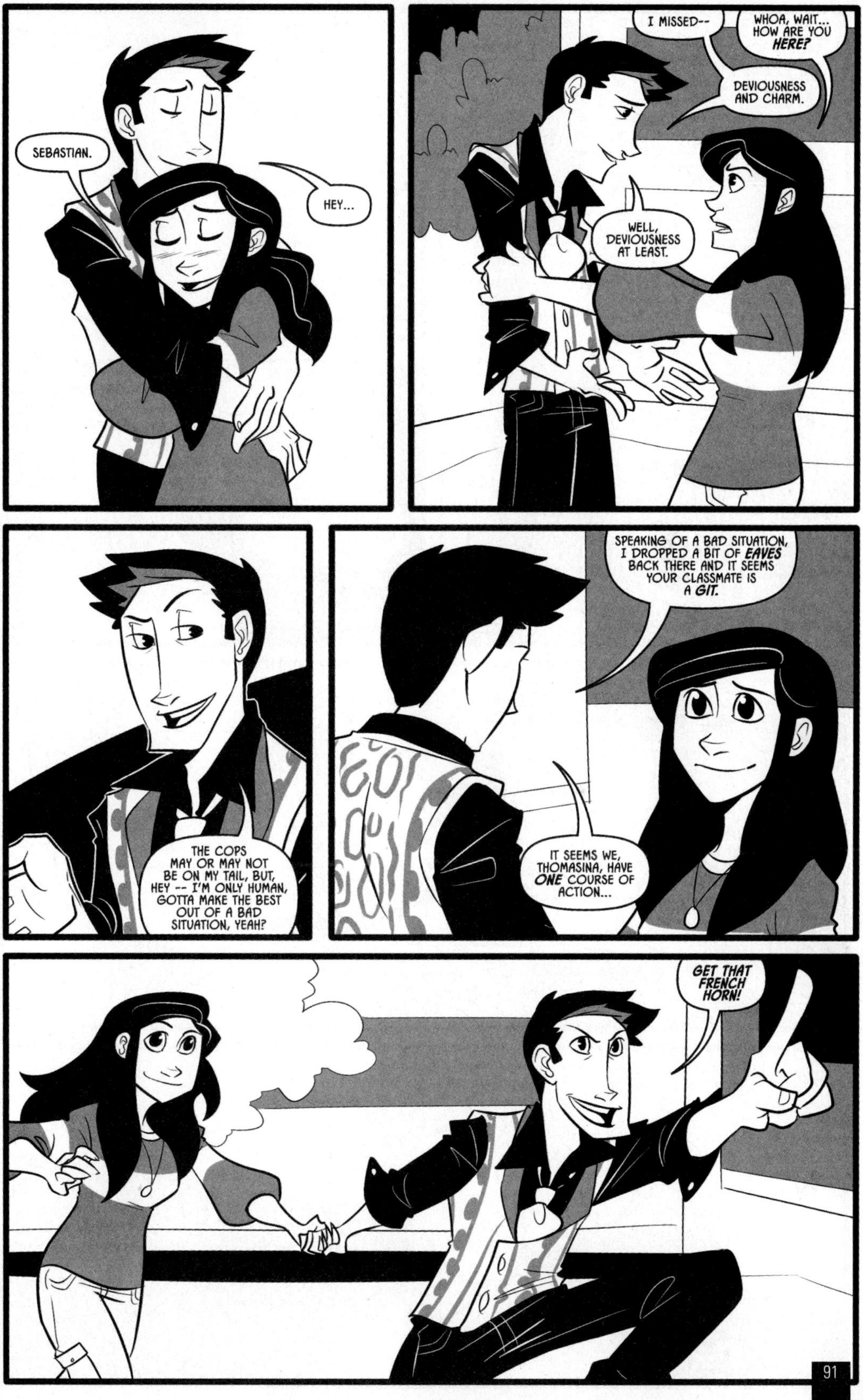
SEBASTIAN.
HEY...
I MISSED--
WHOA, WAIT... HOW ARE YOU HERE?
DEVIOUSNESS AND CHARM.
WELL, DEVIOUSNESS AT LEAST.
THE COPS MAY OR MAY NOT BE ON MY TAIL, BUT, HEY -- I'M ONLY HUMAN, GOTTA MAKE THE BEST OUT OF A BAD SITUATION, YEAH?
SPEAKING OF A BAD SITUATION, I DROPPED A BIT OF EAVES BACK THERE AND IT SEEMS YOUR CLASSMATE IS A GIT.
IT SEEMS WE, THOMASINA, HAVE ONE COURSE OF ACTION...
GET THAT FRENCH HORN!

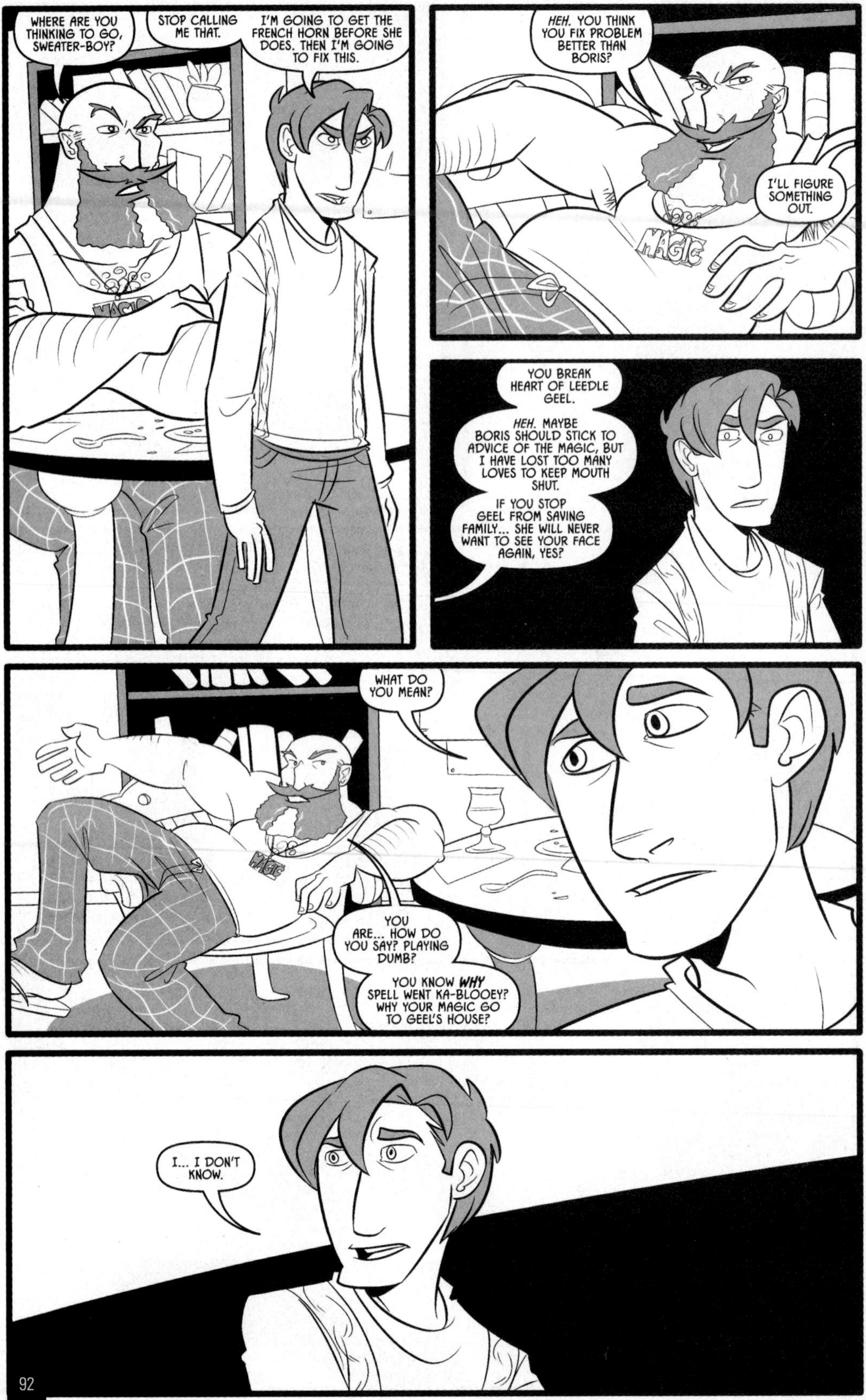
WHERE ARE YOU THINKING TO GO, SWEATER-BOY?
STOP CALLING ME THAT.
I'M GOING TO GET THE FRENCH HORN BEFORE SHE DOES. THEN I'M GOING TO FIX THIS.
HEH. YOU THINK YOU FIX PROBLEM BETTER THAN BORIS?
I'LL FIGURE SOMETHING OUT.
MAGIC
YOU BREAK HEART OF LEEDLE GEEL.
HEH. MAYBE BORIS SHOULD STICK TO ADVICE OF THE MAGIC, BUT I HAVE LOST TOO MANY LOVES TO KEEP MOUTH SHUT.
IF YOU STOP GEEL FROM SAVING FAMILY... SHE WILL NEVER WANT TO SEE YOUR FACE AGAIN, YES?
WHAT DO YOU MEAN?
YOU ARE... HOW DO YOU SAY? PLAYING DUMB?
YOU KNOW WHY SPELL WENT KA-BLOOEY? WHY YOUR MAGIC GO TO GEEL'S HOUSE?
I... I DON'T KNOW.

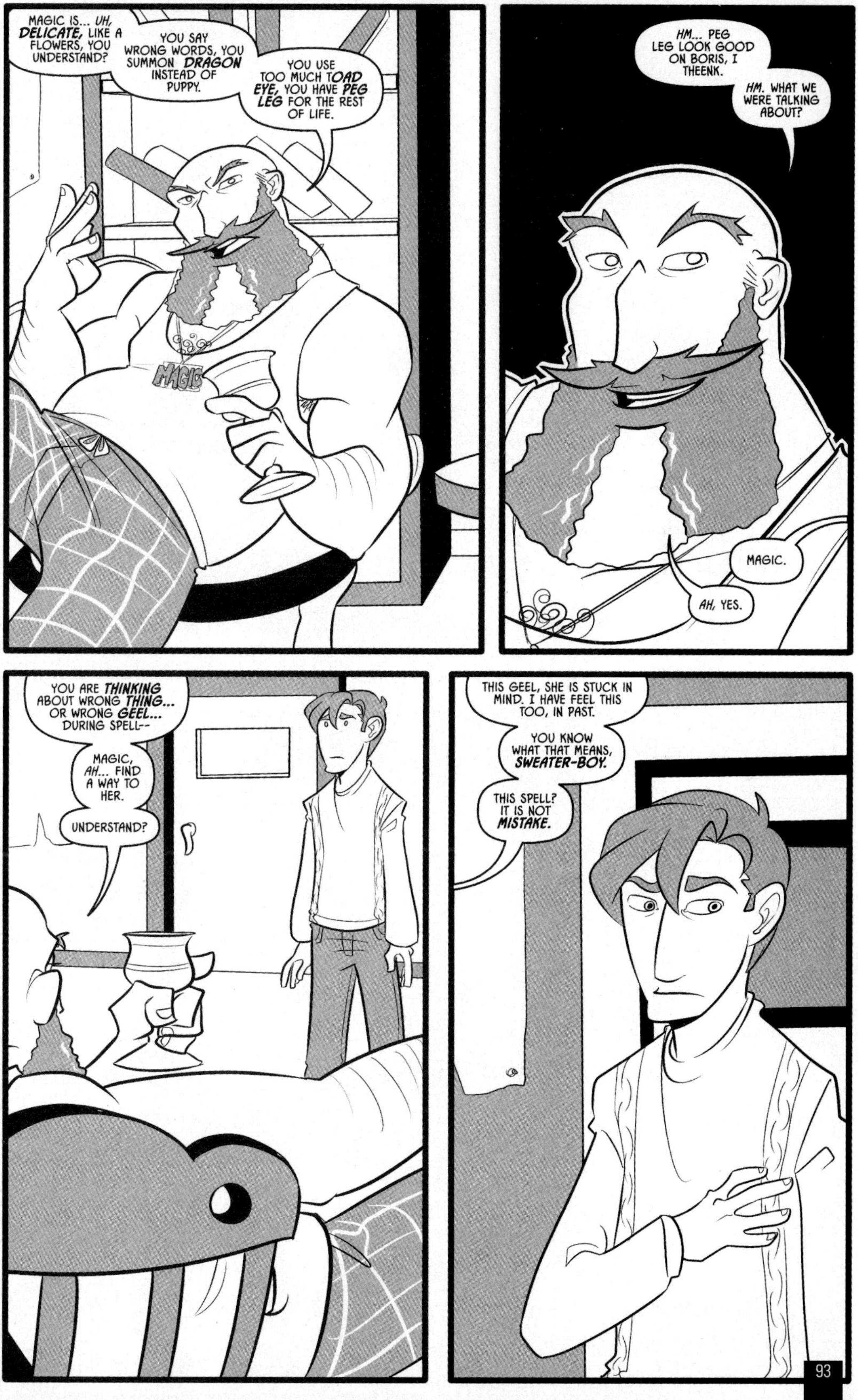
MAGIC IS... UH, DELICATE, LIKE A FLOWERS, YOU UNDERSTAND?
YOU SAY WRONG WORDS, YOU SUMMON DRAGON INSTEAD OF PUPPY.
YOU USE TOO MUCH TOAD EYE, YOU HAVE PEG LEG FOR THE REST OF LIFE.
MAGIC
HM... PEG LEG LOOK GOOD ON BORIS, I THEENK.
HM. WHAT WE WERE TALKING ABOUT?
MAGIC.
AH, YES.
YOU ARE THINKING ABOUT WRONG THING... OR WRONG GEEL... DURING SPELL--
MAGIC, AH... FIND A WAY TO HER.
UNDERSTAND?
THIS GEEL, SHE IS STUCK IN MIND. I HAVE FEEL THIS TOO, IN PAST.
YOU KNOW WHAT THAT MEANS, SWEATER-BOY.
THIS SPELL? IT IS NOT MISTAKE.

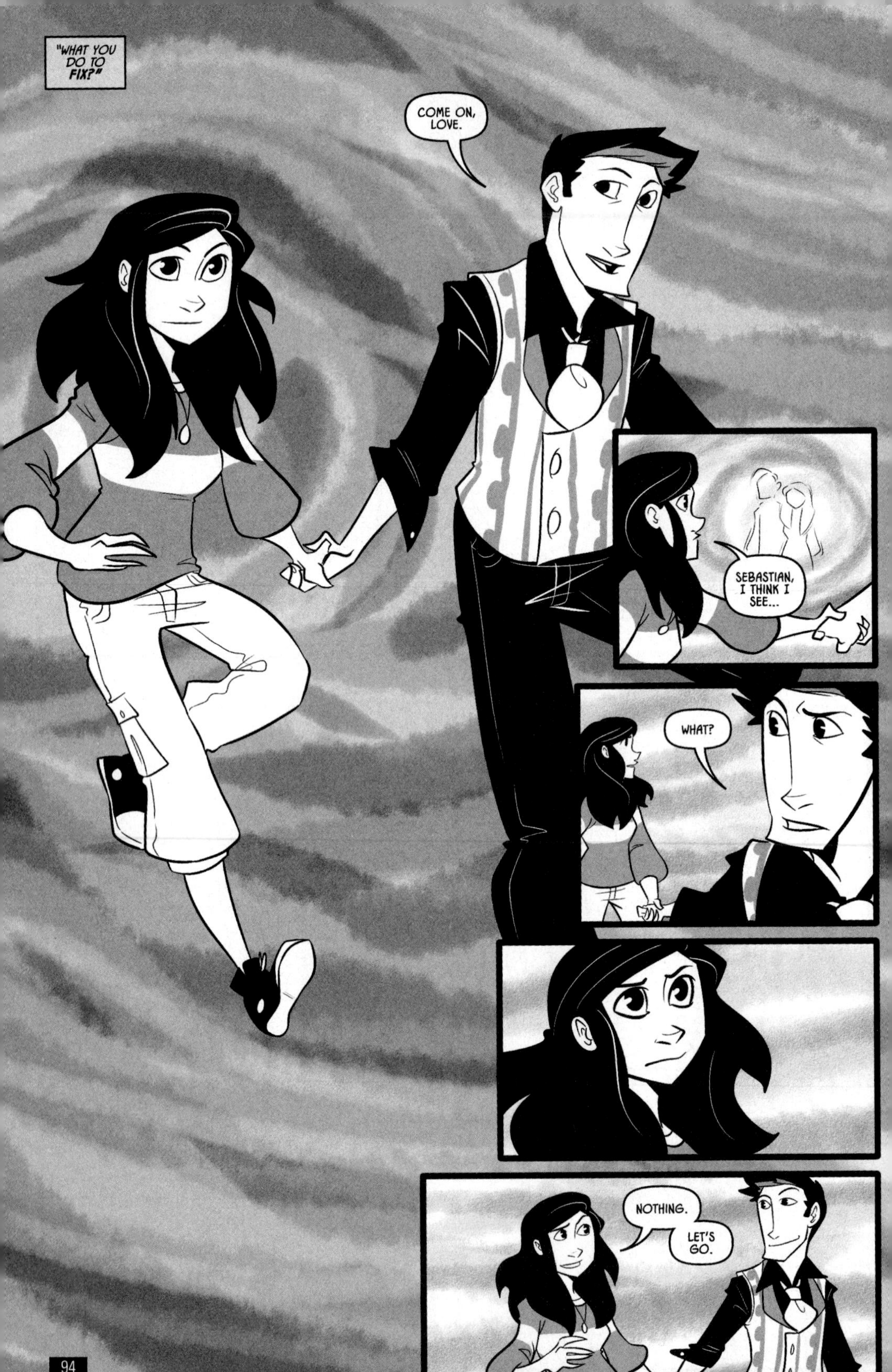
"WHAT YOU DO TO FIX?"
COME ON, LOVE.
SEBASTIAN, I THINK I SEE...
WHAT?
NOTHING.
LET'S GO.

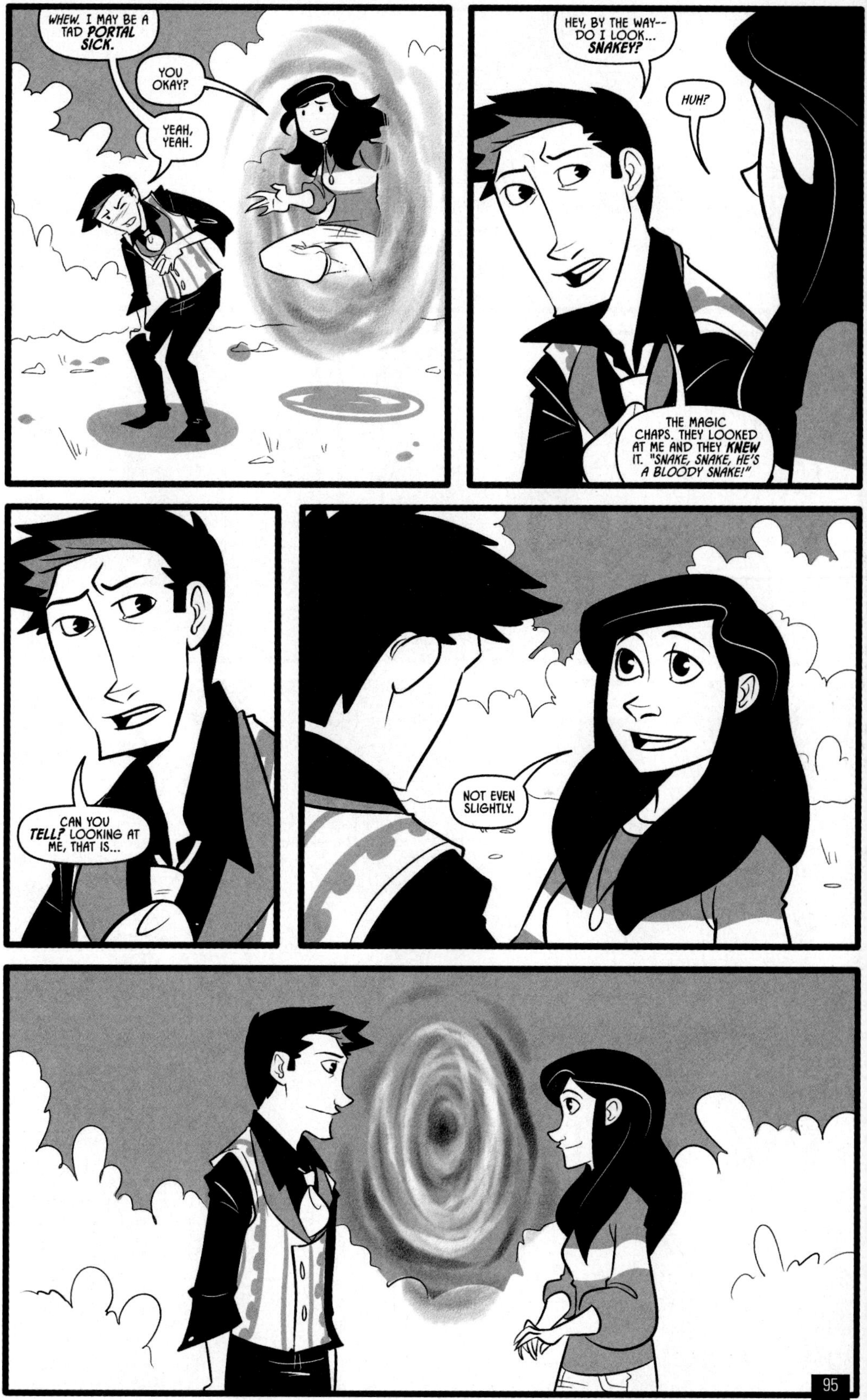
WHEW. I MAY BE A TAD PORTAL SICK.
YOU OKAY?
YEAH, YEAH.
HEY, BY THE WAY-- DO I LOOK... SNAKEY?
HUH?
THE MAGIC CHAPS. THEY LOOKED AT ME AND THEY KNEW IT. "SNAKE, SNAKE, HE'S A BLOODY SNAKE!"
CAN YOU TELL? LOOKING AT ME, THAT IS...
NOT EVEN SLIGHTLY.

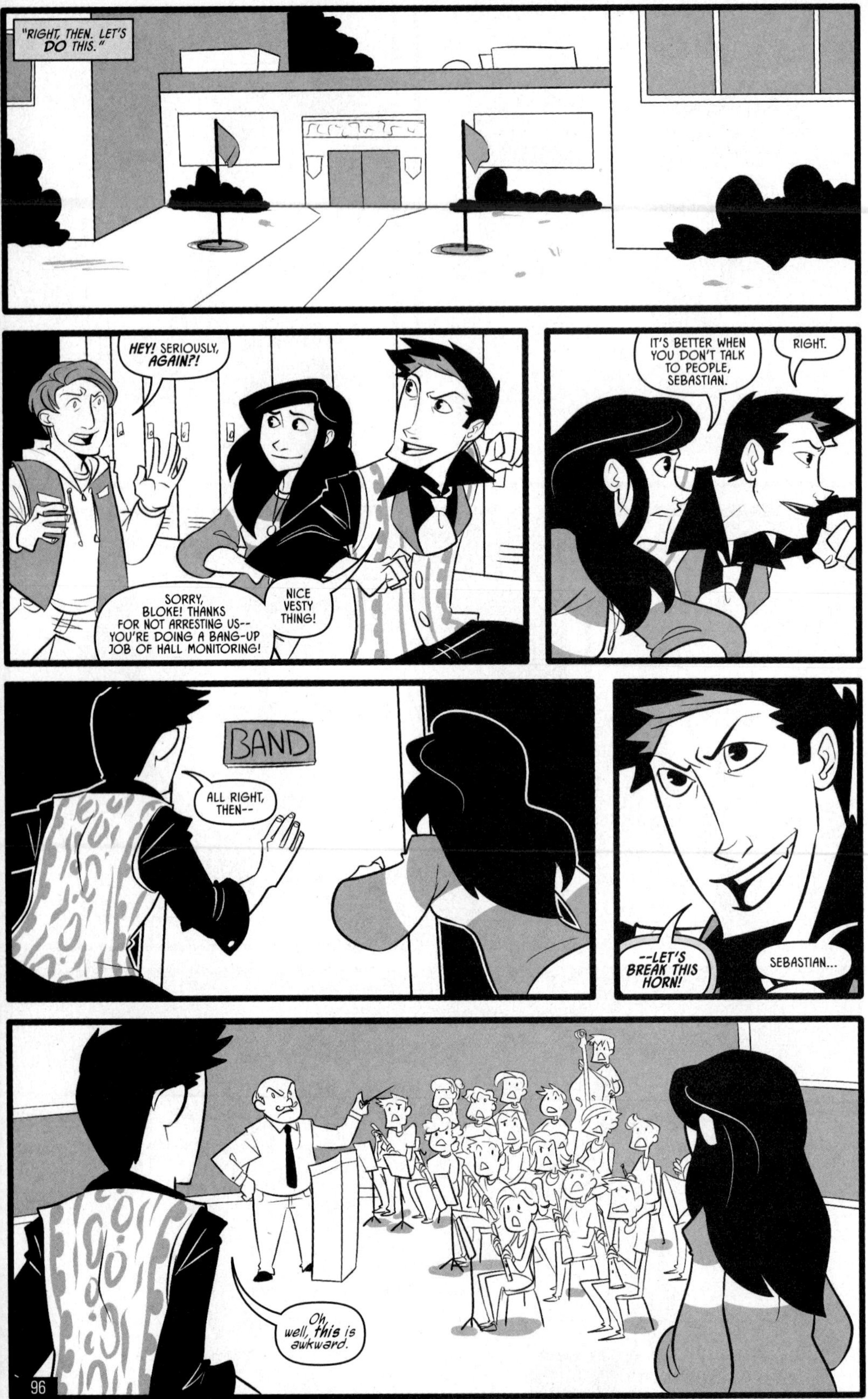
"RIGHT, THEN. LET'S **DO** THIS."
HEY! SERIOUSLY, **AGAIN?!**
SORRY, BLOKE! THANKS FOR NOT ARRESTING US-- YOU'RE DOING A BANG-UP JOB OF HALL MONITORING!
NICE VESTY THING!
IT'S BETTER WHEN YOU DON'T TALK TO PEOPLE, SEBASTIAN.
RIGHT.
BAND
ALL RIGHT, THEN--
--LET'S BREAK THIS HORN!
SEBASTIAN...
*Oh, well, **this** is awkward.*

FAMILY PETS

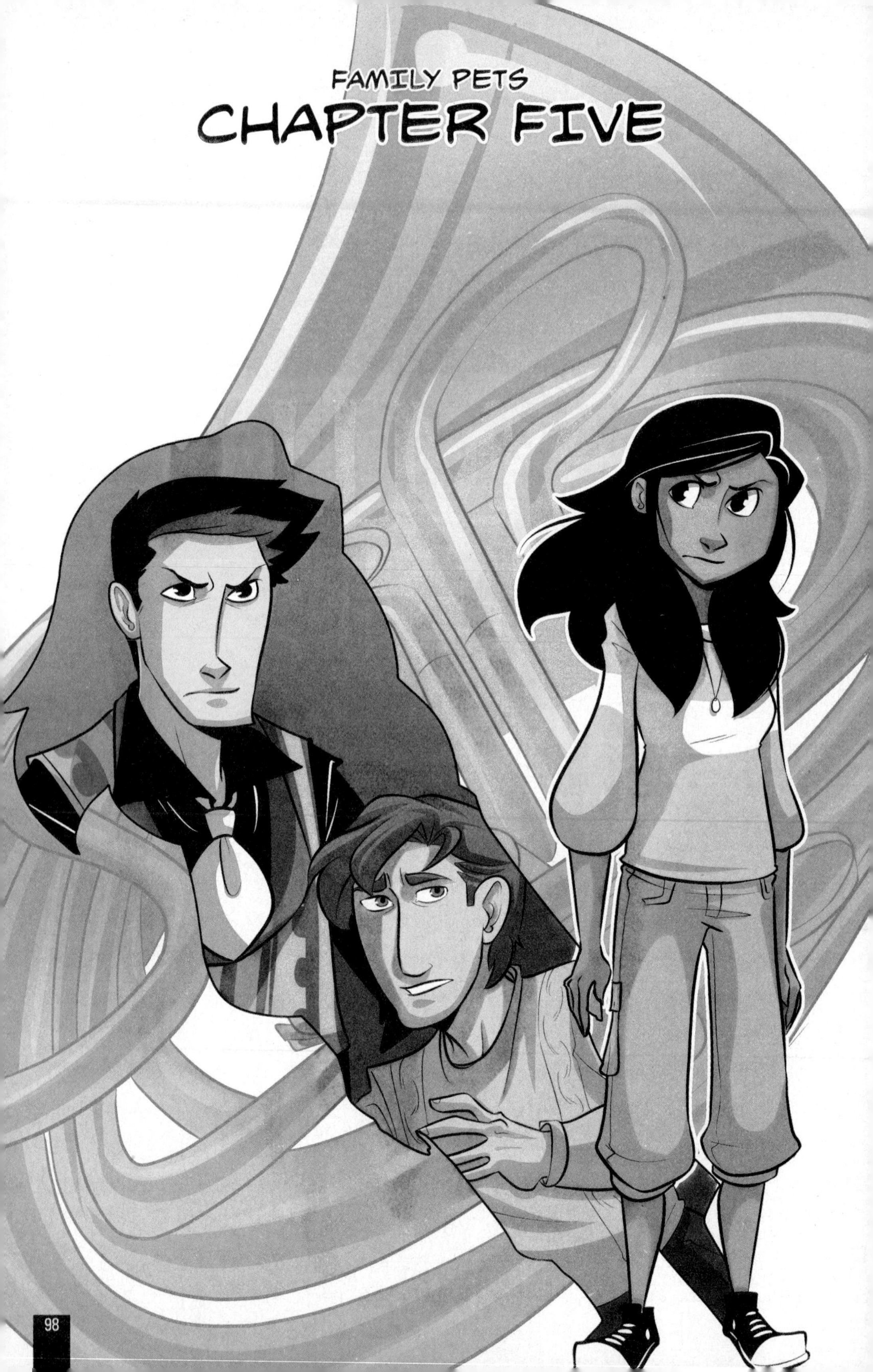
FAMILY PETS
CHAPTER FIVE

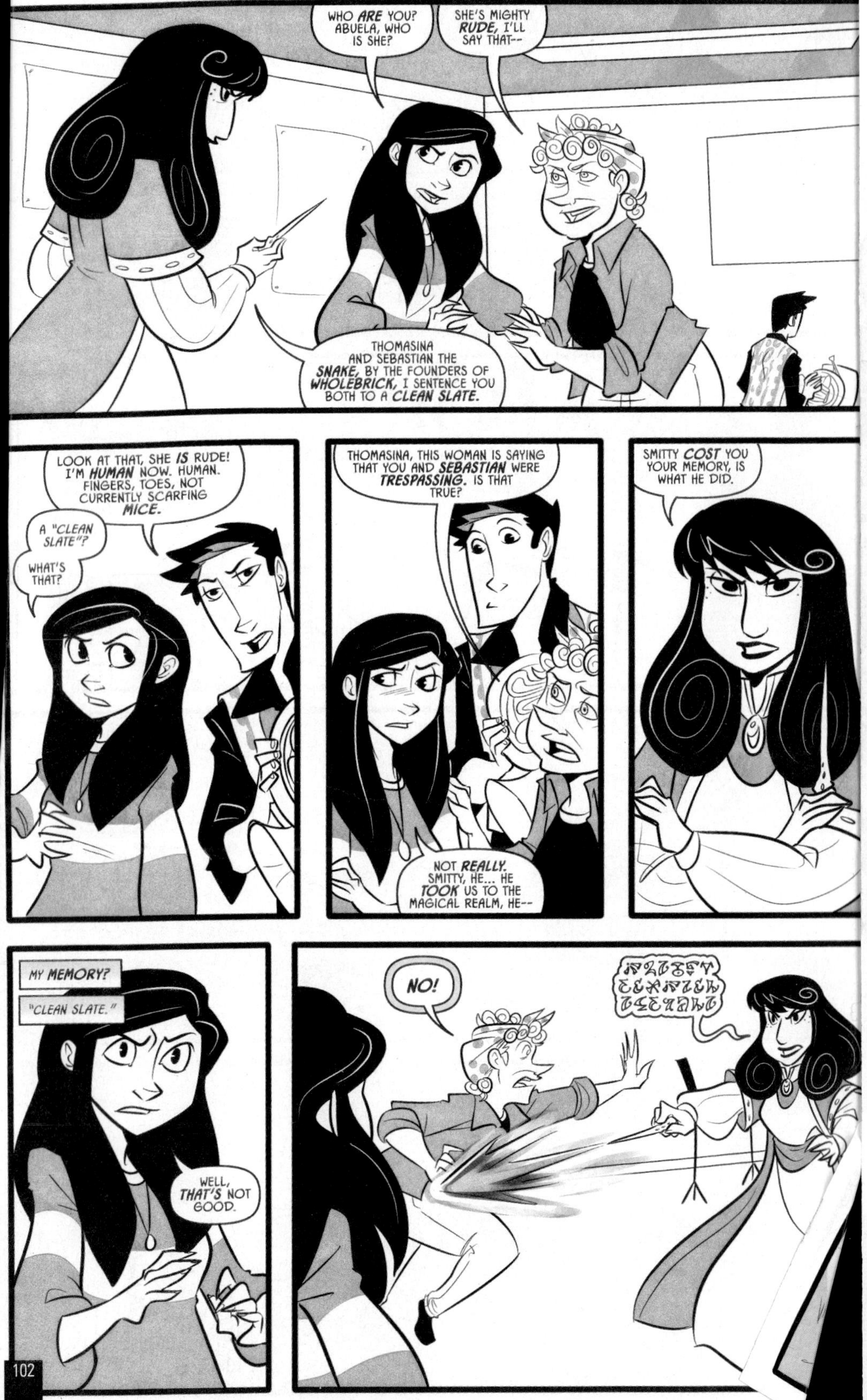
WHO ARE YOU? ABUELA, WHO IS SHE?
SHE'S MIGHTY RUDE, I'LL SAY THAT--
THOMASINA AND SEBASTIAN THE SNAKE, BY THE FOUNDERS OF WHOLEBRICK, I SENTENCE YOU BOTH TO A CLEAN SLATE.
LOOK AT THAT, SHE IS RUDE! I'M HUMAN NOW. HUMAN. FINGERS, TOES, NOT CURRENTLY SCARFING MICE.
A "CLEAN SLATE"?
WHAT'S THAT?
THOMASINA, THIS WOMAN IS SAYING THAT YOU AND SEBASTIAN WERE TRESPASSING. IS THAT TRUE?
NOT REALLY. SMITTY, HE... HE TOOK US TO THE MAGICAL REALM, HE--
SMITTY COST YOU YOUR MEMORY, IS WHAT HE DID.
MY MEMORY?
"CLEAN SLATE."
WELL, THAT'S NOT GOOD.
NO!

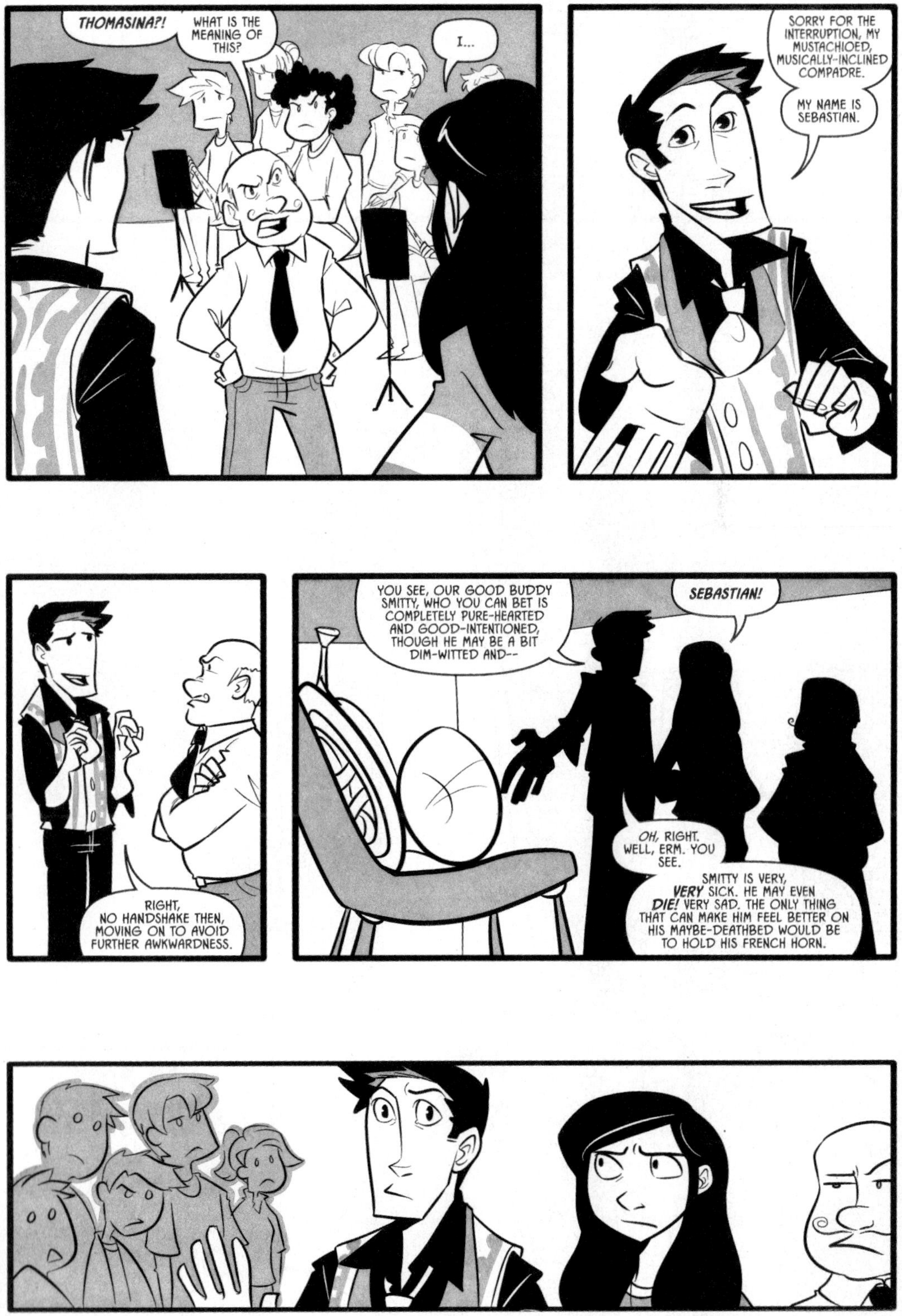
THOMASINA?!
WHAT IS THE MEANING OF THIS?
I...
SORRY FOR THE INTERRUPTION, MY MUSTACHIOED, MUSICALLY-INCLINED COMPADRE.
MY NAME IS SEBASTIAN.
RIGHT, NO HANDSHAKE THEN, MOVING ON TO AVOID FURTHER AWKWARDNESS.
YOU SEE, OUR GOOD BUDDY SMITTY, WHO YOU CAN BET IS COMPLETELY PURE-HEARTED AND GOOD-INTENTIONED, THOUGH HE MAY BE A BIT DIM-WITTED AND--
SEBASTIAN!
OH, RIGHT. WELL, ERM. YOU SEE.
SMITTY IS VERY, VERY SICK. HE MAY EVEN DIE! VERY SAD. THE ONLY THING THAT CAN MAKE HIM FEEL BETTER ON HIS MAYBE-DEATHBED WOULD BE TO HOLD HIS FRENCH HORN.

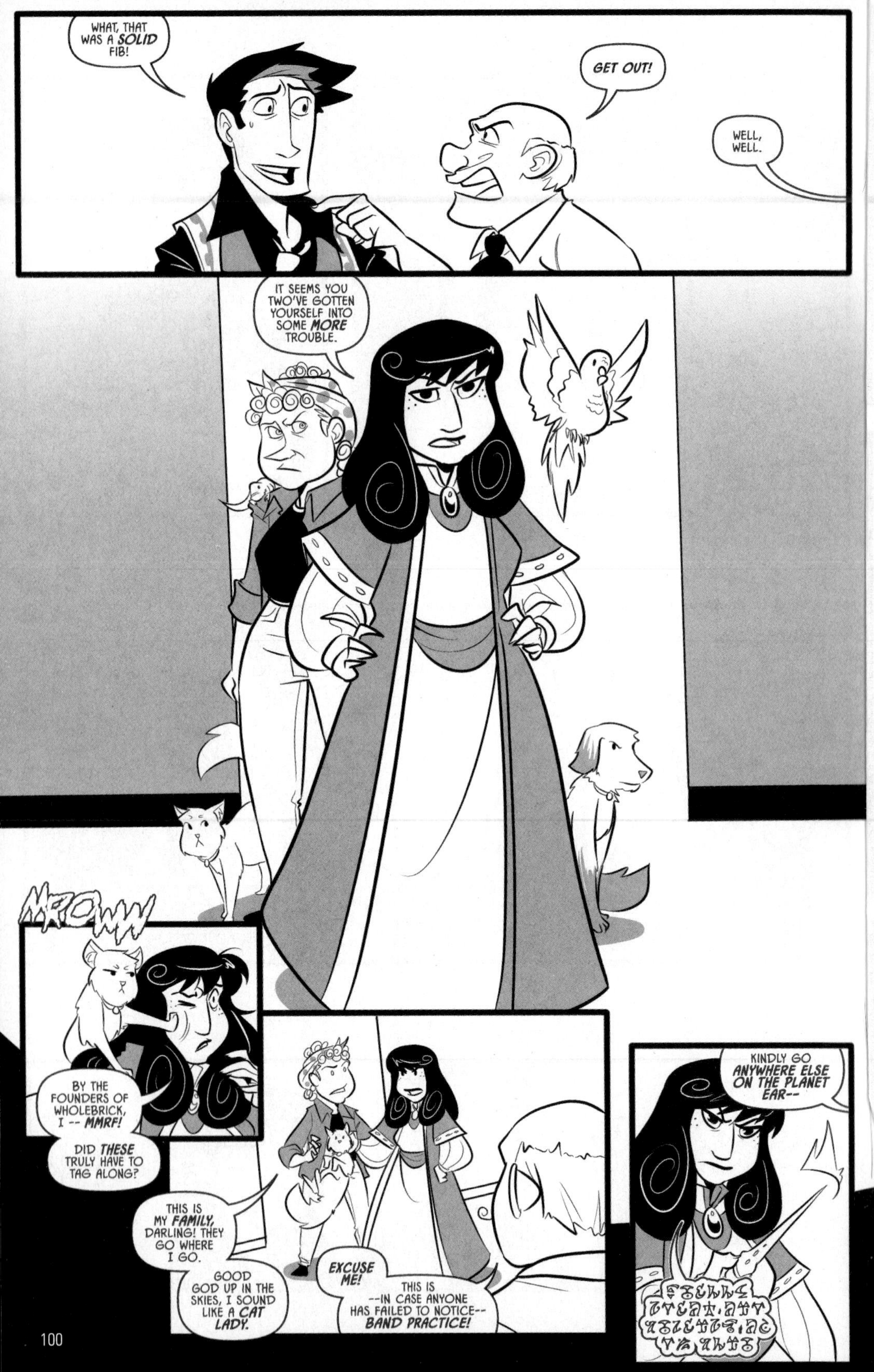
WHAT, THAT WAS A **SOLID** FIB!
GET OUT!
WELL, WELL.
IT SEEMS YOU TWO'VE GOTTEN YOURSELF INTO SOME **MORE** TROUBLE.
MROWW
BY THE FOUNDERS OF WHOLEBRICK, I -- **MMRF!**
DID **THESE** TRULY HAVE TO TAG ALONG?
THIS IS MY **FAMILY**, DARLING! THEY GO WHERE I GO.
GOOD GOD UP IN THE SKIES, I SOUND LIKE A **CAT LADY.**
EXCUSE ME!
THIS IS --IN CASE ANYONE HAS FAILED TO NOTICE-- **BAND PRACTICE!**
KINDLY GO **ANYWHERE ELSE ON THE PLANET EAR--**

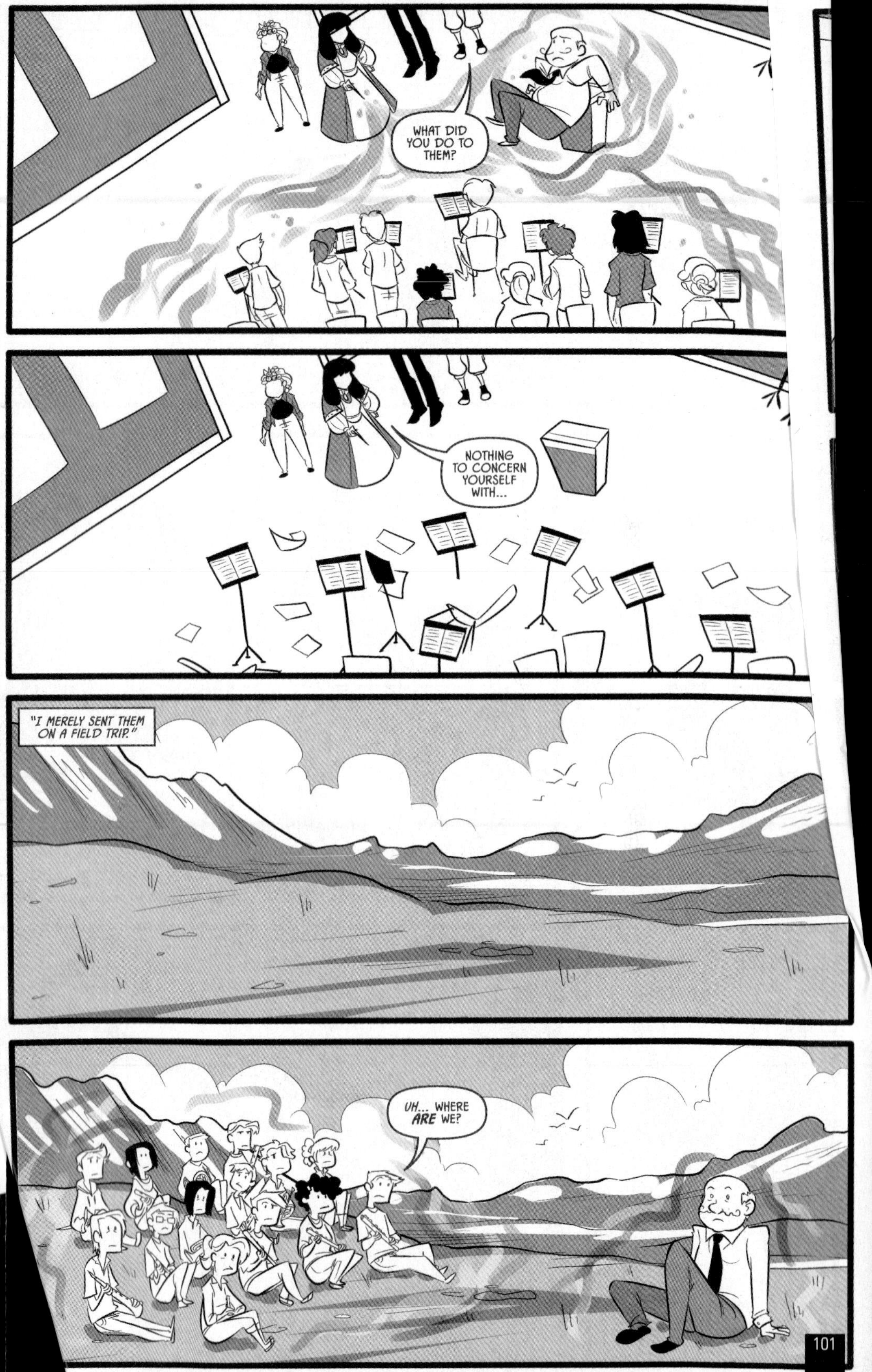
WHAT DID YOU DO TO THEM?
NOTHING TO CONCERN YOURSELF WITH...
"I MERELY SENT THEM ON A FIELD TRIP."
UH... WHERE **ARE** WE?

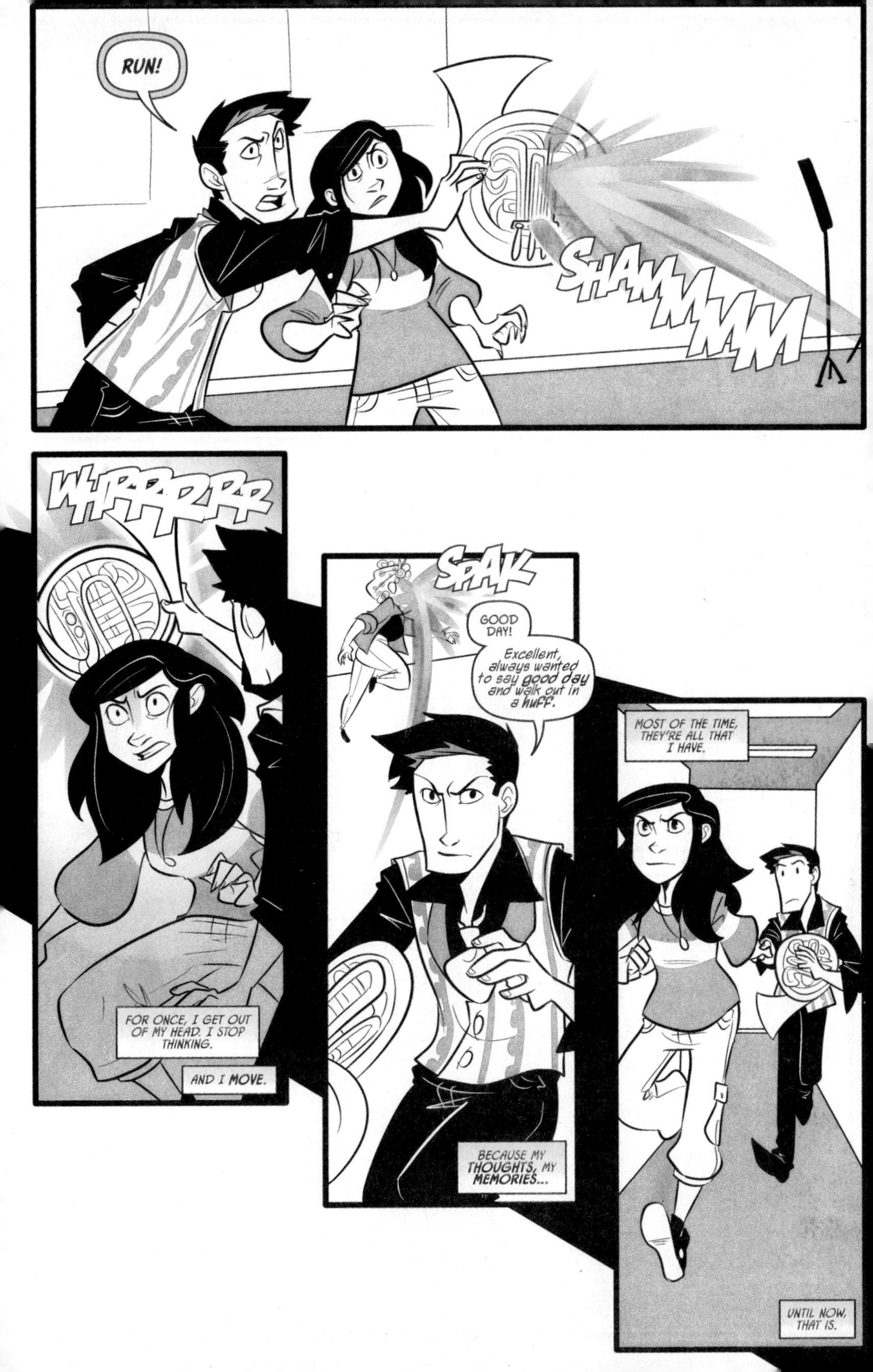
RUN!
SHAMMMMM
WHRRRRRR
FOR ONCE, I GET OUT OF MY HEAD. I STOP THINKING.
AND I MOVE.
SPAK
GOOD DAY!
Excellent, always wanted to say good day and walk out in a huff.
BECAUSE MY THOUGHTS, MY MEMORIES...
MOST OF THE TIME, THEY'RE ALL THAT I HAVE.
UNTIL NOW, THAT IS.

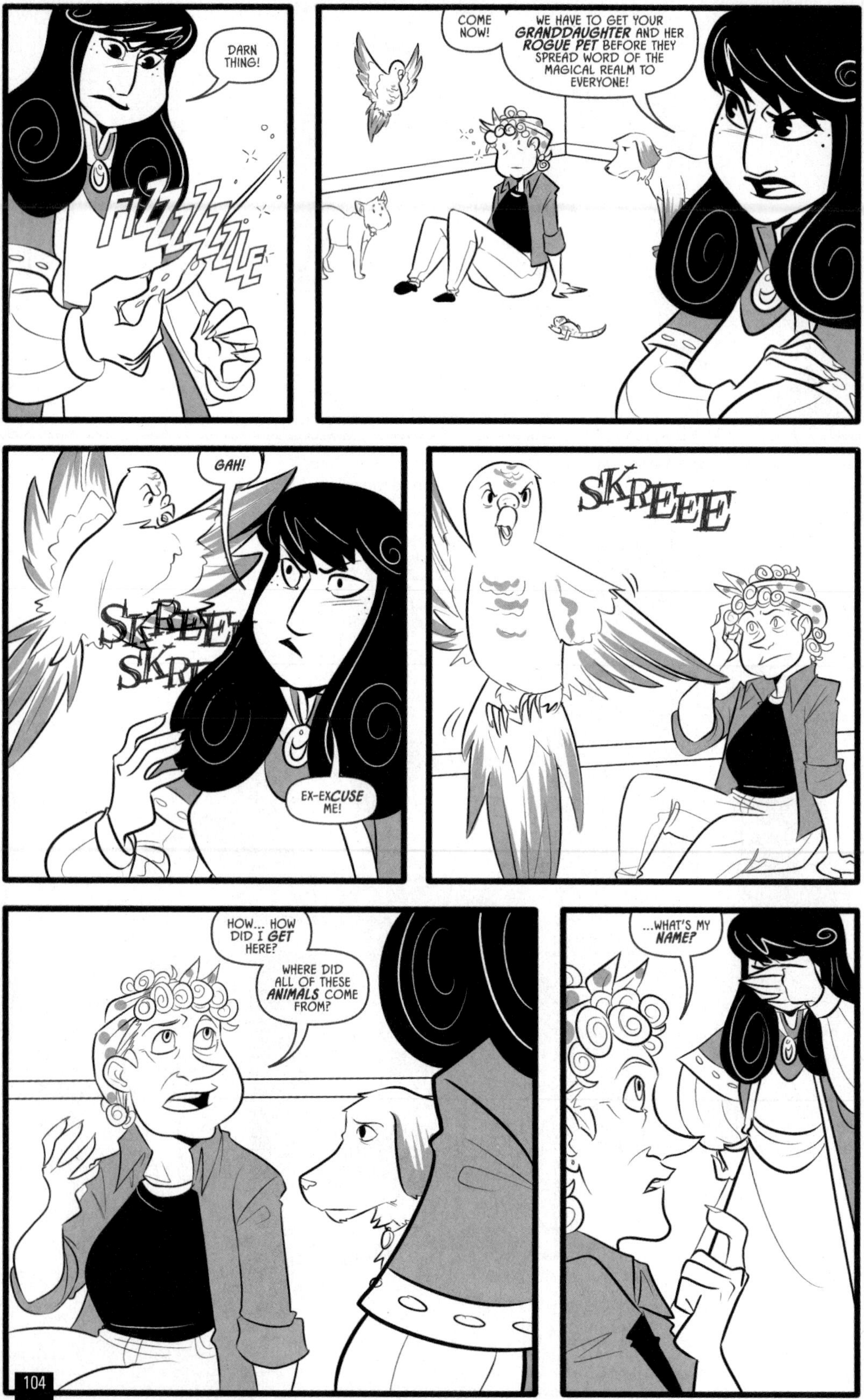
DARN THING!
FIZZZZZZLE
COME NOW!
WE HAVE TO GET YOUR GRANDDAUGHTER AND HER ROGUE PET BEFORE THEY SPREAD WORD OF THE MAGICAL REALM TO EVERYONE!
GAH!
SKREEE
SKREEE
EX-EXCUSE ME!
SKREEE
HOW... HOW DID I GET HERE?
WHERE DID ALL OF THESE ANIMALS COME FROM?
...WHAT'S MY NAME?

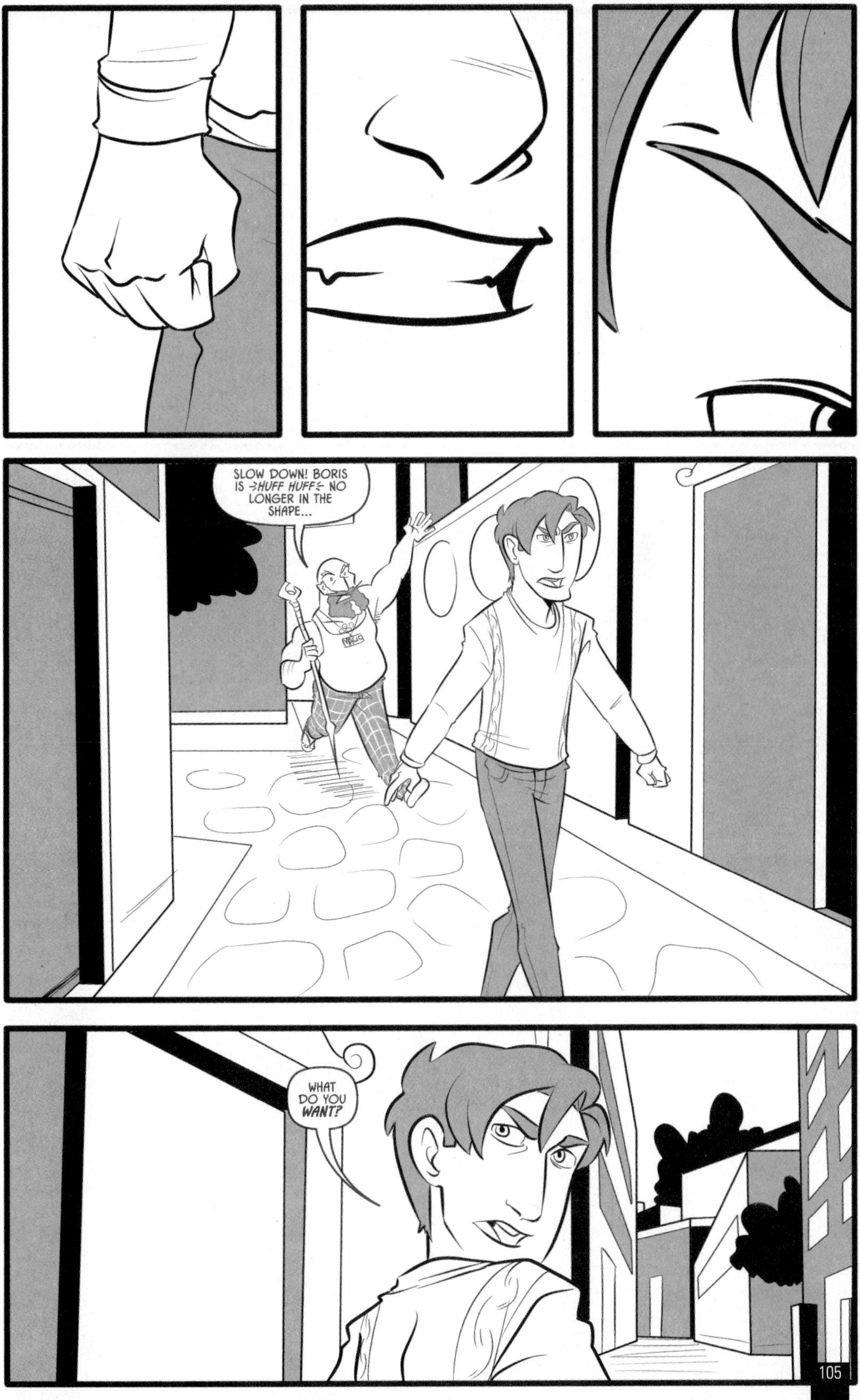
SLOW DOWN! BORIS IS ⇒HUFF HUFF⇐ NO LONGER IN THE SHAPE...
WHAT DO YOU *WANT?*

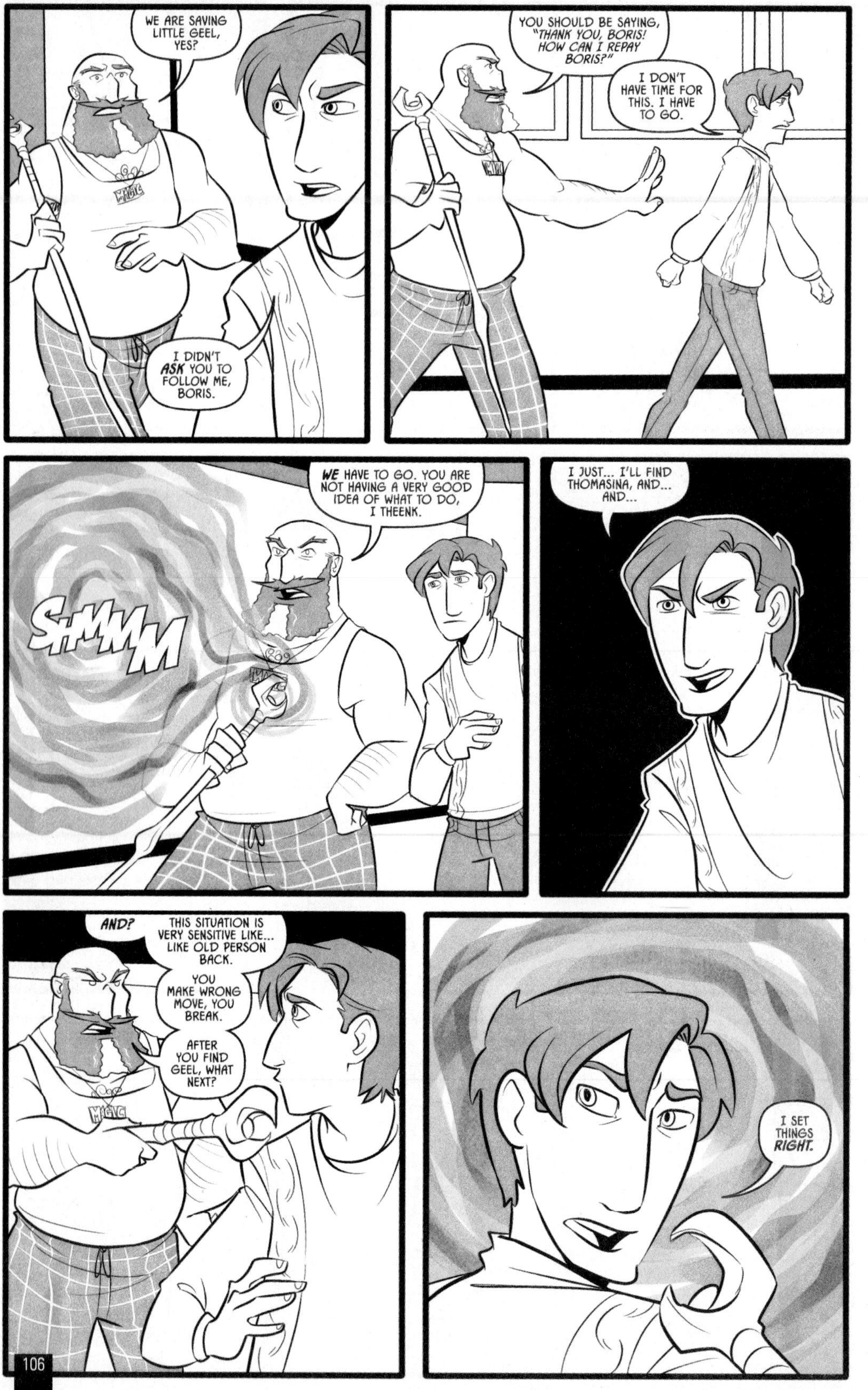
WE ARE SAVING LITTLE GEEL, YES?
I DIDN'T *ASK* YOU TO FOLLOW ME, BORIS.
YOU SHOULD BE SAYING, *"THANK YOU, BORIS! HOW CAN I REPAY BORIS?"*
I DON'T HAVE TIME FOR THIS. I HAVE TO GO.
WE HAVE TO GO. YOU ARE NOT HAVING A VERY GOOD IDEA OF WHAT TO DO, I THEENK.
SHMMM
I JUST... I'LL FIND THOMASINA, AND... AND...
AND?
THIS SITUATION IS VERY SENSITIVE LIKE... LIKE OLD PERSON BACK.
YOU MAKE WRONG MOVE, YOU BREAK.
AFTER YOU FIND GEEL, WHAT NEXT?
I SET THINGS *RIGHT.*

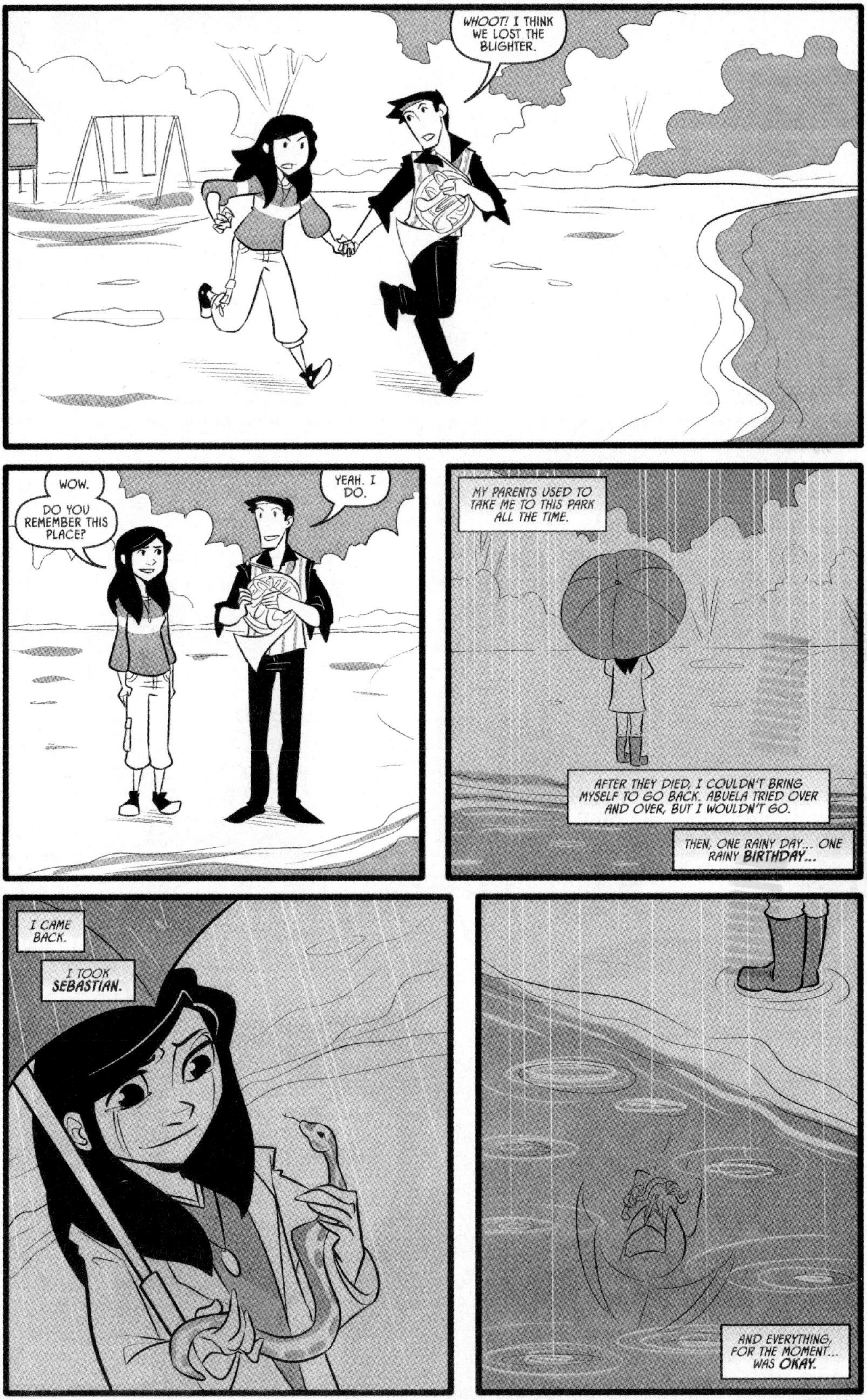
WHOOT! I THINK WE LOST THE BLIGHTER.
WOW.
DO YOU REMEMBER THIS PLACE?
YEAH. I DO.
MY PARENTS USED TO TAKE ME TO THIS PARK ALL THE TIME.
AFTER THEY DIED, I COULDN'T BRING MYSELF TO GO BACK. ABUELA TRIED OVER AND OVER, BUT I WOULDN'T GO.
THEN, ONE RAINY DAY... ONE RAINY BIRTHDAY...
I CAME BACK.
I TOOK SEBASTIAN.
AND EVERYTHING, FOR THE MOMENT... WAS OKAY.

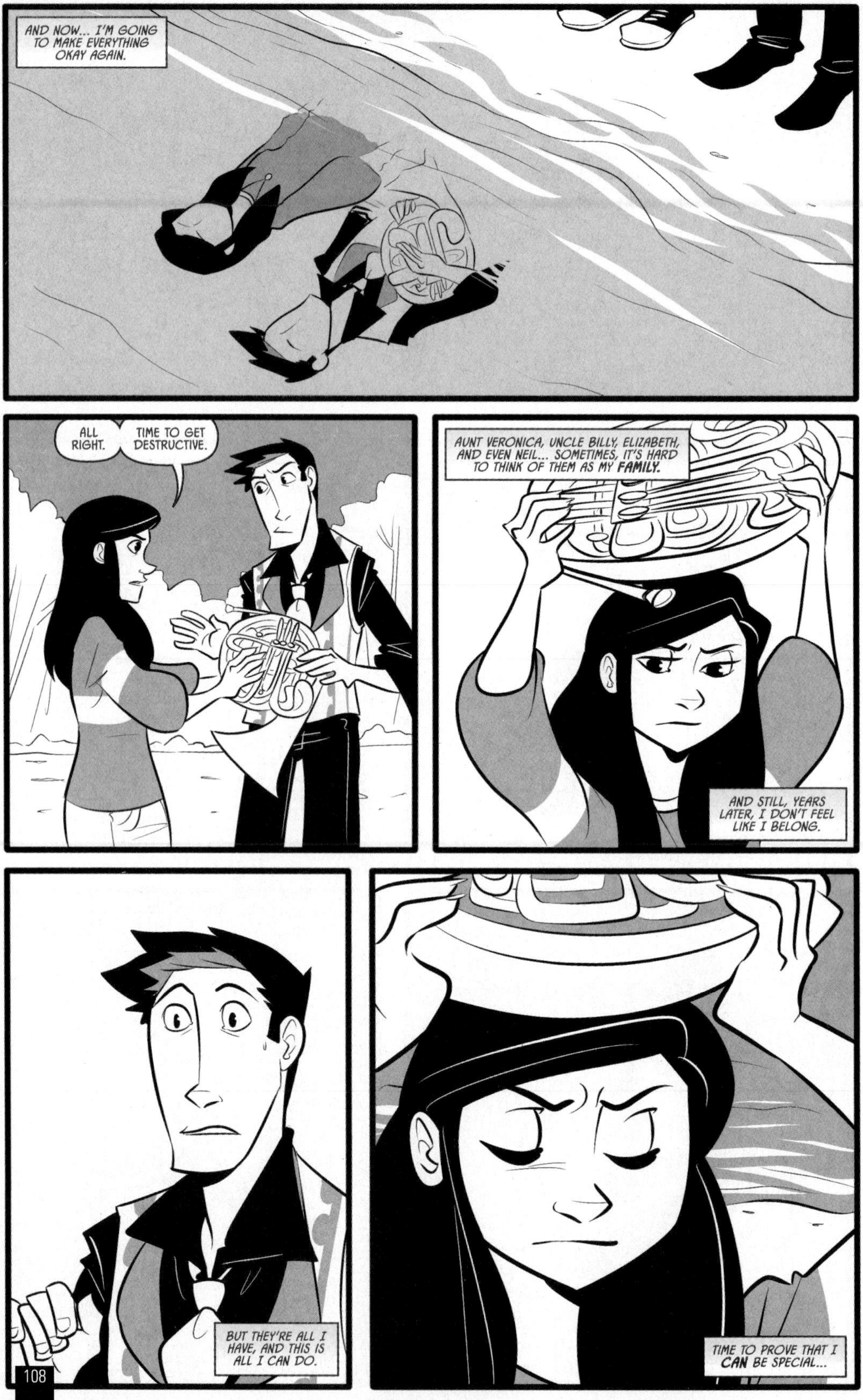
AND NOW... I'M GOING TO MAKE EVERYTHING OKAY AGAIN.
ALL RIGHT.
TIME TO GET DESTRUCTIVE.
AUNT VERONICA, UNCLE BILLY, ELIZABETH, AND EVEN NEIL... SOMETIMES, IT'S HARD TO THINK OF THEM AS MY **FAMILY.**
AND STILL, YEARS LATER, I DON'T FEEL LIKE I BELONG.
BUT THEY'RE ALL I HAVE, AND THIS IS ALL I CAN DO.
TIME TO PROVE THAT I **CAN** BE SPECIAL...

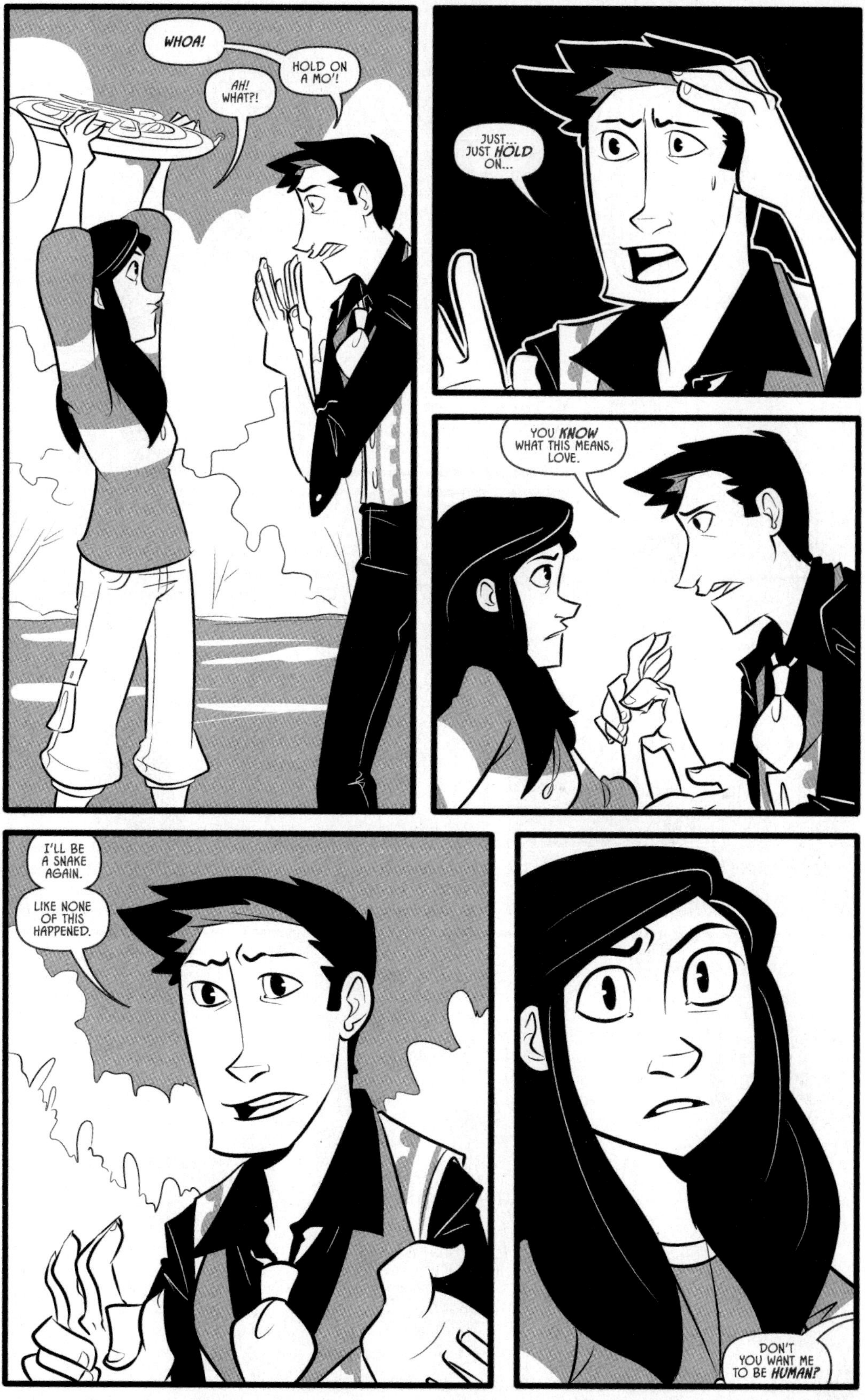
WHOA!
AH! WHAT?!
HOLD ON A MO'!
JUST... JUST HOLD ON...
YOU KNOW WHAT THIS MEANS, LOVE.
I'LL BE A SNAKE AGAIN.
LIKE NONE OF THIS HAPPENED.
DON'T YOU WANT ME TO BE HUMAN?

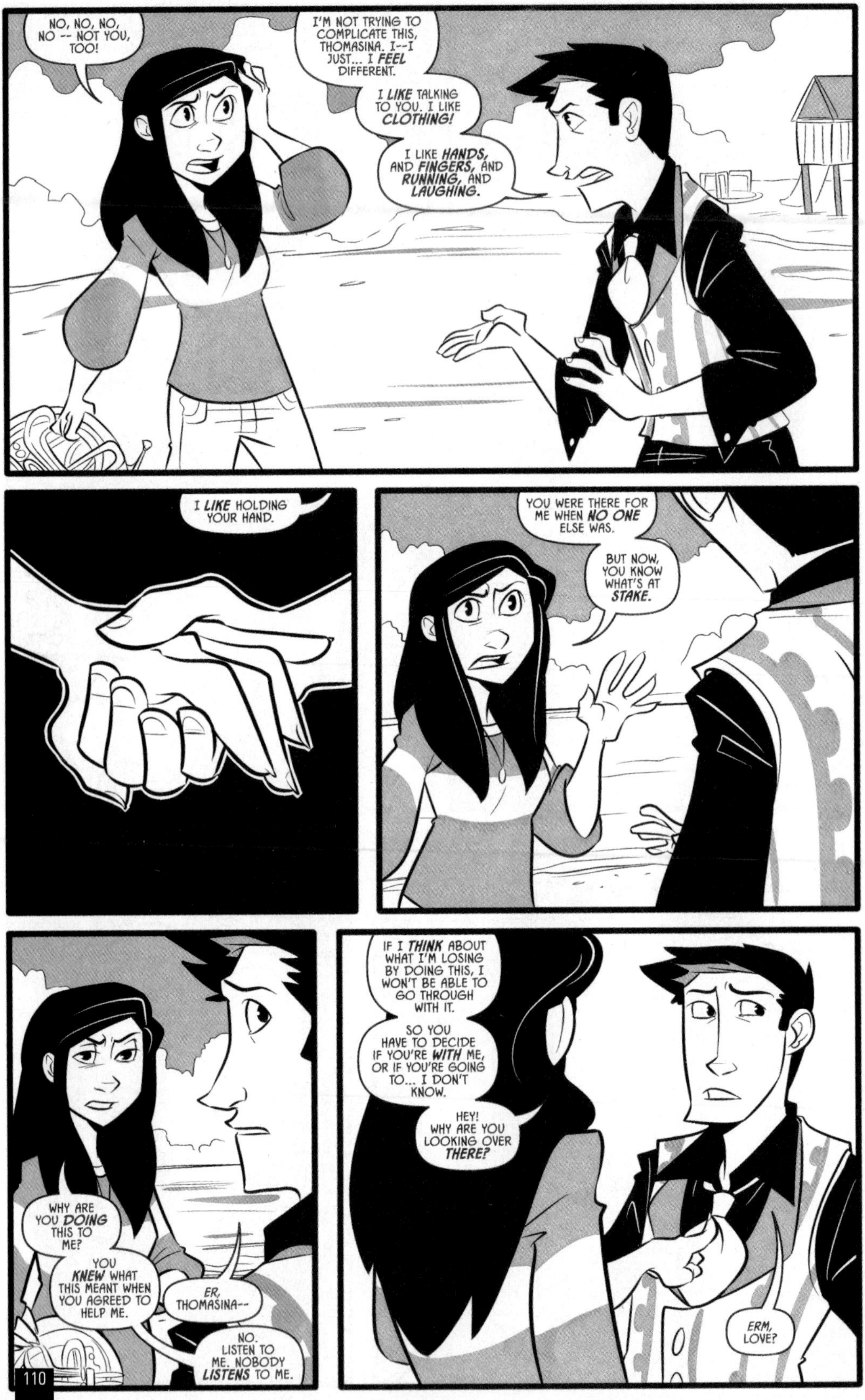
NO, NO, NO, NO -- NOT YOU, TOO!
I'M NOT TRYING TO COMPLICATE THIS, THOMASINA. I--I JUST... I *FEEL* DIFFERENT.
I *LIKE* TALKING TO YOU. I LIKE *CLOTHING!*
I LIKE *HANDS,* AND *FINGERS,* AND *RUNNING,* AND *LAUGHING.*
I *LIKE* HOLDING YOUR HAND.
YOU WERE THERE FOR ME WHEN *NO ONE* ELSE WAS.
BUT NOW, YOU KNOW WHAT'S AT *STAKE.*
WHY ARE YOU *DOING* THIS TO ME?
YOU *KNEW* WHAT THIS MEANT WHEN YOU AGREED TO HELP ME.
ER, THOMASINA--
NO. LISTEN TO ME. NOBODY *LISTENS* TO ME.
IF I *THINK* ABOUT WHAT I'M LOSING BY DOING THIS, I WON'T BE ABLE TO GO THROUGH WITH IT.
SO YOU HAVE TO DECIDE IF YOU'RE *WITH* ME, OR IF YOU'RE GOING TO... I DON'T KNOW.
HEY! WHY ARE YOU LOOKING OVER *THERE?*
ERM, LOVE?

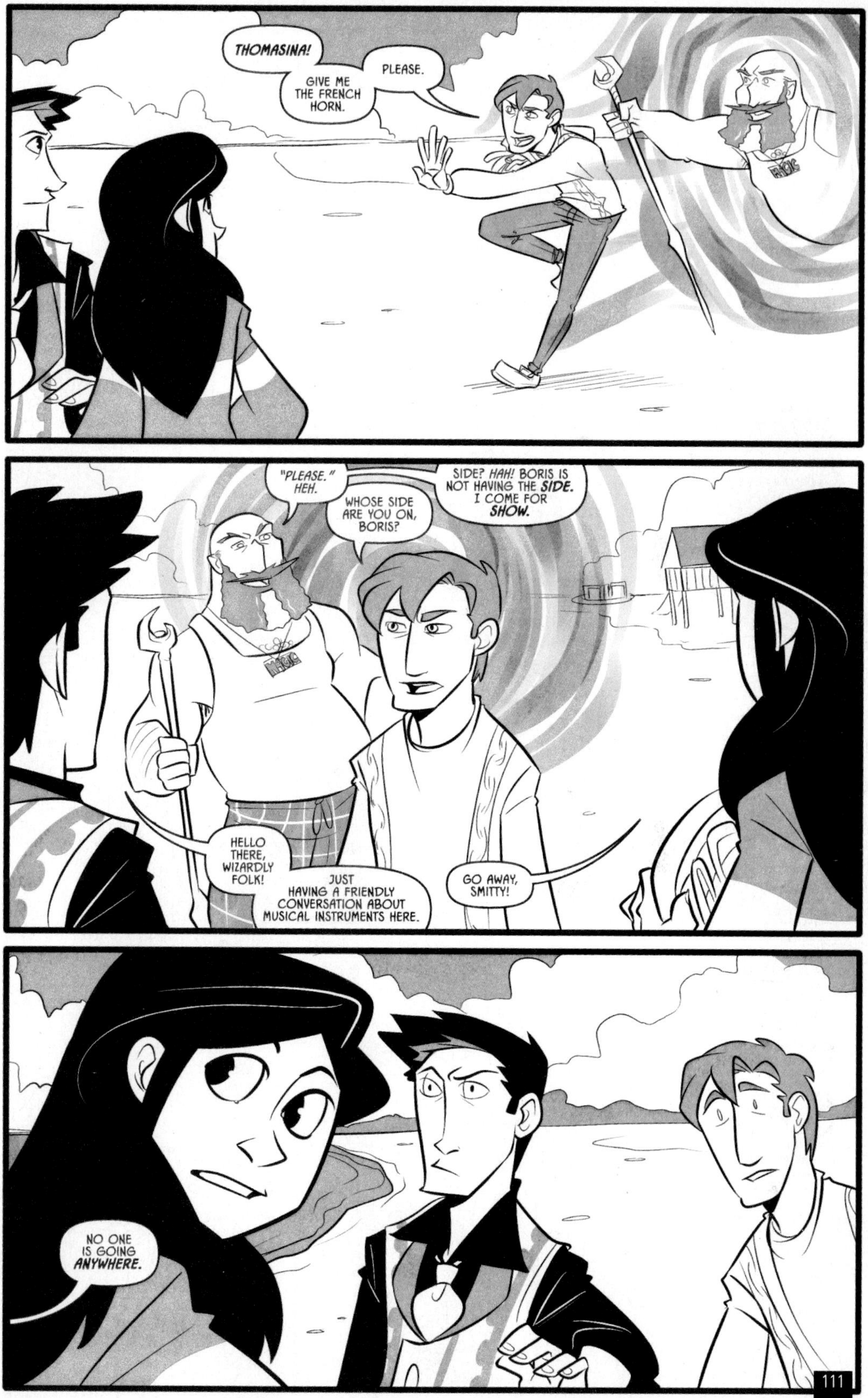
THOMASINA!
GIVE ME THE FRENCH HORN.
PLEASE.
"PLEASE." HEH.
WHOSE SIDE ARE YOU ON, BORIS?
SIDE? HAH! BORIS IS NOT HAVING THE SIDE. I COME FOR SHOW.
HELLO THERE, WIZARDLY FOLK!
JUST HAVING A FRIENDLY CONVERSATION ABOUT MUSICAL INSTRUMENTS HERE.
GO AWAY, SMITTY!
NO ONE IS GOING ANYWHERE.

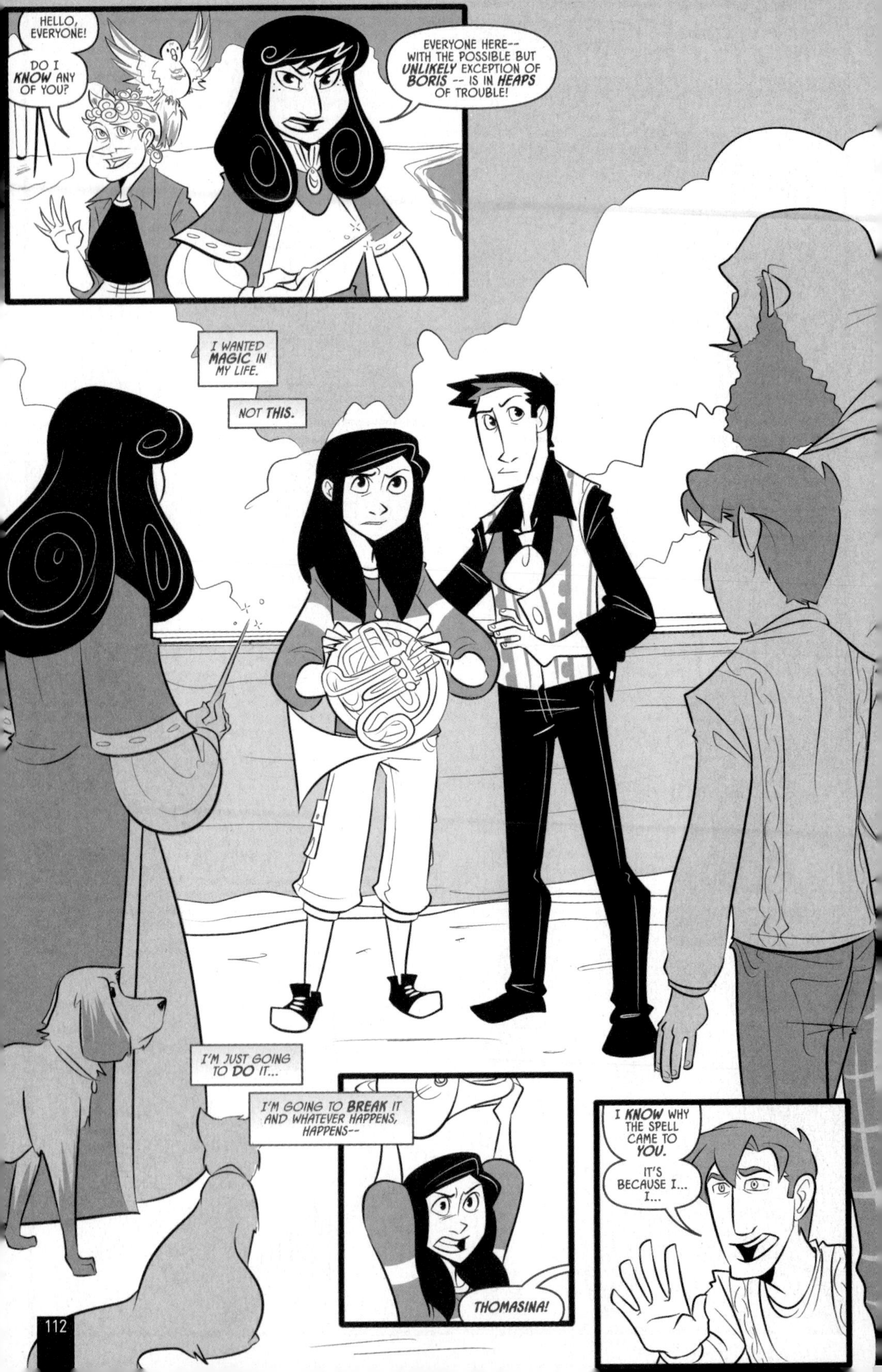
HELLO, EVERYONE!
DO I KNOW ANY OF YOU?
EVERYONE HERE-- WITH THE POSSIBLE BUT UNLIKELY EXCEPTION OF BORIS -- IS IN HEAPS OF TROUBLE!
I WANTED MAGIC IN MY LIFE.
NOT THIS.
I'M JUST GOING TO DO IT...
I'M GOING TO BREAK IT AND WHATEVER HAPPENS, HAPPENS--
THOMASINA!
I KNOW WHY THE SPELL CAME TO YOU.
IT'S BECAUSE I... I...

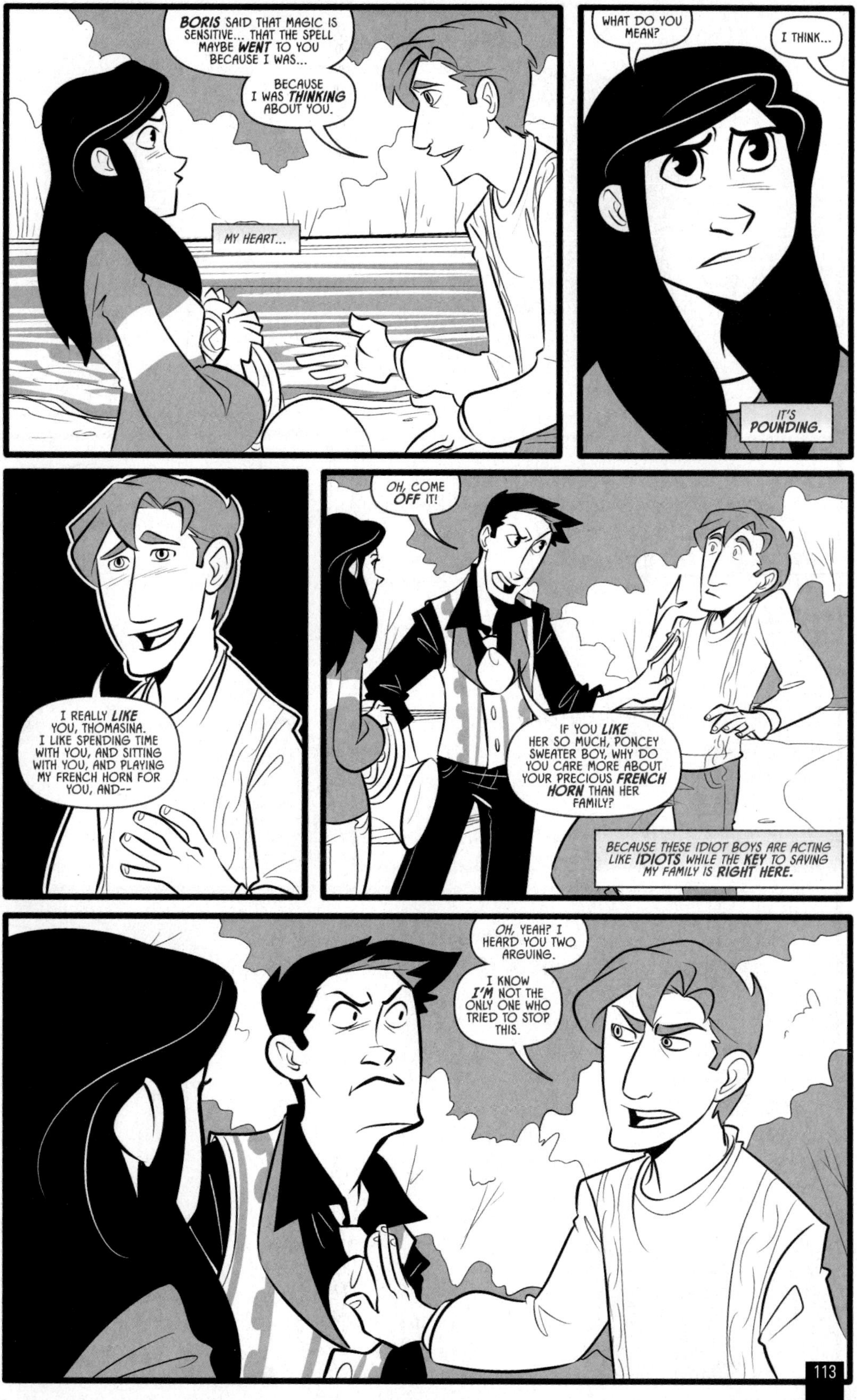
BORIS SAID THAT MAGIC IS SENSITIVE... THAT THE SPELL MAYBE WENT TO YOU BECAUSE I WAS...
BECAUSE I WAS THINKING ABOUT YOU.
MY HEART...
WHAT DO YOU MEAN?
I THINK...
IT'S POUNDING.
I REALLY LIKE YOU, THOMASINA. I LIKE SPENDING TIME WITH YOU, AND SITTING WITH YOU, AND PLAYING MY FRENCH HORN FOR YOU, AND--
OH, COME OFF IT!
IF YOU LIKE HER SO MUCH, PONCEY SWEATER BOY, WHY DO YOU CARE MORE ABOUT YOUR PRECIOUS FRENCH HORN THAN HER FAMILY?
BECAUSE THESE IDIOT BOYS ARE ACTING LIKE IDIOTS WHILE THE KEY TO SAVING MY FAMILY IS RIGHT HERE.
OH, YEAH? I HEARD YOU TWO ARGUING.
I KNOW I'M NOT THE ONLY ONE WHO TRIED TO STOP THIS.

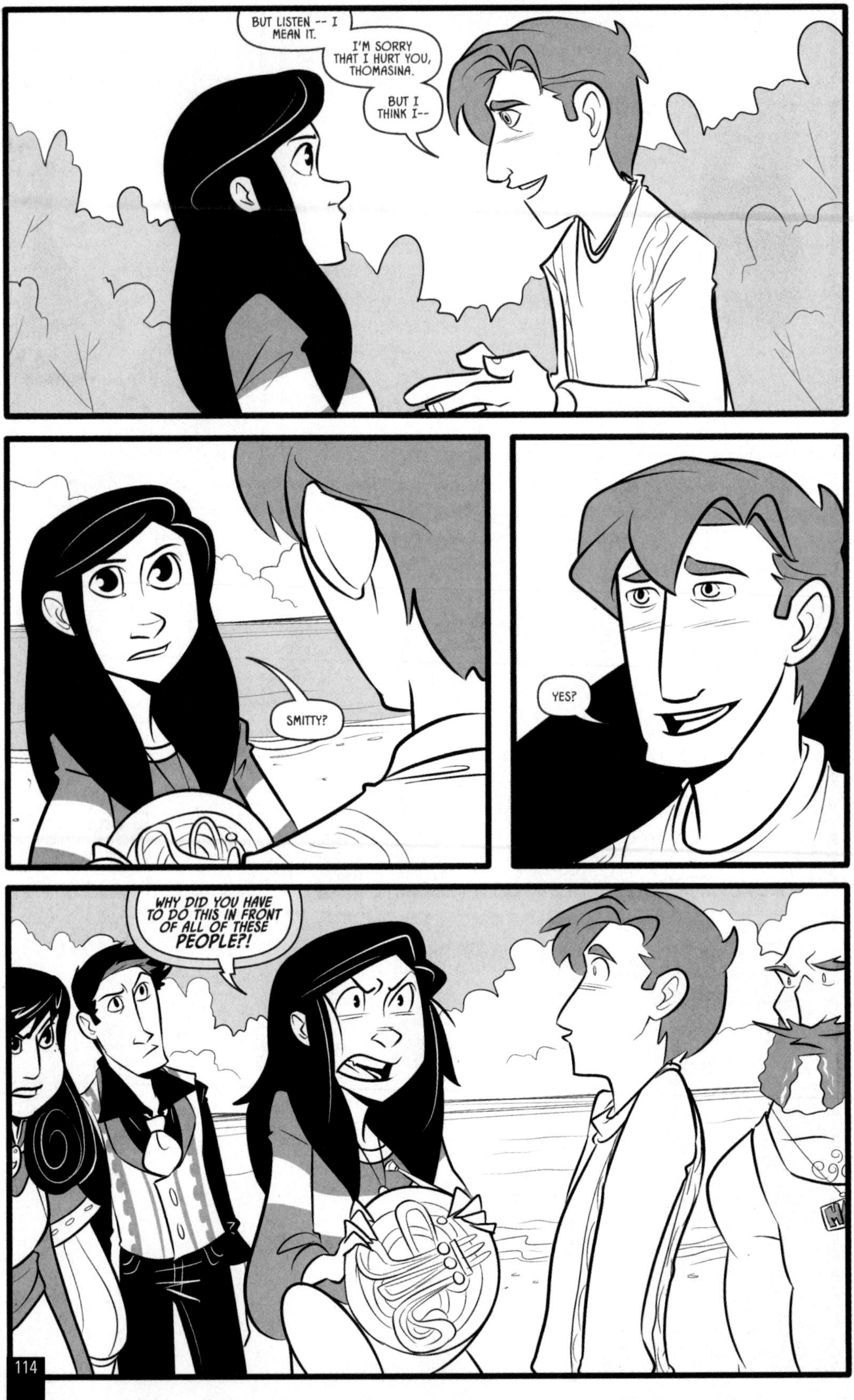
BUT LISTEN -- I MEAN IT.
I'M SORRY THAT I HURT YOU, THOMASINA.
BUT I THINK I--
SMITTY?
YES?
WHY DID YOU HAVE TO DO THIS IN FRONT OF ALL OF THESE PEOPLE?!

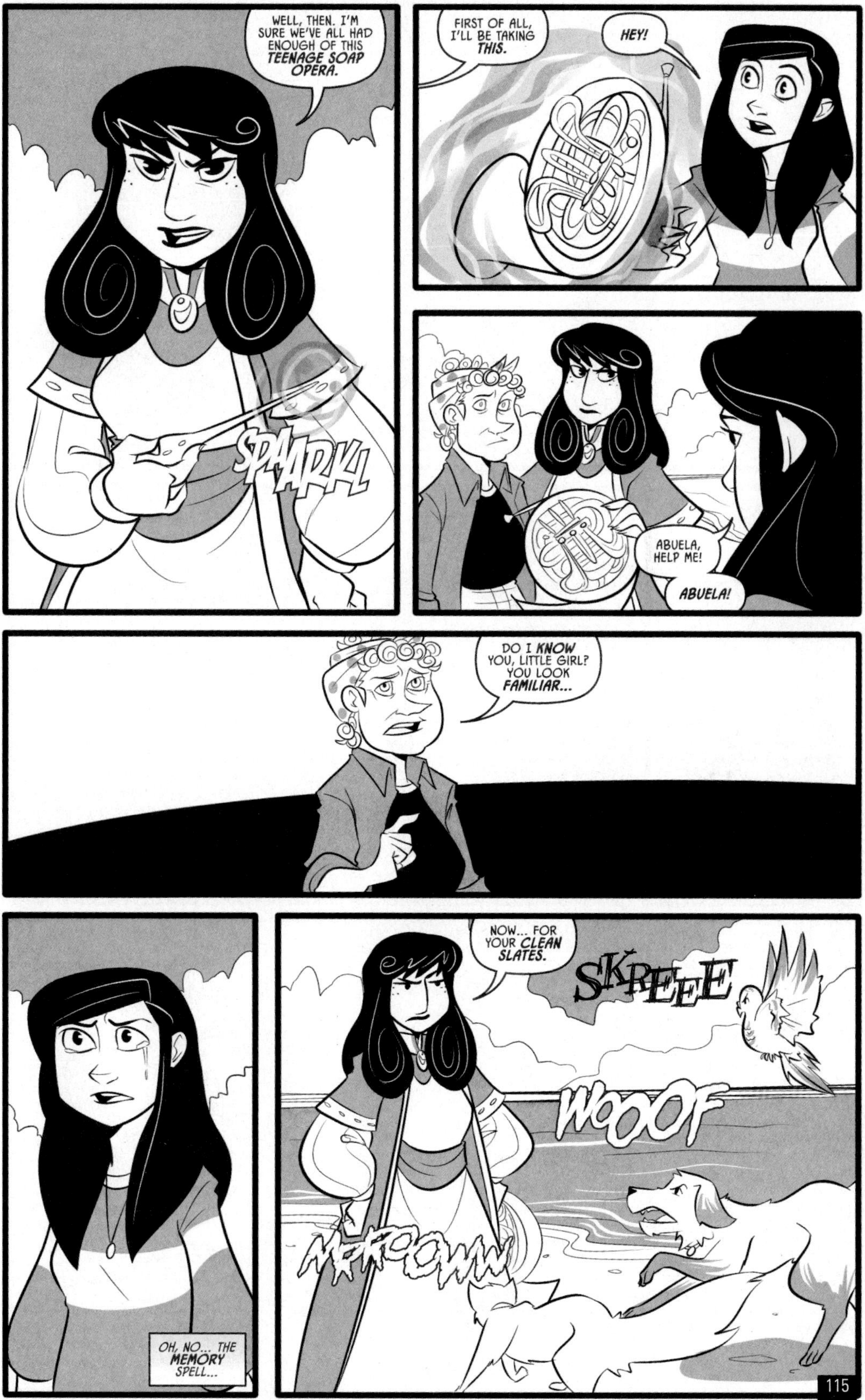
WELL, THEN. I'M SURE WE'VE ALL HAD ENOUGH OF THIS TEENAGE SOAP OPERA.
SPAARKL
FIRST OF ALL, I'LL BE TAKING THIS.
HEY!
ABUELA, HELP ME!
ABUELA!
DO I KNOW YOU, LITTLE GIRL? YOU LOOK FAMILIAR...
OH, NO... THE MEMORY SPELL...
NOW... FOR YOUR CLEAN SLATES.
SKREEEE
WOOOF
MRROOWW

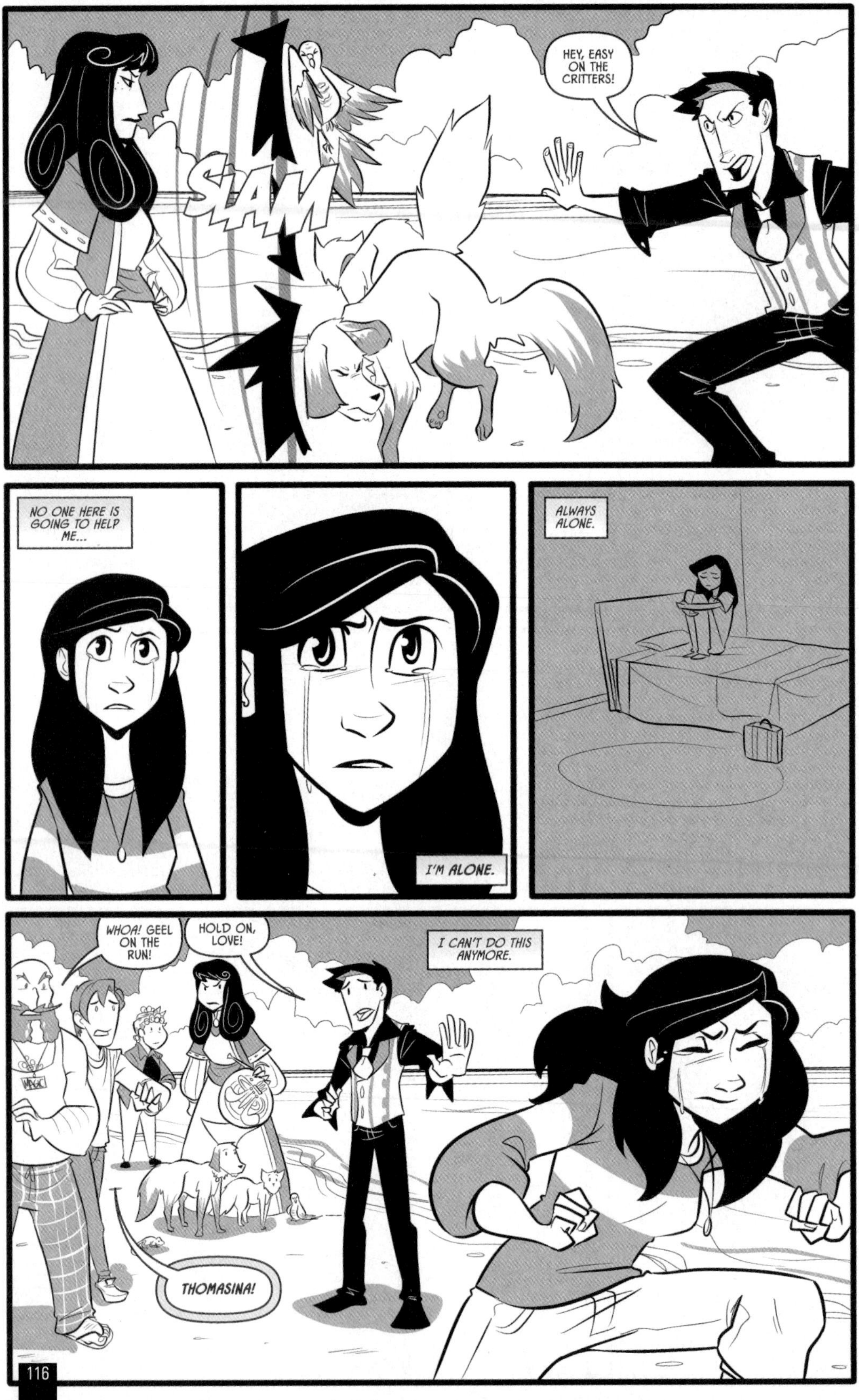
SLAM
HEY, EASY ON THE CRITTERS!
NO ONE HERE IS GOING TO HELP ME...
I'M ALONE.
ALWAYS ALONE.
WHOA! GEEL ON THE RUN!
HOLD ON, LOVE!
I CAN'T DO THIS ANYMORE.
THOMASINA!

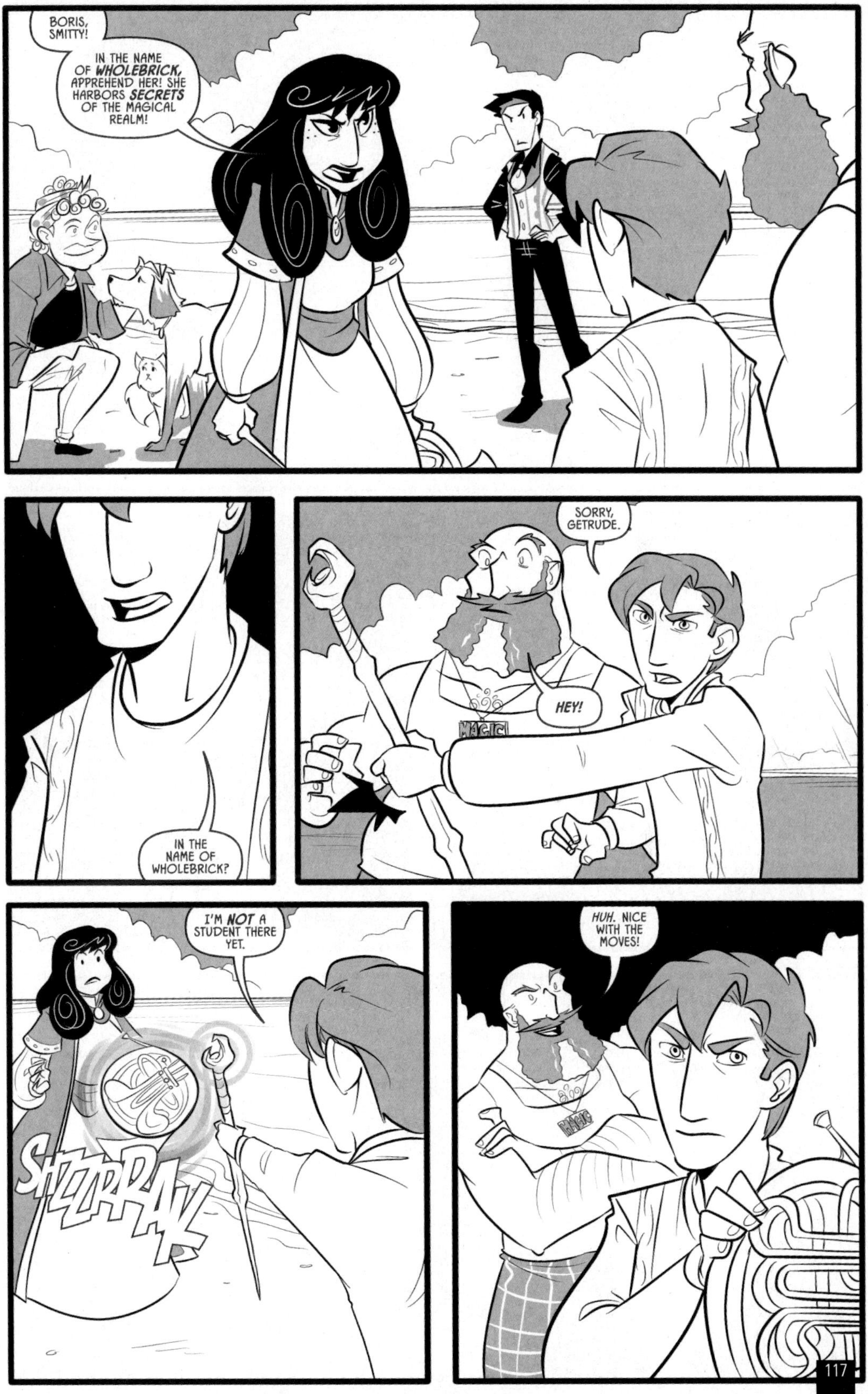
BORIS, SMITTY!
IN THE NAME OF WHOLEBRICK, APPREHEND HER! SHE HARBORS SECRETS OF THE MAGICAL REALM!
IN THE NAME OF WHOLEBRICK?
SORRY, GETRUDE.
HEY!
MAGIC
I'M NOT A STUDENT THERE YET.
SHZZRRAK
HUH. NICE WITH THE MOVES!
MAGIC

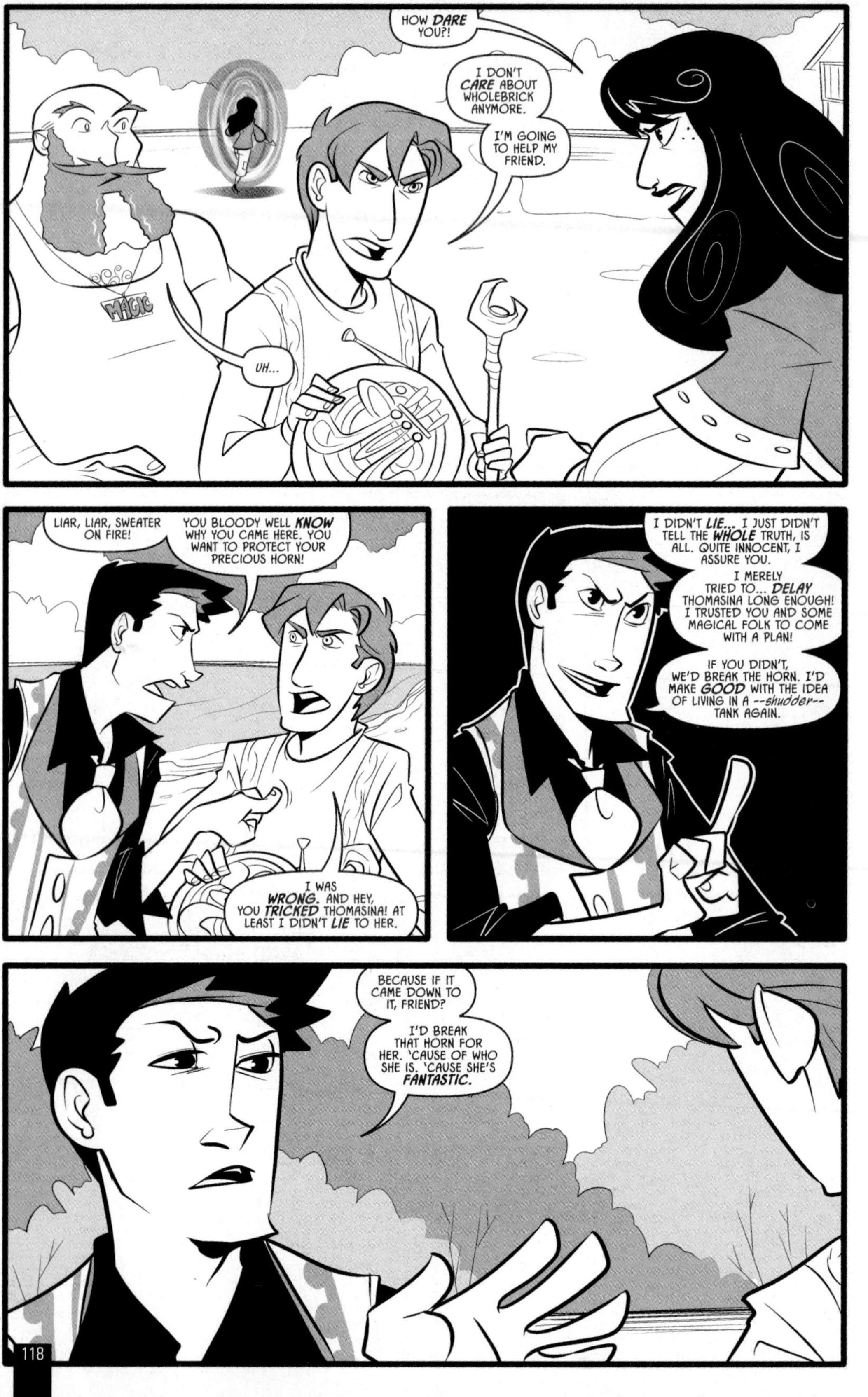
HOW *DARE* YOU?!
I DON'T *CARE* ABOUT WHOLEBRICK ANYMORE.
I'M GOING TO HELP MY FRIEND.
MAGIC
UH...
LIAR, LIAR, SWEATER ON FIRE!
YOU BLOODY WELL *KNOW* WHY YOU CAME HERE. YOU WANT TO PROTECT YOUR PRECIOUS HORN!
I WAS *WRONG.* AND HEY, YOU *TRICKED* THOMASINA! AT LEAST I DIDN'T *LIE* TO HER.
I DIDN'T *LIE...* I JUST DIDN'T TELL THE *WHOLE* TRUTH, IS ALL. QUITE INNOCENT, I ASSURE YOU.
I MERELY TRIED TO... *DELAY* THOMASINA LONG ENOUGH! I TRUSTED YOU AND SOME MAGICAL FOLK TO COME WITH A PLAN!
IF YOU DIDN'T, WE'D BREAK THE HORN. I'D MAKE *GOOD* WITH THE IDEA OF LIVING IN A --*shudder*-- TANK AGAIN.
BECAUSE IF IT CAME DOWN TO IT, FRIEND?
I'D BREAK THAT HORN FOR HER. 'CAUSE OF WHO SHE IS. 'CAUSE SHE'S *FANTASTIC.*

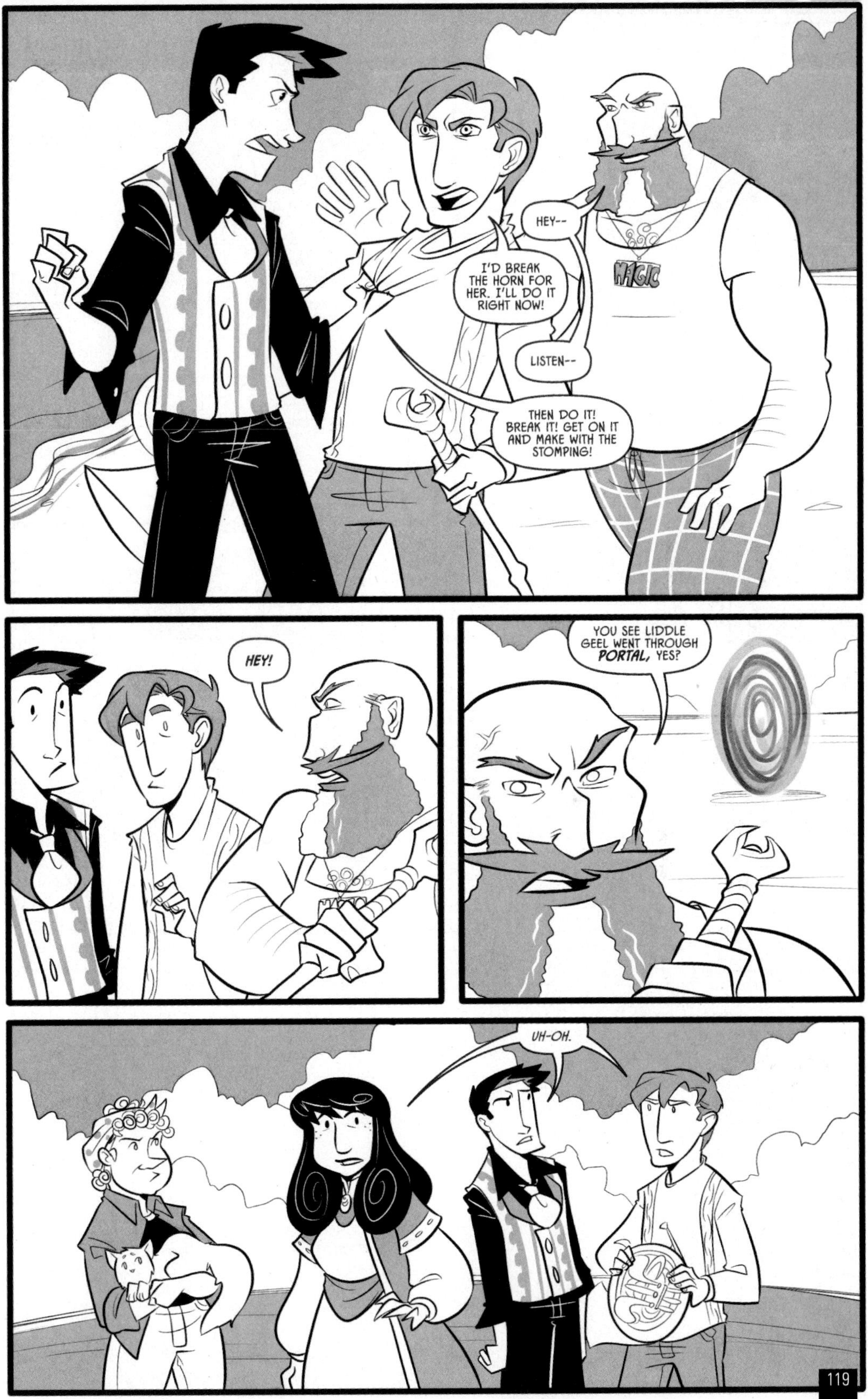
I'D BREAK THE HORN FOR HER. I'LL DO IT RIGHT NOW!
HEY--
LISTEN--
THEN DO IT! BREAK IT! GET ON IT AND MAKE WITH THE STOMPING!
MAGIC
HEY!
YOU SEE LIDDLE GEEL WENT THROUGH PORTAL, YES?
UH-OH.

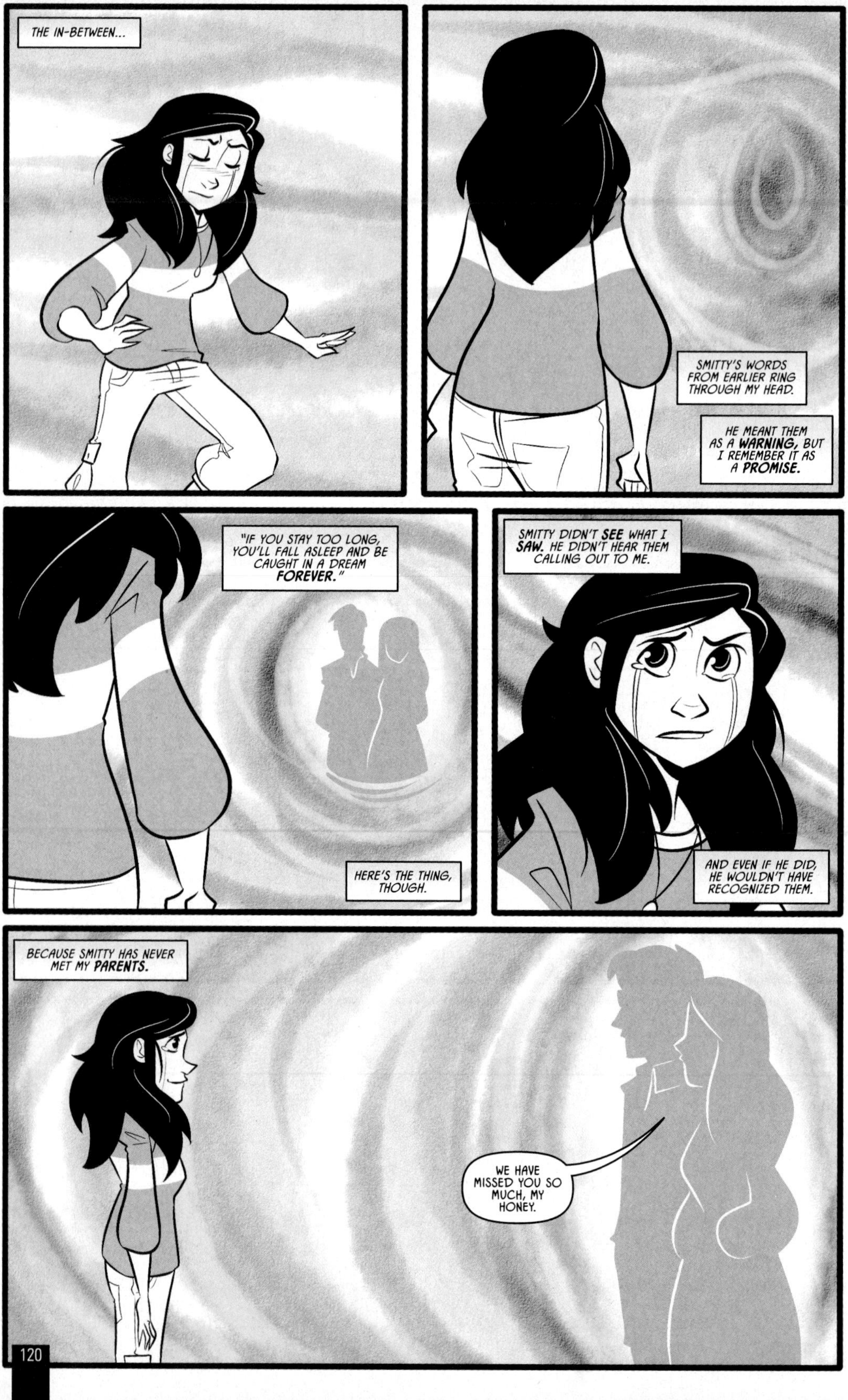
THE IN-BETWEEN...
SMITTY'S WORDS FROM EARLIER RING THROUGH MY HEAD.
HE MEANT THEM AS A **WARNING,** BUT I REMEMBER IT AS A **PROMISE.**
"IF YOU STAY TOO LONG, YOU'LL FALL ASLEEP AND BE CAUGHT IN A DREAM **FOREVER.**"
HERE'S THE THING, THOUGH.
SMITTY DIDN'T **SEE** WHAT I **SAW.** HE DIDN'T HEAR THEM CALLING OUT TO ME.
AND EVEN IF HE DID, HE WOULDN'T HAVE RECOGNIZED THEM.
BECAUSE SMITTY HAS NEVER MET MY **PARENTS.**
WE HAVE MISSED YOU SO MUCH, MY HONEY.

FAMILY PETS

FAMILY PETS

CHAPTER SIX

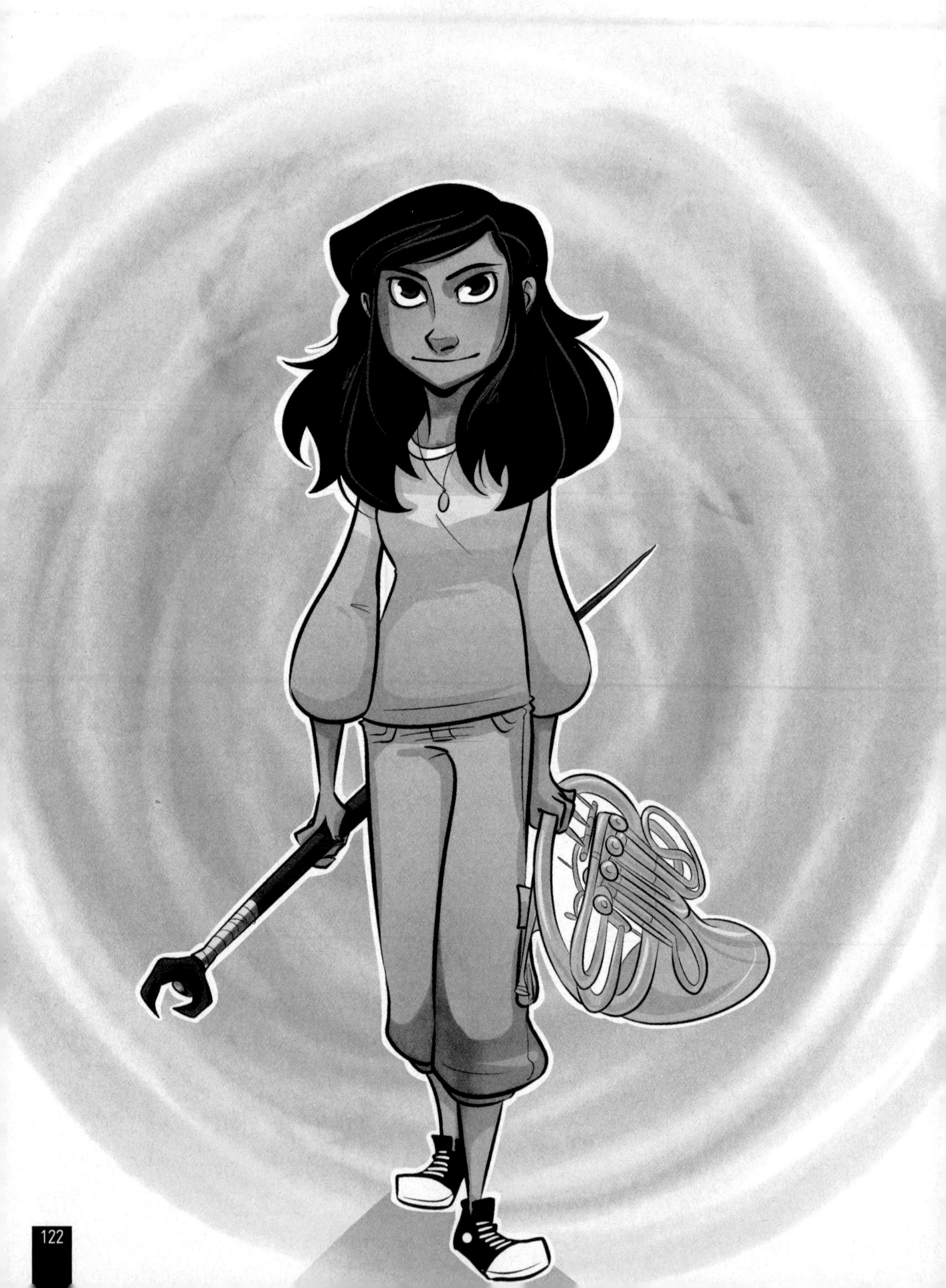

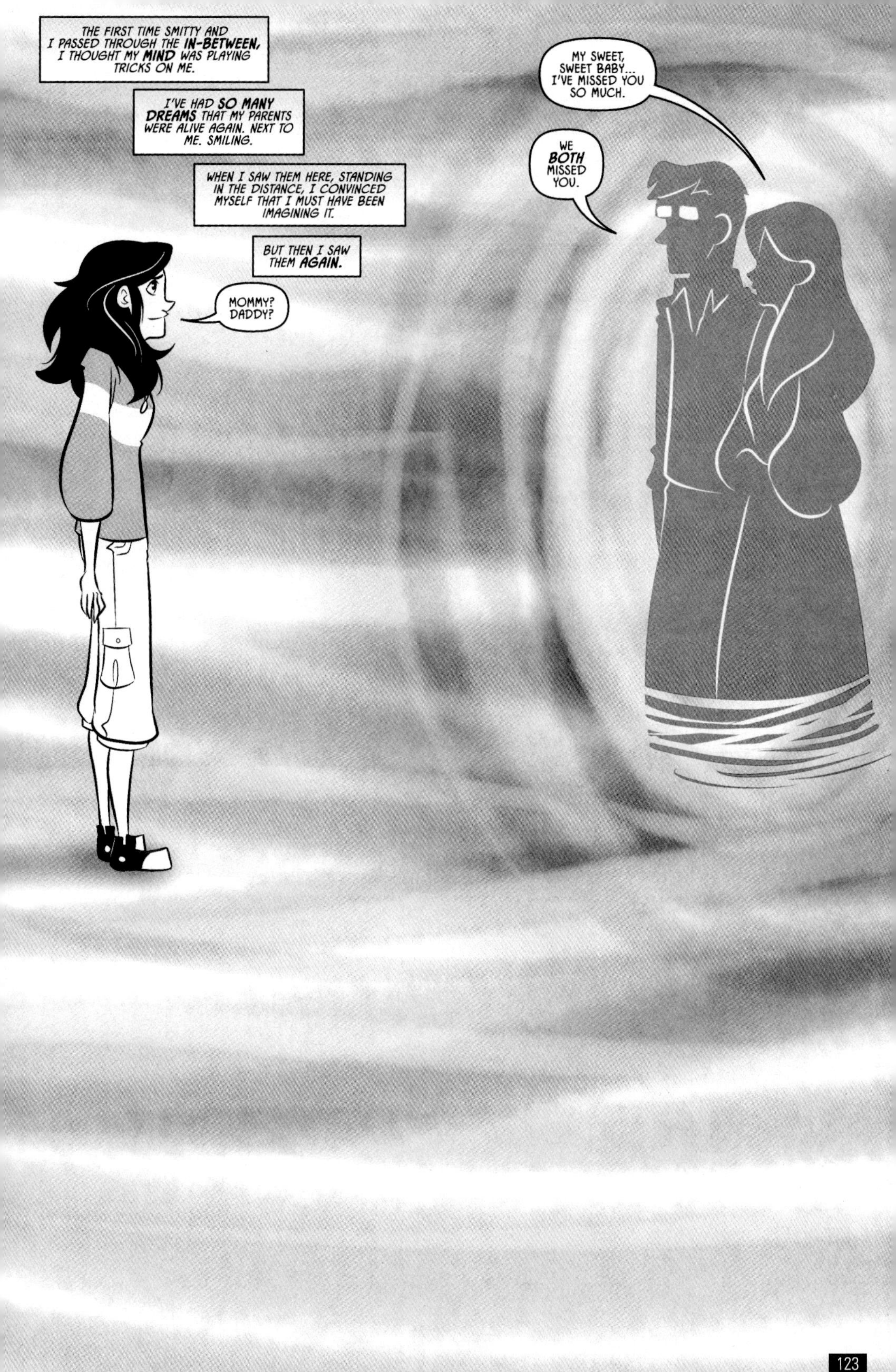

THE FIRST TIME SMITTY AND I PASSED THROUGH THE IN-BETWEEN, I THOUGHT MY MIND WAS PLAYING TRICKS ON ME.
I'VE HAD SO MANY DREAMS THAT MY PARENTS WERE ALIVE AGAIN. NEXT TO ME. SMILING.
WHEN I SAW THEM HERE, STANDING IN THE DISTANCE, I CONVINCED MYSELF THAT I MUST HAVE BEEN IMAGINING IT.
BUT THEN I SAW THEM AGAIN.
MOMMY? DADDY?
MY SWEET, SWEET BABY... I'VE MISSED YOU SO MUCH.
WE BOTH MISSED YOU.

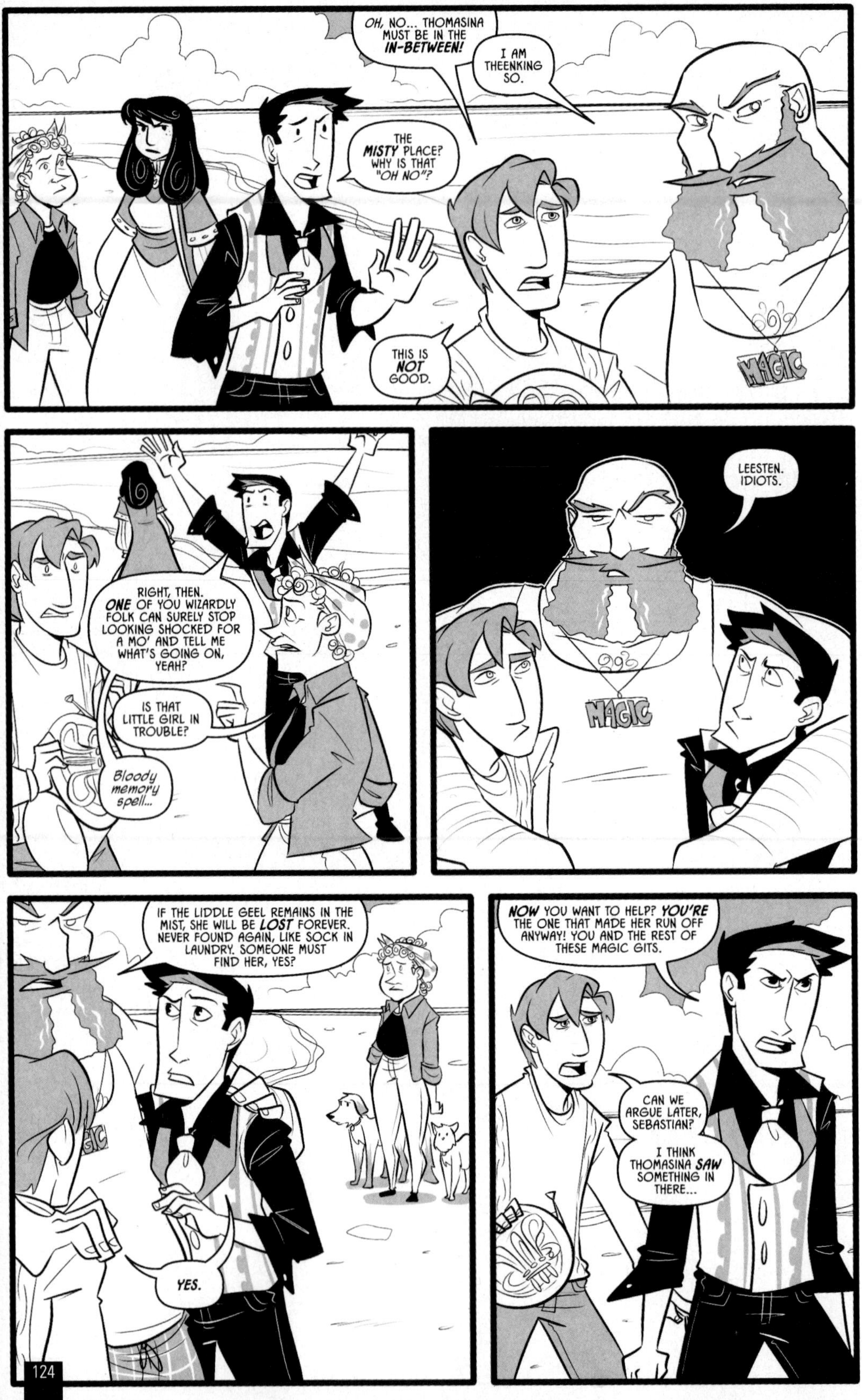
OH, NO... THOMASINA MUST BE IN THE IN-BETWEEN!
I AM THEENKING SO.
THE MISTY PLACE? WHY IS THAT "OH NO"?
THIS IS NOT GOOD.
MAGIC
RIGHT, THEN. ONE OF YOU WIZARDLY FOLK CAN SURELY STOP LOOKING SHOCKED FOR A MO' AND TELL ME WHAT'S GOING ON, YEAH?
IS THAT LITTLE GIRL IN TROUBLE?
Bloody memory spell...
LEESTEN. IDIOTS.
MAGIC
IF THE LIDDLE GEEL REMAINS IN THE MIST, SHE WILL BE LOST FOREVER. NEVER FOUND AGAIN, LIKE SOCK IN LAUNDRY. SOMEONE MUST FIND HER, YES?
YES.
NOW YOU WANT TO HELP? YOU'RE THE ONE THAT MADE HER RUN OFF ANYWAY! YOU AND THE REST OF THESE MAGIC GITS.
CAN WE ARGUE LATER, SEBASTIAN?
I THINK THOMASINA SAW SOMETHING IN THERE...

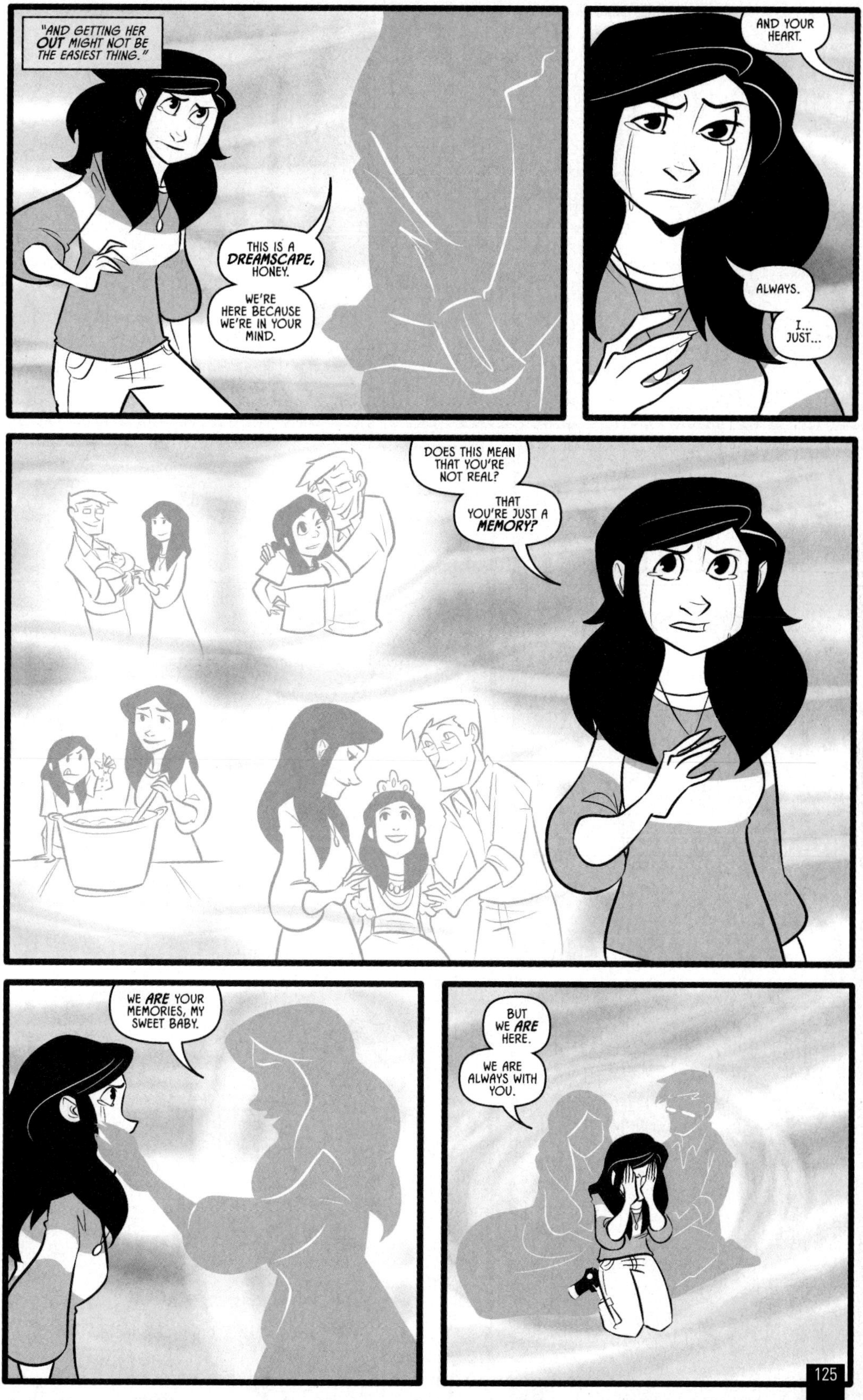
"AND GETTING HER OUT MIGHT NOT BE THE EASIEST THING."
THIS IS A DREAMSCAPE, HONEY.
WE'RE HERE BECAUSE WE'RE IN YOUR MIND.
AND YOUR HEART.
ALWAYS.
I... JUST...
DOES THIS MEAN THAT YOU'RE NOT REAL?
THAT YOU'RE JUST A MEMORY?
WE ARE YOUR MEMORIES, MY SWEET BABY.
BUT WE ARE HERE.
WE ARE ALWAYS WITH YOU.

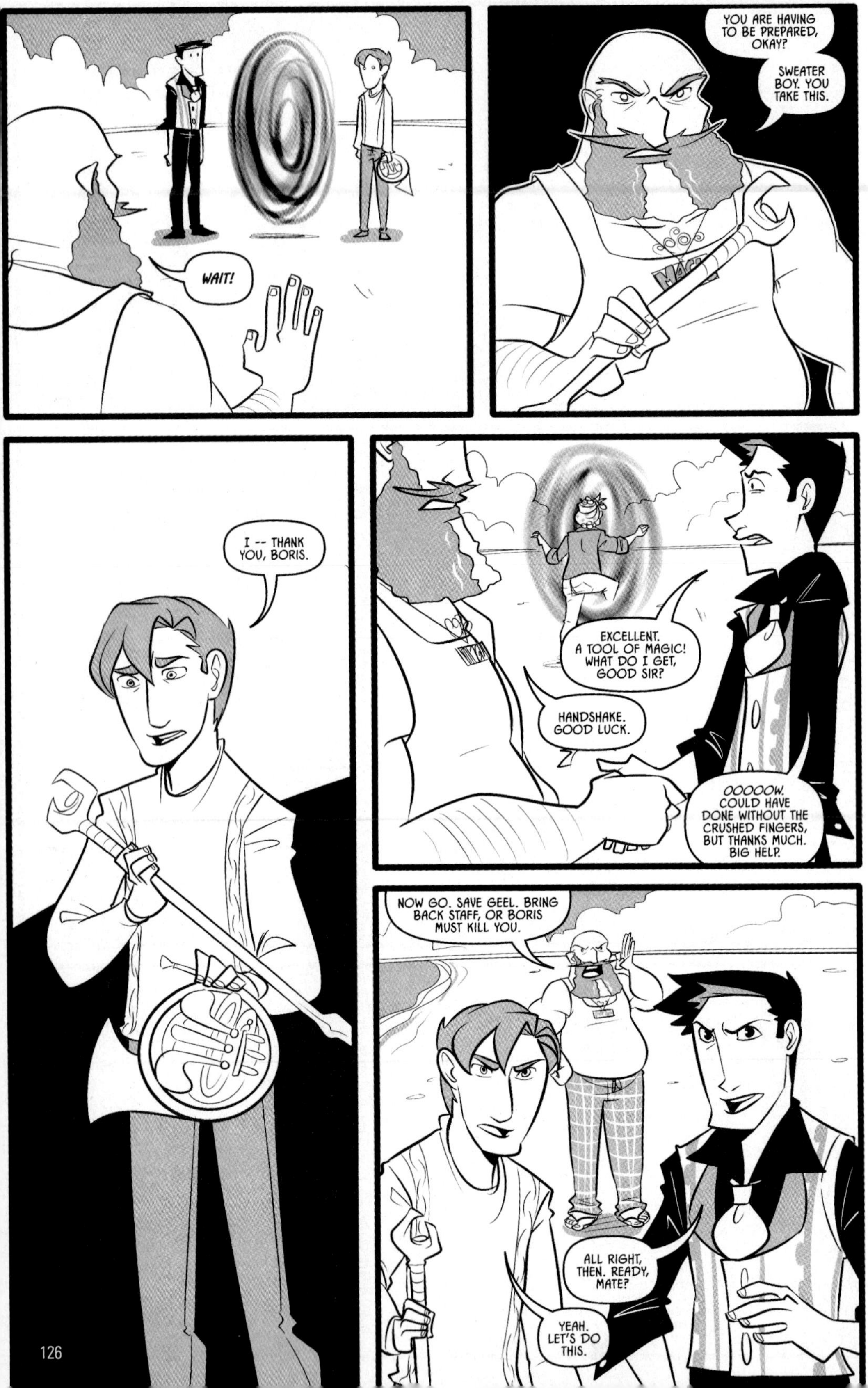
WAIT!
YOU ARE HAVING TO BE PREPARED, OKAY?
SWEATER BOY. YOU TAKE THIS.
I -- THANK YOU, BORIS.
EXCELLENT. A TOOL OF MAGIC! WHAT DO I GET, GOOD SIR?
HANDSHAKE. GOOD LUCK.
OOOOOW. COULD HAVE DONE WITHOUT THE CRUSHED FINGERS, BUT THANKS MUCH. BIG HELP.
NOW GO. SAVE GEEL. BRING BACK STAFF, OR BORIS MUST KILL YOU.
ALL RIGHT, THEN. READY, MATE?
YEAH. LET'S DO THIS.

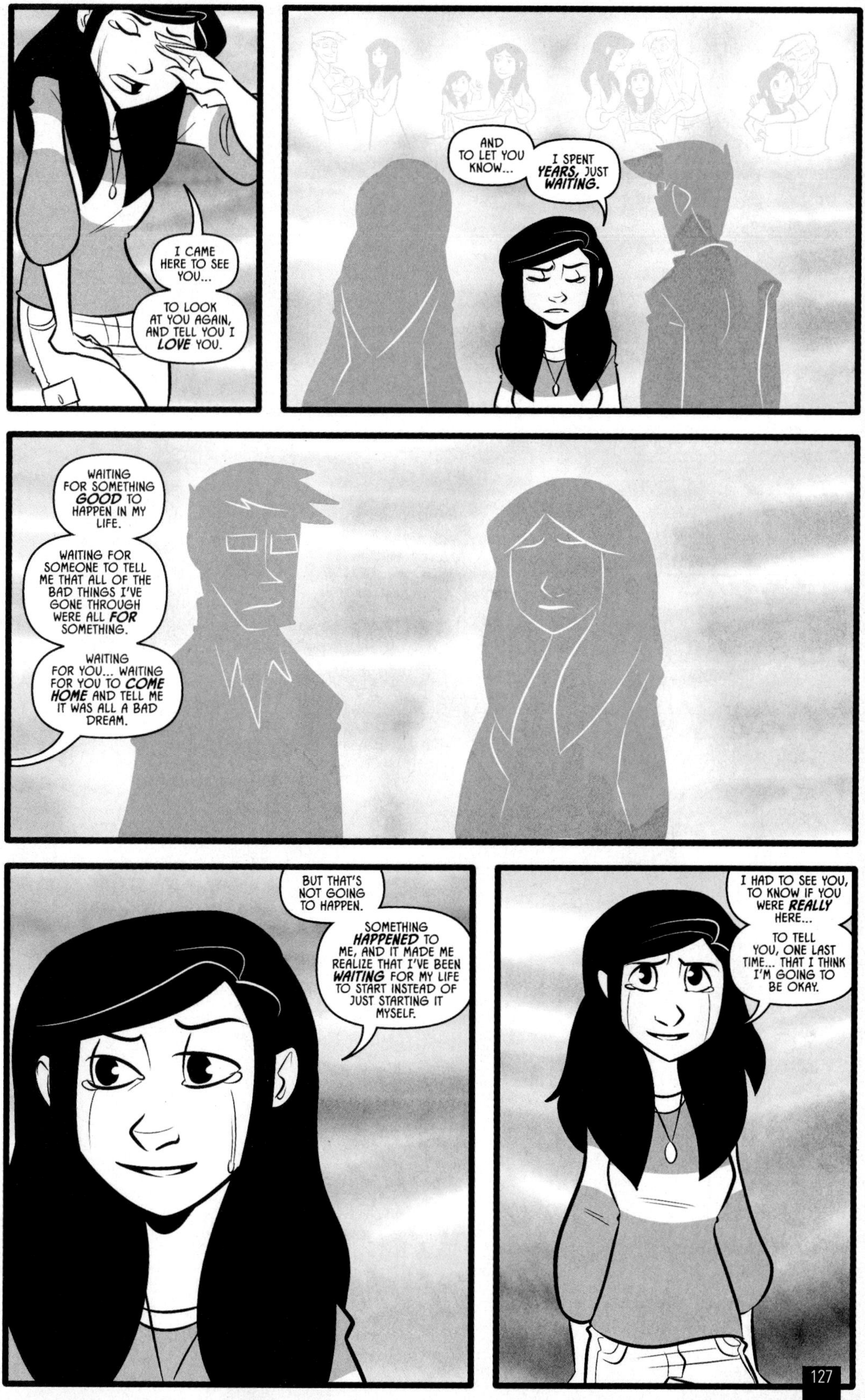
I CAME HERE TO SEE YOU...
TO LOOK AT YOU AGAIN, AND TELL YOU I LOVE YOU.
AND TO LET YOU KNOW...
I SPENT YEARS, JUST WAITING.
WAITING FOR SOMETHING GOOD TO HAPPEN IN MY LIFE.
WAITING FOR SOMEONE TO TELL ME THAT ALL OF THE BAD THINGS I'VE GONE THROUGH WERE ALL FOR SOMETHING.
WAITING FOR YOU... WAITING FOR YOU TO COME HOME AND TELL ME IT WAS ALL A BAD DREAM.
BUT THAT'S NOT GOING TO HAPPEN.
SOMETHING HAPPENED TO ME, AND IT MADE ME REALIZE THAT I'VE BEEN WAITING FOR MY LIFE TO START INSTEAD OF JUST STARTING IT MYSELF.
I HAD TO SEE YOU, TO KNOW IF YOU WERE REALLY HERE...
TO TELL YOU, ONE LAST TIME... THAT I THINK I'M GOING TO BE OKAY.

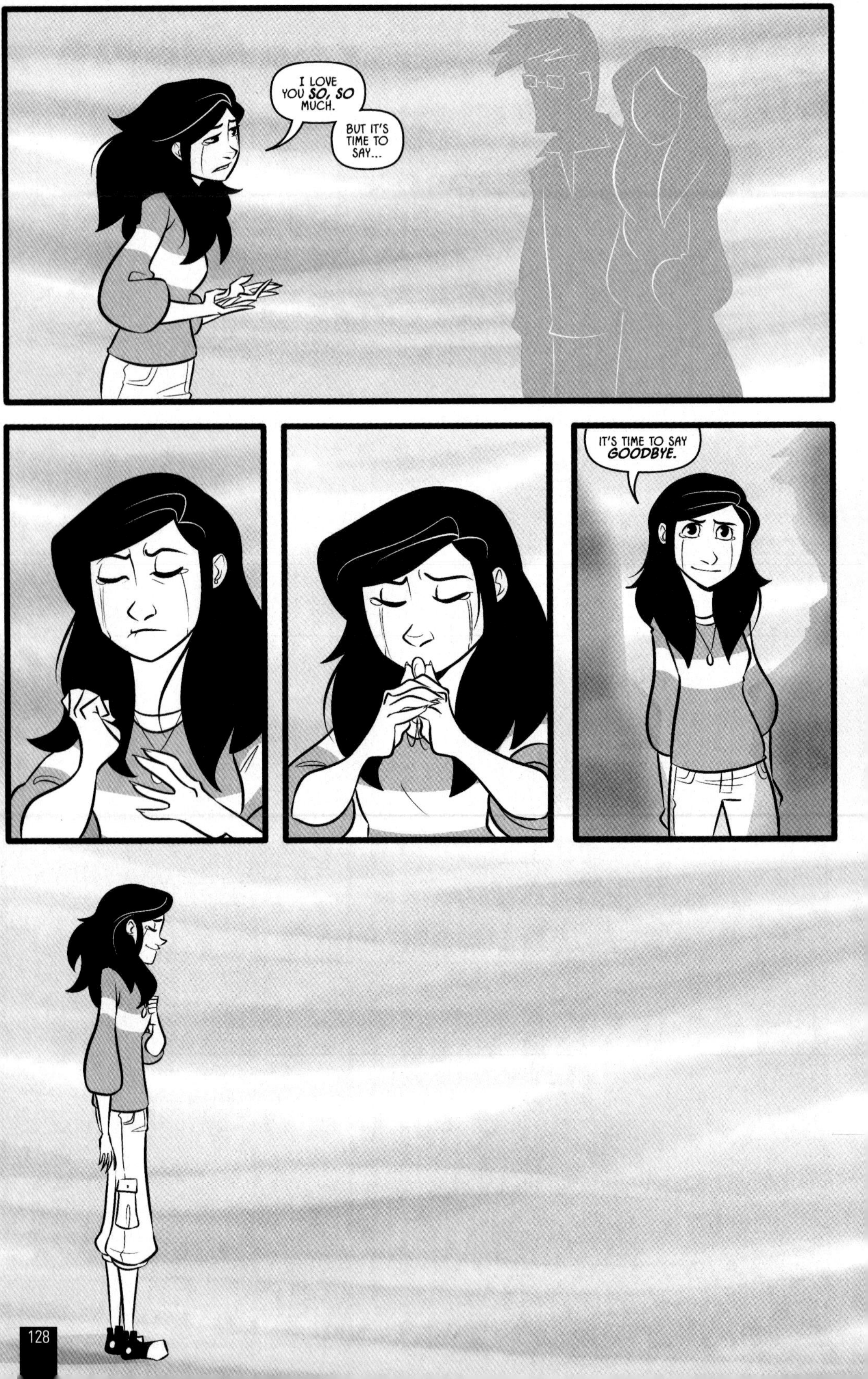
I LOVE YOU SO, SO MUCH.
BUT IT'S TIME TO SAY...
IT'S TIME TO SAY GOODBYE.

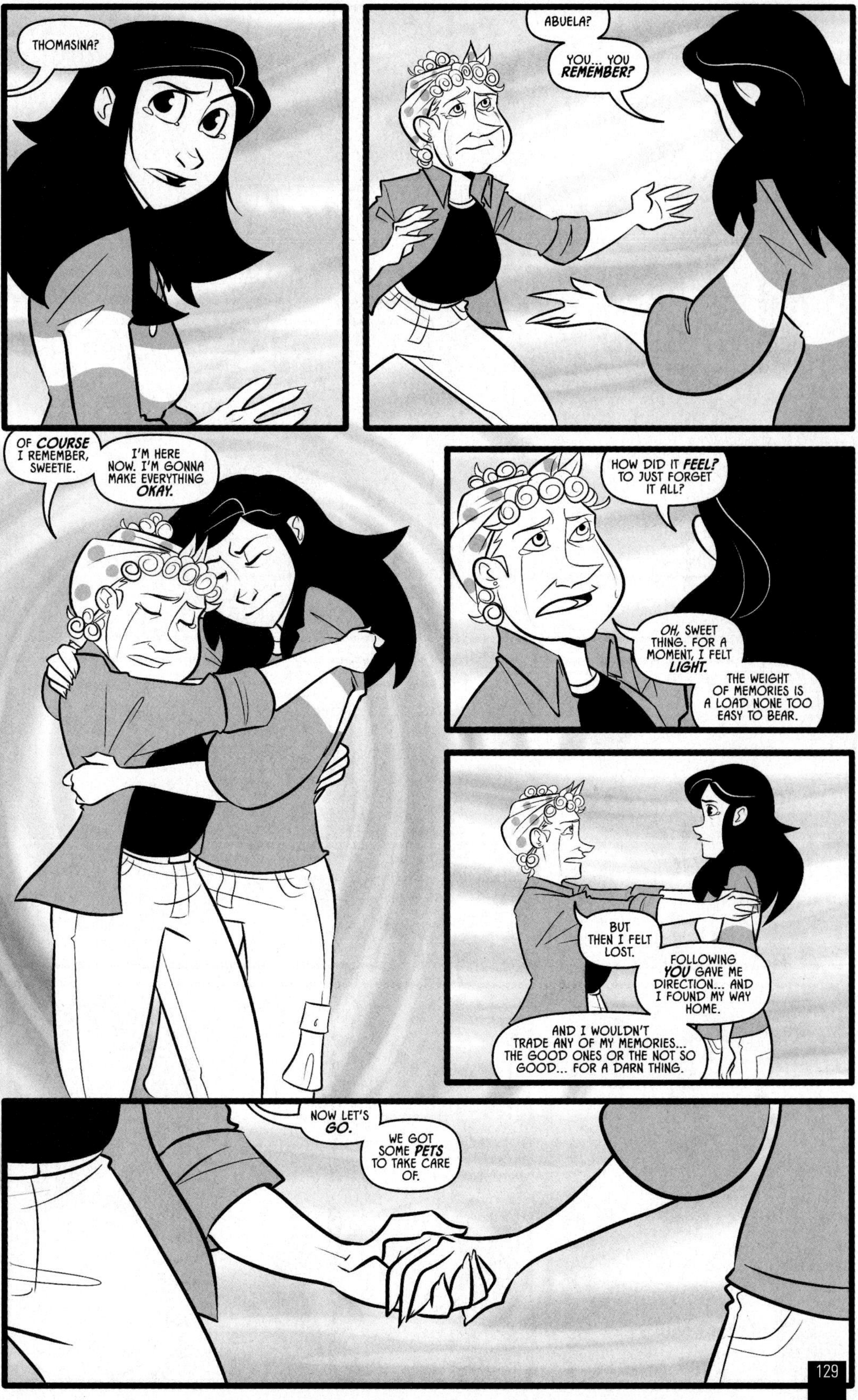
THOMASINA?
ABUELA?
YOU... YOU *REMEMBER?*
OF *COURSE* I REMEMBER, SWEETIE.
I'M HERE NOW. I'M GONNA MAKE EVERYTHING *OKAY.*
HOW DID IT *FEEL?* TO JUST FORGET IT ALL?
OH, SWEET THING. FOR A MOMENT, I FELT *LIGHT.*
THE WEIGHT OF MEMORIES IS A LOAD NONE TOO EASY TO BEAR.
BUT THEN I FELT LOST.
FOLLOWING *YOU* GAVE ME DIRECTION... AND I FOUND MY WAY HOME.
AND I WOULDN'T TRADE ANY OF MY MEMORIES... THE GOOD ONES OR THE NOT SO GOOD... FOR A DARN THING.
NOW LET'S *GO.*
WE GOT SOME *PETS* TO TAKE CARE OF.

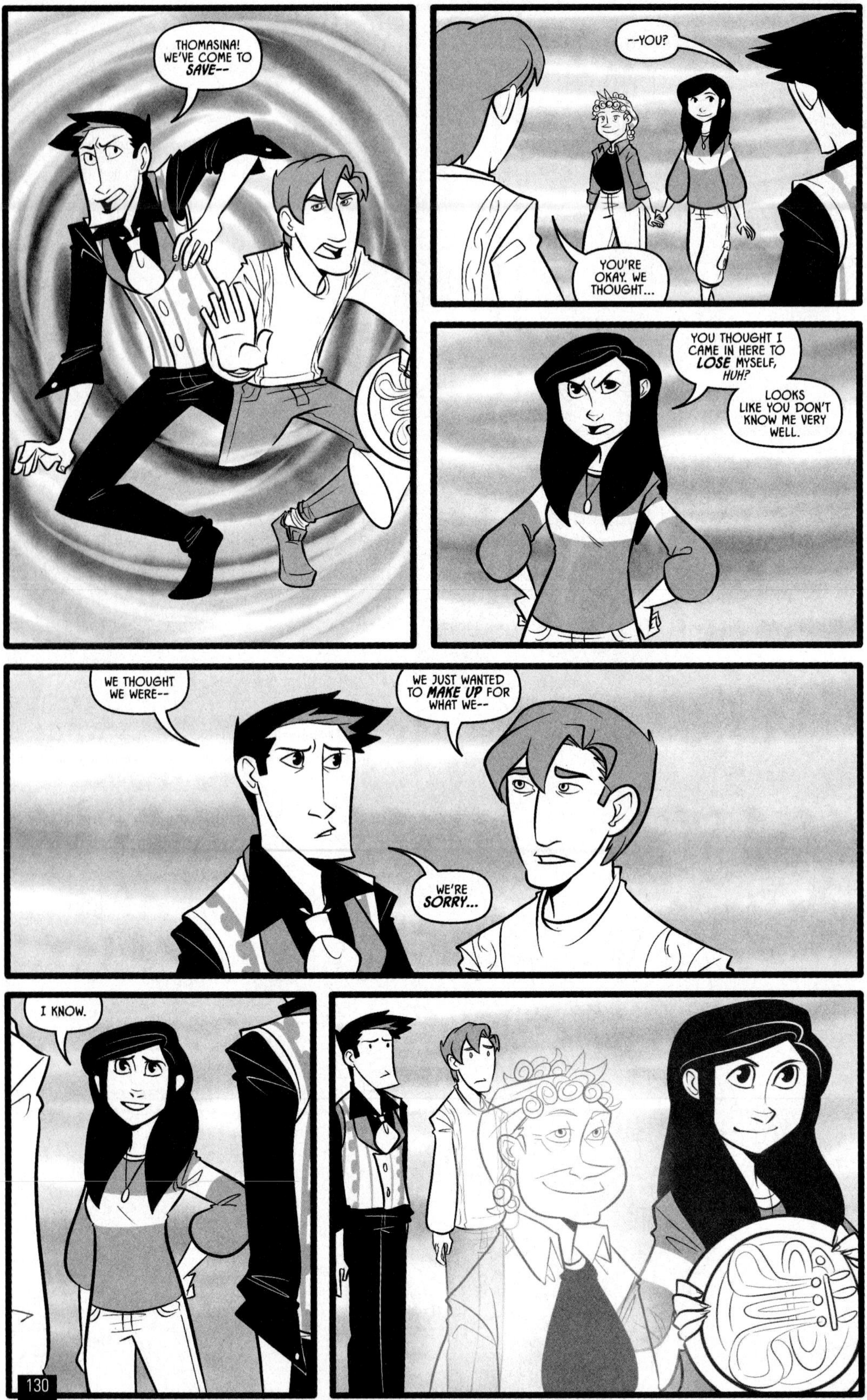

THOMASINA! WE'VE COME TO SAVE--
--YOU?
YOU'RE OKAY. WE THOUGHT...
YOU THOUGHT I CAME IN HERE TO LOSE MYSELF, HUH?
LOOKS LIKE YOU DON'T KNOW ME VERY WELL.
WE THOUGHT WE WERE--
WE JUST WANTED TO MAKE UP FOR WHAT WE--
WE'RE SORRY...
I KNOW.

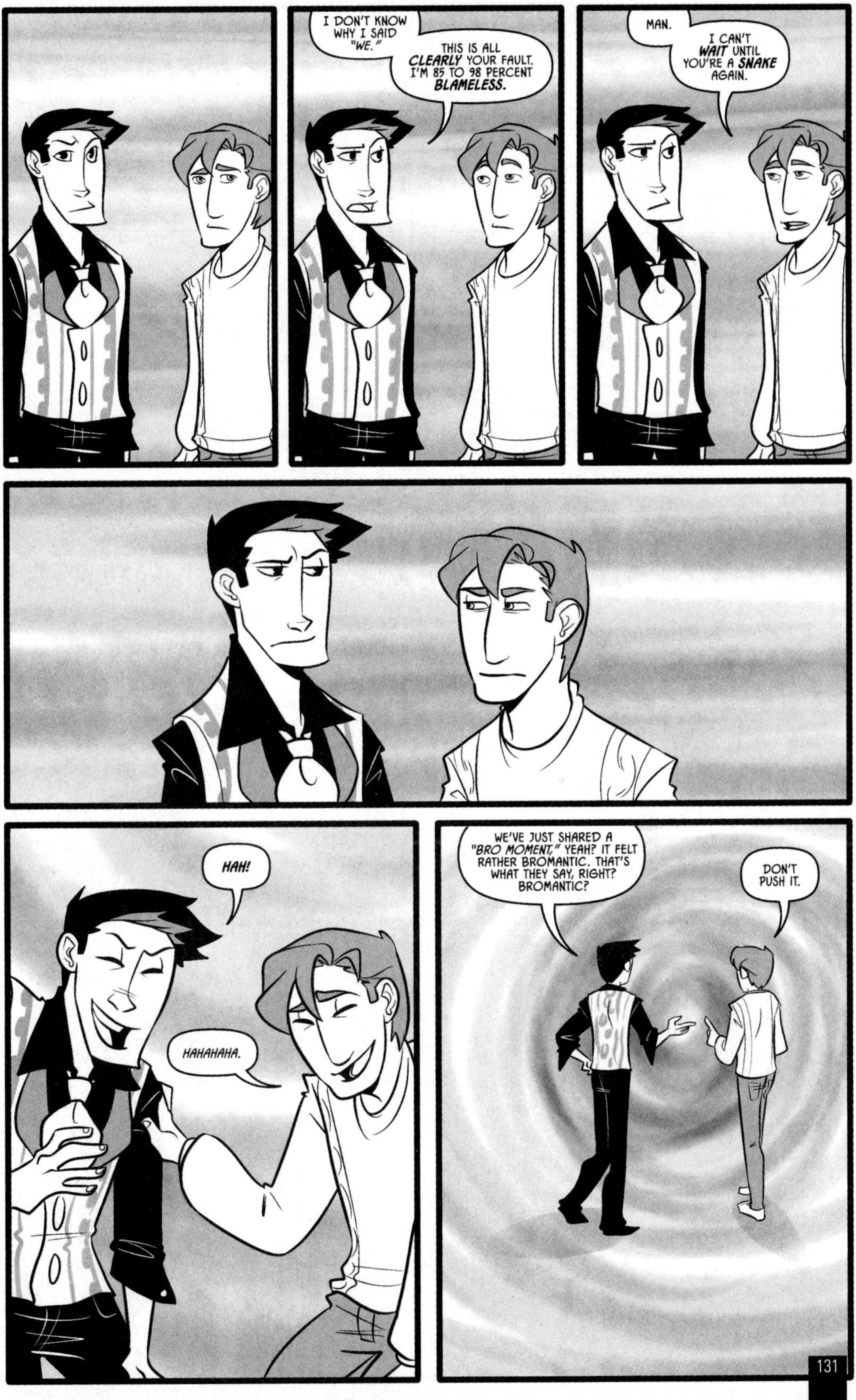
I DON'T KNOW WHY I SAID "WE."
THIS IS ALL *CLEARLY* YOUR FAULT. I'M 85 TO 98 PERCENT *BLAMELESS.*
MAN.
I CAN'T *WAIT* UNTIL YOU'RE A *SNAKE* AGAIN.
HAH!
HAHAHAHA.
WE'VE JUST SHARED A "*BRO MOMENT,*" YEAH? IT FELT RATHER BROMANTIC. THAT'S WHAT THEY SAY, RIGHT? BROMANTIC?
DON'T PUSH IT.

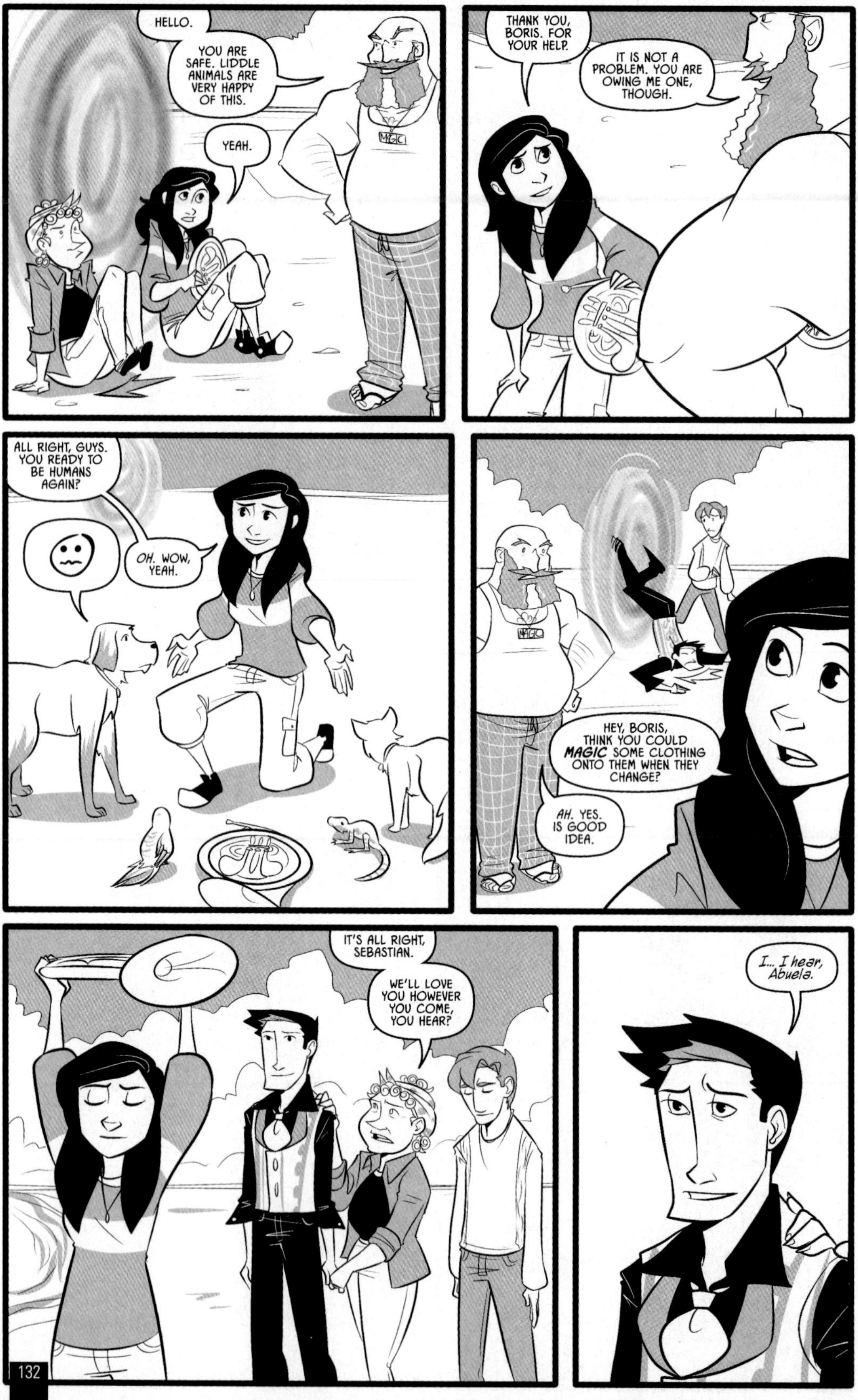
HELLO.
YOU ARE SAFE. LIDDLE ANIMALS ARE VERY HAPPY OF THIS.
YEAH.
THANK YOU, BORIS. FOR YOUR HELP.
IT IS NOT A PROBLEM. YOU ARE OWING ME ONE, THOUGH.
ALL RIGHT, GUYS. YOU READY TO BE HUMANS AGAIN?
OH. WOW, YEAH.
HEY, BORIS, THINK YOU COULD MAGIC SOME CLOTHING ONTO THEM WHEN THEY CHANGE?
AH. YES. IS GOOD IDEA.
IT'S ALL RIGHT, SEBASTIAN.
WE'LL LOVE YOU HOWEVER YOU COME, YOU HEAR?
I... I hear, Abuela.

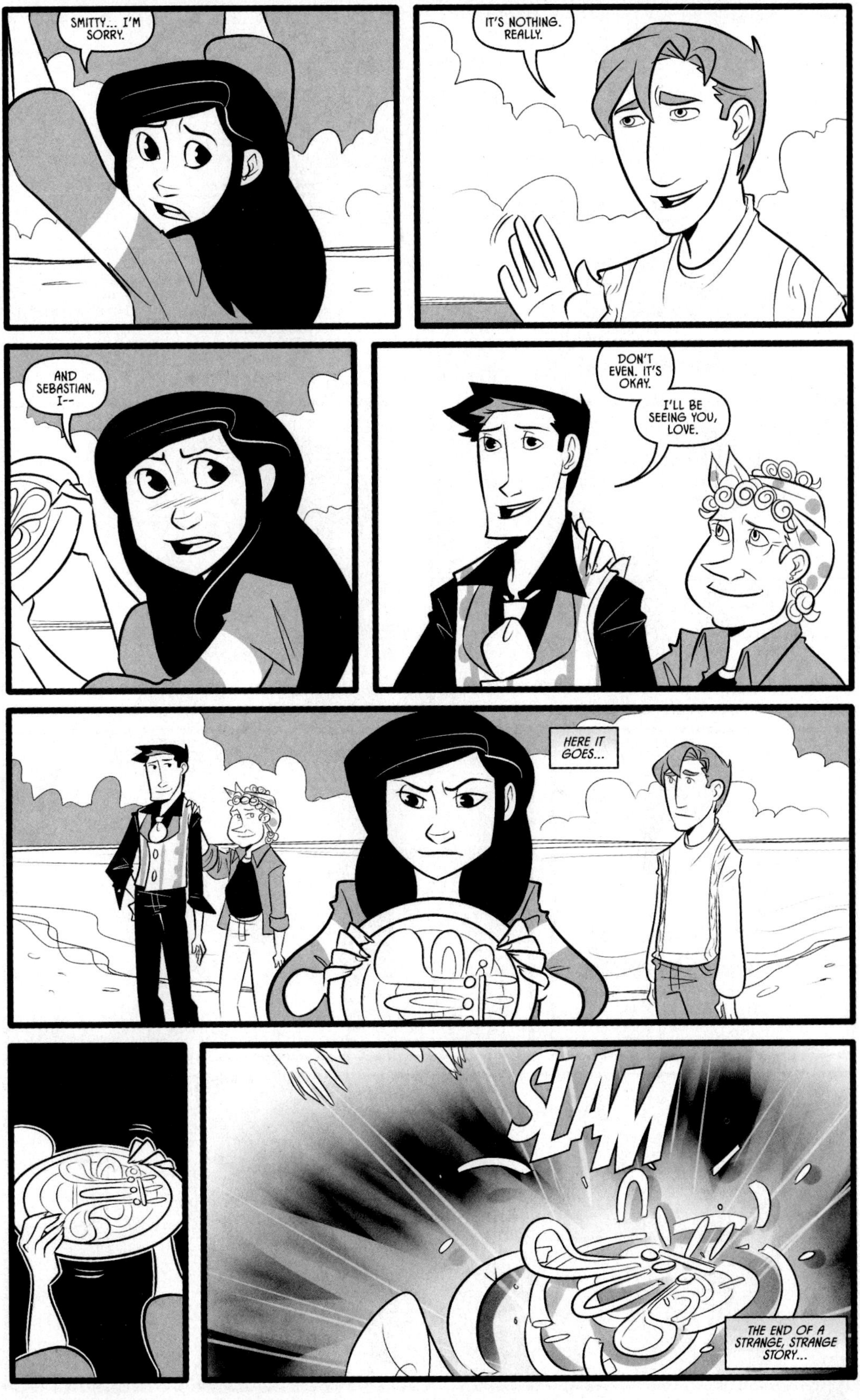
SMITTY... I'M SORRY.
IT'S NOTHING. REALLY.
AND SEBASTIAN, I--
DON'T EVEN. IT'S OKAY.
I'LL BE SEEING YOU, LOVE.
HERE IT GOES...
SLAM
THE END OF A STRANGE, STRANGE STORY...

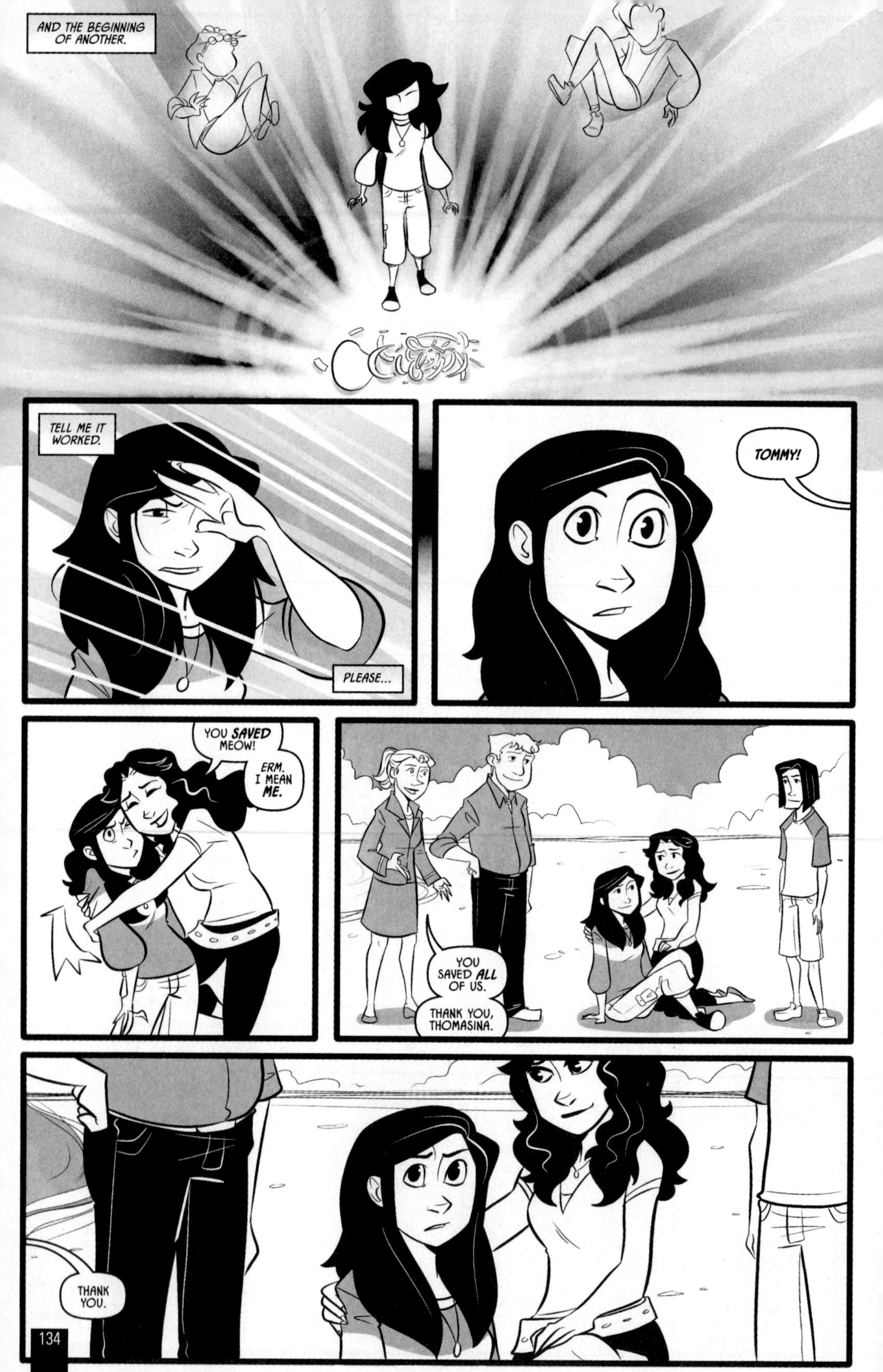
AND THE BEGINNING OF ANOTHER.
TELL ME IT WORKED.
PLEASE...
TOMMY!
YOU SAVED MEOW!
ERM. I MEAN ME.
YOU SAVED ALL OF US.
THANK YOU, THOMASINA.
THANK YOU.

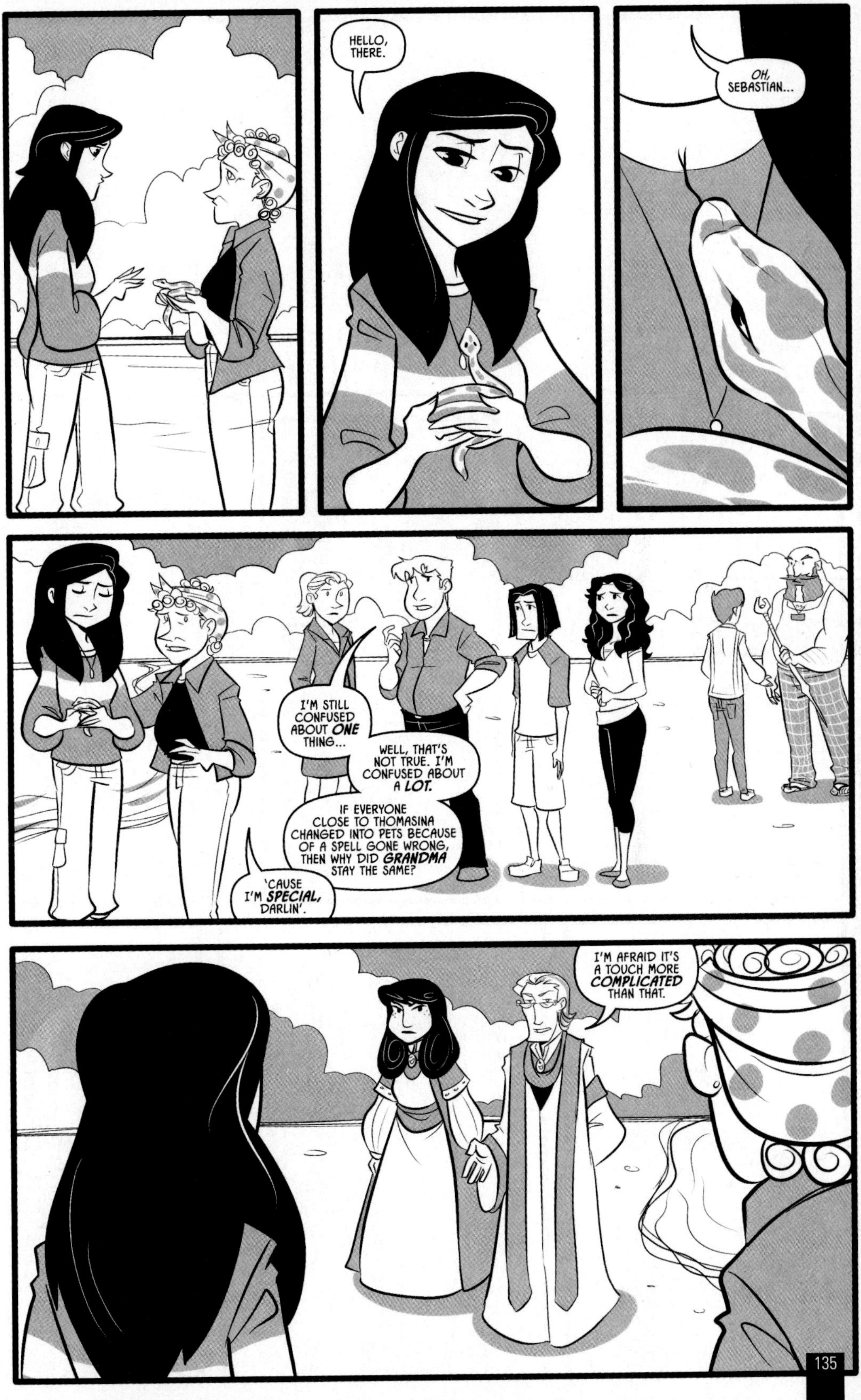
HELLO, THERE.
OH, SEBASTIAN...
I'M STILL CONFUSED ABOUT ONE THING...
WELL, THAT'S NOT TRUE. I'M CONFUSED ABOUT A LOT.
IF EVERYONE CLOSE TO THOMASINA CHANGED INTO PETS BECAUSE OF A SPELL GONE WRONG, THEN WHY DID GRANDMA STAY THE SAME?
'CAUSE I'M SPECIAL, DARLIN'.
I'M AFRAID IT'S A TOUCH MORE COMPLICATED THAN THAT.

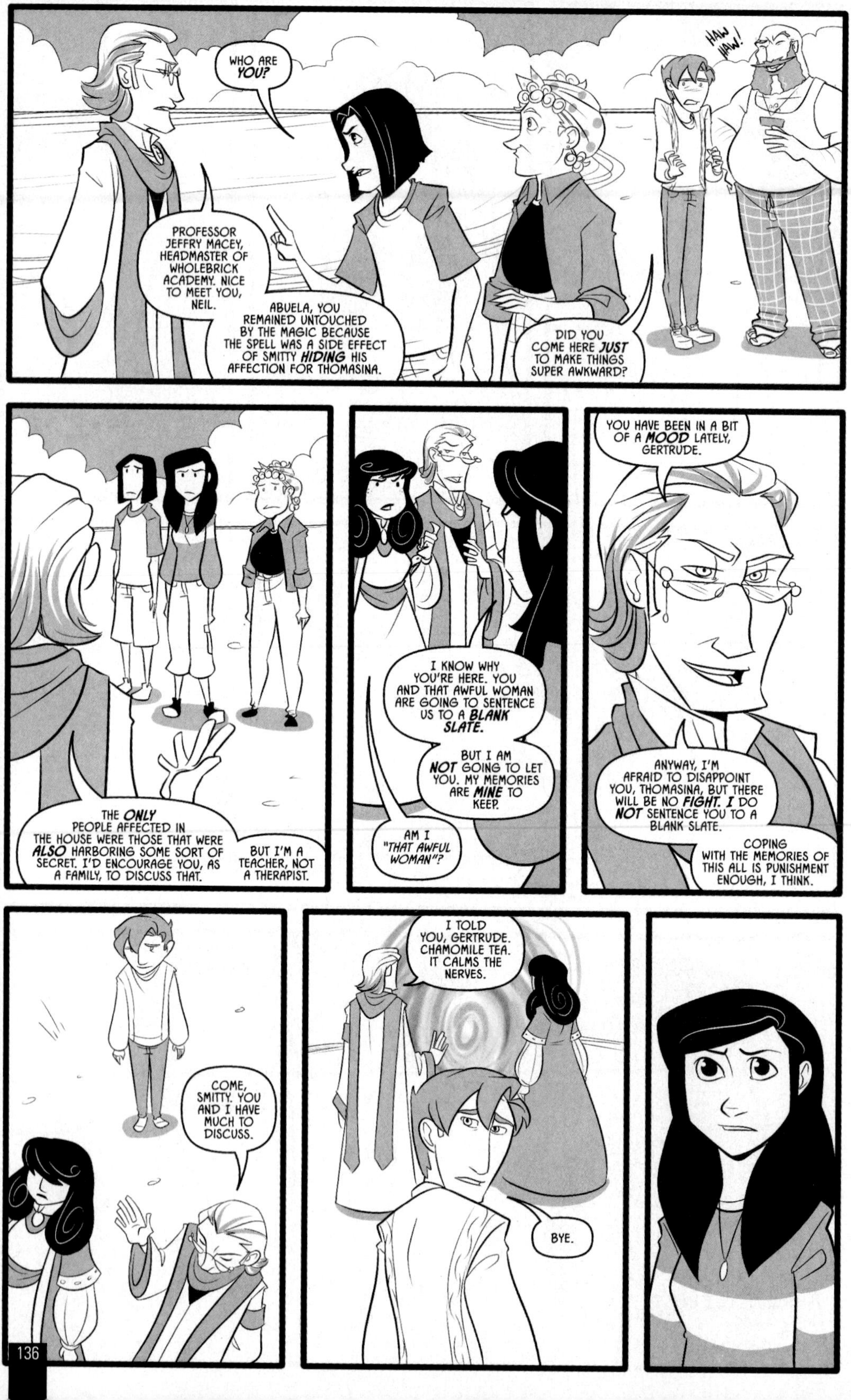
HAW HAW!
WHO ARE YOU?
PROFESSOR JEFFRY MACEY, HEADMASTER OF WHOLEBRICK ACADEMY. NICE TO MEET YOU, NEIL.
ABUELA, YOU REMAINED UNTOUCHED BY THE MAGIC BECAUSE THE SPELL WAS A SIDE EFFECT OF SMITTY HIDING HIS AFFECTION FOR THOMASINA.
DID YOU COME HERE JUST TO MAKE THINGS SUPER AWKWARD?
THE ONLY PEOPLE AFFECTED IN THE HOUSE WERE THOSE THAT WERE ALSO HARBORING SOME SORT OF SECRET. I'D ENCOURAGE YOU, AS A FAMILY, TO DISCUSS THAT.
BUT I'M A TEACHER, NOT A THERAPIST.
I KNOW WHY YOU'RE HERE. YOU AND THAT AWFUL WOMAN ARE GOING TO SENTENCE US TO A BLANK SLATE.
BUT I AM NOT GOING TO LET YOU. MY MEMORIES ARE MINE TO KEEP.
AM I "THAT AWFUL WOMAN"?
YOU HAVE BEEN IN A BIT OF A MOOD LATELY, GERTRUDE.
ANYWAY, I'M AFRAID TO DISAPPOINT YOU, THOMASINA, BUT THERE WILL BE NO FIGHT. I DO NOT SENTENCE YOU TO A BLANK SLATE.
COPING WITH THE MEMORIES OF THIS ALL IS PUNISHMENT ENOUGH, I THINK.
COME, SMITTY. YOU AND I HAVE MUCH TO DISCUSS.
I TOLD YOU, GERTRUDE. CHAMOMILE TEA. IT CALMS THE NERVES.
BYE.

"GOODBYE."

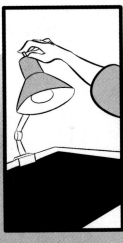

FLIK

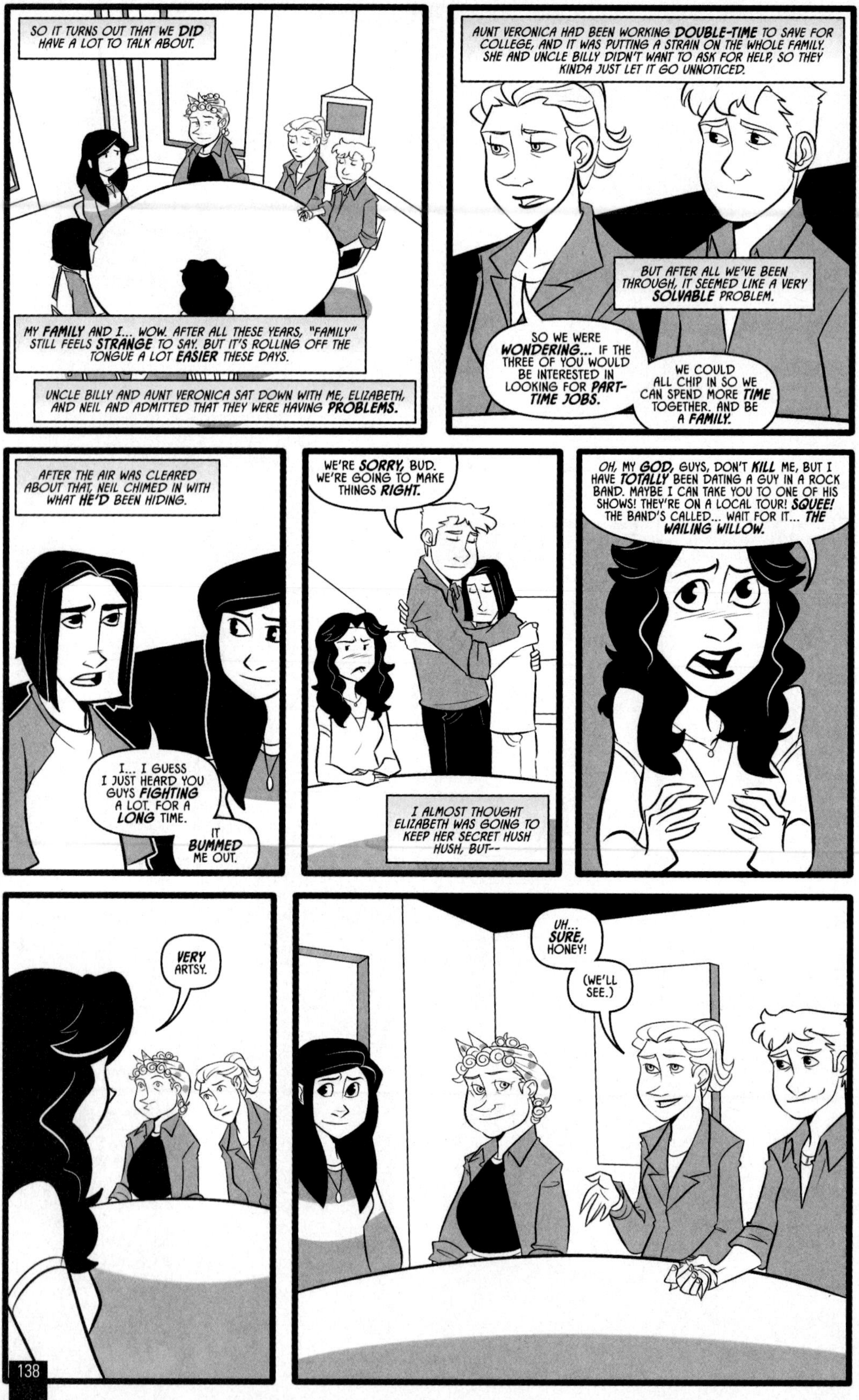

SO IT TURNS OUT THAT WE DID HAVE A LOT TO TALK ABOUT.
MY FAMILY AND I... WOW. AFTER ALL THESE YEARS, "FAMILY" STILL FEELS STRANGE TO SAY. BUT IT'S ROLLING OFF THE TONGUE A LOT EASIER THESE DAYS.
UNCLE BILLY AND AUNT VERONICA SAT DOWN WITH ME, ELIZABETH, AND NEIL AND ADMITTED THAT THEY WERE HAVING PROBLEMS.
AUNT VERONICA HAD BEEN WORKING DOUBLE-TIME TO SAVE FOR COLLEGE, AND IT WAS PUTTING A STRAIN ON THE WHOLE FAMILY. SHE AND UNCLE BILLY DIDN'T WANT TO ASK FOR HELP, SO THEY KINDA JUST LET IT GO UNNOTICED.
BUT AFTER ALL WE'VE BEEN THROUGH, IT SEEMED LIKE A VERY SOLVABLE PROBLEM.
SO WE WERE WONDERING... IF THE THREE OF YOU WOULD BE INTERESTED IN LOOKING FOR PART-TIME JOBS.
WE COULD ALL CHIP IN SO WE CAN SPEND MORE TIME TOGETHER. AND BE A FAMILY.
AFTER THE AIR WAS CLEARED ABOUT THAT, NEIL CHIMED IN WITH WHAT HE'D BEEN HIDING.
I... I GUESS I JUST HEARD YOU GUYS FIGHTING A LOT. FOR A LONG TIME.
IT BUMMED ME OUT.
WE'RE SORRY, BUD. WE'RE GOING TO MAKE THINGS RIGHT.
I ALMOST THOUGHT ELIZABETH WAS GOING TO KEEP HER SECRET HUSH HUSH, BUT--
OH, MY GOD, GUYS, DON'T KILL ME, BUT I HAVE TOTALLY BEEN DATING A GUY IN A ROCK BAND. MAYBE I CAN TAKE YOU TO ONE OF HIS SHOWS! THEY'RE ON A LOCAL TOUR! SQUEE! THE BAND'S CALLED... WAIT FOR IT... THE WAILING WILLOW.
VERY ARTSY.
UH... SURE, HONEY!
(WE'LL SEE.)

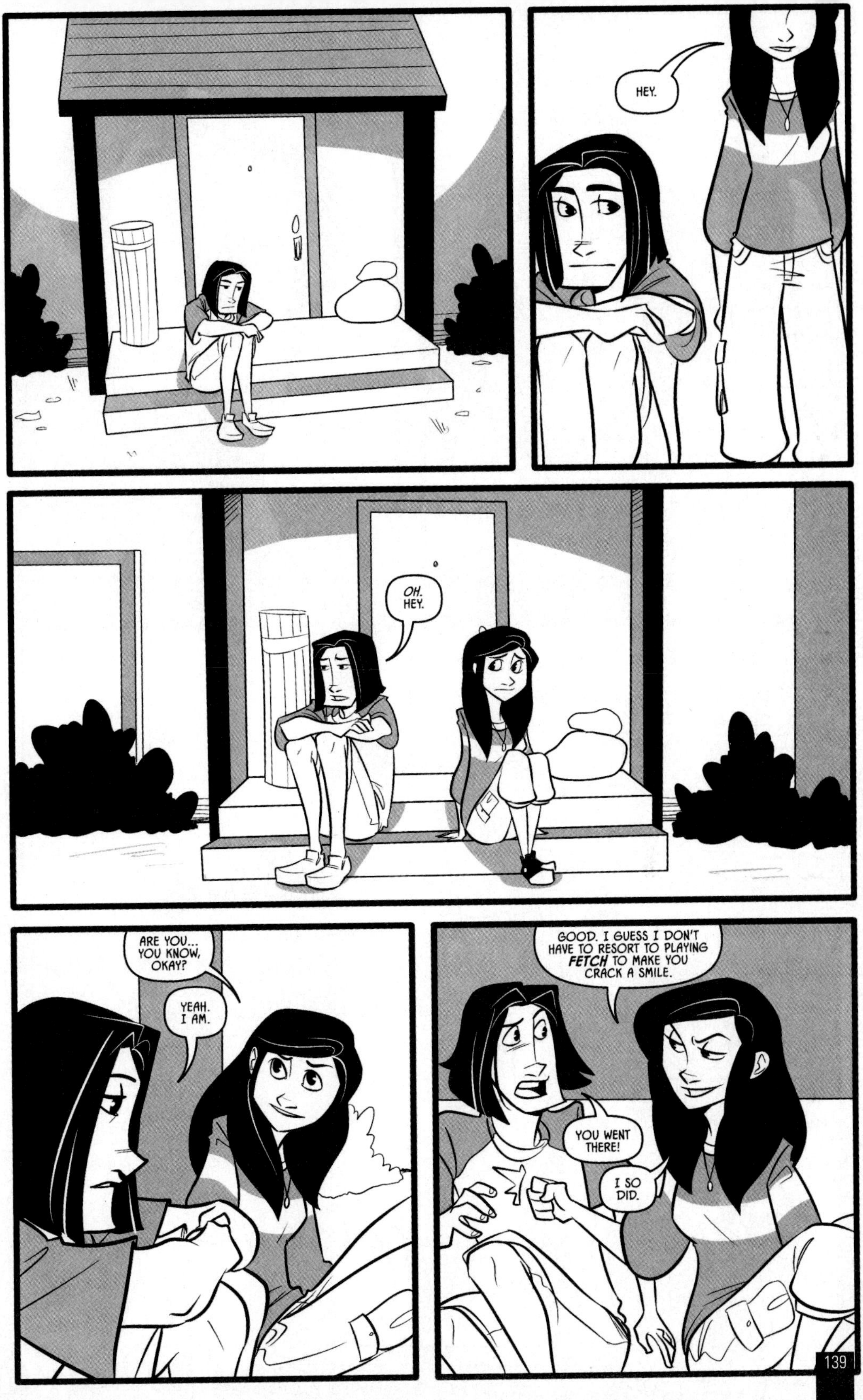
HEY.
OH. HEY.
ARE YOU... YOU KNOW, OKAY?
YEAH. I AM.
GOOD. I GUESS I DON'T HAVE TO RESORT TO PLAYING FETCH TO MAKE YOU CRACK A SMILE.
YOU WENT THERE!
I SO DID.

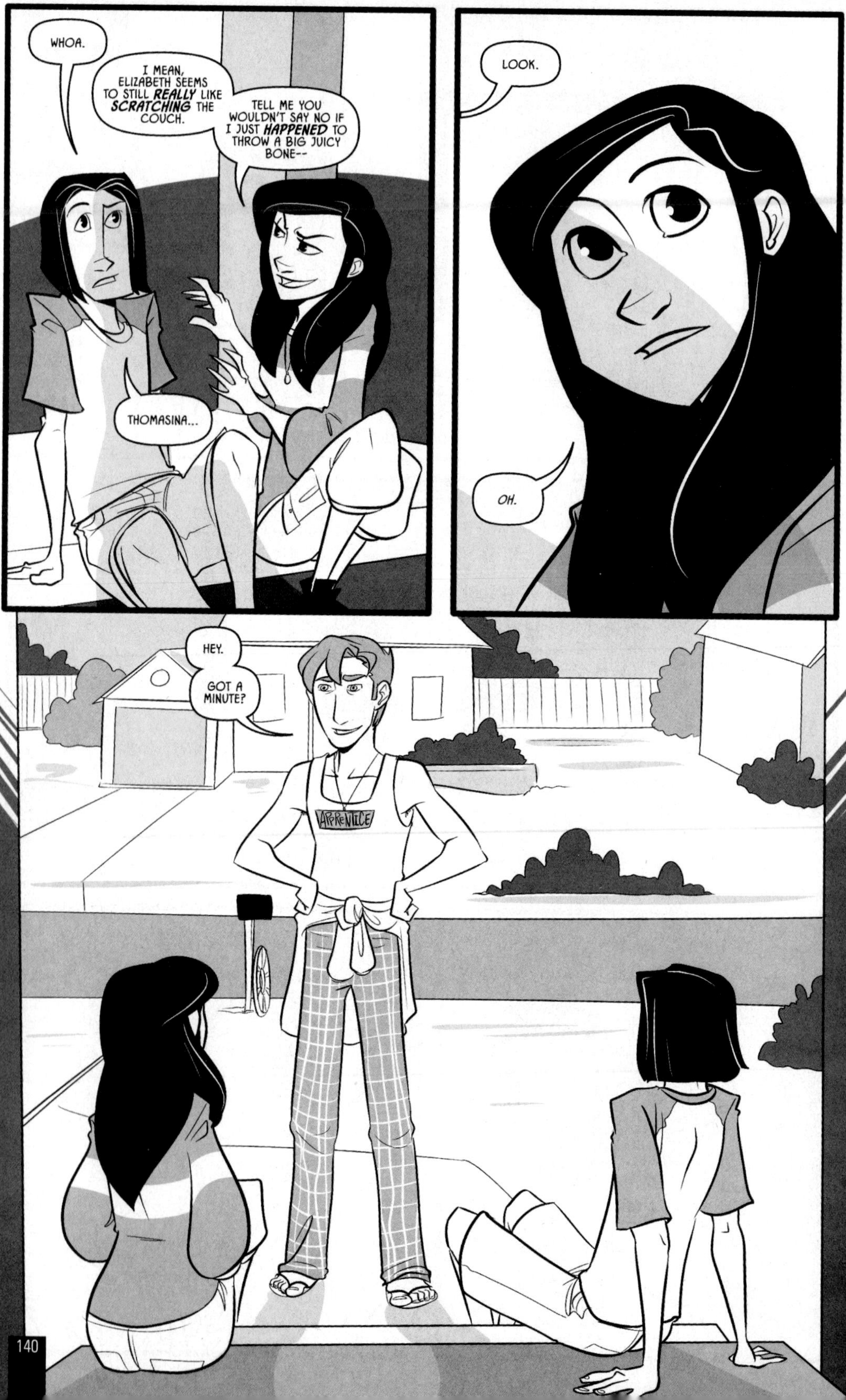
WHOA.
I MEAN, ELIZABETH SEEMS TO STILL REALLY LIKE SCRATCHING THE COUCH.
TELL ME YOU WOULDN'T SAY NO IF I JUST HAPPENED TO THROW A BIG JUICY BONE--
THOMASINA...
LOOK.
OH.
HEY.
GOT A MINUTE?
APPRENTICE

I'LL, UH... LEAVE YOU TWO TO TALK AWKWARDLY.

I AM SPEECHLESS.

I...

APRENTICE

WAIT A MINUTE.

WHY ARE YOU DRESSED LIKE BORIS?!

OH, I--

APRENTICE

HELLO, LIDDLÉ GEEL!

YOU ARE LIKING MY RIDE, YES?

HONK HONK

I DIDN'T KNOW WIZARDS DRIVE CARS.

APRENTICE

OH, WELL... SOME CAN.

I'M STILL NOT SURE IF BORIS IS ONE OF THEM.

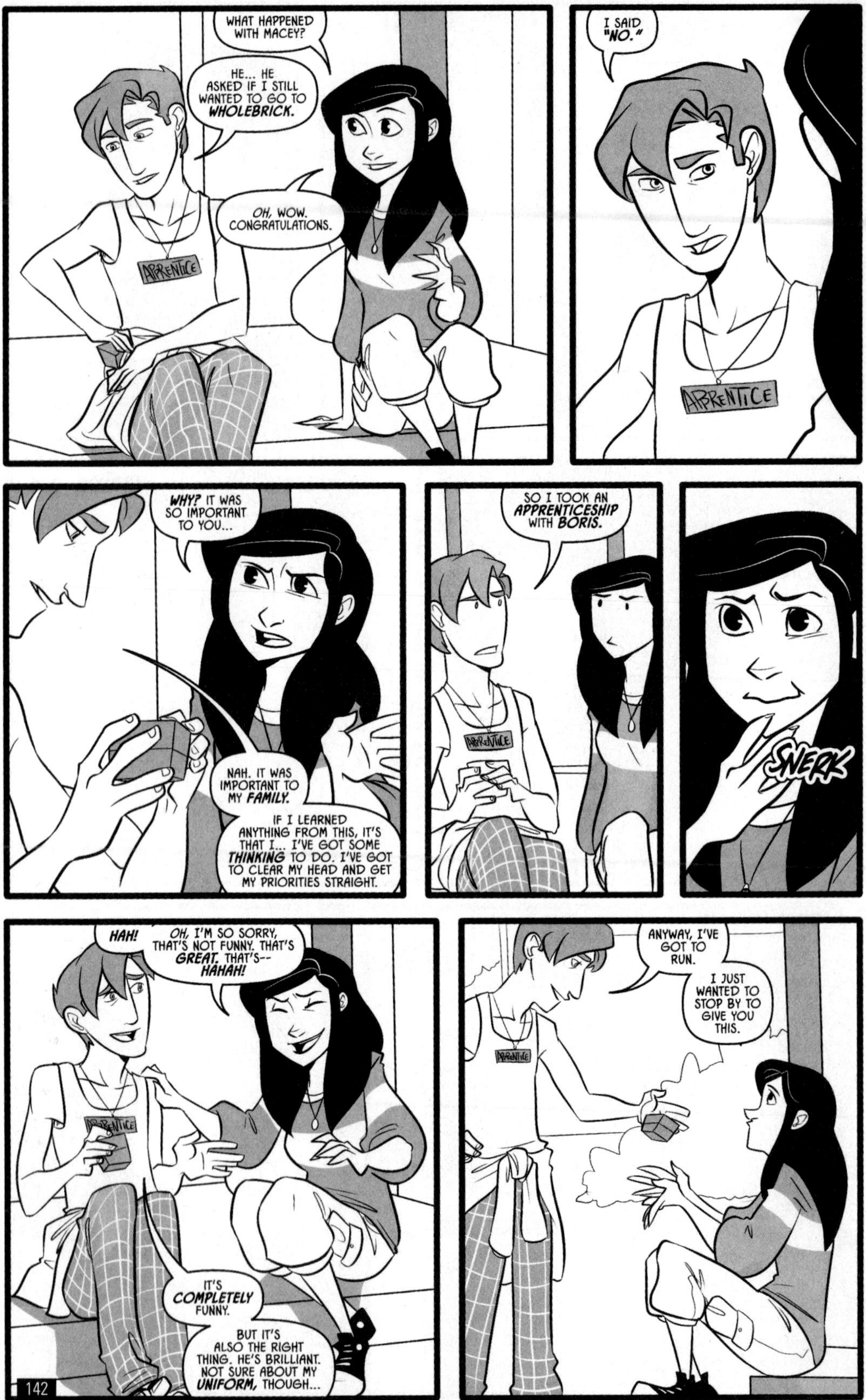
WHAT HAPPENED WITH MACEY?
HE... HE ASKED IF I STILL WANTED TO GO TO WHOLEBRICK.
OH, WOW. CONGRATULATIONS.
APPRENTICE
I SAID "NO."
APPRENTICE
WHY? IT WAS SO IMPORTANT TO YOU...
NAH. IT WAS IMPORTANT TO MY FAMILY.
IF I LEARNED ANYTHING FROM THIS, IT'S THAT I... I'VE GOT SOME THINKING TO DO. I'VE GOT TO CLEAR MY HEAD AND GET MY PRIORITIES STRAIGHT.
SO I TOOK AN APPRENTICESHIP WITH BORIS.
APPRENTICE
SNERK
HAH!
OH, I'M SO SORRY, THAT'S NOT FUNNY. THAT'S GREAT. THAT'S-- HAHAH!
IT'S COMPLETELY FUNNY.
BUT IT'S ALSO THE RIGHT THING. HE'S BRILLIANT. NOT SURE ABOUT MY UNIFORM, THOUGH...
ANYWAY, I'VE GOT TO RUN.
I JUST WANTED TO STOP BY TO GIVE YOU THIS.
APPRENTICE

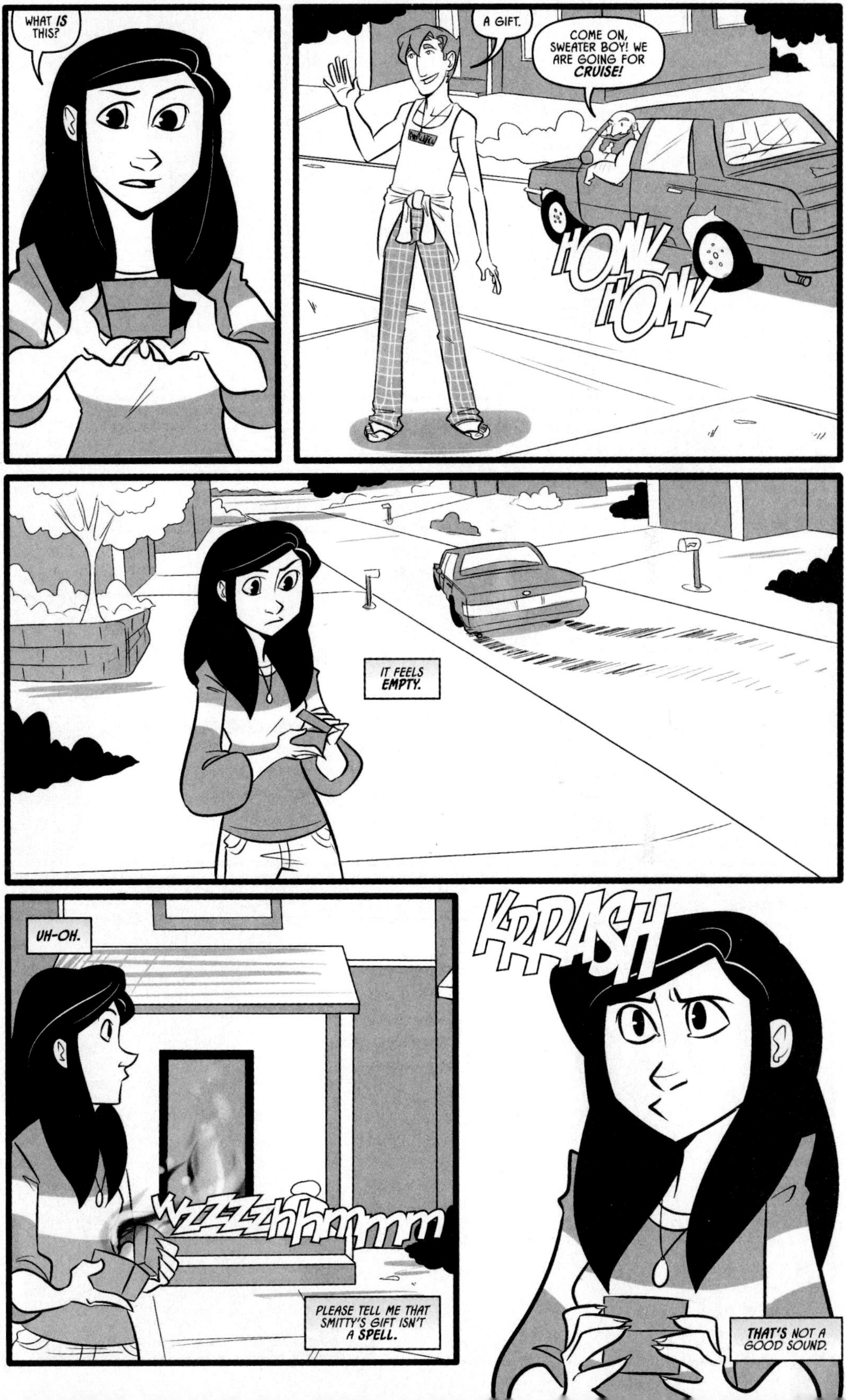
WHAT IS THIS?
A GIFT.
COME ON, SWEATER BOY! WE ARE GOING FOR CRUISE!
HONK HONK
IT FEELS EMPTY.
UH-OH.
WZZZZhhmmmm
PLEASE TELL ME THAT SMITTY'S GIFT ISN'T A SPELL.
KRRASH
THAT'S NOT A GOOD SOUND.

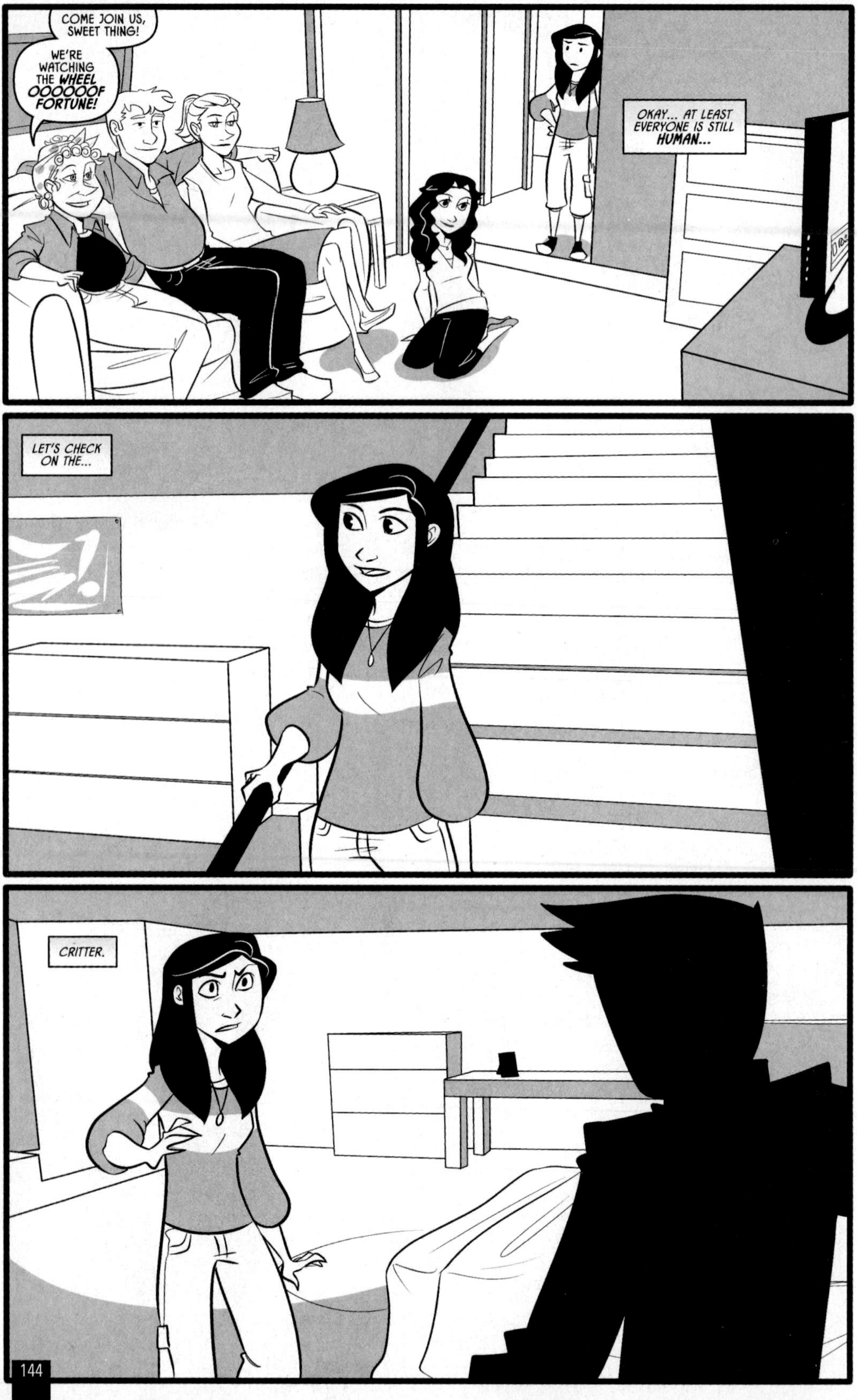
COME JOIN US, SWEET THING!
WE'RE WATCHING THE **WHEEL OOOOOOF FORTUNE!**
OKAY... AT LEAST EVERYONE IS STILL **HUMAN...**
LET'S CHECK ON THE...
CRITTER.

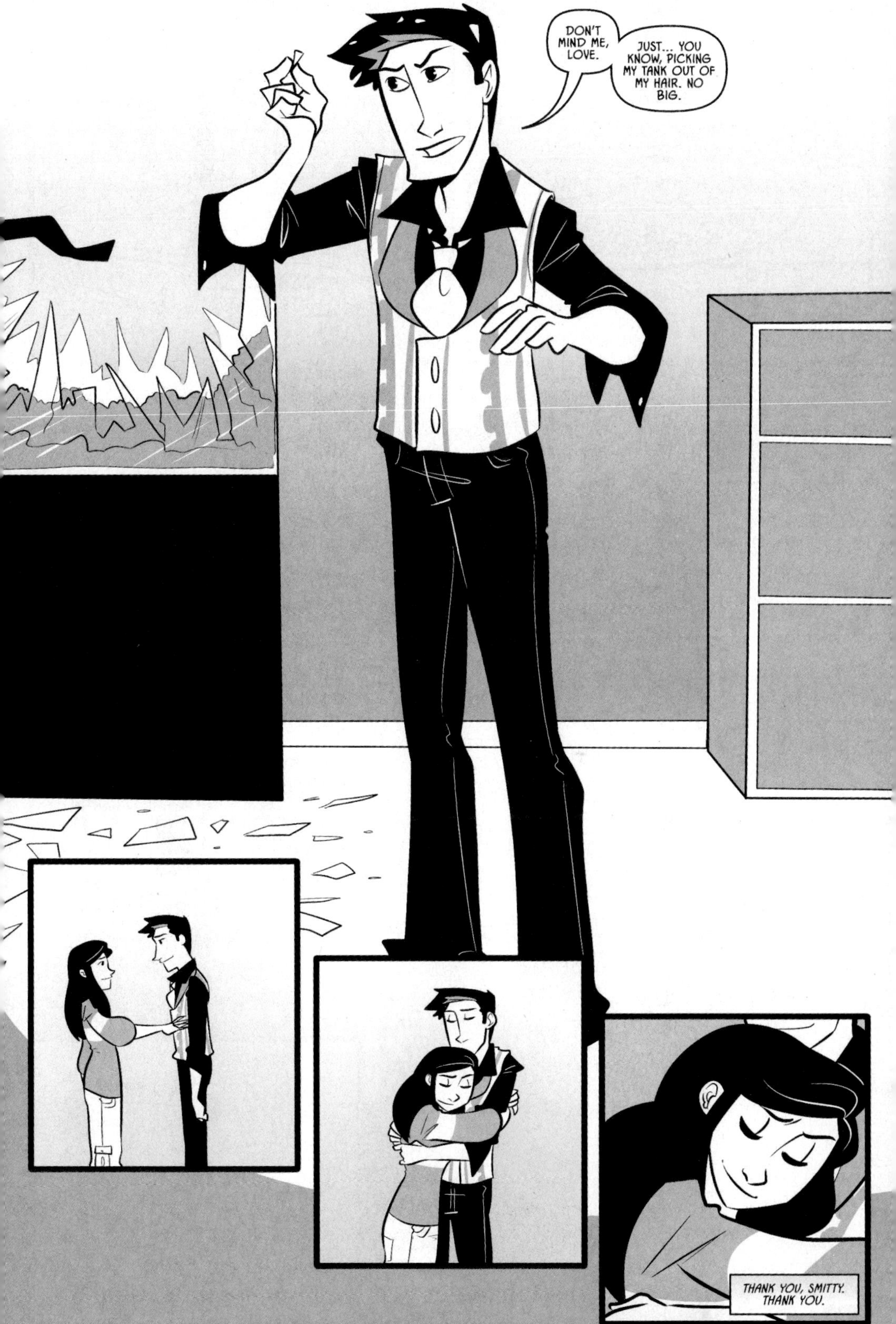
DON'T MIND ME, LOVE.
JUST... YOU KNOW, PICKING MY TANK OUT OF MY HAIR. NO BIG.
THANK YOU, SMITTY. THANK YOU.

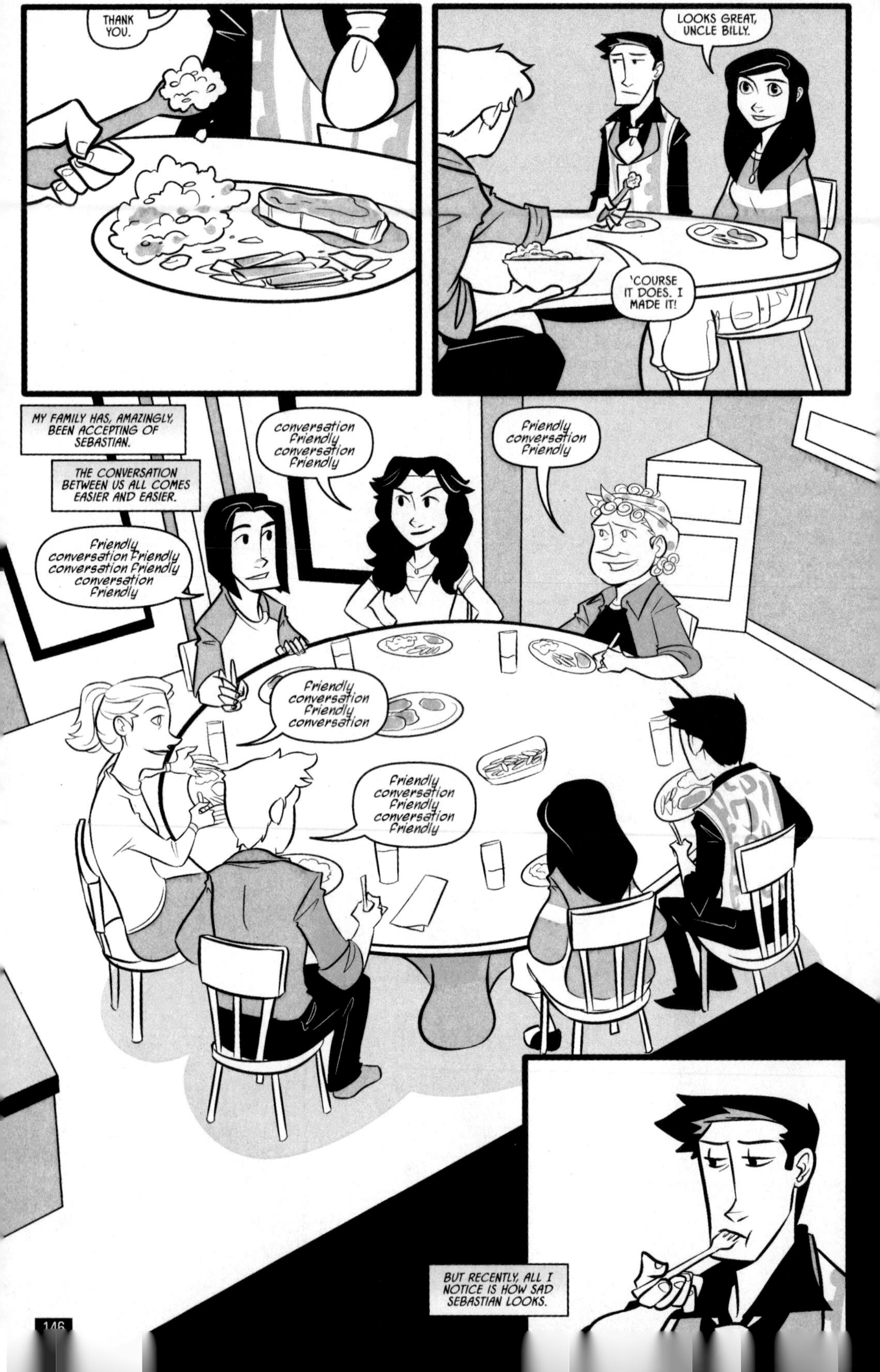
THANK YOU.
LOOKS GREAT, UNCLE BILLY.
'COURSE IT DOES. I MADE IT!
MY FAMILY HAS, AMAZINGLY, BEEN ACCEPTING OF SEBASTIAN.
THE CONVERSATION BETWEEN US ALL COMES EASIER AND EASIER.
conversation friendly conversation friendly
friendly conversation friendly
friendly conversation friendly conversation friendly conversation friendly
friendly conversation friendly conversation
friendly conversation friendly conversation friendly
BUT RECENTLY, ALL I NOTICE IS HOW SAD SEBASTIAN LOOKS.

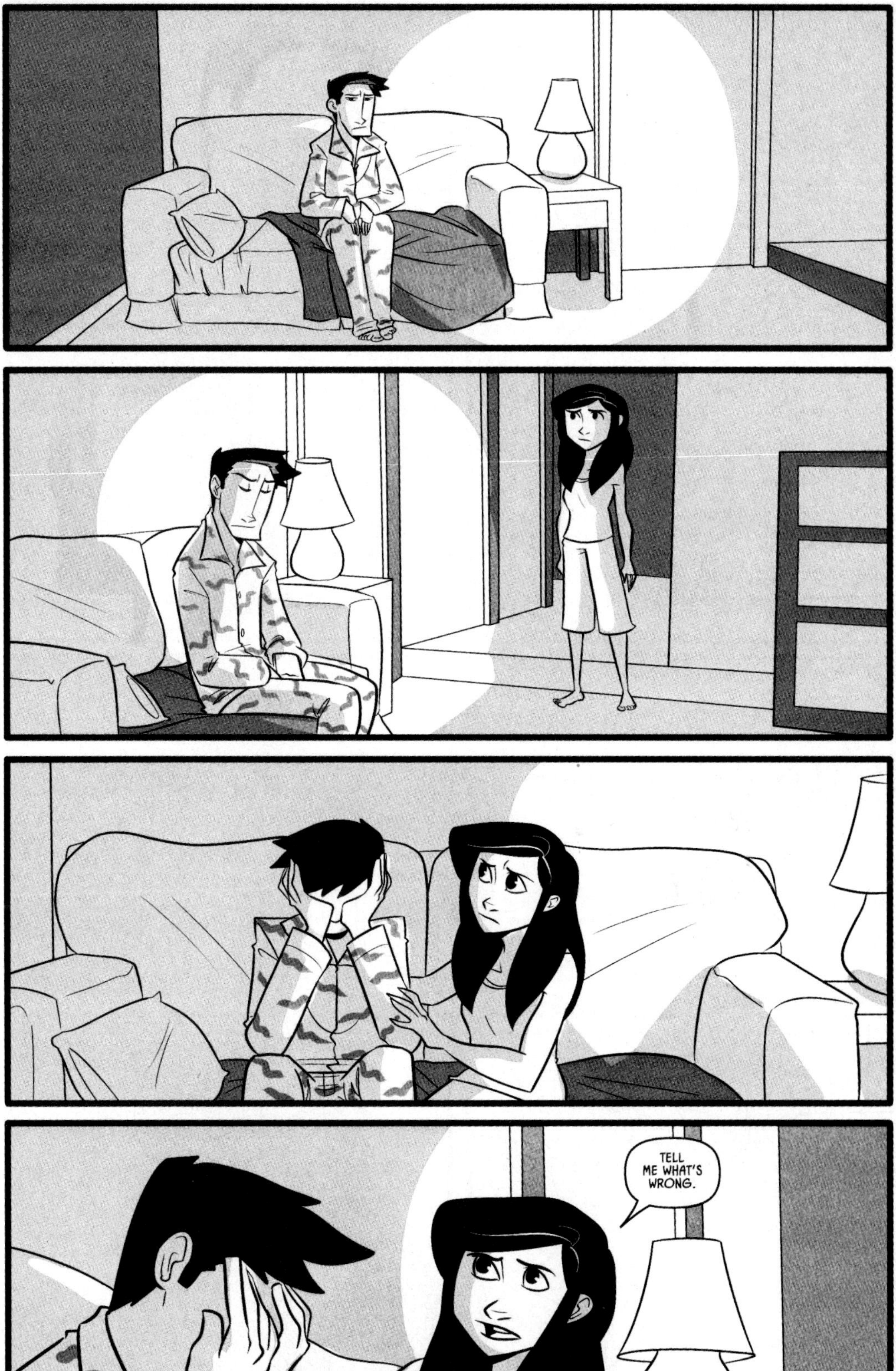
TELL ME WHAT'S WRONG.

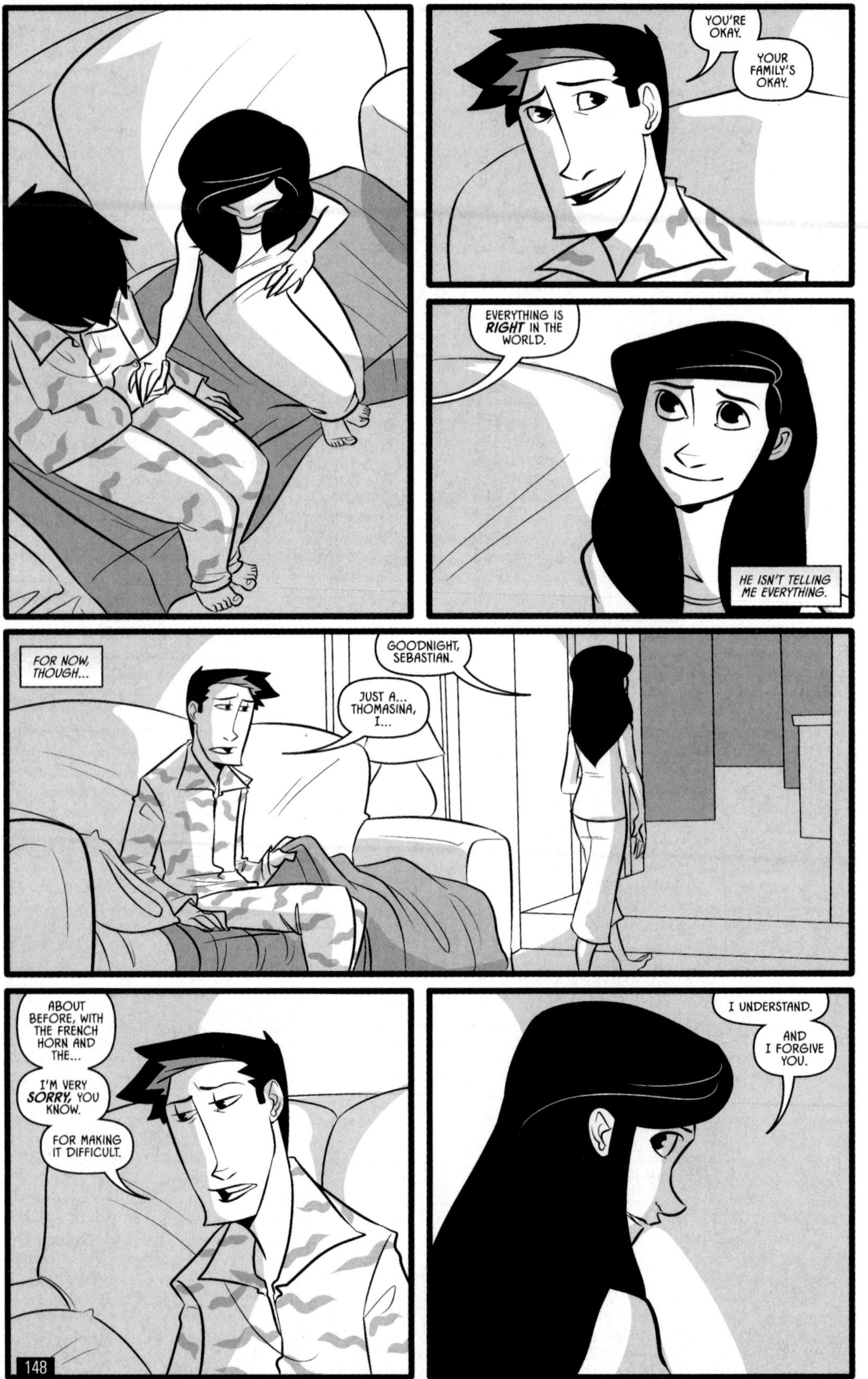
YOU'RE OKAY.
YOUR FAMILY'S OKAY.
EVERYTHING IS **RIGHT** IN THE WORLD.
HE ISN'T TELLING ME EVERYTHING.
FOR NOW, THOUGH...
GOODNIGHT, SEBASTIAN.
JUST A... THOMASINA, I...
ABOUT BEFORE, WITH THE FRENCH HORN AND THE...
I'M VERY **SORRY,** YOU KNOW.
FOR MAKING IT DIFFICULT.
I UNDERSTAND.
AND I FORGIVE YOU.

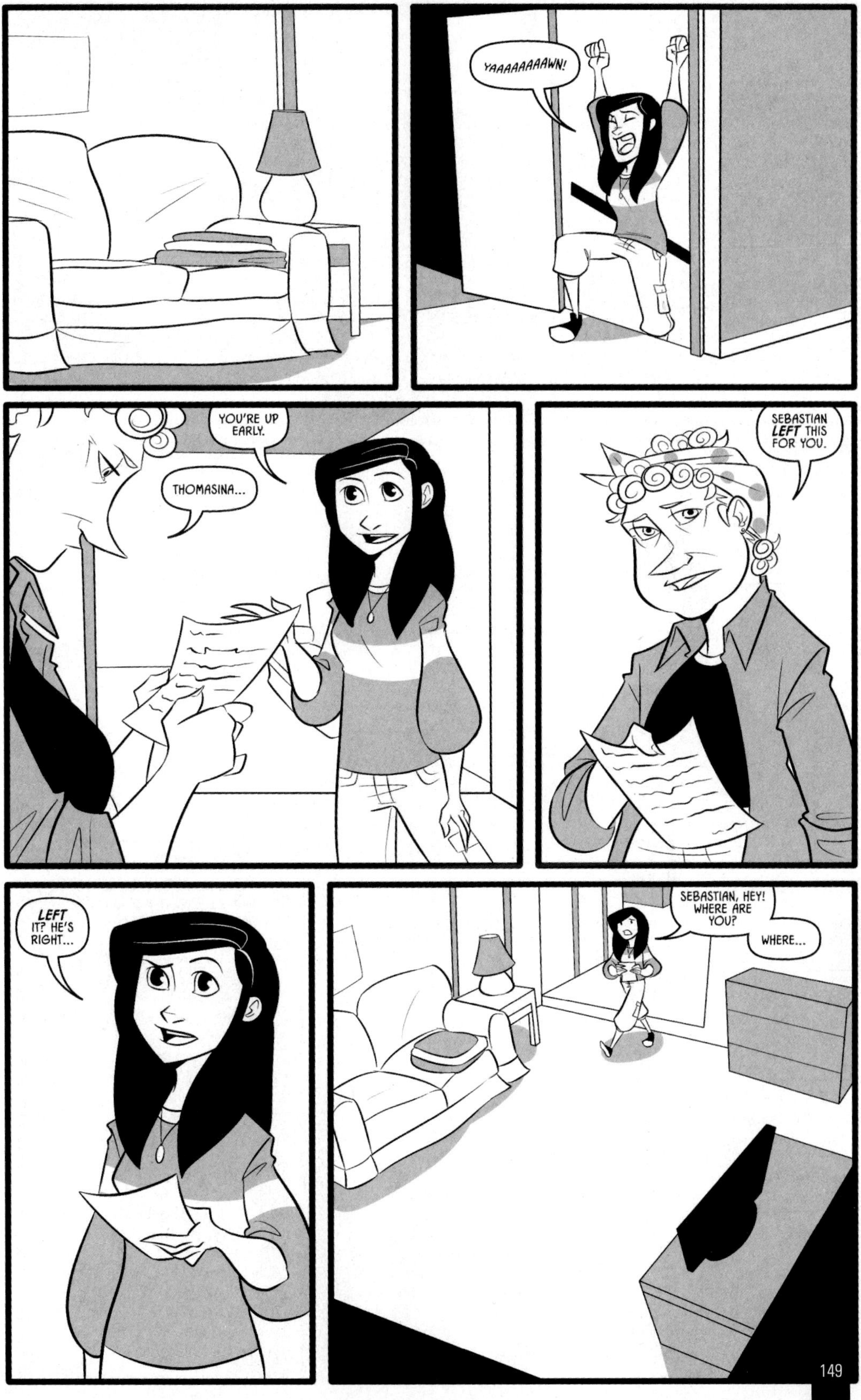
YAAAAAAAAWN!
THOMASINA...
YOU'RE UP EARLY.
SEBASTIAN LEFT THIS FOR YOU.
LEFT IT? HE'S RIGHT...
SEBASTIAN, HEY! WHERE ARE YOU?
WHERE...

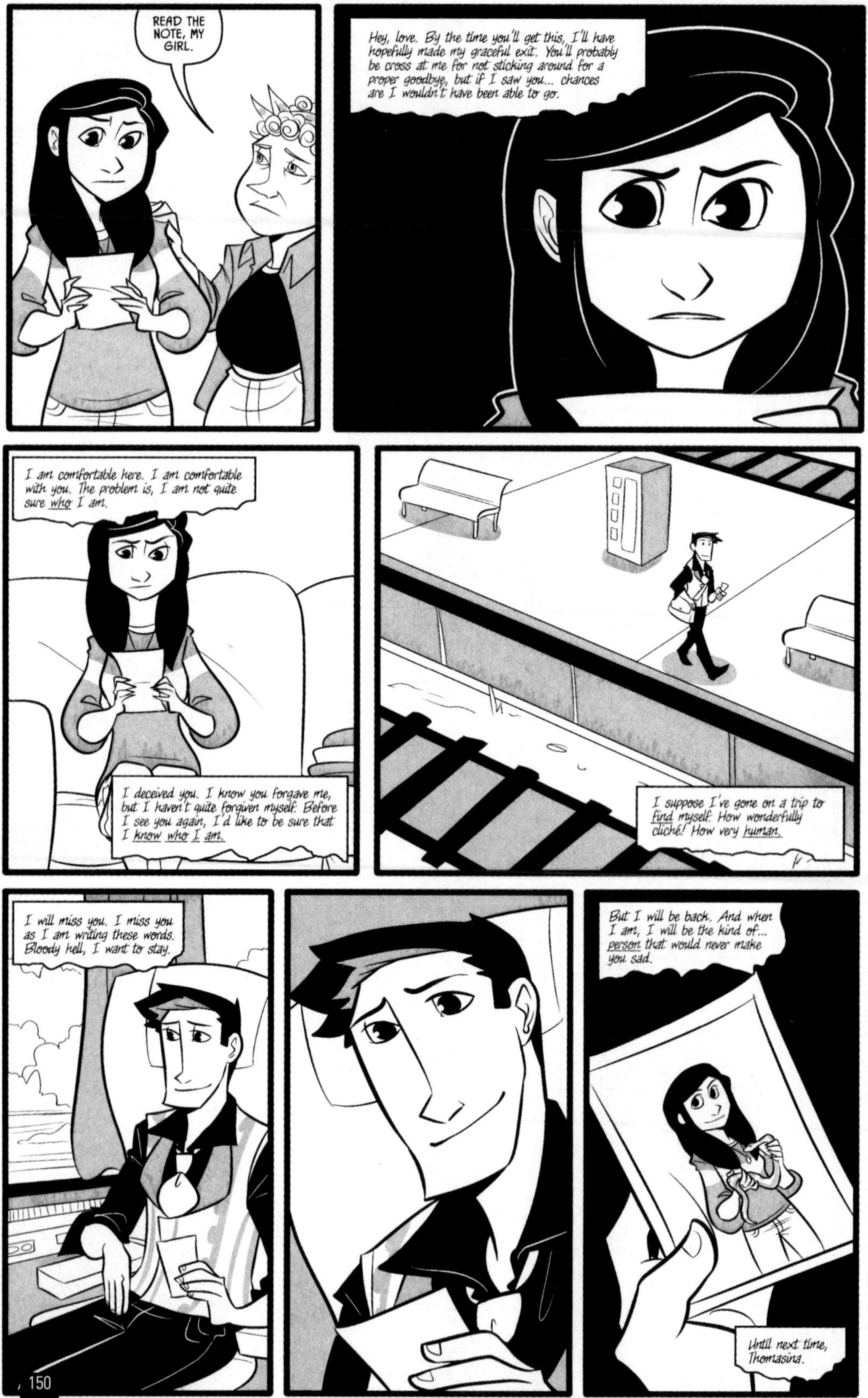
READ THE NOTE, MY GIRL.
Hey, love. By the time you'll get this, I'll have hopefully made my graceful exit. You'll probably be cross at me for not sticking around for a proper goodbye, but if I saw you... chances are I wouldn't have been able to go.
I am comfortable here. I am comfortable with you. The problem is, I am not quite sure who I am.
I deceived you. I know you forgave me, but I haven't quite forgiven myself. Before I see you again, I'd like to be sure that I know who I am.
I suppose I've gone on a trip to find myself. How wonderfully cliché! How very human.
I will miss you. I miss you as I am writing these words. Bloody hell, I want to stay.
But I will be back. And when I am, I will be the kind of... person that would never make you sad.
Until next time, Thomasina.

OH, MY LITTLE GIRL...

ARE YOU OKAY?

I AM.

I'VE SAID "I'M OKAY" MY WHOLE LIFE, AND I'VE NEVER REALLY MEANT IT.

BUT NOW... NOW, I AM.

SOMETIMES THE **WEIGHT** OF MEMORY SEEMS AS IF IT'S TOO MUCH TO BEAR.

IT'S SO EASY TO GIVE UP. TO FALL DOWN.

HEY LOVE.

BY THE TIME YOU G
EXIT. YOU'LL PROBAB
GOODBYE, BUT I
AVE B

IT'S **HARD** TO STAND UP...

BUT I DO IT ANYWAY.

IT LOOKS LIKE A **BEAUTIFUL** DAY, ABUELA.

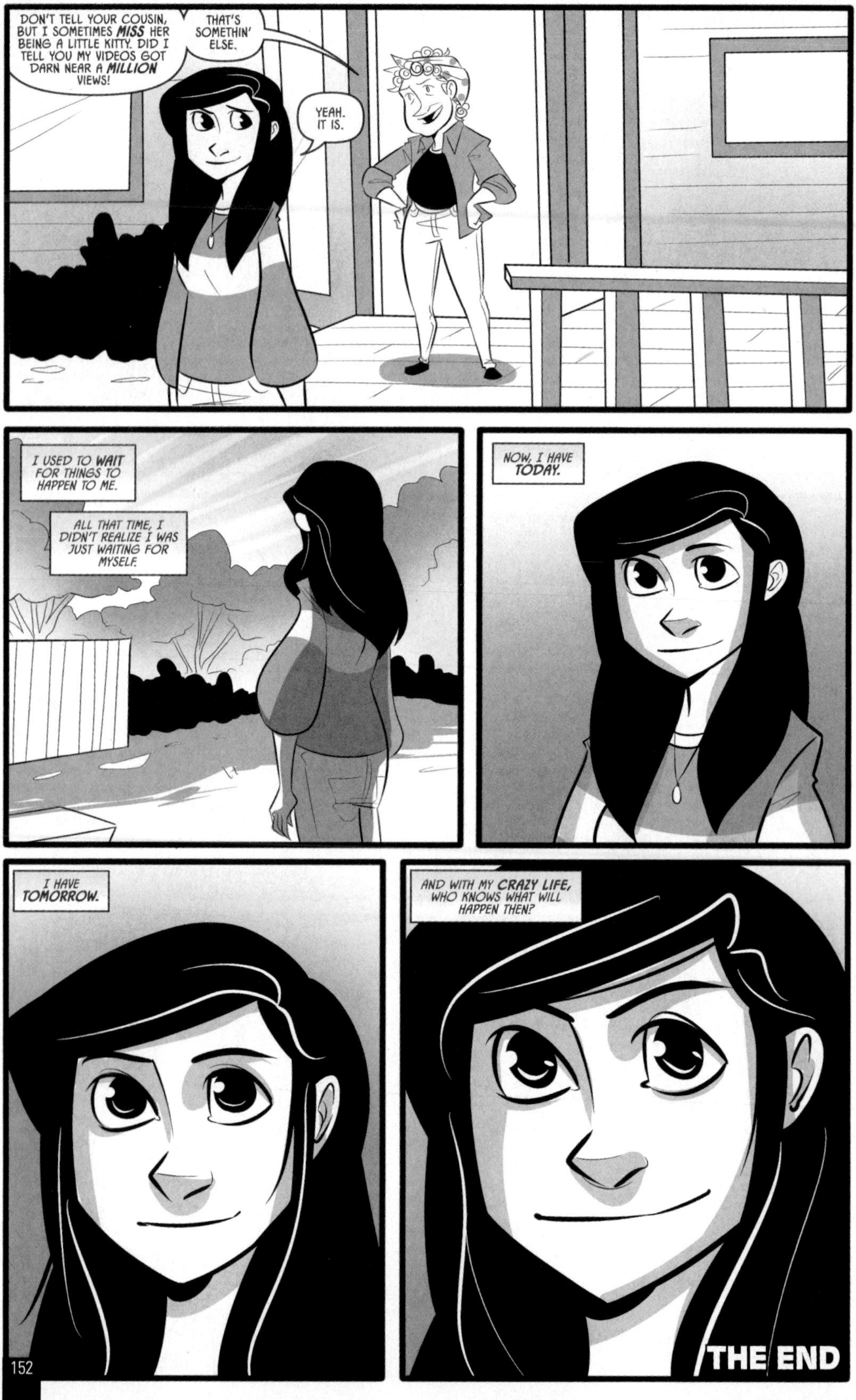
DON'T TELL YOUR COUSIN, BUT I SOMETIMES MISS HER BEING A LITTLE KITTY. DID I TELL YOU MY VIDEOS GOT DARN NEAR A MILLION VIEWS!
THAT'S SOMETHIN' ELSE.
YEAH. IT IS.
I USED TO WAIT FOR THINGS TO HAPPEN TO ME.
ALL THAT TIME, I DIDN'T REALIZE I WAS JUST WAITING FOR MYSELF.
NOW, I HAVE TODAY.
I HAVE TOMORROW.
AND WITH MY CRAZY LIFE, WHO KNOWS WHAT WILL HAPPEN THEN?
THE END

CHARACTER DESIGNS & EXTRAS

WITH COMMENTARY BY
WRITER/CO-CREATOR PAT SHAND

THOMASINA

I've always been inspired by strong characters who have great destinies. Harry Potter, Buffy Summers… the list goes on and on. The idea of a regular kid being given a magical future is appealing for a reason. Who hasn't dreamed of getting mail from Hogwarts on their eleventh birthday? Thomasina is the embodiment of that hope. She's lost a lot, and she's grown up on the same books that we have… and while those stories may have been solace, what happens when that letter never comes? Thomasina, of course, comes out stronger in the end, but I think her journey to get there is one that so many imaginative kids – particularly readers – embark on in their teens.

SMITTY

I remember being in middle school band. I was the only one who played French horn, and I imagine that there has never lived a person with less aptitude for that instrument than me. Even still, I remembered it somewhat fondly, so thought it would be funny to turn this kind of silly, kind of beautiful instrument into an object of incredible power. Also, Family Pets HAS to hold the record for the most times "French horn" has been said in a graphic novel.

SEBASTIAN

Who hasn't wondered what their pets would say if they could talk? What they would be like if they were human? The initial concept of Family Pets was all about that, with Sebastian at the center. The fun thing about him is that snakes are – unfairly, I'd say – always depicted as devious characters! We played with that a bit with Sebastian's arc, but Sarah and I very much wanted to subvert the cliché of the sneaky, tempting snake. Sebastian's journey comes from an emotional place – he wants to be human.

ABUELA

I often toy with the idea of a sequel where Abuela has become a social media celebrity. Now, if I could only get Sarah to draw it…

When Sarah and I first came up with this story, it was very different. We pitched it as Thomasina's Human Zoo, a tale of a lonely girl who surrounded herself with animals. We had Veronica the parakeet, Brian the fish, Schnuckle the turtle, Billy the bearded dragon, Sir Whinesalot the Dog, and... of course... Sebastian the snake.

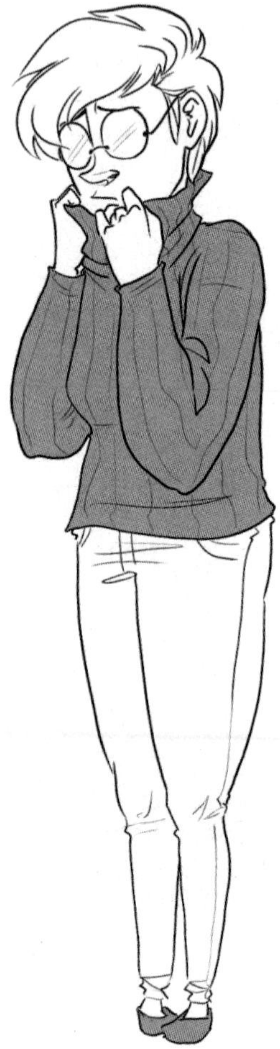

SHNUCKLE,
THE TURTLE

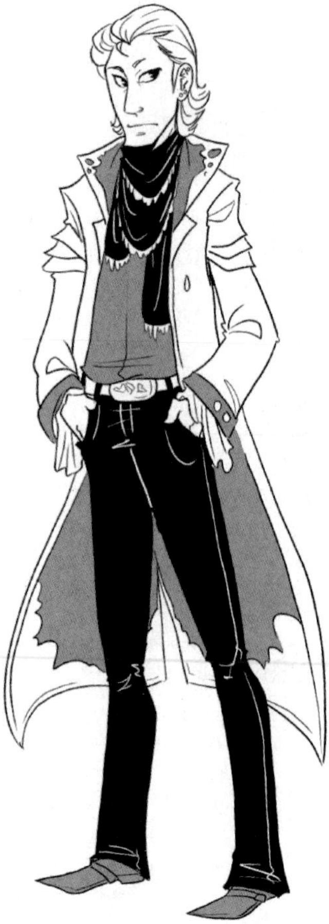

BRIAN,
THE FISH

We were initially going to have all of her pets become human. In that version, she lived alone with Abuela, so we didn't have the plot where her foster family became pets. It was a very different story than Family Pets ended up being, but I still love the character designs Sarah came up with!

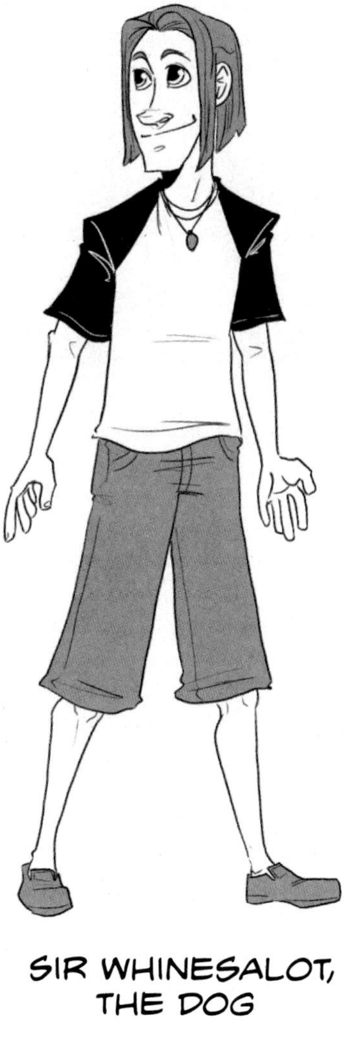
SIR WHINESALOT,
THE DOG

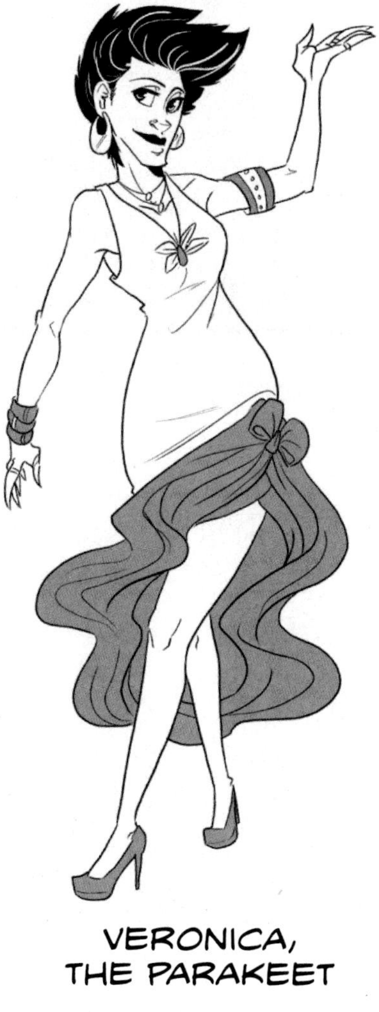
VERONICA,
THE PARAKEET

Sir Whinesalot ended up looking a lot like Neil!

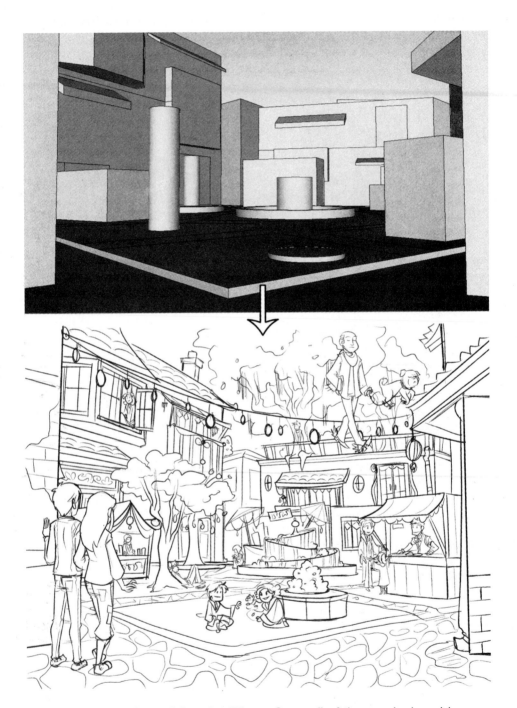

Sarah's process for building the "Times Square" of the magical world.

Here's a scene from the Thomasina's Human Zoo version, where Thomasina discovers that all of her pets – save for Billy the bearded dragon – have disappeared. In the original story, she saw the window open, rushed through it to see if she could chase down the animals… and that's when she would run into the human versions of her pets!

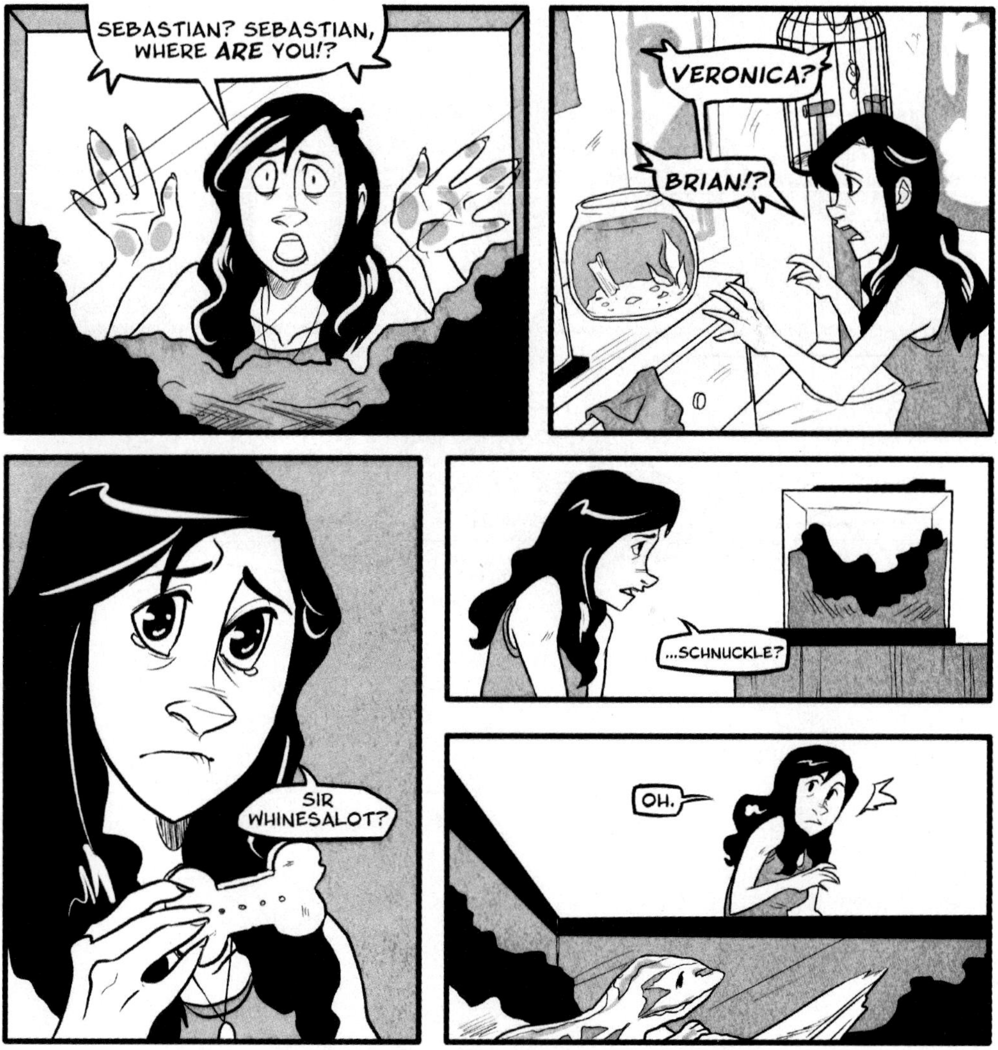
SEBASTIAN? SEBASTIAN, WHERE ARE YOU!?
VERONICA?
BRIAN!?
SIR WHINESALOT?
...SCHNUCKLE?
OH.

The story proceeded much in the same way as Family Pets, but it was a lot more crowded. I think we made the right choice!

FAMILY PETS

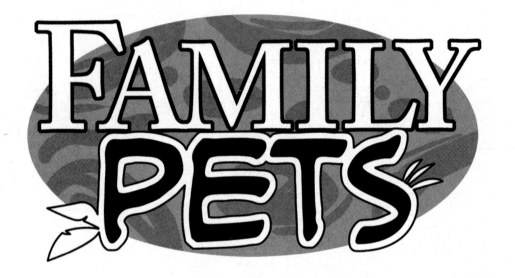